Written by: Christopher Savage

First Edition (1.6) 31/08/2017

Front cover designed by: Nick Savage - Xi Design

Dedication

To my wife and family who continue to patiently weather the storm of my passion to write.

Books in the Angels & Shadows series:

Book 1: Angels & Shadows

Book 2: Forsaken

Book 3: Scorned

Book 4: The Assassin

Copyright: Christopher Sa

CW00551146

Scorned

"The great dragon was hurled down – that ancient serpent called the Devil, or Satan, who leads the whole world astray. He was hurled to the Earth and his angels with him."

Book of Revelation 12:9

And out of chaos, arose Lucifer and the Illuminati....

"Heav'n has no rage, like love to hatred turn'd, nor Hell a fury, like a woman scorn'd."

William Congreve - The Mourning Bride (Act III Scene 2)

And out of necessity, arose Gina Mèdici....

Chapter 1

Bavaria, Germany. June 21st 2017.

It was twenty-one minutes past nine in the evening, when the orb of the burnt orange sun began to set to the east of the Gothic castle, near Ingolstadt in Germany. It was the ancestral home of the Illuminati. The sun's setting marked the end of the summer solstice, but not the end of the pagan rituals that would follow. They would go on until dawn of the next day, by when Satanists around the world would have sated their thirst with the innocent blood of their offerings.

The cavalcade of thirteen black Mercedes limousines passed down the avenue of poplars that led to the castle gate. As they passed, each of the magnificent trees flickered in the mysterious orange light, as if caught on an old acetate film of the silent movie era. There is something strange and sinister about nature. Much in the same way that the atrocities at Auschwitz forever blighted the land such that wildlife never fully returned, the birds around the castle fell into an eerie silence as the procession passed as if sensing danger.

The gate opened without command, as if they were expected. The cars drove on and pulled into the courtyard beneath the battlements that cast their long shadows across the yard, like the teeth of a giant dragon. A single person, dressed in the cowl and black habit of a monk, exited each of the cars. They walked in silence to the grand oak doorway of the castle. Again, there was no command. The door opened, and the thirteen filed through. One lingered and looked back at the lead car. He simply nodded to the driver and then followed the others into the gloominess of the ancient fortress.

They stayed in file as they walked through the arched hallway to the chambers facing them. The walls were clad with old tapestries and weaponry of bygone eras. Suits of armour stood to attention in columns on either side of them, as if still on duty after hundreds of years in obedient silence. The door to the master chamber was as massive as that of the main entrance. The oak was black with age and bore the scars of past battles, where aggressors had breached the castle demanding the blood of those within.

The only lighting to the chamber was a cartwheel of one hundred candles, hoisted above a rough stone altar with an annulus of thirteen chairs set around it. They were all identical but for the one furthest from the door. Whereas the others were of simple hewn oak, numbered one through twelve in an anti-clockwise direction, this was a grand and ornate throne. The legs and arms of it were wrapped in carvings of serpents and the back support depicted a fire breathing dragon. The bodies of its victims were crushed beneath its clawed feet. At the top of the backrest, was a carved shield with the letter 'L' prominently declaring its owners name. *Lucifer*.

Twelve of the thirteen took their places and sat in silence, waiting for their master to take his throne and start proceedings. These men and women were the heads of the twelve most powerful families on the planet. Together with their master, the *Pindar*, they made up the Council of Thirteen. Depending on how they threw the dice, wars would be fought and world-changing, globalised deals made. Each would be strategically chosen to strengthen the Council's hold and control of political, economic, social and religious matters of world consequence. Those at the table included representation from the oligarchs, corrupt politicians, bankers, religious zealots and royal families. Even the Vatican was represented. They and their forefathers were, and have been, re-shaping the world and its politics for centuries.

The Pindar arrived after several minutes. Those men and women assembled there stood respectfully. They remained cowled, with no need to submit their identities to him. The Pindar knew them by where they sat in the room. They would only drop their cowls when a new member was introduced to the Council, and then only the once. After that each would know the other.

The Pindar was himself cowled. The glint of the candles reflected sinisterly on the golden mask that he wore beneath. It was symbolically sculpted to show only one of his eyes, the eye of Osiris. The All-Seeing Eye of the *Novus Ordo Seclorum,* more popularly known as the 'New World Order'. At his bid, the Council of Thirteen sat in anticipation of his address.

"It is the sacred night of the solstice," began the Pindar, his Slavic voice deep and resonant, "the time to renew your vows of allegiance to Lucifer. It is our duty to send him the gift of life in appreciation for the latitude and fortune that he has given us here on this Earth."

They all remained silent. The Pindar, if not Lucifer, was his chosen ambassador on Earth and with that, he had the delegated power of Satan himself.

"As is custom the girl has been chosen from one of your families. As heads of family, you will appreciate the honour bestowed on you, should you be the one to part with your loved one. You and your family should exult in that choice and embrace Lucifer as your God. Rejoice that she is committed to him for all eternity and trust her to his care."

To disobey or deign to oppose the Pindar would be in the knowledge that to do so would be an unforgivable sin, punishable by death and an eternity in Purgatory. The Illuminati is based on a pyramid of power. It feeds up through the various levels from its base to the Council of Thirteen, and on to the Pindar himself at the top. Included in the layers of power, are the three Brotherhoods of Satanism, the Knights Templar and the Freemasons. All there were sworn to absolute secrecy on pain of death.

There was an air of expectancy. All those sat around the crude stone altar had been there before, except for the new incumbent of the Dracul family, Illya. Without his cowl, you would see that he was a strikingly handsome young man with Slavic features and eyes so dark that they were almost black. His short cropped blonde hair, pale skin and perfect white teeth, were incongruous with the colour of his eyes but completed his striking appearance. He had the accolade of being the youngest ever member of the Council of Thirteen and had succeeded his late uncle, Alexis. He was a man of great intelligence and fortitude. The Dracul bloodline went back well past their ancestor, Vlad the Impaler, and the fabled House of Dracula. Although only just in his twenty first year, Illya Dracul had no global equal in how to use the manipulative power of the Internet and media to influence and control the population; particularly its youth. Meeting final global Illuminati expectations would fall squarely on Illya Dracul's shoulders. All in the room were aware of that, apart perhaps, from Illya Dracul himself.

The Pindar was sat with his back to the old oak door. He raised his arm and beckoned, even though there seemed to be no one in the room to see his command. Somehow there was a response and the grand door creaked open. A man and a woman entered the room, dressed in white robes and cowled as was the protocol. The woman seemed to need the man's support, as if drugged. He steered her in front of him, past the Pindar to the stone altar, where he sat her and dropped her robe. The young, blonde and petite girl was naked but for the silver fitted mask that covered her face. The expression on the mask was an ambiguous grin. It gave no clue whatsoever as to the girl's identity, or her personal crisis. The mask was cutaway at the eyes, allowing her to view her audience.

There was a different demeanour about the thirteen after the girl's robe dropped. Their attention was now totally drawn to her. Although excited by the occasion, each was concerned and secretly trying to ascertain as to whether the girl was of them. She was clearly young but in her womanhood. She seemed unaware of her nakedness and the look in her eyes showed that she was confused and scared. The girl responded to the man's demands in a robotic way as he arranged her position to best display her sex to her audience. He dropped his own robe revealing his naked and muscular body. His readiness for the act that was about to take place, was profoundly evident and all had view of his impressive manhood. The man had a shock of red hair. He was masked in the same way as the girl, but the expression on his mask depicted the face and leer of a devil.

The man turned the girl on to her back and spread her. She offered no resistance. Her head rolled to one side and her gaze seemed to fix on the man sat in the sixth chair, to the right of the throne. It was as if she had sensed who he was. Her body tensed and she screamed out as the well-endowed man penetrated her. His hand went instantly to the girl's mound, then to his silver mask striping his forehead with the evidence of her virginal blood. The young stud began his rhythm and drove powerfully into the girl's slack body, whose only protest was to whimper pathetically. The rape lasted several minutes. Throughout, the girl's eyes never left the man in the sixth chair. The girl's violator at last withdrew and demonstrated his fulfilment to the Council by means of showing his sated manhood, leaving the girl still spread in that humiliating pose. His last act was to remove her mask and reveal her shame.

The man sat to Illya Dracul's left, in the sixth chair, gasped out loud. He dropped his hood. He had now recognised the girl as his sixteen year old niece who was as precious to him, as his own daughter. Still her eyes were fixed on him, but now he could see the tears flowing down her stricken face.

"Number six," prompted the Pindar, holding out a ceremonial dagger, "do your duty."

Even though each of the twelve members of the Council knew each other by name, it was a protocol, raised for security reasons, not to refer to given names. It also marked their ranking in seniority within the Council. Number six was deep in shock and slow to respond to the Pindar's direct order. Dracul sat next to him in the seventh chair shook him by the arm.

"Six, do as you are ordered, the Pindar is growing impatient."

The girl's uncle stood reluctantly, seeming to have aged in those few minutes. He shuffled rather than walked to the Pindar, who was proffering the Jewel-crusted ceremonial dagger. Number six took it from the Pindar's outstretched hand. He noticed, for the first time, that his skin seemed to be reptilian and too pink, red even. He glanced into the Pindar's single uncovered eye and his blood ran cold. It was not the eye of any human that he had ever seen. The blink was unnatural, it seemed to close from the sides and there was no emotion in his look. It was like staring into the black eye of a shark, hoping for a sign of compassion. There was none. Six turned with the dagger in hand and walked with a heavy heart towards his niece, whose eyes were imploring him to help her. The red headed man, still naked, had gagged her. He was tying her hands to iron rings set in the top corners of the stone and then her feet to those at the bottom, until she was spread-eagled on the altar. His job was done. He picked up his robe and walked naked out of the room.

Six took his place at the side of his niece. Her terrified face was exploring his for hope of salvation but he could give her none. He raised the dagger high above his head with both hands clasped around the jewelled handle. Tears of guilt and grief were streaming down his face.

"I'm sorry darling. Please forgive me," were the pitifully inadequate words to take with her to eternity.

Her passing was swift. Six drove the dagger down through her chest until it came to a halt with a chime on the altar stone. Lucifer had his reward. The girl was dead. Six began shaking violently, then collapsed going into a fit at the side of the altar. Again, the Pindar rose hinews arm and beckoned. The door creaked open and two cloaked men appeared. They crossed to the altar and took the convulsing man, who was now screaming incoherently, out of the room. Moments later there was the sound of a single gunshot and then silence. Without prompt, Illya and the others to his right, stood and moved one chair closer to the Pindar, leaving chair number twelve empty. They had all been promoted one place in the seniority ranking of the Council of Thirteen. The Pindar spoke.

"Six has broken his vow of silence and has paid the ultimate price. Let that be a lesson to you all. I will not tolerate any who disobey the absolute rules of this Council."

There was an uncomfortable silence. Most knew that their own personal greed had taken them to the very edge of their own interpretation of 'the rules' and we're thankful that it was another who had been found guilty of treason, not them. The Pindar looked at each of them that remained in his Council. In truth, he could find a reason to kill most of them, but if they weren't corruptible, then they would not have been of any use to him in the first place. Only two people flinched when the dagger was driven through the girl's heart. One was a woman sat in chair number five and the other was Illya Dracul who had now moved next to her in chair number six.

It wasn't squeamishness though from his part, far from it. As young as he was, Illya Dracul had already taken lives. He and his family line were accomplished swordsmen. Duels to the death were a matter of family honour and tradition that dated back to their notorious ancestor, Vlad the Impaler. Illya had flinched through muscle memory. When he was sixteen, Illya was in a duel to the death with a boy of the same age but from a different

8

race, a benign race that had usurped the role of *Protector of Mankind. Angels* they had called themselves. In Illya's mind, and indoctrination, the Angels were evil and their archenemy. Ben Robinson was the boy's name. After the sword fight of Illya's life, he had been run through by Ben's sabre. It had entered below his sternum and exited below his left shoulder. It was the only sword fight that Illya had ever lost and he vowed that it would be his last. Illya Dracul had practiced every day since. Ben Robinson had gone on to kill his beloved uncle Alexis, who Illya had succeeded as a member of the Council of Thirteen. Illya had already sworn vengeance. In his mind, Ben was already a dead man in the waiting.

"But there are degrees as to what is acceptable," the Pindar mused and raised his arm. The great door opened yet again and he addressed the Council.

"I want you to meet the new number twelve," the timbre of the Pindar's voice was unaffected by the recent events and it rang out loud and emotionless in the cool air of the stone room.

All heads turned to the cloaked man entering. They all dropped their cowls respectfully as was the custom, except for the Pindar who never showed his identity, ever. Number twelve moved like a predator. His feet seemed to only caress the floor as he walked silently by. His cowled head turned in every direction along the way like a raptor taking everything in. He was constantly accessing the inherent risk of his predicament and looking for escape routes. He was a survivor and these instincts had kept him alive, often in cases of extreme adversity. He was known as the 'un-killable man'.

The newcomer took his chair to the left of the Pindar and dropped his cowl. He was of indeterminate age, possibly fifty. The desert had burnt all excess flesh from his bones and his skin was like parchment. He did however have the brightest, most intelligent amber eyes that you could possibly imagine but there was cruelty in them too.

All there recognised him. It was the Mullah Ismail Alansari, one of the deadliest men in the combined African and Asian continents. His connections reached into the very heart of every Arab state or caliphate, touching every Sheikh, Emir and terrorist faction there. The Mullah's influence in the Middle East was legendary. It went right up from ISIS to the arms dealers and their sponsors and to the White House and the Kremlin. Even to the Russian President himself.

More importantly from the Pindar's point of view, the Mullah was recognised by the Muslim warring factions as a prophet. His vitriolic speeches proclaimed that the End Time prophecy could only be fulfilled through uniting with the Islamic State leader, Muhammad Akhbar, a religious zealot and charismatic jihadist. The Pindar knew that the Mullah's religion was false though, just a way of controlling and uniting the Muslims in his own personal cause. That cause was the pursuit of power and money.

The Pindar needed a credible *False Prophet* and a plausible *Mahdi* to fulfil his vision of a New World Order. The Mullah would be that False Prophet for him and Muhammad Akhbar, the much-awaited Mahdi. The one the Koran predicts will lead a global revolution and establish a worldwide Islamic empire. They were perfectly suited to deliver the Pindar's plans. Akhbar also bore the name Mohammed, which was fortuitous and in line with common Sunni and Shia beliefs. Once the masses believed that he was the Mahdi, the Twelfth Imam, then the Pindar would be invincible and the world would fall under his control.

The Mullah looked back implacably at his audience. He recognised all there and smiled un-affectionately back at them through his long grey beard and gappy teeth.

"Welcome to the Council of Thirteen number twelve. You have been chosen for your skill-set and Middle East influence."

The Pindar had insight and influence into all things. He knew also of the Mullah's machinations and of his connections to both the CIA and the Kremlin. Both used the Mullah as their conduit for the destabilisation of the Middle East and as their ambassador for arms trading with the warring Muslim factions that they had created. He continued.

"Yours, the Russian's and the CIA's manipulation and escalation of the ISIS crisis, is the springboard that we need to destabilise the Middle East to the point that America will put troops on Arab soil. The holy war that follows, as the radical Islamists try to fulfil the End Time prophecy, will suck in the rest of the world into the biggest, deadliest and most lucrative war in history; World War Three."

There was an exchange of conspiratorial glances and smiles amongst the Council, apart from the elegant woman who was now seated in the fifth chair. She remained expressionless. The only other woman present at the Council was number one, sat at the Pindar's right hand. She was now watching the elegant woman with great interest. Her name was Hydie Papandreou, also elegant and the most powerful woman on the planet.

"Now that the Pindar has put the Mullah amongst us, you will be my ally young lady," she decided and smiled openly at the woman who gave no response in return.

The future and security of Hydie Papandreou's world had changed monumentally from the moment that the Mullah walked into the room and she knew it well.

"War is the biggest business," the Pindar continued, "and our plans for total globalised economy and control depend on it. It is a three-year plan and you all have pivotal parts to play in it. When we meet here to celebrate the summer solstice of 2020 it will be complete and ready to execute," he paused for emphasis and continued," or the Council will have twelve new members."

Everybody in the room knew exactly what that meant. Nobody disappoints the Pindar and lives, neither do their loved ones.

The Mullah considered the Pindar's words carefully and smiled baring his teeth that stood like individual tombstones in his mouth. His amber eyes shone with the passion of a zealot, but he spoke calmly and authoritatively.

"But Pindar, you only talk about the first of the three steps required for total world domination, which of course is globalisation. It is indeed the key strategy of the twenty first century conqueror where you create an economy where self-sufficiency is no longer sustainable, then control the trading through powerful conglomerates. After that its dog eats dog until you are left with only a few conglomerates. That is when the ultimate financial war begins as they fight it out until only one dog is left."

The Mullah looked into the Pindar's single uncovered eye, the All-Seeing Eye and held it.

"I am expecting that the dog left standing is you Pindar."

"You can count on it number twelve," The Pindar was secretly amused and respected the Mullah's clear and apparent lack of fear for him. It was refreshing.

"Not another lapdog," he mused.

There was a mumbling of accord around the room, but also a discord. The Council, being formed of such rich and powerful people, had the idiosyncrasies and characteristics of their type; jealousy and fear of being out-gunned, out-ranked and overtaken. The Mullah continued.

"It doesn't work on its own without the support of the other two steps though."

"Go on," instructed the Pindar.

He was indulging the Mullah. He already knew of, and had plans in place for, the other two.

"The second step is to control of the people. This is done in two parts, firstly through the media. They control our perception of everything and therefore control our minds and our actions. The second part is through religion. This is where extremist organisations, such as ISIS come into it. Give people fear and religion and you can control the masses. Unite the masses and you can control the nation. Unite the nations and you can control the world."

The Mullah paused and considered his audience. He decided that it was already time to go out on a limb. The Mullah was afraid of none and knew no other way.

"I presume Pindar that I have been chosen to orchestrate the control of the people through religious indoctrination and the management of the warring Arab factions."

The Mullah waited for the almost imperceptible nod from the Pindar before continuing.

"And the recently promoted number six is to deliver the other aspect of control through the media and manipulation of the people's perception of reality."

"And perhaps you presume too much number twelve."

It was a gentle rebuff by the Pindar's standards and a disappointment to the rest of the Council. They were secretly hoping that the new incumbent of the twelfth chair would be heavily chastised for his presumptuousness.

"Do continue," the Pindar added with growing curiosity. All in the room however knew that it was the truth.

"The third, final and simplest step is to control the politicians and leaders. They are all corruptible through their greed for money and power. This is where the three steps are entirely dependent on each other. The first buys the second and the third. The politicians and leaders cannot govern their countries without world infrastructure, banking, food, employment and medicine, nor expect to be re-elected when they fail. The ruling conglomerate funds and enables all this and everybody is happy just as long as the politicians and leaders do as they are told. The religious factions used to cause the insurgence in the first place, such as ISIS, are brought back under control. The result is a New World Order led by one man at the top of the pyramid of power, the Pindar."

Every man and woman around the table wished that they had said those words. The Mullah had summed up their mission so succinctly.

The man to the right of number one tapped her on the shoulder and whispered to her.

"Don't get too comfortable in that chair young lady. You are only keeping it warm for our new number twelve."

Number one already knew that he was a threat and she was more than up for the fight. Nobody ever crossed Hydie Papandreou, or *the Hydra* as she was known, and lived to tell of it. The Hydra was aptly named after the multi-headed serpent in Greek mythology that guarded the entrance to the Underworld. If you cut off one head, then two would grow in its place. Even its poisonous breath would kill. This Hydra was also known for having identities over her lifetime, changing to another each time that the identity was compromised. She was looking again at the elegant woman sat in the fifth chair.

"Yes number five, we will be friends," she said to herself.

Chapter 2

It was midnight when they finally filed out of the castle gate, marking the end of the summer solstice. A lone owl hooted hauntingly, but otherwise the night was silent. The footsteps of the thirteen fell heavily on the cobblestones that had been polished by several hundred years of people trafficking, destroying the peace and tranquillity of the moment. Their cars were parked in their new order of seniority, with the Pindar's at the front. None bid farewell or exchanged niceties as they reached their own chauffeur driven vehicles. All that had needed to be said publicly had been. Anything else was included in the personal large brown envelopes that each member of the Council was carrying. They were to be opened in privacy and obeyed to the letter. The woman entering the fifth limousine was Gina Mèdici.

The cavalcade pulled away as one, circling in the courtyard before making its way back out through the avenue of poplars. The cars once again flickered as they passed down the avenue of impressive trees but now it was in the light of the silver moonlight rather than the burnt orange glow of the setting sun. There were fourteen of them now, not the original thirteen. The fourteenth was a hearse with two coffins inside, uncle and niece, united in death.

When the cavalcade reached the main road, it divided, part heading north and the rest, south. Gina's car headed south, beginning the six hour overnight run down through Switzerland to her home in Milan. Gina leaned forward to the privacy divider.

"Drive safely Luigi and stop if you need to. I'm turning in. Goodnight and thanks," Gina's voice had that endearing musicality that is characteristic of the Italian language.

"Goodnight Donna Gina," Luigi closed the divider and set his mind on the long journey south.

Now alone, Gina was free to take off the coarse black, shapeless habit. Beneath it, she wore a white long sleeved shirt and dark grey, pinstriped pencil skirt cut to above her knee. The shoes were an attempt at sensible, but only as far as Gucci does *sensible*. Gina was in her mid-thirties and one of Italy's most sophisticated and photographed women. Unusually for the celebrities chosen by these magazines, Gina was voluptuous. She promoted the image of *well-woman* and was evidence apparent that you didn't have to be skinny to be beautiful and sexy.

By no means did she have the build of an athlete, but Gina had fenced since she was a child. She had competed in the World Fencing Championships and the Olympics, winning gold medals in both. Her preference was the sabre but she had collected medals in the epée too. That was before the Council of Thirteen and the Pindar had come into her life. Gina hadn't picked up a sword in over two years now.

You couldn't pick up a magazine without finding her somewhere in it. *Grazia* and *IO Donna's* sales thrived on the personal interviews and photo-shoots that she gave with generosity. The paparazzi followed her relentlessly for any scraps and to get that photograph in a million that would set them up for life.

Gina had worn her black hair up in business-like fashion for the meeting. Now, she unpinned it letting it drop past her shoulders. She shook it out, stretching her long neck as she did so, relieving the built-up tension. Gina could feel a migraine coming on and searched her bag for the lifesaving painkillers. She popped two capsules in her mouth and took them dry. Gina was an elegant woman with the face of an angel. Although she had the fuller figure that she had become famous for, she was fit and toned. Amazonian would describe her. Gina's vivid blue eyes set beneath her arched and well-groomed eyebrows were incongruous with her black hair and dark Latin skin. This striking combination was a hand-me-down that went back through the Mèdici family line to at least the thirteenth century. At that time, and until the seventeenth century, the House of Mèdici was one of the most powerful families in Italy. During that period their family could boast three popes and marriages into both the English and French royal families.

Like other signore families in Italy, the Mèdici's had dominated their city's government and finances. This often required a degree of ruthlessness and not everything was done entirely in accordance with the law. On numerous occasions the law needed a certain amount of *revision* to accommodate their business arrangements, but this was never a problem for such a powerful and influential family as the Mèdici's. They also had the accolade of leading the birth of the Italian Renaissance and humanism in Italy. Perhaps more memorably, they founded the Mèdici Bank in 1397 which traded for the next 100 years. At that time, it was the most prosperous and prestigious bank in Europe. The Mèdici's capitalised on its wealth and the power that money can buy. In more recent times Gina's direct family had banking interests of their own and had financial control over most of the banking institutions in Europe, the Middle East and Africa. It was for this

16

reason that her late husband, Antonio, had been invited into the Council of Thirteen.

Gina buried her face in her hands and began to cry. She wondered how things had ever got this crazy. Two years ago, she knew nothing of the Illuminati or the Council of Thirteen; nothing of blood sacrifices and nothing of the New World Order. Since her husband's death, under mysterious circumstances, she had been invited to take his place on the Council. It wasn't even an invitation, she recalled, it was a demand. Life had changed beyond recognition since then. Gina was on a roller coaster that she didn't understand and couldn't get off. She only knew that it was headed for disaster.

Tonight, at the solstice meeting right up until the man had unmasked the girl, she thought that it was her daughter Isabella on the altar. Everything about her was the same. She had found herself desperately searching the girl's body for some difference, some hope. There was nothing to convince her that it wasn't Isabella. Gina knew now, that blood sacrifices were part of the payback for the wealth and the privilege that the Illuminati assured them, but she had never seen it personified. When the mask was removed, Gina had gasped out loud, "Thank you God," she was immediately ashamed that the abuse and death of somebody else's daughter, was less important than her own.

All that Gina could think of now, was to get home and hold Isabella with all her love as if it was the last time that she would ever see her. Gina and her family line were prone to premonitions and she was filled with dread. She knew now that a dark cloud hung over her family and that Isabella was not safe and neither was her beloved son, Sasha.

It was half past six in the morning. The black limousine turned into the drive of Castello di Mèdici, situated just outside of Milan. It would be another five minutes before the car wound its way through the vineyards, up to the grand family home. These vineyards only produced forty tons of grapes in a year, equating to a mere 60,000 bottles. Mèdici wine however, was sought after by the rich and famous all over the world. Pre-orders alone exceeded production annually, even though the price was 80 U.S. Dollars a bottle.

This was no big business for the Mèdici's though, only a drop in the ocean of their wealth. It was simply done for prestige and to use the land to its full potential. Gina was a humanist above all things. The vineyards also served to give employment to the local community. She was the patron and benefactor of numerous local charities and a staunch supporter of the local Catholic Church. Gina was a natural invitee to all major functions, not just because of her financial and social position in the community, but simply because she lit up the occasion and was fun to have around. The locals adored her.

Gina had only slept fitfully on the journey home. She was tormented by guilt fuelled dreams that were still vivid and real in her mind. In her dreams, the girl being raped on the sacrificial altar was her daughter Isabella. She was reaching out to her with both arms crying, "Mummy," repeatedly.

"Baby!" Gina had called out as she tried to run to her daughter's aid but it was if she was wading through treacle. Then somehow, it all changed as dreams do. Gina was now knelt across her daughter's naked body with the dagger held high in her hands. Isabella's face was contorted in horror as she looked up at her mother and screamed out, "Mum!" as Gina drove the dagger down through her daughter's heart.

Gina had woken in a cold sweat, as if the scream was real. She called out to her daughter in panic, "Isabella!"

Gina was stuck in a loop. Each time she dozed off, she immediately went back to that same dream until she was too terrified to close her eyes. But her terror was well founded. Gina's premonitions were all too often real glimpses into the future and she dreaded that this dream might be one of them. Her fear was further reinforced in that, until that night, number six could never have imagined that he would have sacrificed his own flesh and blood to appease the Pindar. Now both he and his niece were dead.

Gina couldn't help replaying the horror of the Council's meeting through her mind. It wasn't just the barbaric murder and rape of an innocent child; it was *everything* about the meeting. There was nothing about the Council's objectives that bore any similarity to her personal doctrine. It was all abhorrent to her. Perhaps it was a man's world she wondered? Then she recalled that the only other woman in the meeting, a rare sophisticated beauty, had been watching her. She had even invited her with a smile.

"Perhaps she was different to the others?" Gina hoped.

The limousine pulled up in front of the impressive entrance tower of Castello di Mèdici. It was an early seventeenth century palace built in the ornate Moorish style with battlements and spires that mixed both the Anglo and Arab influences. Each side of the main tower, were the east and west wings that gave extensive accommodation for family and guests. The orange and red sculpted stonework reflected the morning sun in the most pleasing way and Gina immediately felt safer for being there.

Gina bade Luigi goodbye, turned and climbed the steps up to the intricately carved front door. Luigi had called ahead and the staff there was expecting her. The housekeeper, a plump African woman in her early forties, met her at the door with a genuine smile that lit up her face.

"Donna Gina, 'tis lovely to have you back. Life's not the same when you go leave us. Ain't no sunshine when you gone, only shadows," she had that gentle West Indian lilt to her voice.

It was typical African flattery but Asmina meant every word of it. She regarded Gina, Sasha and Isabella as her family and their care to be entirely her responsibility. That was particularly so, since the unexpected and unexplained death of Gina's husband, Antonio. Asmina had never quite taken to him though, so her concerns about his passing were entirely about how it would affect Gina and the children.

Although a staunch Catholic, Asmina still had deeply embedded tribal roots and dabbled in the mystic. Even before the shock news of Antonio's death, Asmina had seen it in the cards. Tarot was her passion but she often used it to simply explain other supernatural visions that she had. Her mistress, Gina, had the same fascination with Tarot and they often used to indulge in it together. Asmina though, was an adept in the art and Gina, yet a novice; a sceptical one at that. Asmina had never divulged the dark secret that she carried about having foreseen Antonio's death, nor those that she had glimpsed that were yet to come.

Gina took Asmina in a welcoming embrace that was just a little too urgent. Asmina sensed it immediately. She pushed Gina away to arm's length and looked her in the eyes.

"Somethin' wrong *bibi*, tell me?" Asmina used the African word for 'mistress' affectionately when they were alone or in moments of concern.

"It's nothing honestly, I'm tired is all. It was a stressful meeting and I hardly slept on the way back," Gina smiled innocently but as usual Asmina saw right through her.

"Just as you say bibi, we talk 'bout it later."

It would have sounded patronising to another but it was simply Asmina's mothering instinct and Gina needed that, particularly as she had been an orphan since her late teens. It was latitude that Gina gave her when they were alone.

"I'm starving," Gina said quickly to divert the conversation.

"Luigi already call me, as the man does, an' breakfast's ready. Kids are still sleepin' bibi. Shall I call them?"

"No Asmina, I will go. Thank you," Gina needed to see them to reassure herself that they were safe, particularly Isabella.

When Gina opened the door to Isabella's bedroom she stirred but didn't rouse. Gina sat on the bed and watched her sixteen year old daughter as she slept peacefully. Gina genuflected. Her fingers gently touching her head, chest and shoulders.

"Thank you, God, she murmured," the guilt, grief and relief that she felt at that moment were a heady mix that was suffocating her. Tears of immense gratitude streamed down her face.

Gina ran her fingers through Isabella's golden curls and kissed her on the forehead. She felt blessed that it was not her daughter that had been chosen by the Pindar. All this was at total odds with her Catholic beliefs. She needed to somehow find a way out of the Council of Thirteen before it was too late. Gina knew though, deep down, that it would put them all in even greater danger if she did. She silently cursed her husband for having got them involved in the first place. The Pindar was not a man to disappoint.

"Stay safe baby," Gina whispered, and then quietly left the room.

Sasha's bedroom was down the hallway, through the tower to the west wing of the building. As she walked there, Gina felt the weight of fear begin to lift from her shoulders. Seeing her daughter safe and peaceful in her bed went a long way towards allaying her fears and mending her spirit. Gina didn't have to be quite so careful as she opened the door into Sasha's room. He was like most eighteen year old boys and could sleep like the dead until midday or beyond. Gina crossed the room and knelt on the floor beside him. He was lying on his stomach with his face turned to her. She laid her head on the pillow next to him, looking into his face and breathing his scent in. He was simply an Adonis. Blond, like his sister, but with angular Roman features. He had recently turned man and his morning stubble was evidence of that. The nights were still hot in Milan and Sasha had dragged the covers down to his waist to cool. Gina idly marvelled at how her little baby now had a muscular back.

"They grow up too quickly," she mused, planted a kiss on his cheek and left his room.

The breakfast room was at the back of house. It led out into a decked area outside with cheery orange parasols and high backed chairs set around rustic tables that were cushioned in the same brightly coloured material. In good weather, Gina preferred to dine outside. She enjoyed the ambience of the immaculately kept gardens and the view of the vineyards as they tumbled down the hill in tiers to the main road, over a mile below.

"The trappings of wealth," she mused. "And the trap that is wealth," she added ironically.

Right now, Gina would have given it all up if she could just take her kids and run. But she couldn't, the trap was truly set. Both Sasha and Isabella had enviable lifestyles and expectations. Their educations were going impeccably and the fees astronomical. They had made some special friends and their social lives were extraordinary. The vineyards employed almost a quarter of the people in the village, either directly or indirectly. The community depended on it, on her. Even the upkeep of the homestead of Castello di Mèdici provided a living for six local families. The Mèdici banking and financial institutions employed thousands. They all depended on her, now single handed, to steer the business through the aggressive, globalised and corrupt world that they traded in. No, she couldn't run away, she knew that. Too many lives depended on her. But then, if she didn't, she would become as corrupt as the Pindar and his Council herself. It was Catch 22.

Gina needed advice but couldn't confide in anyone. Number six and a dear relative of his died last night because of some breach of confidence and suffered the ultimate price. Gina knew that it would ultimately be her fate too or that of her children. Blood sacrifices were obligatory for all who wished to stay in power or to be famous. Monthly the news reported the deaths of the wealthy and celebrities in unusual circumstances. Invariably, when you researched the detail, the celebrity who died either had direct or indirect links to the Illuminati. It was way past coincidence. The happenings of last night were evidence of the truth of it. Even more damningly, so many happened around the solstice, at the time of sacrifice.

When people are desperate they often turn to religion or to the occult. Gina needed Asmina to read the cards for her, she was desperate. At that very moment, as if Gina had called out to her, Asmina walked out onto the decking carrying her breakfast tray.

"Your breakfast bibi."

Asmina was quite an actress. She put the tray on the table theatrically and set about placing Gina's breakfast in front of her in a business-like fashion. She over-emphasised pouring the coffee and moved the plates into position more swiftly than was necessary. It was Asmina's way of gently punishing her mistress for being dishonest with her and not sharing her secret. Gina took Asmina's hand and stopped her antics.

"I'm sorry," she said smiling back at her, "can we start again?"

"Don't know what you talkin' 'bout Donna Gina," Asmina was still being off-hand and playing hurt.

"You never call me *Donna Gina* in private Asmina unless you are cross with me."

Asmina's face was stern. She put her hands on her hips and thrust out her chin. She looked for all the world like she was about to let rip, then her face transformed and melted into the biggest grin. Asmina tipped her head to one side in quizzical manner.

"You holdin' out on me bibi?" they laughed conspiratorially. Asmina put her big arms around Gina. It felt like heaven to her, so safe.

"Oh Asmina I don't know where to begin or how much I can say."

"Tis trouble brought on by that no-good husband o' yours, an' now you takin' on the Devil's own work for him."

23

Asmina was a simple woman but she had seen and heard things in the house that she knew just weren't right. The cards had shown her that troubles in the Mèdici family were far from over. Asmina had dutifully held her tongue until now but she sensed the moment.

"You gonna lose everythin' bibi, 'less you be strong."

Asmina hoped that she hadn't gone too far. It was in the balance for several seconds while Gina agonised over her response.

"He wasn't so bad," Gina said defensively.

"An' I ain't black," Asmina retorted mockingly. "You got family to think on bibi, I knows you in trouble, I seen it in the cards an'..." Asmina stopped abruptly. She had let her mouth run away with her.

"What have you seen Asmina? Tell me," Gina's expression was a mixture of anger, fear and panic.

"Things is all," it was Asmina's turn to be defensive but now there was no turning back.

Gina held her own counsel while she thought on it. Asmina had worked in her household for twenty years and she did have an uncanny knack of divining some truth from the cards. It was mostly trivial though, or at least what Asmina told her was. She had predicted both of Gina's pregnancies and was right about their sexes too. There had been a miscarriage between the births though. Gina remembered when she first found out that she was pregnant that, on this occasion, Asmina had acted strangely and had not enthused as she had with Sasha.

"Tis early days bibi," she had said. "Hold your 'citement 'till baby's good'n fixed an' you feel him kickin' in your belly. Then you rejoice."

Gina had never felt her baby kick and she lost him in her twentieth week. Strangely it was a boy and Asmina had said *him*. At last Gina had decided.

"Asmina, will you read the cards for me tonight? I don't know what to do anymore; I'm lost and out of my depth. I know that this doesn't end well."

Tears welled in Gina's eyes until they were fat and full. Finally, they erupted into a river that fell down her beautiful face, finding the angles of her high cheek bones that turned them down the side of her face to her chin.

Asmina looked at her mistress with a love that was as big as the moon. The cards had shown her that her mistress had the mother of all battles ahead of her if she had any hope at all of saving herself and her children. Even then, she had divined that she had precious little.

"You not as helpless as you t'ink bibi. You got somethin' in you, somethin' strong. Somethin' 'bout yourself that ain't nobody got. You just got to dig deep 'n find it girl. You just gotta fight is all bibi. You just gotta fight!"

Asmina had long ago recognised that Gina wasn't altogether *normal*. There was something in her nature that wasn't entirely human. Something in her blood that dated back to ancient times. Asmina had sensed that heritage in others too, but they were rare indeed. It wasn't anything sinister or of the occult, Asmina had divined. No, it was as if the girl had come from the very stars above her, or at least her ancestors had. Gina was not altogether of this world; she decided and prayed that it would make the difference when the time came.

Chapter 3

Thessaloniki, Greece. June 22nd 2017.

Hydie Papandreou was still towelling her wet hair as she walked out onto the balcony of her luxury town house in Thessaloniki. She was an elegant woman, dark and mysteriously attractive. She appeared to be in her early forties but this woman had seen civilisations rise and fall. She was not of us or caring of us. The colonisation and integration of their *kind* happened significantly before the birth of Christ. They had gravitated to be the ruling power infiltrating governments, religious and terrorist organisations, conglomerates, world banking and the media. It was for all these reasons that Hydie sat to the right-hand side of the Pindar as his number one.

The journey back from Ingolstadt had taken a fatiguing six hours and Hydie had been desperate to shower and get into the comfort of her white silk robe. She leant against the balustrade and feasted on the view, as she wrapped the luxurious white towel around her head in turban fashion. The sun was just rising in the eastern skies, silhouetting the foothills and peaks that grew into Mount Olympus, bathing her in its warm orange light.

There had been two women present amongst the Council of Thirteen's meeting of the summer solstice. They shared only one thing in common, they were both widows. Otherwise, they were entirely different beings; genetically and spiritually. The view out towards Olympus always reminded Hydie of her late husband Demitri. It evoked a feeling of great sadness, but somehow comforting too. It had been a view that they had shared over the centuries and a backdrop to their lovemaking, on countless summer evenings. But that was many years ago now. Hydie had thought about leaving the house but she still found great comfort in the memories that they had shared there. It was only for this reason that she had stayed.

A young slender, somewhat effeminate man walked out onto the balcony. He was carrying a tray with coffee and hot croissants. Vassos set the tray down and poured the hot, sweet Turkish coffee.

"Coffee is served *Kyrie*. Can I get you anything else?" Vassos's voice was soft and almost apologetic, matching his gentle nature.

Hydie stayed with her back to him looking out across the mountains in thought, ignoring his presence, as was usual. At last she raised an admonishing hand, signalling his dismissal and Vassos duly left. He had grown accustomed to being treated in that condescending way and wondered why he had never left. That would have needed courage though, and he knew that he had none. Besides, there were things that he had witnessed in the house and knowledge that he had gained. This would have made him a threat and his mistress had a way of neutralising *threats*.

"Off-handedness was just her way," he conceded. She was the one that they called *the Hydra,* and probably the most powerful women on Earth. It was not Vassos's place to take offence.

Hydie Papandreou gazed up at the mythical mountain of Olympus and considered the events of the night of the solstice. The human sacrifice had left her unmoved. She was accustomed to death and the administering of it. Death was a natural part of maintaining her position as Supreme Senator in the Shadow organisation. It was an ancient organisation, that had undergone numerous attempted *coups d'état* over the millennia and was significantly more enduring than the Illuminati. The Hydra had dealt with all and every conspiracy ruthlessly, using the dark powers of her birth right. There was now only one in her organisation that didn't fear her and that was the new number twelve. That man was the Mullah Ismael Alansari, but then he feared no one, nor death.

It was a conundrum. The Hydra had superior inborn powers to the Mullah's because of her pure Shadow genes, so he was no *physical* threat to her. Her network was all but impregnable so to be toppled from the inside was unlikely. Her problem was the Pindar. He had chosen the Mullah to be one of the Council of Thirteen. That now placed the Mullah beyond reach. To kill him, or have him killed, would evoke the rage of the Pindar and she was not ready for that. Not yet. There was something supernatural about the Pindar, something profoundly dark and dangerous. The Hydra had not yet fathomed it. He was not entirely human and not a Shadow either, nor a man to cross; but then nor was she. Number two's words echoed in her mind:

"Don't get too comfortable in that chair young lady. You are only keeping it warm for our new number twelve."

Those words were hauntingly prophetic.

The Hydra turned away from the mountain holding those thoughts. She sat and picked up the brown envelope the Pindar had given her. She took a sip of the sweet coffee and placed a long, painted fingernail under the flap and levered it open. It was not in the Hydra's nature to take orders. For now, she would do as she was told and bide her time. There would be more favourable occasions when she could press her advantage. Right now, she was safe because the Pindar needed her. The Hydra's network of financial, political and military control was unsurpassed. She knew that if she gave it to the Pindar, she would be dead in the days that followed.

"Dog eats dog," the Mullah had said, she reflected. "Until the last dog is standing."

In his rhetoric, the Mullah had gone on to imply that the *dog* in question would be the Pindar. He had already declared his allegiance to him in that statement despite being a fellow Shadow and one of her subordinates.

"Yet another *coup*," the Hydra sighed. "Bring it on!" and then with a sadistic grin, "Move over Pindar, your chair is mine. And you, Mullah Ismail Alansari, are a dead man in the waiting."

Hydie went on to reflect on the only other woman present at the meeting. She needed an ally on the inside, one of the Council of Thirteen. The Hydra pushed the brown envelope to one side.

"That can wait," she said under her breath and reached for her iPad. She typed the name, "Gina Mèdici", into the browser. By the end of the day the Hydra would know all there was to know about the beautiful and enigmatic number five.

Chapter 4

Asmina laid the dinner table lovingly for her surrogate family. She had endured a hard life up until being 'adopted' by the Mèdici's. There were things that had happened to her, both as a child and a young woman, that she couldn't have confided in anyone but Gina. Somehow Gina had the ability to listen, advise and not judge her. Without that advice Asmina knew that she would have sought solace in death. It was that closeness to ending her own life that had opened her mind to all possibility and inspired her relationship with God and, perhaps, with the Devil.

Because Asmina could read the cards and cross into that *other world*, she knew without doubt that nothing in the present was as it seemed. She could see the conflicts. She could see that certain things were divined and that something's were within our remit of choice; things that we could change. Asmina could also see that few of us had the strength of spirit to fight against the inevitable. Her mistress, Gina, was one of those exceptions. Asmina had long since sensed that Gina was of another kind, not of her blood. She had sensed others too but not benevolent and caring like her. The others that she had encountered, that were alien to us, were of a dark and menacing nature. Gina's late husband had been one of those. Fortunately, Gina had the dominant gene and Sasha and Isabella had taken after her.

"It was a blessing," Asmina mumbled to herself, deep in her thoughts.

"What was a blessing?" Gina asked. Asmina nearly jumped out of her skin.

"Holy Mary, mother of God bibi! You gimme such a fright creepin' round like that," Asmina's eyes were wide open at the shock of it. Gina just chuckled at her dilemma.

"I wasn't creeping Asmina, you were just lost in your thoughts as usual."

"Someone round here need to worry 'bout things," Asmina said defensively with an expression of mock hurt. "Shall I call the children?"

Gina found it endearing that Asmina still referred to them as *children* even though they were already worldly and stood taller than her. She was like a grandmother to Sasha and Isabella and they loved her for it. This meant the world to Gina, as she had lost her own parents while only in her late teens. Her late husband's parents had no interest in him, let alone his kids. So Asmina was their only source of nurture, apart from herself. It was a fragile support network and Gina constantly worried about how things would go if she were to become ill or die. This made the current danger about being a member of the Council of Thirteen even more poignant. She needed an exit plan and she needed it now.

Sasha and Isabella walked in sharing some gossip. Isabella had her hands theatrically over her mouth gasping the word "no", and then laughed conspiratorially. Sasha dropped the story and embraced Asmina. Their size difference was significant and he planted a kiss on top of her head, something that always had the effect of infuriating Asmina. Secretly though she loved his uninhibited show of affection and wouldn't have had it any other way.

"I'm starving Asmina, just put a horse between two slices," he smiled at her fondly.

It was hardly a joke though. Sasha was always working out, either bulking up or stripping down. Right now, he was off the carbs and eating more meat than a pack of wolves. He looked good.

"What are you having Mum?" Isabella asked, kissing her mother's cheek.

"Hello darling. The fish and salad alas, but only so that I can have some of Asmina's Pavlova," it was a family favourite, even though Gina and Isabella were always counting calories.

"Mm same for me please Asmina," then, turning to Sasha. "It's a shame about you being off the carbs Sasha. That Pavlova looks wicked. What price vanity, eh?"

Their sibling relationship revolved around friendly jibes and point-scoring, much as it does for most teenagers.

"Just remember that when you are out shopping and have to buy the next size up," Sasha grinned. Isabella just crossed her eyes and poked out her tongue.

"How did your meeting in Germany go Mum, it must have gone on late?" Isabella was keen to change the subject.

"Oh, pretty mundane really. Just the usual players and aspirations, mostly around greed really," well at least some of that sentence was true, thought Gina.

"Do they miss Dad?" Isabella looked pained.

She had idolised her father, although Gina had never understood why. He was neither a giver nor a carer. Somehow Isabella had forgiven that, "Blind love," Gina had concluded.

"It's not that kind of caring organisation darling, though I wish it were," Gina replied. "It's all about acquisition, balancing the accounts and the bottom line. They don't much care who does it," and that was the truth. They were all expendable at the right time.

"It is enough for your father that *we* miss him," Gina continued, placing her hand over her daughter's supportively. "And what about your day, how are your studies going?"

Isabella was a bright student and had already chosen her career. She had begun her extracurricular studies and wanted to specialise in international law. She wanted to make a difference to people's lives, just like her mother had done.

"I love them Mum. At last it all feels *relevant* and I know where I'm going."

"Defender of the people," thought Gina but didn't say. "She would be good at that."

"You will make your father proud Isabella," Gina squeezed her hand and turned to Sasha.

"And have you broken any more hearts?" Gina raised an immaculately groomed eyebrow at him accusingly.

"Mother, I collect them, I don't break them," his smile was easy, although mischievous.

"*Jar of Hearts*," Isabella interjected pointedly. It was one of her and Sasha's favourite songs, so she knew that he would *get* the jibe.

Sasha didn't want to be drawn in. He knew that his mother enjoyed the shenanigans of his love life and guessed that it was in part driven by her own isolation. There had not been another man in her life since his father had died.

"Not much to report, although I do have to make a choice for the end of year university dance. I wonder who the lucky girl will be?" it was said to bait his mother, rather than in earnest. She bit.

"So you don't break any hearts eh?" Gina could never help herself from drawing the comparison of Isabella having her heart broken by some Cavalier boyfriend.

It was Sasha's turn to change the subject.

"Hey Sis, have you seen the latest development in LuminaGames, the *Dream App*?"

"I've heard about it, but it will never happen Sasha. Too much legislation," Isabella replied authoritatively but playfully. "Trust me I'm a lawyer.

"What's this Sasha?" Gina felt out of the loop.

"It's a new idea by LuminaGames," began Sasha, "it comes from their subliminal learning research where you embed suggestion into a documentary, film or even an advertisement. They implant images and words throughout, that you don't realise you see or hear, but you do. They reckon that it will revolutionise education and make cool games too."

"It's been going on for years in advertising Sasha. They banned it then as unfair and *contrary to the public interest*, and they will ban this one now," Isabella was confident in her statement. "Its mind control, *intentional deception of the public*, as they called it then."

"Help please," Gina asked, "I'm definitely behind the curve here," Isabella continued.

"In the early seventies, subliminal messaging was used in various TV ads and presidential campaigns. They flashed an image at a rate of about one a second, which is not possible to see consciously, but your subconscious mind picks it up. They can do the same with sounds too, and games apparently."

Gina was always amazed at her daughter's power of retention; she was a sponge for random information and soaked it all up. But then that was a talent that was universally shared in her family line. Sasha was the same but he focussed too much on gaming, girls and trivia. It worried her.

"Thank you Issie. And so, Sasha, what is so special about this Dream App then?"

"It's going to be awesome."

Sasha was still holding on to the positive despite his sister's certainty that it would never be allowed.

"You choose a character apparently, in a list of subscribing movies that you want to be in and watch it before you go to sleep. They have done some stuff like Issie says to the movie like inserting suggestive frames. Then when you go to sleep, you are programmed to re-run the movie in your dreams. But this time, you are the hero," Sasha's grin showed that he was sold on it.

"It sounds perfectly dreadful to me Sasha and really quite dangerous," Gina could see all sorts of issues. "I think, well I sincerely hope, that Issie is right and that they ban it."

"Don't worry Mum," Isabella interjected, "it's a non-starter. Even this morally bankrupt world will fight against something as Orwellian as this. Sorry, Sasha but you must fulfil your own dreams."

Chapter 5

Illya Dracul walked through the entrance to the LuminaGames research and development facility in Berlin. It had been yet another media acquisition by the Illuminati. It now gave them almost total control of the gaming and video industries. Dracul's brown envelope from the Pindar had set out his objectives. One of them was to complete the development of their new and revolutionary Dream App and commence manufacture at the soonest. In parallel he was tasked with producing a globalised marketing strategy and distribution plan. Dracul was already well advanced in all areas of his programme and today was going to be a major milestone in the project; proof of science. He had carefully selected three young couples from disadvantaged backgrounds, who had little or no family support. They were the kind of people who could *go missing* without raising too many questions. They were living in the facility rent free with nominal pay and the promise of a significant completion bonus; one that they would be unlikely to receive.

When Illya Dracul walked into the proofing studio at seven o'clock in the morning, his technical team were already hard at work. Ali Getz was his graphics man, a self-taught genius. He had a natural affinity for knowledge and an empirical understanding of even the most complex gaming design software. Ali Getz was so well respected in the industry, that software designers would come to him to troubleshoot for their own products. Haru Kishimoto was the audio man who came with the highest possible credentials and experience. He was a master in synthetic sound and related software design. Then there was Simon Farley, their editor. His remit was to pull it all together, working closely with Doctor Walter Schwartz, the brains behind building the mental and physical addictions into the game.

The gaunt and stooped doctor was a vastly experienced man, now in his high nineties but still as sharp as a knife. He mostly worked covertly in a top-secret wing at the Max Planck Institute for Medical Research in Heidelberg. He only visited the LuminaGames facility at key decision making moments. Today was one of those key moments, the start of human trials.

Doctor Schwartz was not unfamiliar with trials of this kind. In the Second World War, he had worked in the German concentration camps with Ernst Rüdin, one of the leading Nazi physicians at the time, specialising in the field of human experimentation. Those experiments, included mind control through subliminal messaging, hypnosis and the use of hallucinogenic drugs. In more recent years, he had used his wartime experiences to inform his studies into cognitive psychology. He supported the theory that the human mind behaves like an organic computer, and therefore can be programmed and reprogrammed as such. In other words, careful selection and control of input data, through the five human senses, will result in the desired output or response.

These were the men that Illya had chosen to deliver his mission. That mission was to create a game with the potential to be as addictive as heroin and that could enslave the masses to do as the Pindar pleased; electronic narcotics.

Bjorn and Heidi were sat in the comfortable chairs in front of the impressive 3D TV. The lights were dimmed and mood music was playing through the cinema effect sound system. They were runaways at just sixteen, lovers who had exchanged Berlin for their small village in Sweden. Both their parents had disapproved of their love affair, "Puppy love," they had called it and put every obstacle possible in their way. When they had learned that Heidi was pregnant, their fury was beyond measure. The young lovers had then sold all their personal possessions discretely and scraped up enough money to get to Germany, but little more. When Illya Dracul had found them destitute and offered free accommodation and the promise of a good completion bonus after some TV based experiments, it was manna from heaven and too good to refuse. It seemed safe enough to them, dream research was all. Illya had promised them future opportunities too. They had every reason to be sat happily cuddling each other, sharing a bottle of beer in front of the big screen TV.

Both had been given a brief about what to expect. Apparently, the film would inspire their dreams and they would experience some kind of pleasurable virtual reality. After that, in all probability, the dream would live as a lasting memory. Just as if it actually happened.

Bjorn looked at the DVD cover and read it to Heidi as the film started to boot in the game module.

"It's an action, adventure Heidi," Bjorn was clearly pleased with Illya's choice and beamed lovingly at her.

"Sam Stone is an undercover agent working for the CIA. Through a staged FBI raid on an illicit arms deal with one of the Arab nations, Stone gets arms boss, Carlos Mendes, clear of the fray. Stone is invited to join Mendes' organisation as one of his bodyguards and gets close to Mendes but even closer to his wife, Angelina. A dangerous and tempestuous liaison with Angelina ensues, as Stone enters into a web of deceit to entrap Mendes and expose his organisation."

Bjorn selected 'play' and tossed the controller onto the sofa.

"Right up my street," he said placing his hand proudly on Heidi's tummy. "Baby is under age though. Do you think he will mind?"

"*She* will be just fine, it's me you should be worrying about," Heidi cocked an accusing brow. "I've seen films like this before and I hate them. Angelina will definitely get killed by her husband, for being a traitor and Sam Stone won't even shed a tear. I should be watching Disney in this condition, not murder and suspense."

Heidi pulled her long blonde hair over her shoulder furthest away from Bjorn and snuggled into him. She placed her hands over his and pulled it to her belly, then kissed his cheek.

"I think *she* kicked today but I'm not sure," Heidi said proudly, emphasising the 'she' again. They were in friendly dispute over the matter. "At least this movie might make her do it again in silent protest to support her mother. You might feel her for the first time."

Bjorn grinned with pleasure at the news of the new development. The abstract thought of being a father was slowly becoming a reality. All he knew was that he would do anything to give the woman that he loved and their baby a safe and happy home; anything.

Chapter 6

Gina and Asmina were sat in the chapel in Castello Mèdici that had not changed significantly in over 400 years. The chapel was where Gina often went to reflect. It was Spartan in appearance, just a simple altar covered in a white linen cloth with a red silk tapestry draped over. A crucifix was centred upon it along with a single candle that burned feebly, barely illuminating the room. The only other lighting was from a stained-glass window set high on the wall that depicted Jesus on the cross. It allowed the dying embers of the sun to fall colourfully on their faces. They sat on two rudely cut wooden stools at one end of the altar, with the pack of Tarot cards in front of them. Gina always chose to have her reading done in the Chapel in the hope that God might lend a hand in the outcome.

"You ready bibi?" Asmina's voice was whispered. Even in the holiness of the chapel she felt the presence of both God and the Devil.

In terms of Tarot, Asmina was a bit of a fraud. She mostly used the cards as a theatrical prop for what she really had. That was an ability to look into the future through her own eyes as if she was there and an ability to converse with the spirits. This unfortunately brought with it much heartache. She already knew how her loved ones were going to die, including Gina, and even how she herself would meet her maker. It wasn't preordained though. Alternative futures could be made but that was by exception, not by rule. To change the order of things you needed fortitude, you needed to endure. Courage, foresight, conviction and good fortune were prerequisites. Asmina wondered if her mistress had enough of these qualities. She hoped to God, and the Devil, that she did.

Gina was filled with superstitious and religious dread but she had no choice. She had no answer for her predicament. If she did nothing, then she would eventually lose all. If she went against the Pindar's will, he would certainly have her and her family killed. *De facto*.

"I'm ready," Gina said unconvincingly.

She looked like a frightened child as Asmina handed her the deck of Tarot cards.

"Take them and change their faces bibi. Free your spirit an' mix them so they' of your makin' an' tell your story."

Asmina's manner had changed dramatically. She had become business like and distant, opening her mind to infinite possibility. Her eyes rolled back until all Gina could see was the whites of them, then exhaled with all the gusto of a bull in the ring readying itself to take on the matador. Asmina had begun the journey that would take her to that dimension that exists between worlds, the twilight zone. It was a place where restless spirits exist in purgatory, until they have repented and earned their place in the next world. In this place, time has no structure, no order, no meaning. It is a place where past, present and future meet as one. Deep guttural sounds came from within her that rumbled around the stone chapel like distant thunder. Her face reflected the pain and suffering of all those that she met and conferred with, in that unholy place. At last she slumped onto the altar and fell into a deep sleep, snoring peacefully.

As she slept, Gina's religious dread consumed her such that she feared for her very soul. As a Christian, she knew that she was inviting the Devil into the sanctuary of this holy place. She knelt at the altar, genuflected and began praying for forgiveness. It was sometime before she felt Asmina's hand on her shoulder, bringing her back from her God.

"Tis actions you need now bibi, not penitence. Your god'll understand. He made you mother an' give you strength to fight. Now you fight bibi, you fight for all of us."

There was something in Asmina's bountiful smile that was different, mischievous even. Gina couldn't quite fathom it. She had seen something, Gina was sure of it.

"Hope perhaps?" Gina mused.

It certainly wasn't hopelessness. Asmina tipped her head towards the cards prompting Gina to pick them up again. Gina gave them a final shuffle, cut them and handed them back.

Asmina turned the first card over and placed it purposefully, almost theatrically, in front of her mistress. It depicted a crowned woman sitting between two pillars holding a book. It was the Torah, written by the prophet Moses, expounding the Jewish people's covenant with God. Her flowing blue dress turned into running water at her feet where a crescent moon, symbolising her ruler, lay adjacent. It was the second and most controversial card of the Major Arcana of Tarot. Asmina sucked in her breath at the magnitude of it.

"*The High Priestess*," Asmina said authoritatively. "She is you. Tis the sign of ability an' help. Maybe you gonna find a teacher bibi, someone to lead you on your journey.

They both understood the significance and the danger of this powerful card. Asmina turned over the next and placed it below and to the left of the first. It was *the Magician*. It portrayed a young apprentice starting his journey towards knowledge and enlightenment. He was stood behind a table on which were placed symbols of the four suits of the Minor Arcana; the pentacle, cup, sword and wands. All that he would need to succeed on his journey. The card reinforced the attributes of Gina's personal card, the High Priestess and they both knew it.

"You not gonna be alone on your journey bibi," Asmina said simply.

Asmina smiled encouragingly at her mistress as she turned over the next card and placed it to the right and in line with the Magician. It was *the Fool*. The image on it was of a young man walking over difficult terrain and about to step over a cliff. He is seemingly unaware of the dangers of his surroundings. The young man carries a bag with his possessions on a stick and his dog is at his side.

"Tis the card of discovery bibi, new talents an' abilities. You's yet an embryo bibi an' you still growin'," the smile that crossed Asmina's face told Gina that the cards were fortunate so far.

The next card caused Asmina to falter and hold her breath. The card was *Death*. She placed it reluctantly to the right of the Fool. The card showed a black night on a white horse carrying a flag with a heraldic rose embroidered on it. The horse is trampling people beneath, not caring of creed or class.

There was an unnatural pause. Gina could tell that Asmina was considering her words very carefully. At last Asmina exhaled.

"There be death comin' bibi, much death," Asmina looked stricken and Gina more so.

"My babies!" Gina howled, as if her heart had just been ripped out.

"We don't know bibi, that for you an' fate to decide.

Asmina moved on quickly and turned the last card, placing it to the right of Death. The card showed a man and a woman stood naked together in Adam and Eve poses. The trees around them bore the forbidden fruit and serpents were entwined around them. An angel in the sky above them is seemingly nurturing their love.

"*The Lovers*," Gina said in a whisper. She knew that she must be the woman on the card and immediately felt a reflex action in the base of her stomach as if in preparation for the encounter. "Who is the man?" she wondered and felt sure that she had only thought it and not said it out aloud.

"We never know bibi," Asmina had *read* her. In these intense moments Asmina's psychic skills were highly tuned. "Maybe he be your white knight bibi, your saviour, or maybe the very Devil himself? We must consider the cards as one, as a story bibi, then we know where you goin'."

"And if I come back," Gina said ironically.

Despite the coolness of the chapel, Gina was glowing with perspiration. It was fear. The flickering light of the candle played on her face, accentuating her high cheekbones and angular Roman features. It also brought out the blueness in her otherwise black hair. Gina's pupils were large in the dimness of the room and reflected both the candle and her religious dread. It was the face of a rare beauty, which somehow accentuated the pain of her expression. Asmina put the rest of the cards down and came to her rescue, cupping her trembling hand with hers. She cleared her throat in readiness to tell Gina what else she had divined from the cards enhanced by what she had learned from the restless spirits and their ravings. She pointed to the cards almost reverently.

"All your cards be from the Major Arcana of Tarot bibi; powerful cards. They tell me your futures mixed with forces of good an' evil an' that you have choice an' then no choice at all."

"That's really helpful Asmina, thanks a bunch. Good and evil, choice but no choice. What the hell is that supposed to mean?" it was an uncharacteristic tirade from Gina, evidence of her anxiety. Asmina decided to gently return the punishment.

"An' you ain't listening Donna Gina," it was her formal address again, a rebuff.

Asmina had become business-like again. She was about to undertake the difficult task of combining the mystical prophecy of the cards with the knowledge that she had gleaned from somewhere between Heaven and Hell. By the very nature of their damnation the spirits were at best unreliable but Asmina had learned to interpret their lies and half-truths. She touched the image of the High Priestess and began to talk in the third person.

"She's on a journey bibi but she don't know where an' she has abilities that she don't know neither. She born of Angel blood an' need enlightenment and direction to find who she is. The girl need teachin' bibi!" Asmina's chubby fingers moved to the Magician card. "He, or she, gonna bring that but maybe the High Priestess just don't listen. She stubborn."

In the sombre of the chapel the whites of Asmina's eyes shone from the black anthracite of her face. They seemed like saucers as they fell accusingly on Gina. She knew Asmina well enough to know that the *stubbornness* comment was a minor scalding for her earlier tirade and let it go.

"Do I know him?" Gina asked a little timidly.

"Girl you don't even know if it's a man!" Asmina was becoming theatrical. "Might not be, but you must find him, or her, an' you gotta know where to look.

"But how..." Asmina cut her short as her hand passed to the Fool card.

"The girl still a fool bibi, but this card be discovery an' change. She gonna find her talents an' abilities and she ain't gonna be a fool for too long. She gonna learn all she can. The Magician has

Angel blood too an' gonna show her. But she gotta listen bibi, she gotta listen an' believe. If she don't believe in herself, then ain't nobody walkin' outta here. Not you, not the kids an' not even me," Asmina had *seen* their deaths. She knew how each would be taken if the Pindar wasn't stopped, including herself.

Gina felt the truth in Asmina's words and the chapel seemed to chill at the mention of it. The next card was Death. Asmina's fingers trembled as she touched it.

"Death have two meanin's bibi. It don't mean it's hopeless. Can be just a change, a new beginning," Asmina didn't sound convincing and Gina's response even less so.

"Of course," there was a tremble in her voice. She changed the subject. "And what of the last card, the Lovers?" again Gina felt that contraction in her lower stomach as if in premonition.

"Simple," Asmina's black face broke into the biggest smile and she giggled showing a mouthful of oversized white teeth, "you gonna fall in love bibi an' with a better man than before."

Gina flared for a moment about the slight on her late husband, but she didn't know even a fraction of what Asmina knew about him. There are none as blind as those who will not see...

"That's unfair Asmina and you should be ashamed of yourself. Anyway, a chapel is no place to speak ill of the dead," Gina couldn't help herself and asked. "Will it be true love?"

"It'll be true love," Asmina replied nodding her head. Her gaze was enigmatic and distant.

She had divined more from the spirits than she was telling her mistress, not just in this but in all things.

"Sometimes, we need to know less 'bout things or they jus' become self-fulfilling prophecies," Asmina said authoritatively.

"Bibi, you wanna see the face of your enemy an' who he is?" the question was rhetorical. Gina simply nodded her head but she already knew.

"Cut the cards bibi an' take one."

Gina did, almost in slow motion. She placed it face up below the other Tarot cards of her reading. Her face was stricken. It was *the Devil* card.

"The Pindar," Gina barely mouthed the words.

The candle guttered eerily and then extinguished, leaving them both terrified and clutching each other in the gloom and chill of the old Mèdici chapel.

Chapter 7

"I'll fix us a coffee," Bjorn said, hitting the pause button. "Think we both need a break after that."

It had been a tense thriller and Heidi had enjoyed it too, despite herself. The action was violent but well done and the love scenes, past graphic although artistic despite the brutal content. The sex was not gentle and loving like theirs, but it was in keeping with the violent nature of the movie. It had left them both a little breathless and highly turned on, which was entirely Illya Dracul's intent.

"I guess I'm going to be in a lot of trouble when we go to bed Bjorn," her face was flushed and her expression, expectant.

"If we hadn't promised to see this film through and report on it, we would already be there and you would be mine," his look reflected the yearning that he was feeling.

"Hurry up with the coffees then, I'm not sure how much longer I can wait," Heidi meant every word. Pregnancy had increased her sex drive and the movie was like igniting the blue touch-paper.

They cuddled through the last twenty minutes. Bjorn's hands were paying increasing attention to Heidi's ample breasts that early motherhood had enhanced tantalisingly. The moment the film ended and dedications began to roll up the screen, Bjorn took Heidi's engorged and highly sensitised nipple in his mouth and began to suck and tease it with his mouth. The effect on Heidi was immediate and she cried out at the sheer ecstasy of it. She reached down and slid her hand under the elastic waist of his jog bottoms finding the hardness of his manhood. Heidi encircled him with her long slim fingers and began her rhythm. Bjorn gasped and increased the intensity of his assault on her breasts.

"God I need this inside me Bjorn. Take me to bed and make me feel loved and safe. Now Bjorn, do it now. Please."

He broke from her breasts and looked into the face of the woman that he loved. The look in Heidi's eyes told him that there could never be any other man for her and they kissed. Her hand stilled and they were lost in that kiss. It was something that they shared, an ability to kiss to the exclusion of all else. In that moment, there was nothing but that kiss. At last their mouths parted and it was over, but their want for each other was not. He rose from the sofa and swept her up into his arms. Even though he was yet young, he was already muscular and Heidi, petite. Bjorn carried her through to the bedroom, unaware of the array of cameras secreted there. He laid her on the bed and Heidi moaned in anticipation of the moment.

"Tonight, I'm going to show the mother of my child to be, just how much I adore her."

Heidi giggled and pulled him toward her. The night was yet young and so were they.

"Jesus Christ! Heidi, Heidi, wake up!" Bjorn was horrified and uncomprehending.

The bed was covered in the blood of her miscarriage. She was battered and bruised all over and there were angry red marks around her throat. Bjorn anxiously raised the lid of one of her swollen eyes. To his immediate relief, her iris contracted to the light. She was still alive.

"Thank God," Bjorn choked out the words.

Suddenly he felt vulnerable. Bjorn left the bed in a single move, looking furtively around him in case the perpetrator of this foul act was still in the room. There was no one. He checked the other rooms. There was nobody. The front door was still locked and there was no other way in. They were on the third floor, so nobody could have come in through the windows. It was a conundrum. Now, sure that they were safe, Bjorn quickly filled the kitchen bowl with warm soapy water and poured a glass with cold water. He grabbed the tea towel and ran back into the bedroom. Bjorn lifted Heidi's limp body into a sitting position and propped her with pillows.

"Wake up Heidi, please wake up," he shook her until her eyes opened.

She looked at him but there was no recognition in her eyes, only fear. Bjorn made her drink and she choked back the cool water hungrily.

"We have to get out of here Heidi, before they come back."

The words echoed around Heidi's head for some time, not making any sense.

"Who's going to come back Bjorn?"

"The men that did this to you of course," he replied as he began to clean Heidi up with a soapy cloth.

Tears were rolling down his face in rivers of grief and anger. They had taken his baby, the most precious thing in the world to him other than Heidi herself, who remained silent throughout. She didn't even wince at the pain. She just looked at him in disbelief.

46

When Bjorn had done all that he could for her, he began to throw their things into a suitcase. All Heidi could do was watch. Bjorn opened the front door and looked both ways.

"It's clear Heidi. Can you walk if I help you? We've got to get you to a hospital," despite the beating and the miscarriage, there was still no show of emotion from Heidi.

"Why did you do that to me Bjorn? Why did you kill our baby?" Heidi's face was devoid of all expression, such was the depth of her shock and horror.

"What do you mean, I didn't. I couldn't have," at last there was an expression on Heidi's face but it was an expression of accusation, hate and disgust.

All at once Bjorn had a flashback. His hands were around Heidi's throat; her eyes were bulging under the pressure of his grip and full of fear. Then another flashback as he repeatedly punched her in the stomach. She was screaming at him, "Stop it! You're killing my baby, stop it!"

"Oh, my God," Bjorn's hands went to his mouth as the enormity of it sank in. "Oh, Jesus Christ what have I done? I didn't know what I was doing I swear. You must believe me."

All Bjorn could see was the look of hatred in Heidi's eyes and her desolation. There was no way that he could mend her, no way of redemption for the foul deed that he had done. No way back. He had shattered their perfect world in a moment of madness. It was too much for a gentle soul like Bjorn's.

"Please forgive me," Bjorn cried out in despair, his heart was at breaking point.

There was only one thing that he could do to make the pain go away. Without looking back, he ran at the window and dived headlong through it, glass shattering and wood splintering under the impact. Bjorn's frenzied scream was suddenly silenced by a sickening thud as he hit the cobbled street three floors below.

Illya Dracul was sat with Doctor Walter Schwartz reviewing the CCTV video recordings of their first human experimentations. There were three experiments conducted during the night and that of the Scandinavians' was by far the most pleasing. The two men made an unlikely pairing. Illya was tall, young and athletic with his short cropped blond hair, black eyes and youthful swagger. Walter Schwartz however was stooped, almost bald with tufts of unruly wispy grey hair that were almost comical. He had several brown teeth only that seemed too long for his mouth and skin that appeared to be turning to parchment, testament to his great age. Incredibly though, his eyes were still the darkest brown, piercing and alert. You would be a fool to contradict or dismiss this man for he had the mannerisms of a predator and a black heart to go with it.

"So, Doctor Schwartz, to recap; what have we learned and what must we change?"

Illya's question was more to formalise the conclusions that they had already come to, rather than to continue the debate. The ancient doctor leaned back in his chair. He put his thumbs in his shabby waistcoat pockets, as he considered Illya's question.

"Well, we have proof of science. The game will deliver our objectives, of that there is no doubt. It was interesting that the boy radicalised in his sleep as was intended, and that the subliminal messages were not received by the girl. It means that we can be entirely gender specific when targeting our audience. To be honest I wasn't expecting that," there was a sadistic smile of professional satisfaction on his face.

"What did you make of the loving sex that they had prior to sleeping?" It had puzzled Illya. "It was totally in contrast with the boy's behaviour in sleep."

"Totally as expected Illya" the old doctor began. "In consciousness, the boy loved his woman. He could never be manipulated to do those things in that state. His lovemaking was

48

demonstration of his nature. It is as simple as that. He would have clearly lain down his life to protect her. But that is in his *conscious* state when he has control. Our subliminal messages that were inserted into the film only stimulated his subconscious mind, which is when he has no control and becomes our puppet. He fulfilled his instructions to the letter, even his own suicide, which was most gratifying."

Walter Schwartz loved his work. He felt blessed that he had enjoyed over seventy years of human experimentation, delving into all kinds of pain and suffering. Every time he thought that he had reached the pinnacle of his career, he would exceed himself and find something even more perverse. Walter Schwartz had no soul. It even sent a chill down Illya Dracul's spine, and he was a man who was also morally barren.

"What news of the woman, have you found her?" The doctor asked. He had further plans for her.

"Not yet. She has gone to ground, or died in the gutters somewhere from her bleeding," Illya could sense the doctor's anger over his security guards' sloppiness. He continued reassuringly. "We will find her Walter, we always do."

The old doctor looked far from convinced.

"OK," Illya began, moving on quickly, "so we know we can meet the ultimate goal of the Dream App, which is total mind control of the masses. First though, we have to get the masses addicted to it. What are your early conclusions on that front?"

"Well none from the Scandinavians of course, that was not our intent. The monitors did however pick up hyper-dream activity by the other two couples. On interview, they described it as having the most realistic dreams of their lives. One of the women went as far as to state that she had the best sex ever in her dreams. It goes without saying that her partner wasn't too pleased about that," the doctor chuckled. "So, it's not hard to imagine that she could become addicted to that alone, besides any adventure and intrigue. That would be even without the introduction of our planned game upgrades and the illicit sales of mild hallucinogenic drugs to enhance the dream experience."

It was exactly what Illya wanted to hear. He couldn't wait to report their successful trials back to the Pindar. It would mean a promotion of at least three seats around the table the next time the Council of Thirteen met. He needed one more piece of information first.

"What time scale are we looking at for completion of human trials and getting the Dream App onto the market?"

"Three months. That gives you nearly three more before your meet with the Council of Thirteen for the winter solstice. At that point you will have proven sales and field results to boast," the doctor said with confidence, then frowned as he cautioned Illya. "That is assuming three billion U.S. Dollars are transferred to my Swiss bank account by the end of this month."

"It will be done," Illya confirmed with equal confidence.

Chapter 8

Gina Mèdici sat at her desk in the Milan office of her banking consortium. She was gazing thoughtfully out of the window. The outlook was Milan's business district that hosts Italy's Stock Exchange and the headquarters of some of the largest national and international banks and companies in the world.

She watched everyday people getting on with their everyday lives and wished to God that she was just one of them, another everyday ant in the anthill. One woman was trying to manage her little girl eating an ice cream that was migrating faster down the child's arm than into its mouth. The mother was stressing about it and trying to tidy her up and hurry her at the same time. Gina suddenly missed that simplicity and tears of regret and hopelessness began to roll down her face.

The brown envelope, given to her a week ago by the Pindar, was still unopened. She had felt that to do so, would result in the final damnation of her soul. Leaving it any longer though, could further jeopardise her family's safety. Gina reluctantly picked it up. She idly noted that it was soaked with her tears and lamented that it could so easily be with her family's blood. She took a deep breath and opened it.

There were no niceties to begin with. The text went straight into procurements and a schedule of delivery. The long list of acquisitions included the last remaining bastions in the software industry, social media, the film industry, computing and micro-processor technology. The long-term strategy, already in place, was to attract them with the most favourable of financial conditions, via Mèdici loan arrangements, then to acquire a controlling number of shares in the companies. The plan was for Mèdici to turn the screws and make re-payment difficult to impossible. The principal shareholder, the Illuminati under another name which was to be her banks name, would then step in and bail them out. Globalisation of those industries achieved, just as laid down by the Pindar and endorsed by the newcomer, the Mullah Ismael Alansari.

Gina's late husband, Antonio, had made all the deals on behalf of the Pindar. He had used the prestige and trust of the Mèdici name to secure each and every client. It was only now, since Gina had been dragged into the business, that she could see the game plan. Now it made her doubt everything that she had ever taken for granted about her husband. If all this had been a lie, then what else had even a glimmer of truth about it? And then there were things that Asmina had said, or only half said.

"Have I been a fool?" she wondered.

There was an immediate link to her Tarot reading with Asmina the night before. The Fool card, it was supposed to mean 'discovery and change', not just being one as she currently felt. Just then, the phone rang. It was her secretary, Phoebe.

"I have a Mr da Vinci here. He wants to talk to you about investing in some of his inventions. He's talking helicopters, scuba gear and things," the young, blonde and petite girl turned her head to one side to whisper discretely into the phone. "He's a little strange and most persistent. Shall I call security?"

"No Phoebe just tell him to leave his card and I'll get back to him," there was an exchange that Gina couldn't quite hear.

"He doesn't seem to know what a *card* is, unless you are referring to the *Fool* Tarot card he says. Apparently Asmina asked him to meet with you."

"Holy Mary, mother of God!" Gina gasped, "It's not possible."

The young secretary heard the phone drop. She left Mr da Vinci stood at the desk and ran into Gina's plush office.

"Donna Gina, are you alright? You look like you've seen a ghost," phoebe was close to panic.

"No, I haven't Phoebe, but maybe I'm about to," Gina genuflected. She needed a few minutes to collect herself and Phoebe waited patiently.

"Show him in please," Gina said at last, then held her breath.

She could no longer trust her knees, so Gina took to her seat behind the large polished onyx desk. Moments later, a tall dark man walked in confidently. He appeared to be in the middle of his life and striking to look at. His face was handsome with long angular features, typical of the Romans. A short-cropped goatee beard covered his strong chin in a most dignified manner and his tanned skin shone with health. He had lively blue eyes that danced below his broad intelligent brow and a ridiculous slouch hat that did him no favours at all.

"Perhaps he was just a mad man," Gina wondered and then became objective.

"Please sit Mr da Vinci," Gina pointed towards the comfortable chair in front of her. Da Vinci looked at it, hardly recognising it as a chair. He sat reluctantly and looked most uncomfortable as the soft upholstery engulfed him.

"Would you mind if I stand, only I have never been consumed by a chair before," the twinkle in the rather *proper* gentleman's eyes showed character.

"Of course," Gina smiled and pointed to a small table with two hardback chairs. "I hate those soft chairs too. Perhaps this would better suit our needs?"

"Absolutely," da Vinci stood with alacrity.

They moved to the table and sat facing each other. No words were spoken as one appraised the other. Somehow that didn't make Gina feel uncomfortable in the slightest. It seemed that this man could look inside her mind and she didn't want to resist. There was something benign about him. She felt his presence deep within her soul, but it wasn't in the slightest way an invasion.

"Hello Leonardo," she said at last, offering her hand with the broadest of smiles. "I see now that it really is you, but how?"

After that experience, Gina felt like she had known Leonardo da Vinci for years and didn't even think that it was strange or unnatural. Somehow, unfathomably, she was sat in the present with one of the most intellectual men from the past, who was about to help with her future; or at least to even have a chance of one. She had no way of knowing that time wasn't mapped out as she had perceived it. No idea that she lived her life in only one possibility amongst infinite others. Gina's known world, and all that she had held sacred, was about to become unravelled. All that she would have to see her through the next few months was faith; blind faith.

Leonardo took Gina's offered hand, but rather than the shake that she was expecting, he kissed it in the old-fashioned way. Gina was unaccustomed to his gentlemanly manner and blushed. She paused to collect herself before continuing.

"How did Asmina contact you Leonardo?"

"Through possibility Gina, if you are open to possibility, then all things can happen."

"I need more," Gina said simply. "That's not enough for an enquiring woman's mind of the twenty first century. Surely you must know us ladies better than that?" Gina smiled disarmingly, immediately knowing that she could be informal with this extraordinary man.

"Ah, the guiles of a woman," you have grown over the centuries to better us.

He let out an endearing chuckle. Leonardo had visited this time once before, although in an entirely different country, but the scenarios were not too dissimilar: power, avarice, destruction and a woman alone in the world who had to endure and overcome.

"The world is not quite as you perceive it little one," the endearing and familiar diminutive was not meant in a patronising way and Gina accepted it in the spirit that it was meant. "All men are not born equal. Some have advantages through their birth right. You have advantages Gina, but you just don't know that yet."

Gina interrupted; it struck a chord. It wasn't the first time that she had been told that.

"Asmina said that too, she talked of me being an *embryo*. What exactly did she mean?"

"Just that, you are as yet a novice Gina," he paused, considering how to best deliver a scenario that would seem beyond credibility. "Maybe it is better that I start at the beginning, in times long ago when our ancestors first colonised this planet," Gina was intrigued, or maybe aghast but certainly captivated.

"Our ancestors colonised, this planet? You are not for one moment implying that I am an alien, are you?"

"Well, in part. Your genes go back to a time on Earth that significantly predates Christ, when first they came; the three hundred. They were of two races and came to be known, by the enlightened few, as *Angels* and *Shadows*. Both races were much more genetically advanced than humans and with that came certain *abilities*. You are a direct descendant of those Angels, as am I; a benign race that have always endeavoured to lead us to our better side."

"Angels from Heaven then?" Gina asked incredulously.

"No, but Angels from *the heavens*," Leonardo corrected. "The destroyed planet *Angelos,* to be precise. They integrated with the human race and produced many hybrids, including us. The others, the Shadows, didn't and their bloodline is still pure; pure evil. You may already know some of them as the *Illuminati*. Their infiltration of that organisation is rife," Gina shuddered. It was like someone had walked over her grave.

"I know them," she whispered, as if admitting it only to herself.

The intercom sounded, it was Gina's secretary.

"Your two o'clock appointment has arrived; Mr Verdi, of Afonso & Verdi Acquisitions. What shall I say?"

"Give him my apologies and tell him that I have an emergency on my hands and that I will call him in the morning. Then cancel my other appointments and take the rest of the day off. I don't want to be disturbed. Thank you, Phoebe."

Gina cut the call. She didn't want to dwell too long on the Illuminati, that could wait for now. She needed to know more about herself, who she was.

"I'm sorry about the interruption Leonardo. So, what are my abilities? One must be that I'm able to make an unholy mess of things," Gina said self-effacingly.

"But those things might at last be coming together," she thought, feeling optimistic for the first time in a long time.

"I need to be Superwoman right now. I'm not sure anything else can cut it."

Gina was making light of it to help buoy her through the enormity of what was being presented to her.

"Superwoman?" Leonardo was puzzled. He had never heard that expression.

"Forget it, it's a bit after your time Leonardo you must have had your equivalent, the goddess Athena maybe?" Gina offered but Leonardo still looked puzzled. "Never mind, please continue," Gina regretted the flippant comment.

"Your abilities, well that will depend on your genealogy," he began, "how many mixings of blood outside of the Angel bloodline that have created you. To my knowledge, it seems few. Angels have always tried not to dilute their bloodline as it also dilutes their powers. Your blue eyes and black hair are testament to that. Angels always have blue or green eyes. But your abilities could include mind reading, mind control, levitation, and telekinesis; even shape-shifting. Certainly, you will have experienced some kinds of premonition or *déjà vu* perhaps? The original colony had powers on a biblical scale though, but they number only two now, Maelströminha and her sister Crystalita. Pure blooded Angels endure millennia."

"I'm intrigued," Gina felt like she needed to pinch herself to prove that it wasn't a mad dream. "But how does any of this explain how Asmina contacted you and how you are here six centuries outside of your time?" Leonardo considered her question and how he might best answer it.

"I have spent a lifetime researching quantum physics, the universe and the laws that bind it all together. As soon as you answer one question it begs more to be asked. In truth, I still do not know the answer to your question," it was an honest and modest observation on Leonardo's part. "But I can tell you, that time doesn't have a beginning and an end and that all times coexist. You just have to know how to step between them. That is how I am here. I know how to take that step. It was science brought to us from those of our bloodline five thousand years ago."

Leonardo paused to let Gina reflect on the magnitude of what he had said. At last he continued.

"How Asmina contacted me? Well, I don't exactly know. There are some of us, rare though they be, that can glimpse other times and places; other dimensions even. Perhaps Asmina can transcend these in her spiritual world. It matters only that she did and that I am here."

"But here to do what?" Gina needed a small army more than an intellectual artist.

"To help you find yourself and to build on that *embryo* that Asmina and you referred to. There are others of your kind who can help. You are not alone Gina and your journey is more significant than you think. It is about much more than saving your family and yourself Gina. It is to avert World War Three and rid the world of the Pindar and banish him back to Hell from whence he came."

Again, Leonardo waited for Gina to assimilate all that he had said. It was a massive ask for her to come to terms with the fact that nothing that had appeared to her to be true, now was. At last Gina felt ready to reply. Her first thoughts were of her own religious beliefs. And whether they were still valid in this new world of Angels and Shadows she now lived in.

"You said, 'banish the Pindar back to Hell where he belongs'. Does that mean that there is a God and Heaven?" there was hope in Gina's voice.

It was the hardest question that she could have asked Leonardo and it showed in his thoughtful expression.

"I hope so Gina. I have spent my life believing that to be so. In all my studies, I have found nothing to refute it, but then not enough to prove it either," Leonardo spread his hands on the table in thought. They were the long slender fingers of an artist. "You are thinking that I died hundreds of years ago, and therefore I must know. But for me, my death is yet to come. All I can say, is that I am not afraid of my own death but I am deeply afraid of the death of humanity and that, in part, is why I am here."

It wasn't a complete answer but it was enough for Gina. If one of the most intelligent and gifted men that ever walked the Earth had faith, then that was sufficient for her.

"You mentioned World War Three Leonardo. What did you mean by that?" Gina already knew in part, as the Pindar had talked of it in their meetings and the New World Order that would follow.

"When we look through time Gina, the future holds many possibilities. The one that occurs in most all of cases is a catastrophic war that begins in the year 2020 and lasts a decade. There is not much left in the end to have, but what is left is owned by the Pindar and his New World Order."

There were no words to describe the look of sadness on Leonardo's face. Above all he was a fellow humanist, like Gina. They were kindred spirits. He continued gravely.

"I can't offer you 'a small army' Gina," she gasped out loud, realising that he had read her thoughts earlier. They were only in her head, never voiced! "But I can connect you to people who can be more than that to you, if that is what you want. But only if you are prepared to fight for humanity and not just for your children."

"I want," Gina answered simply. "I want that with all of my heart."

Chapter 9

Saudi Arabia, Middle East. June 28th 2017

The implacable Mullah Ismael Alansari sat cross-legged on the Persian rug in the humble Bedouin tent. He drew from the antique copper hookah, held the breath for several seconds before blowing it out in streams through the gaps in his teeth, like some mythical dragon. The sweet smell of hashish scented the hot, dry air in the tent making it even more oppressive for the two suited men sat in front of him.

Hashish was considered as *haram* under Islamic dogma and not permitted. But then the Mullah was not a man of faith, despite the image that he publicly portrayed as being a staunch defender of it. To the Mullah, religion was just a tool like many others, used to manipulate the people.

As he smoked, he was assessing the strengths and weaknesses of the three men sat in front of him. The Mullah needed to know which way they would fall when push came to shove. Who he could depend on the most and who he could sacrifice, should the need arise. There are always traitors who sell out at the last minute but it didn't matter to the Mullah though, just as long as he knew in advance. No surprises. He had replacements for all of them, if necessary. All he needed to do for now, was to get the ball rolling.

The air in the billowing tent was stifling despite the brisk desert wind blowing relentlessly outside. The American and Russian sat in front of him were showing signs of heat stress, tugging at the collars of their shirts to find something resembling air to breathe. Their jackets were stuck to their backs, making them feel even more uncomfortable. Their breathing was laboured and stress levels, high. In contrast, the Arab sat between them in cool, loose-fitting black robes, looked confident and at ease. His attire was entirely typical of the ISIS ruling elite and well suited to life in the desert. Of the three, this was the man that the Mullah already knew he could trust implicitly. That was because they both shared the same agenda; a thirst for power.

Muhammad Akhbar was also a great friend and ally of the Mullah, having fought side by side for mutual gain. It was never about truth or justice. He was the self-elected leader of the Sunni militant jihadist organisation known as the Islamic State. His power, influence and terror had already spread through western Iraq, Syria, Libya and Afghanistan. He was already an unstoppable force.

Since seizing power after a bloody coup in the spring of 2017, Muhammad Akhbar had secured the full unofficial support of the CIA and the Foreign Intelligence Service of the Russian Federation, once again operating under the name of KGB. He was responsible for Arab intelligence and espionage activities outside the Russian Federation's ability to control. The two suited men, Karl Ivanov and Brad Harper, were of those agencies and unofficially there to represent Russian and American interests in the Middle East. Everything was about money and power, not freedom from oppression and certainly not about the wants or beliefs of the American and Russian citizens. The Mullah took another puff from the hookah and held it.

"Min fadlik," the Mullah bowed respectfully as he handed the hose to the other Arab there and then exhaled the scented smoke through his teeth.

"Shukraan," Akhbar replied in gratitude, then took a deep drag from the hookah.

The two foreign agents there could have no more taken from the hookah than fly to the moon. Both were feeling nauseous from the heat and sickly fumes. They both wanted to do business and get back to the air conditioning of Saudi's famous Makkah Hilton Hotel. Brad Harper took the hard line.

"Excuse me for breaking up the party, but we didn't come thousands of miles to watch you guys get shit faced," Harper was a product of the CIA, a no nonsense man and afraid of no one, but then he hadn't met the Mullah face to face before.

"Had we met in *your* America Harper, we would have been fed cupcakes, taken to the casino, given alcohol and saddled with high class hookers. Do not deign to tell me how to do business in the Arab world!" there was fire in the Mullah's amber eyes and his expression was murderous.

The big Russian raised his hands in peaceful gesture to pacify the situation. It was ironic though, as they had met for the sole purpose of talking war. His English was heavily accented in typical Russian manner.

"Does it ever drop below forty degrees here?" the question was rhetorical but served to open the conversation between them. "Tell us more about the Illuminati's three-year plan and what more you need from us."

Karl Ivanov dabbed at his forehead with an already moist handkerchief. He had short cropped blonde hair above a square face and a strong angular chin. Sweat was running in rivulets down his face, channelled by his chiselled contours, until they fell from his chin like a dripping tap. The fire in the Mullah's eyes died to a mere smoulder.

"Your continued and anonymous support as usual," the Mullah began graciously in the typical Arab way. "A massed landing of American and Russian foot soldiers in Syria is being orchestrated to happen in the fall of 2020. By that time, we want American and Russian arms in the hands of every Muslim and every caliphate on board ready to fight the infidels."

The Mullah turned his gaze to his friend Muhammad Akhbar, a wiry Arab with cropped beard and furtive black eyes. The real work would be done by him and his jihadists.

"Your part, as we have already discussed, is to unite all the warring Arab factions into one army under one caliphate, Islamic State. Then to indoctrinate, radicalise and train and arm them. The Pindar wants them massed at Dabiq, where the scriptures tell us that the holy war will take place and where the Muslims will be victorious," there was a flare of fanaticism in the Mullah's voice. Akhbar picked up on it.

"Do you really believe that, even in their millions, an Arab army could possibly be victorious over the combined might of the American and Russian forces?"

It was a strange concept that the American CIA and their equivalent, the Russian KGB, had for decades been in close dialogue in matters outside of their national interests. Such is the world when organisations become more powerful than the governments that employ them, irrespective of who is in power. It makes them above the law, virtually unaccountable and infinitely corruptible.

The Mullah smiled through his gappy teeth. His parchment skin crumpled into a grin and there was fire in his amber eyes.

"Of course not, the Arabs will be slaughtered. But that is of no consequence," the Mullah was unconcerned about the collateral damage. "What is of consequence though, is that it will evoke a Third World War. Our soldiers and citizens are only expendable pawns in a much bigger war and that is the fight for global financial power."

The Mullah took back the tube from the hookah and drew another deep breath. He found that the opiate gave him clarity of thought.

"Your part, Muhammad Akhbar, is to lead that holy war. You will be the Mahdi, hailed by all Muslims as the Twelfth Imam and I will be your False Prophet endorsing everything that you do as being in God's holy name. You will poison the minds of your followers with your charisma, half-truths and false hope. Your doctrine will be as it is laid down in the scriptures; to unite world under one religion, Islam, and under one religious leader, the Messiah."

All there knew that the *Messiah* was the Pindar in waiting, and that it would be Islam in name only and nothing like its peaceful doctrine. The religion that they would actually be united under would be Satanism.

"Together we will strip humanity of its identity, its freedom and its suspicion, thereby ushering in an age of blind acceptance," the Mullah continued. "The Illuminati will have all else in place to create the New World Order and there will be a seat there in the Council of Thirteen for us all under the Pindar's reign."

There was at last unity and an accord at the meeting. They were all united in one thing, they had been chosen by the Illuminati to execute the Pindar's vision. All would reap their rewards when the New World Order was achieved or execution if it wasn't.

The American stepped into the conversation. He was a man in his early forties, strong looking and handsome, in a rugged way. He had an easy smile and good teeth.

"You've gotten the CIA's full but unofficial support on the weapons front. Containers of so called 'Agricultural Machinery' are being loaded as we speak, bound for whatever port you say is the most secure at the time and free of customs inspections."

Brad Harper quaffed the iced water in front of him and sighed as if it was nectar. He continued.

"On top of that we've got reinforcements for your training camps. There ain't no shortage of disgruntled GIs that want a piece of the action for a fist full of Dollars. If you got the money, I can find you fighting men."

"Money is no problem," Muhammad Akhbar began, drawing deeply from the hookah. His words that followed came out in gusts of smoke. "Our sponsorship from Saudi Arabia and the Gulf states is secure and dependable. Oil revenue from ISIS controlled oilfields flows reliably and lucratively, despite the American bombings."

The black robed Arab couldn't help directing his remark to Brad Harper. It was ironic that the CIA's unofficial stance was so in contrast with that of American declared policy. He continued.

"Then taxation, extortion, ransom and drug trafficking count for a further two billion U.S. Dollars per annum and growing. No Mr

Harper. Money is not an issue for the Islamic State," none doubted him, their tyranny and resourcefulness was already legendary.

"And what of Russian supplies?" the Mullah asked turning to the big Russian.

"More or less the same as our American colleague," Ivanov began. "Containers are being loaded on a weekly basis at the Black Sea port of Novorossiysk, where there are no customs issues. We have reciprocal agreements with Turkey and assured passage through the Bosporus Strait into the Aegean Sea, without any scrutiny."

Karl Ivanov finally succumbed to the heat. He shed his charcoal grey suit jacket revealing his sweat soaked white shirt and his SPS pistol in shoulder holster. It was considered bad manners to openly display weaponry as a guest in Arab company. Ivanov read the look on the Mullah's face and quickly divested himself of the offending weapon, secreting it under his jacket. He continued.

"We can assist in training and of course our ongoing air strikes are strategically aimed at frustrating those forces that are massed against the Islamic State initiative. Russia will continue to side with Syria, partly because of our president's special relationship with their president Assad, but ultimately to have a foothold in the Middle East. It suits our government to have the instability of Islamic State so you can consider Syria remaining our safe-haven," Karl Ivanov concluded his part.

"Excellent," the Mullah already knew that, but praised the Russian anyway. "Turkey is strategically our most important ally though. Notwithstanding the importance of controlling access in and out of the Black Sea, their land based army is massive and potent. We need them on board. I already have that agreed in principal through guarantees of crushing Kurdistan resistance and handing them their territory after the war. Kurdistan, despite their resources, are proving to be the only real thorn in the side of Islamic State. Even their women are fearsome in battle."

Despite their political differences, the Mullah admired the Kurds and their 'fight to the death' approach to defending their country.

"The jewel in the crown will be the annexation of Iran to our cause," continued the Mullah. "They are less than three years away from achieving offensive nuclear capability and producing nuclear warheads in the quantities needed to unite the world in war," his voice once again reflected his fanaticism.

They all knew that, if the other Arab countries rallied to a holy war, Iran would naturally follow. The rest of the world would then have no choice but to unite against the Arab uprising, particularly with their new-found nuclear capability. It would be the End Time scenario as prophesied in the Koran. The Pindar's plan for a Third World War was on track and almost inevitable.

Chapter 10

It was a week since Gina had talked with Leonardo and nothing had happened. The only things that evidenced that it wasn't just some crazy dream were the business appointments cancelled in her diary and the smug look on Asmina's face.

Gina was in her office, sat at her grand onyx desk looking at her screen. It was displaying the accounts of the newly set up acquisitions that conformed to the Pindar's latest expectations. She had managed to open accounts with all but felt sullied by the lies that she had to tell them to secure those agreements. They were unwittingly succumbing to the Pindar's plan. The trap was set. Gina's job now was to pump up their borrowing to the point of no return, then pull the rug. It made her feel sick and deeply ashamed. These clients had trusted her judgement implicitly as they had her fathers before her. Now she was nothing but a traitor to them and her father's memory; the Pindar's puppet.

Gina closed the 'New Accounts' page in the Pindar's portfolio and opened 'Existing Clients'. Her eyes idly fell briefly on the name *LuminaGames*. She recalled fleetingly that it was the company that were trying to market the new Dream App that Sasha had talked of. Unfortunately, it didn't set any hares running and she carried on looking down the list. There were more than one thousand of them, each valued at above one billion U.S. Dollars on the stock exchange, or if they didn't, they had something unique that the Pindar needed to execute his insidious plan. She looked at the clock; it was ten minutes before one. Phoebe called right on cue. She always did at that time, to make sure that her boss didn't need anything before she left for lunch.

"Sorry to disturb you Donna Gina, but I have a Mr Callum Knight here to see you. He says that you are expecting him but it's not in the diary. Maybe I missed it, he seems so sure," Gina could sense Phoebe's concern in that she might have been remiss and less than efficient.

"My diary is full Phoebe and I still have things to do. Could you ask him to re-schedule for tomorrow morning please?" Gina had become reluctant to take on too much work. She wanted to maximise her time with her children, as she was far from convinced that she could save them from the Pindar. Every moment with them was now even more precious to her.

There was a short delay while Phoebe discussed the alternative with Mr Knight.

"He says that he has flights arranged for you and him to go to Moscow late this afternoon and so a meeting tomorrow won't be possible," there was another short exchange. "Oh, and he said that the Magician had sent him and that *no* wasn't a possibility."

"He said that *the Magician* had sent him?" Gina was in a spin and unsure that she had heard correctly. "And tickets to Moscow?"

"Yes, Donna Gina, he seems most insistent."

Gina was re-playing Asmina's Tarot card reading through her mind. The Magician was to be her teacher, to bring enlightenment and help her manifest her abilities, whatever they were.

"But this man was not the Magician, only *sent* by him so who is he?" Gina wondered.

"Show him in please," Gina was full of superstitious awe and crossed herself to ward off any evil spirits, like she always did.

Moments later Phoebe returned with a strikingly handsome man. He was in his late forties, strong of build with fair, salt and pepper hair swept back from his broad brow. His eyes were blue, lively and welcoming. Judging by Phoebe walking beside him, Gina estimated the man to be a little over six feet tall with a confident stride. His smile was natural and honest, creasing his face in an appealing way.

"Mr Knight to see you Donna Gina," Phoebe said formally, then retired respectfully.

"*The Lovers*?" Gina whispered in awe under her breath. She felt her body flush with anticipation, just as it had in the chapel when Asmina first turned over the Tarot card.

"I'm sorry, I didn't quite catch that?" Callum said innocently.

He had heard Gina loud and clear but could see her dilemma and allowed her time to compose herself which, after her next clumsy sentence, she clearly needed.

"Err, I said 'you can leave us', to Phoebe I mean, not to you of course. That would have been quite silly, wouldn't it?" Despite Gina's dusky skin she felt sure that she was blushing. Then to herself she said, "Just shut up woman, you are babbling. He must think you are a fool."

Callum rescued her gallantly.

"I've been so looking forward to meeting you Mrs Mèdici. I have read so much about you and am most impressed, I must say," his smile was easy and reassuring.

"Thank you, Mr Knight. It's all probably exaggerated. The press you know? And its Gina by the way, it hasn't been *Mrs* for a while."

"Another gaff," thought Gina and wished she could take it back." He must think I'm underlining my availability."

"Gina, it is then," he said offering his hand. "In which case, it's Callum," there was a mischievous twinkle in his eye and she wondered if he was mocking her, but in the nicest possible way.

Gina took his hand and shook it laughing easily.

"That was clumsy of me Callum. I can talk sensibly, I promise."

"And I don't doubt it Gina. It's fortunate too, as we have a lot to discuss on the way to Moscow. There is a woman there that I want you to meet."

Below Ingolstadt's Gothic castle lays a labyrinth of dimly lit tunnels and chambers that the Pindar had made his earthly home. Over the centuries, he had used this as his lair; a place of exile and solitude. It was a place to wait and endure, while he coaxed the world into preparedness for his return, for the time when he could drop his guise of Lucifer and become his full being. Satan. The Pindar had eternity on his side. This wait for the time to be right was only fleeting in the grand scheme of things. The Third World War would be so barbaric and horrendous that it would cause the people to seek God and humanity would be easily fooled to accept Satan as Jesus Christ and the Mahdi as the false leader of Islam.

To be totally sure that mankind would fall for his lies, was the reason the Pindar was so interested in the Dream App. Once the game had become viral, he would be able to control the masses through subliminal messages on game upgrades. There would no longer be freedom of choice, no way for mankind to opt out of damnation. Soon all souls would belong to the Pindar, to Satan. His reign on Earth would be secured after more than six thousand years of banishment from Heaven, when he was cast down. The key to ultimate success though, was in the hands of the Mullah Ismael Alansari. He opened the Mullah's brown envelope with his scaly fingers that were more akin to claws, and read the report.

At last, he pushed the Mullah's handwritten dossier away and exhaled in a sigh of deep satisfaction. The End Time prophecy had been initiated and would now become self-fulfilling. But still it needed a little help. He needed Muhammad Akhbar to join the Council of Thirteen.

The Pindar was pleased with his choice of the new number 12, his False Prophet, and with his work in the Middle East so far. He would promote the Mullah to number five at the Council of Thirteen's next meeting of the winter solstice. By then the present incumbent, Gina Mèdici, would be of no further use to him. He sensed too that her bloodline was not that of her late husband's and that she was becoming a security threat. His clawed fingers reached for the jewel encrusted ceremonial dagger that was secreted in his loose-fitting habit.

"You will drink the blood of a young Mèdici virgin soon my friend," he hissed.

The Pindar couldn't wait to put the dagger in the hand of Isabella's mother and enjoy the look on her face as she sacrificed her own daughter to Satan. That would leave her chair free for the Mullah and number twelve, for Muhammad Akhbar. The Mahdi!

Chapter 11

Gina Mèdici had just enough time to go home, change and pack her suitcases before leaving for the airport to meet Callum. She was in a fluster. Gina desperately hoped that Sasha and Isabella would be back from their studies at the usual time. She couldn't stand the thought of not saying goodbye to them, not in the dangerous world that they were now caught up in. Luigi was loading the bags while Asmina stood with Gina on the steps that led up to the grand front door. She was trying to steady and reassure her mistress.

"They be here soon bibi. I knows it," Asmina was the calming influence that Gina needed right then.

Gina took Asmina in a meaningful embrace and shed a little tear as she did so. Asmina was her rock.

"Don't ever leave me Asmina, I couldn't live without you, I just couldn't cope," Gina meant it.

"I ain't goin' nowhere bibi. You the one with the ticket to Moscow," Asmina laughed to lighten the moment. "You goin' to find the Magician an' learn who you are bibi."

Asmina let out a loud belly laugh that sounded like the rumble of distant thunder and her bulk shook with the intensity of it.

"An' you still gotta play the Lovers card too bibi. Maybe it's this Mr Knight?" Asmina howled with delight.

"Don't be ridiculous Asmina, I barely know the man," Gina found herself at a loss for any credible words of denial.

The sudden reddening of Gina's throat and cheeks was proof enough to Asmina that she was right.

"Here they are!" Gina shouted. She was glad to divert the conversation.

Isabella was waving from the pillion seat of Sasha's Lambretta, looking puzzled about the suitcases being loaded into the Mercedes.

"You didn't say that you were going away again Mummy," Isabella said quizzically.

She swung a shapely limb off the saddle and unbuckled her crash helmet, letting her long blonde hair tumble around her shoulders.

"Oh, baby I didn't know myself until two hours ago," Gina's relief was palpable as she took Isabella in her arms. "I kept calling you both but you didn't answer and I couldn't leave not knowing that you were safe."

"We were on the bike in traffic is all. Is there something wrong?" Isabella was suddenly concerned. Her mother's embrace was just a little too urgent.

"No darling, it's just that I've been called away on business unexpectedly and I don't know how long for," there wasn't much more that Gina could tell her daughter.

At that moment, Sasha came bounding up the steps and gave her a crushing hug.

"Where're you going Mum?" he asked cocking a quizzical eye.

"Err, Moscow. Well to start with, but then I don't know. I will FaceTime you as soon as I do though. I promise."

Isabella smelt a rat. It was unheard of for her mother not to know *exactly* what she was doing and where she would be.

"You're not telling us something Mother," Isabella never used the word *Mother* unless there was an issue.

Gina wondered who was the adult in this conversation and hadn't the time to concoct some placatory story.

"Look darlings I'm late and have to go. Promise me that you will watch out for each other and I want you to call me every night. I won't go to sleep until I know that you're safe so promise me," Gina wanted to explain but didn't want to panic them more than she already had.

"Mum, I'll look after baby sister for you and tuck her in at night. Just get in the car and go. We will be fine, just like always," Sasha grinned at his sister who looked miffed at his patronising comment.

They hooked their arms lovingly through Gina's and led her down the steps to the Mercedes.

"Hope you get time to go to the Bolshoi while you're there, Mum. I know how much you love the ballet. It will help you to relax," Isabella offered, then kissed her mother goodbye affectionately.

Sasha did the same then handed Gina into the car and closed the door. Luigi promptly pulled away, conscious of the fact that they would already be hard pressed to get to the airport. Sasha and Isabella waved until the limousine was out of site. Isabella turned to Sasha with tears in her eyes. She had experienced one of her premonitions.

"There's something wrong Sasha, something dreadfully wrong."

Gina let out a sigh of relief when her bags were quickly accepted by the baggage check-in girl at the Milan Malpensa Airport. Callum Knight had arranged for fast-tracking through security in anticipation of her tardiness.

Gina flew down the corridors to the departure lounge. She was towing her hand baggage behind her, careering around the corners precariously on high heels. The last of the passengers were going through their boarding card checks at the gate when Gina came in sideways into the lounge, skidding to a halt.

Callum smiled with comical relief, as Gina slid into view. Their eyes met at the same instant and Gina immediately felt foolish, again. It was becoming a habit. He rescued her quickly with a disarming comment as he took her bag.

"Remind me not to try and keep up with you if we ever work out together in Moscow," his smile was easy and his blue eyes shone with the genuine pleasure of seeing her.

It caught Gina's breath, adding to the physical confusion that she had been feeling ever since she met him.

"Don't you know that it's fashionable for a girl to be a little late?" Gina countered. "But not the most elegant of entries that you've witnessed I don't suppose," she conceded offering her smile to him, and her passport and boarding card to the pretty Asian hostess.

Moments later they were walking down the jet bridge to the waiting fight crew. Callum let Gina into the window seat in the second row of the first-class section, while he placed their hand luggage in the overhead locker. As he sat down next to her, the cabin intercom pinged.

"'Arm the doors and cross-check," the pilot's voice was authoritative and the cabin crew went dutifully to their stations.

"There's *fashionably late* and missed the plane late, "Callum quipped. "That must have been the very pinnacle of fashion."

"It's not every day that a girl gets told out of the blue that she's off jet-setting with a stranger and only hours to get herself packed and ready," she raised a perfectly groomed eyebrow accusingly at him.

"*Touché!*" Callum had to concede defeat. "Guilty as charged but I couldn't have missed this opportunity to get you to Moscow, though I must confess that it was perhaps an unnecessarily punishing schedule."

"Forgiven," Gina wiped the slate clean with a bright smile and a caveat, "but only if you get me a glass of champagne at the soonest."

Callum caught the young blonde air hostess's eye easily and she came over with a smile.

"Can I get you anything sir?"

She seemed to be all legs, eyes and smile Gina noticed. Clearly women found Callum desirable, even the younger ones, "Are you a player?" she wondered suddenly feeling insecure.

"Champagne as soon we reach cruising height please. I'm assuming that it's already on ice?" Gina was pleased to observe that Callum's smile was engaging but not flirtatious.

"Why am I thinking like this?" Gina wondered.

It was so out of character for her. She had no claim on this man, nor any reason to have any expectations and certainly not to be jealous. But then there was the Tarot card, the Lovers. Gina suddenly became aware that she was watching his strong chin and how his cheeks dimpled as he talked to the particularly attentive female. She immediately felt that blood rush to her groin, a feeling that had been alien to her for so long. Gina was feeling completely unnecessary and had to quickly divert her thoughts from Callum's evident masculinity. She addressed the girl.

"Would you get me a glass of water now please, before we take off?" Gina interrupted. She had already allowed the pretty girl to chat for too long.

The hostess left with alacrity, sensing the discrete but territorial rebuke. Callum turned to face Gina and immediately *read* the look on her face.

"She's interested," he thought with an element of surprise. "That was definitely a possessive dismissal of the hostess."

Callum had felt Gina's awkwardness over it and let it pass. He had read up on her. Callum already knew of her late husband's unnatural death and that she had not had any serious relationships since. Not even casual ones, it would appear. That struck a chord with Callum. His on-off relationship with Kayla Lovell was definitely in the *off* stage currently, and had been for over two years now. She was a woman to love but one that you could never keep. Each time she had broken his heart he had sworn that it would be the last. Callum also knew what it was like to be out in the wilderness, when it came to love and matters of the heart.

The hostess returned, passed the water to Gina with a half apologetic look, politically avoided Callum's engaging smile and left quickly to take her seat for take-off. Moments later the powerful jets of the Alitalia Airbus A320 roared, hurtling it down the runway in a southerly direction into the brisk headwind. The jet climbed steadily and banked to the port side, then headed off in a north easterly direction over the Alps towards Moscow. The fight time was three hours and twenty minutes, more than enough for Gina and Callum to become acquainted.

Once they had reached cruising height and the seat belt sign was off, the pretty blonde hostess returned with the champagne and her professional smile. Callum thanked her and poured two glasses, handing one to Gina. For the first time in years he was stuck for an appropriate toast. 'Bottoms up' would definitely be inappropriate and 'to us' presumptuous.

"To your successful journey," he decided and tipped his glass in her favour.

"To a successful Tarot reading," Gina countered with a look in her eye that Callum couldn't read.

"I'm sorry, I don't understand," Callum looked perplexed, "am I being obtuse?"

"No Callum, I'm being flippant. You don't need to know. Honestly," Gina clashed glasses and changed the subject. "You left me guessing when you left my office. Exactly *why* am I going to Moscow?"

"Firstly, there's a girl I want you to meet there. She's not too dissimilar to you, in that until a couple of years ago, she was just a pretty normal woman but with some basic and unexplored extrasensory perception."

"Psychic powers you mean," Gina looked quizzically at him, "like telepathy and precognition?"

"Yes, but there can be more, depending on your genealogy. In her case, she had kinetic powers too, but we are still unsure of your handed-down potential. This was explained to you by Leonardo I'm sure."

"Yes, it was but only in brief. I was going to talk to you about that. I was starting to think that I had invented the meeting with him, that it was just a dream driven by despair. Now I find myself on a jet to Moscow with a ridiculously handsome man and a glass of champagne in my hand," Gina laughed at the nonsense of it. "So now I really do know that it must be a dream!

Gina became reflective, "Where is Leonardo, will I see him again?"

"Well firstly thank you for the compliment even though it was satirical," he moved quickly on. "Regarding Leonardo, probably no. He was just a messenger. Asmina somehow found him and we don't exactly know how. Clairvoyance is outside the skill-set and experience of our kind, you see."

"That's sad, he was the most amazing man," Gina looked genuinely sorrowful.

"He still is Gina. You have a lot to learn, that's why we need you in Moscow, to explore you. Time doesn't run in the consecutive manner that you imagine. All things happen in parallel, with many alternatives and nothing is lost. We just live in one of those alternatives. Some of us can move in between those alternatives when shown how. Leonardo is one and you might be another. We will soon find out"

It was heavy stuff. Gina already knew through her experience with Leonardo when they joined minds briefly, that Callum was telling the truth. She was thoughtful for a while, until Callum broke the silence.

"There is a man I want you to meet too, our second in command under Maelströminha. His name is Emanuel Goldberg, head of MI6. We need to find a way to ensure that you and your family are safe in the short term; bodyguards maybe, and some kind of an insurance policy, while we work on the bigger picture. There is no one more knowledgeable and resourceful than him."

Gina was lost for words, out of her depth. She had to place her trust in this stranger. Somehow, she felt that she could and that it was the right thing to do. Gina was watching his lips forming the words while he spoke and had to drag her eyes away.

"How long have I been doing that?" she thought, panicking at her indiscretion. "He must think I'm easy," Gina was distracted and had lost track of what Callum was saying. She needed to find a way to redeem herself.

"Am I being presumptions?" Callum asked concerned that he might have over-stepped the line.

"Presumptions about what, Callum?" Gina hadn't heard, she had been too lost in him.

"About dining with me after we check-in at the Metropol. Or there is the Bolshoi across the road if you like ballet," Callum suddenly felt foolish and it didn't help that Gina had visibly panicked.

"I'm sorry, but I will just have room service tonight and FaceTime the kids if you don't mind? Long day and all that," Gina couldn't believe the words that were coming out of her mouth. It was such a cruel and ungrateful rejection.

"Quite. Of course, how thoughtless of me," Callum looked mortified that he had offended her. "We can meet at breakfast and get started."

"I need the bathroom, do you mind?" Gina asked. She needed some breathing space and time to collect her thoughts.

Callum stood and let her out into the isle. Gina walked unnecessarily quickly to the restroom, stomped almost.

"That went well," Callum thought sardonically. "She nearly broke into a gallop escaping up the aisle," Callum was angry with himself for being so forward and presumptuous.

The problem with Callum was that he was an all or nothing man. When he was *interested,* he really was, and he fell in love all too quickly. He had suffered the broken hearts that went with it but never learned, nor wanted to. But then he was a passionate man. From the moment that he had met Gina in Milan, he was smitten. Apart from being shapely and gorgeous, Gina had an air of positivity and energy about her that was infectious. He found her fascinating with facial expressions that already squeezed his heart. Now Callum rued putting her under pressure to meet socially so quickly. He decided that he would apologise as soon as she returned.

"Shit, shit, shit!" Gina chastised herself all the way, as she strutted to the restroom. "Where has your brain gone woman? You are much brighter than this."

Gina hadn't experienced this physical and mental confusion since she was a teenager. Not even when she first met her late husband. Gina felt it necessary to find excuses for her behaviour.

"It's just that I'm desperately reaching out for help to protect my children," she said to herself as she bolted the door, trying to believe her own propaganda. "It's not like I'm looking for a man, I'm not."

She ran the cold tap, soaked a towel and refreshed her face and neck with it. Gina immediately felt the cooling effect and it cleared her mind. She looked at her reflection in the mirror critically. She had probably never looked so good apart from in her first flush, when she was a teenager but time was passing. She knew that she had wasted her womanhood. There was an early and passionate first relationship. He was several years older than her and it had ended acrimoniously. It transpired that the man was already married and couldn't commit. He was the love of her life; the only man to ever truly make her feel like a woman. Gina had married Antonio on the rebound, feeling discarded and unattractive. She had pledged, as a devout Catholic, that she would honour her wedding vows whatever and had conceded to his needs on many a lonely night. She had two adorable children to show for it though, but not one moment of pleasure or fulfilment.

Right now, Gina wished with every fibre of her body that she could take back those stupid words that she had said to Callum. Tonight, she could have been in his pleasant company for dinner or even watching the ballet at Moscow's famous Bolshoi with him. Instead she would be tolerating yet another night of her own tedious company.

"Pride comes before a fall," she whispered to herself then exited the restroom. She drew a deep breath and walked back as serenely as she could to her seat and Callum.

He stood to let her in and refreshed her champagne. Gina accepted it with a gracious smile, then took another deep breath and ate humble pie.

"Callum, can we re-wind?" she began nervously. "I apologise, that was most ungracious of me under the circumstances. I just panicked I guess. Would you do me the honour of dining with me tonight? And yes, I would love to go to the ballet with you but perhaps on another night when we haven't already had such a full day?" Gina's smile was honest but her eyes were averted in shame.

For a change, Callum considered his response carefully before replying so as not to make it any harder for Gina.

"There is nothing to forgive Gina. If I had to endure what you have had to over the two years since you lost your husband and the threat to your family that lies ahead, well I'm not so sure that I could have fared so well."

Callum was famous for his sentimentality and Gina felt his sincerity.

"And on top of that I put you in a compromised situation by rushing you onto a jet to Moscow, without any warning. And then I sat you next to a ridiculously handsome man, apparently. It is me who should be asking for forgiveness Gina," there was now a mixture of sincerity and mischief in Callum's eyes.

Gina clapped her hands together and laughed the most natural laugh that she had in a long time. It felt so therapeutic.

"I have no idea what the future holds for me Callum Knight, but I do know that it will be a joy working with you and your colleagues," then as an afterthought. "You said that we would meet Emanuel Goldberg tomorrow and a woman, but you never mentioned her name. Who is she?"

"A very close friend and colleague of mine Gina," Callum replied. "Ava. Ava Alexandrov-Kaplinski."

Chapter 12

After checking in at the Metropol, Gina had an hour to get ready to meet Callum for drinks.

"Damn, is this the best that you could pack woman?"

Gina stood in front of the full-length mirror. She held a variety of dresses against herself with one hand and pulled her long black hair up with the other, pouting as she did so. Finally, she settled for the three-quarter length black dress that was cut radically at the back and a little more modestly at the front. A safe cut for her ample figure to not invite a wardrobe malfunction. It was when she wore dresses like this that she wished she wasn't quite so well blessed. Skinny girls could wear their dresses slashed to the waist and still look elegant.

"I would just look like a whore," she thought wryly.

Gina brushed her long, black silky hair and then piled it up high on her head into an up-do. She was deep in thought as she did so, mostly about her children but Callum's enigmatic smile was haunting her too. As she came out of her reverie and studied herself in the mirror her eyes opened wide in shock and her jaw dropped. She had inadvertently styled her hair in the same way that she had on the morning of her wedding, nearly twenty years ago. It was a style that she had never used since. Gina was about to unpin and re-brush it when she stopped and laughed a joyous laugh.

"So, you are not looking for a man then Gina Mèdici?" she asked the girl in the mirror.

Gina decided to stick with the up-do. She sprayed her hair and painted her smile with red lipstick.

"Perhaps it's a good omen this time?" Gina wondered. "Anyway, it can't be worse than the last time," she added ironically.

Gina put on her black heels, grabbed her diamond studded clutch bag and blew a kiss at her refection.

"Go out and get him girl!"

She turned and walked confidently to the door and left her suite. Gina couldn't recall ever feeling this excited, or this nervous.

Callum idly stirred his gin and tonic. He was deep in thought and his thoughts were of Gina. The ice rattled pleasingly against his glass to the rhythm of his stir and condensation ran enticingly in rivulets down it. Gina was late and Callum was delaying the moment to savour the drink with her. He looked up just as Gina's shapely figure appeared in the doorway, at the far end of the lounge. Her enigmatic smile transcended the distance between them and Callum felt bathed in the warmth of it. The Mona Lisa smile could not have been more unfathomable. She walked towards him elegantly with a natural sway of her hips. Callum wasn't the only man in the lounge that had noticed her arrival. Several others had turned their heads. One of them was being reprimanded by an irate partner. Gina had a serene beauty about her that made her entirely photogenic, which was partly why the paparazzi were constantly pursuing her.

Gina's bright blue eyes never left Callum's face as she approached. She could see that he was already captivated and it boosted her confidence. When they met, she offered her face to his to exchange kisses and needed to stretch her long neck up to him to do so. When their faces touched, Gina could smell the invigorating scent of clean man and the sensuous gentle grazing of his stubble on her skin. It sent delicious shivers down her spine and caused her heart to flutter.

"You look beautiful," Callum said. It was a statement of fact, rather than flattery. Gina could tell that he meant it.

"Why thank you, kind sir and you are looking suave and dashing in that rather expensive suit. I like a man who dresses well for his date," Gina's eyes twinkled mischievously under the directional lounge lighting.

"Mm, I like it that you refer to it as a *date*. It does feel like that, doesn't it?" Callum returned the spirit of Gina's smile. "Perhaps tonight we should keep it light and concentrate on small talk and getting to know each other. Tomorrow is likely to challenge everything that you have ever taken as truth or holy, so you will need to be fresh for that."

Gina felt the change that had come about him and it reawakened her to the dark and sinister reason that they were in Moscow. Survival. Callum realised with regret, that he had broken the magic of the moment and the need to divert her from her sombre thoughts.

"So, I'm guessing gin and tonic, Bombay Sapphire of course?" his smile was convivial.

"Spot on Callum, it seems that I must try and be unpredictable or you will quickly tire of me," it was just a nonsense statement, designed to unbalance Callum. It worked.

"You are far from predictable Gina. I only took an educated guess...," Gina was already laughing before he had finished his sentence.

"And I am only playing with you Callum. A gin and tonic would be perfect," that immaculately groomed eyebrow was raised again but this time it was in humour.

Callum called the barman over to fix Gina's drink. He passed it to her and proposed a toast.

"To the success of your Tarot reading then Gina, whatever that means," Callum tipped his glass to hers and took a long-awaited quaff. His sigh of pleasure was un-abandoned.

"I might tell you one day if fate plays its hand," Gina returned and again Callum couldn't read the meaning of her smile or the look in her eyes.

"You are definitely not predictable Gina, quite mysterious in fact. I like that about a woman," in comparison he was an open book to Gina and she was perfectly aware of his infatuation.

"I'm famished. Can we go through to the dining room? Travelling always gives me an appetite," Gina suppressed making a reference to a double entendre and wondered what she might have had for breakfast that had made her so uncharacteristically horny?

"Of course," Callum obliged, totally unaware of Gina's confusion.

Callum took her glass. They chatted idly as they walked through to the impressive Art Nouveau dining room. Its scrolled ironwork with curving lines, floral shapes and drapes were set out in themes of leaves and flowers, all picked out in pleasing colours such that it was a visual extravaganza. They sat and chatted easily in the ambience of the room about unimportant things and observations. Such as the decorations, the interesting people in the room, the idiosyncrasies of one of the waiters who they both found amusing. Even the Moscow weather was encompassed by their trivia. It felt to both that it would be a crime to spoil the moment by talking business, and so they mutually avoided doing so.

Gina was a well-travelled woman but had not been to Russia before. After asking Gina what her likes and dislikes were, he steered her through the menu and ordered for them both. As an *entrée,* Callum had chosen the pan-seared scallops, served on a bed of blanched spinach with a drizzle of lime and coriander. A bottle of Grand Cru Chablis was his natural choice to compliment this. After establishing that Gina loved red meat, the chateaubriand to share was a must, rare of course. Callum had chosen the Châteauneuf-du-Pape for its full body to accompany.

They were elated when it turned out to be the idiosyncratic waiter that served them. He had the movements and mannerisms of a clockwork doll. Everything he did was in slow motion, like he moved a frame at a time. Even his smile spread in phases across his face; lips, cheeks, eyes then teeth. It had become an in-joke and it was as much as they could do to keep a straight face when he served them. Neither dared look at the other for fear of laughing inappropriately.

"Good choice Callum, these scallops are divine," Gina sipped her wine, "and the Chablis, just perfect."

Gina had been harbouring a little guilt and it was playing on her conscience.

"Callum, I have a little confession to make. I Googled you before dinner," even with Gina's dark complexion, it was clear to Callum that she was blushing.

"Interesting Gina, so what did you find?" Callum cocked an inquisitive glance that felt like an arrow to Gina.

"Well, not so much more than I already knew," Gina quickly qualified that statement. "We often appear in the same magazines, you see. It would seem that you are quite a heartthrob Callum."

"Well I don't know about that," it was his turn to feel a little flushed.

"Yes, you do Callum. You were quite the talk amongst the air hostesses on the plane. It certainly didn't need two lovely receptionists to help you check in here and several hotel guests have already looked you over. I call that being a 'heartthrob'," Gina accused.

"And you didn't notice all heads turn to you when you walked into the bar. Men and women?" returned Callum.

"Did they?" Gina was good at *aloof* and diverted the subject. "My point was that there has never been a Mrs Knight, something that I find strange about a man who is so obviously attractive to women, charming and attentive."

Callum considered Gina's question for a moment. The honest answer was difficult to admit, particularly to a woman that he already had a shine for. He momentarily considered a white lie but that would have got them off to a bad start.

"I guess I'm not very good at choosing the right type. Maybe I fall in love too quickly and lose my advantage," Callum looked distant for a moment. "My friend's advice is 'treat them mean and keep them keen', but my women seem to beat me to it," Callum offered a wry smile.

"Oh Callum, I shouldn't have asked. That was painful for you, I'm so sorry."

That hadn't gone quite how Gina had hoped and she felt clumsy. Once again, she wished she could stop and rewind. Callum saw her awkwardness and once again came to the rescue.

"No, you should. If things are out in the open, then it avoids any confusion later," Callum felt the need to bare his soul. He was one who always wore his heart on his sleeve.

"I have hit an impasse in my life, someone I can't quite get over. Every time I nearly make it she comes back and I have no defence. She's my Kryptonite, my vulnerability," Gina could see in his eyes that he loved even the mention of her.

85

"What's her name, and is she on the scene now?"

It was partly a selfish question on Gina's part. What she really wanted to add was, "Is she pretty?" Callum sensed it.

"No, we're having time out again. It can go on for months and sometimes into years like that. The catalyst is normally when I find someone new. Her name is Kayla Lovell, an American woman. She's a black girl with attitude; a real beauty. She has a crazy mix of bloods to go with it and she's much smarter than me."

"So," Gina thought, "Kayla was just about the most passionate and manipulative woman that a man could ever meet and abundantly intelligent. Note to self, 'Google that one too'."

"Sounds like you are not a quitter Callum. Or that you just don't know when to jump ship," Gina said pointedly. She had at that moment declared her hand. The question was, had Callum noticed?

"Well you can see that I am a hopeless case when it comes to love Gina, but what about you? I must confess that I have also researched you, but for professional reasons of course," Callum's grin showed that his comment also had a self-interest side to it. "I needed to know all of your weaknesses and strengths. I couldn't help wondering why you are still not romantically involved so long after losing your husband."

That was a little blunter and more to the point than Gina had expected from a gentleman like Callum. It unbalanced her.

"I deserve this," Gina admitted. "Well, to be honest, it wasn't great the first time round and I didn't think that I could do it twice."

Gina's face showed that there was more and Callum gave her time to come to terms with herself.

"It wasn't just the lack of romance, or the bereavement of losing him," Gina was struggling with her confession. "It was him bringing danger into our home. I don't think I could ever forgive him for that, nor ever trust a man to take that much control again."

"The danger was the Illuminati you mean?" Callum didn't really need to voice that but it got the subject out into the open.

"Yes."

Despite trying to fight it back, a single tear squeezed out from the corner of Gina's eye and rolled down the olive skin of her cheek. Callum picked up his napkin, reached across the table and dabbed the rogue tear away. Gina subconsciously leant into the comfort of his touch.

"It's not hopeless Gina," Callum said reassuringly. "We are a very resourceful organisation and you are not an island anymore. Trust us and we will come through for you," the thin smile that Gina returned was as fragile as her confidence.

"I will try Callum, I will try."

Gina desperately needed to share her secret of the summer solstice with someone. To talk about that desperate night of terror when an innocent child was raped and murdered. It was too much for her to support alone. She needed to exorcise it through confession in the Catholic way. She was one of the Council of Thirteen and therefore guilty by association. Until now there had been nobody that she could confide in, not even Asmina. It was too monumental.

"I have done a terrible thing," she began. "I stood by and watched a young girl as she was raped and killed. I didn't even raise a finger to help her or even utter protest," the tears of grief and guilt were now flowing freely down her face. "All I did was thank God that it wasn't my daughter. I'm so ashamed of myself Callum, so ashamed."

Callum offered his serviette but Gina pulled away and sat back in her chair, increasing the distance between them. She just looked at him, now a ghost of her former self.

"How can you even bear to sit at the table with me knowing what I have done?"

"Where did this happen Gina?" Callum asked calmly.

"In Germany, near Ingolstadt. It was at the summer solstice meeting of the Council of Thirteen. I'm sure you know who they are?" Callum nodded. "We were all there. I thought it was Isabella right up until they took her mask off. I thanked God for his mercy when it was not. As if some other child's life was less important, less precious than mine. I find it hard to live with myself for that."

Callum knew much more about Gina and her late husband's involvement with the Illuminati than he would like to admit to her. Her late husband had been a prolific fundraiser for the Illuminati for over twenty years. He also knew that the Pindar had sanctioned his death for misappropriation of Illuminati funds, or *theft* as the Pindar had called it. Callum also knew that Gina was indeed fortunate that Isabella had not been sacrificed at the time for his crime, much in the same way as the girl was that she had referred to.

"Gina," Callum began, "you have no reason to carry guilt. You were placed out of your depth by circumstances beyond your control. Nothing that you could have done would have saved that girl's life and anything that you might have tried would have resulted in extreme danger for you and your family," he paused looking for some acknowledgement from Gina, then added, "at best."

Callum's words were rejuvenating for Gina and she seemed to come out from where she had regressed to.

"I suppose I know that, but I have never been so weak that I have not risked all to help someone in need," Gina lamented.

"But then you have never been up against someone as ruthless and heartless as the Pindar, have you?"

Gina was shocked that Callum knew their master by name.

"You know him?" she said incredulously.

"I know of him and little more," Callum admitted, "but across the next few months we will all learn everything that there is to know about him. His strengths and his weaknesses, then together we will defeat him."

It was sabre rattling to a degree on Callum's behalf and he knew it. All that the Angel organisation really knew of the Pindar was that he was the uncontested leader of the Illuminati and that he was untraceable; invisible even. There wasn't a single photograph of him, not even by any of the world's most secret services. It was as if he didn't exist.

Gina held her own counsel. She had met the Pindar and had never, ever felt the clear and present danger and evil that was transmitted by him. She had very little hope that this lovely and gentle man sat in front of her, had even a snowball's hope in Hell of besting the Pindar.

"Thank you, Callum, and I believe in you," she lied, smiling feebly back at him. Gina had run out of options and this was simply her last chance saloon.

After that the evening passed most cordially and their conversation slipped back into trivia. By the time that coffees were served, each knew the other's life like intimate friends. Neither held back and they shared honesty without shame or embarrassment. It was late and the day had been long.

"Will you walk me back to my room Callum, only I'm falling asleep despite your undeniable charm," there was no hint of sarcasm in Gina's comment. She literally was dead on her feet.

"Of course," Callum stood and came around the table to her side, easing her chair backwards as she stood.

"Thank you, Callum. I like a man who is gentlemanly," her fond smile was all the reward he could have hoped for.

They thanked their idiosyncratic waiter as they left. Callum discretely handed him his tip disguised as a handshake. They were immediately rewarded with his clockwork smile that ticked in stages across his face. Gina stifled a conspiratorial laugh as they walked out of the dining room towards the foyer and lifts. She slipped her arm inside Callum's and leaned against him as they walked, both out of affection and the combined effect of the Chablis and Châteauneuf-du-Pape.

When the lift doors opened and they stepped in, Gina had the overpowering desire to kiss Callum. How she did not, she had no idea. Nor did she know that Callum was himself struggling with the same instinct. They walked slowly down the corridor to her suite, still deep in conversation and delaying the moment. Gina waited until they were at her door before searching for her key. It was yet more procrastination.

"Ask him in for a coffee," she told herself, but her modesty would not allow the words to form at her lips. She was hoping that Callum would take the initiative.

"Well goodnight then," Callum offered reluctantly, "it's been a pleasure."

As Gina placed her key card to the lock he leaned down and kissed her cheek.

"Breakfast at eight then and don't be late. I will have missed you for long enough by then," his smile was brief and shy, Gina thought.

"My pleasure too," Gina replied but Callum was already walking back to the lift.

Gina let herself into her suite and closed the door behind her, leaning with her back against it looking at the grand four-poster bed.

"Alone again," she thought but this time there was a smile on her face.

For the first time since she was a teenager, Gina felt desire and being desired. She couldn't wait for breakfast and of course to see Callum again.

Callum poured himself a drink from the minibar and sat on the bed loosening his tie. He took a mouthful of the chilled Jack Daniel's rinsing it around his mouth, enjoying the subtle liquorice flavour. He kicked off his shoes and lay back against the pillows piled against the headboard. The smile on his face said it all. He was totally captivated by this dark, elegant and sophisticated woman. It had taken all his willpower not to spoil it and suggest a nightcap. He was pleased with himself that he hadn't, but not too sure that it could happen twice.

His mobile chirped as a message came in. He reached for it, certain that it would be Gina. His jaw dropped when he saw the name on the display. Kayla Lovell.

"What the hell?" Callum was floored. "How on Earth did she choose this moment to get back in touch?"

It was uncanny, but then Kayla was *uncanny*. She was a half breed, neither Angel nor Shadow. Coupled with that, she was part African and part European. With that heady mix of genes, came psychic powers that beggared belief. Somehow, she always knew when he was ready to move on and then she would be back on the scene. Callum loved her so much that he fell for it every time. She would swear that she had finally seen the light and that he was the only one, then it would happen over again. Each time Callum lost part of his soul and a lot of his heart.

He opened the message:

"Darling! I'm coming to Moscow and I hear that you are there? I've missed you so much and can't wait to see you. I'm counting the days.... xxx"

Callum tossed his mobile on the bed. Just one word left his lips, "Christ."

Chapter 13

Breakfast was animated and Callum wholly attentive but Gina had sensed that something had changed, or that something was on his mind. She held her own counsel.

"It was too good to be true anyway," she told herself defensively.

The taxi stopped outside the impressive tower in Russia's newly constructed International Business Centre, or "Moscow City", as it had come to be known. It was only two miles from Moscow's Red Square and the Kremlin, which brought with it numerous political advantages. Callum's organisational offices for the whole of Eastern Europe occupied the eleventh floor of this prestigious building.

Gina had been quiet on the taxi journey there but it wasn't because of personal issues or Callum's unaccountable change of mood, she was steeling herself for the enormity of what was to come. Asmina's words, in her endearing West Indian lilt, echoed in her head:

"'Tis the card of discovery. New talents an' abilities. You's yet an embryo bibi an' you still growin'."

Leonardo had endorsed that statement, so it wasn't just hocus-pocus on Asmina's part. Soon she would know what the world *really* looked like and what she was. It scared the hell out of her. Gina genuflected as she walked up the steps, something that appeared to have become habitual. It was a giant leap of faith and one that was certain to make an enemy of the Pindar. She looked at Callum for reassurance, and hoped to God that she had put her money on the right horse.

After passing through security, they crossed to the lifts. Callum called the car and pressed the button adjacent to a plaque that simply said, "*Angelos Associates*".

Gina remembered that Leonardo had referred to the Angel's lost planet as *Angelos* and so the name on the plaque made sense to her. That was reassuring.

When they arrived at the eleventh, Gina was impressed with the plushness of her surroundings. A spacious reception with coffee lounge and comfy chairs gave way through subliminal partitioning to open-plan offices on each side. Beyond that, corridors led on to individual offices and lounges. Callum went straight to the receptionist. She was a tall elegant woman in her twenties with blonde hair, startling blue eyes and a generous smile that she used copiously on Callum.

"Everything that I am not," Gina noted as the girl engaged enthusiastically with Callum. "Perhaps he prefers blondes?" she thought with more than a hint of jealousy.

The pretty young receptionist turned her smile on Gina with just as much enthusiasm.

"Let me get you a coffee Mrs Mèdici while they prepare for your meeting," she spoke perfect Italian, albeit with a heavy Russian accent.

"I won't be long Gina," Callum called across to her, "I just want to bring Emanuel up to speed, hope that's OK?" he seemed reluctant to leave her alone, which Gina felt most reassuring.

"Of course Callum, it'll give me a chance to catch up with Sasha and Isabella. Take your time," he left her with a smile.

The Russian girl took Gina into the lounge with the comfy chairs and gave her a coffee. She was really sweet and Gina felt a little guilty for having pre-judged the elegant blonde receptionist. As she sat there engulfed in the luxurious chair, Gina couldn't help but wonder if Leonardo might have visited these offices at some time too and what he might have thought of them.

"He would have hated these," she decided and smiled fondly.

She imagined his consternation at being 'consumed' by the furniture and him standing awkwardly as a preference. Gina once again felt a little bereft that this extraordinary man from the past, wasn't to be part of her present and help shape her future.

"Mr Knight and Mr Goldberg are ready for you now Mrs Mèdici."

The pretty Russian girl led the way and Gina followed her down the sumptuously carpeted corridor. An avenue of sculpted busts was mounted on dwarf columns on both sides, with paintings in the style of the old masters in between. As they turned the corner into yet another corridor, Gina gasped as she came face to face with a bust that was the very image of Leonardo da Vinci. She smiled and ran her hand fondly down his marble face.

"It's a good omen," she thought as the receptionist knocked on the door of the *Crystalita Room.*

That name was also familiar. Leonardo had said that Crystalita was one of the two true blood sisters that were still alive today. The concept of longevity seemed totally impossible to Gina and beyond her comprehension. It was something that she was now just going to have to accept as fact.

"At least there is some consistency in this madness, "Gina thought and again it was reassuring.

A deep, friendly and unfamiliar voice called them in. Gina found herself in a comfortable meeting room. A round table was set in the middle, with four chairs set around it and comfy sofas to her right. On the wall behind the sofas, was a big and impressive ornamental mirror with carved cherubs set in a gilt frame. Gina was immediately drawn to it but she couldn't understand why. After all, it was just an old ornate mirror. There was a panoramic window in front of her that occupied the whole of the wall. From it, was an amazing view that looked out over the old town to the Kremlin and Saint Basil's Cathedral, a beautiful example of ornate Renaissance Russian architecture. The eight ornamental and brightly painted domes of the churches, surrounding the core, shone in the morning sun like beacons proclaiming the faith that had lovingly commissioned them. Gina was consumed by its beauty. As magnificent as Castello di Mèdici was, it seemed to pale into insignificance by comparison.

Callum was stood next to a bear of a man with a shock of white curly hair and an angelic smile. He looked like the grandfather figure that Gina always wished for, but never had. It was strange, but Gina immediately liked him and felt as if they were already friends, even though there was no reason at all for her to do so.

"I have been looking forward to meeting you so much Mrs Mèdici. Your reputation precedes you. I am honoured," his bright blue eyes were kind, honest and welcoming.

"You are too kind Mr Goldberg and I'm Gina by the way. Pleased to meet you," she said offering her hand and her smile.

"*Enchanté* Gina. Please call me Emanuel. Will you sit with us?"

Callum withdrew Gina's chair and seated her to his right, facing Emanuel. The chair to Emanuel's left was vacant.

"Are we expecting company?" Gina asked, cocking a fine brow in the direction of the empty seat.

"We are hoping so but alas Ava is stuck in Moscow traffic. We can start without her though. She has her own ways of catching up as you will no doubt see."

Gina's curiosity was aroused about just how 'her own way' might be. Emanuel continued.

"Perhaps that start could be by you telling us what you know about the Illuminati and what your role is in their organisation?"

Gina suddenly looked like a rabbit caught in the headlights. She felt accused, like a naughty school girl. Callum sensed her uneasiness and put his hand over hers in comforting manner.

"Relax Gina, we are not here to judge you. It's just that we must understand what brought you to the Council of Thirteen and what the Pindar is asking of you, what his strategy is and who his key players are. Armed with that we have a reasonable chance of protecting you and your family, or at least stall him," it was meagre fare for Gina but she recognised it as a life line, albeit a slim one.

Gina let out a sigh of resignation and began. She decided to go right back to the beginning, as if to do so would help her own understanding of it.

"My connection to the Illuminati is through my late husband, Antonio. I met him when I was in my early twenties. He seemed to come out of nowhere and found me I suppose. I certainly wasn't looking for him," Gina looked regretful. "I was on the rebound from a relationship that had turned sour and vulnerable I guess. My parents hated him and warned me off, threatened to cut me off in fact. But I didn't listen. Strangely enough I didn't even like him, but he had a hold on me. Not physical," Gina added hastily, "it wasn't that sort of relationship, he was in my head. Sometimes I couldn't think without him. I became dependent. When he proposed I naturally said yes despite my parents' protests. I never even considered that I had the right of refusal."

Gina had lost her self-consciousness now. The story was all important. She was at last, after many years, beginning to question her understanding of things.

"We married and went on honeymoon. For a while Antonio was an ardent lover, and a good one at that. He was adamant that we didn't use contraceptives. *Life was holy*; he had said and insisted that we had children and how important that was to him. Well it came as no surprise when months later I was with child. That was when the sex and the romance dried up."

Admitting the intimacies of her personal life to almost total strangers was like a counselling session to her. It was immensely cathartic and in some ways, an epiphany. For the first time in her life she was beginning to realise that she hadn't made a life decision since she had met Antonio. She resumed her story, but this time not under duress. Her openness was leading somewhere, she knew it.

"Antonio was then equally adamant that I should devote my time to growing *his* baby as he called it and give up my job at the Mèdici bank. I argued that my work was too important but he torpedoed that by saying that he would do it for me until *his* baby was born and settled."

Gina looked distant again and perhaps angry. But it was herself that she was angry with.

"I didn't argue. I wanted to but somehow, I just couldn't. I remember being so frustrated with myself for my lack of spine," Gina shrugged her shoulders. "Somehow the words of protest never came. Antonio had become a big success at the Mèdici bank by then and even my father had come to admire him. After that he seemed to have little time for me. Even my mother took sides with Antonio and became distant."

Gina was in full swing with her *petite histoire* such, that Emanuel and Callum had no need to intercede.

"My parents had become secretive. There was some problem at the bank that was never discussed with me, but I could tell that Antonio had fallen out of favour. I never did find out why because their accident happened shortly afterwards."

"I'm sorry Gina, your pain is more than evident to both of us," Callum said sincerely. His hand had once again crept over hers, "but what do you know about the circumstances of your parents' accident?"

97

Gina looked like tears were about to flood her face but she fought them back. She didn't want them to perceive her as a weak woman.

"Mum and Dad were holidaying in France, just outside Nice. They had gone sightseeing and took the Grande Corniche, a narrow mountain pass. Apparently, a truck had lost its brakes coming down and they met head on. Both vehicles left the road and fell nearly five hundred metres. There were no survivors and no reliable witnesses either."

Gina hurried on so as not to let the moment overcome her.

"That left the Mèdici bank like a ship without a helm in stormy waters. I managed to get Antonio to agree for me to go back to work and strangely he became quite supportive and even amorous. I believed that he had changed now we were a couple, alone in the world," Gina sighed. "Again he wouldn't countenance contraception and needless to say I got pregnant again. I was naive to think that he would change, he didn't. The tenderness and sex dried up again. I was ordered to be the doting mother of *his* two kids, this time without the mediation of my mother. Antonio now had total control of the Mèdici bank and me. He ran the bank at his own discretion for the next twelve years until his death two years ago."

Gina's face looked pained and the pain turned to anger.

"That was the episode when Antonio brought the Pindar into our lives and endangered our children and me. Now I am a forced member of the Council of Thirteen carrying out his dirty work. Damn him to Hell!"

There. It was out in the open and Gina felt the load come off her shoulders. At last she didn't have to pretend anymore. Emanuel shook his big shaggy head in sympathy.

"You are a woman of great strength and fortitude Gina, and have my utmost respect and admiration."

Emanuel had an intuitive nature. He could completely read and understand the human side of Gina's ordeal that her words had not spoken.

"I'm sorry to press you further, but what do you know about your husband's unexpected death?"

"I don't know much more than was published in the newspapers really. He went out at six o'clock in the evening on business, as he regularly did, and didn't return. I had thought for a long time that he was having an affair. No, I will reword that. He *was* having an affair, with whom, I didn't know and had long since passed caring. When he didn't return that night, I just assumed that he was with her. It wasn't until he didn't return the next, that I raised the alarm."

"If that truly is all you know then the rest is well documented," Emanuel began. "Your husband's car was found on the cliff-top at Genoa with a suicide note written to you in his own hand. It basically asked for your forgiveness for misappropriating bank funds and that he couldn't live with the shame. There was no body recovered, only scattered possessions in the waters below the cliffs."

"Yes, that about sums it up," you might have expected some sign of remorse from Gina but there was none. "I never believed that he wrote that note, or at least didn't mean what it said. Antonio was not a man to ask for a woman's forgiveness and particularly not mine. Nor was he the suicidal type. It never rang true."

"And it would also be a documented first for a Shadow to commit suicide," added Emanuel, shaking his main of white hair. Gina's jaw dropped.

"Antonio was a Shadow?" She looked shocked. "But Leonardo said that they were pure evil. How could I not have seen that? He was secretive, yes and dishonest too, but not evil. That, or he was a good actor."

"The latter I'm afraid," Emanuel lamented. "You were his route to gaining control of the Mèdici bank, its prestige and its clients. As

99

a race the Shadows have an ability to control the minds and actions of others. That explains why you never refused his proposal of marriage or indeed any other of the impositions that he put on you."

It was time for Emanuel to deliver the cruellest news of all, but he had to do it. Gina needed to know what she was up against.

"Your parents had no choices either after meeting him. He would have got into their minds and they would have been powerless to resist his will. When your parents seemed to distance themselves from you it would have been through his control, not because of them not loving you."

A rogue tear squeezed from Gina's eye at the mention of her deceased parents love for her. She swept it away with a finger, hoping that they didn't see it. Emanuel continued.

When the Board of Directors at the Mèdici bank exposed his nefarious transactions, your parents must have woken up to it all," Gina felt Callum's hand increase its pressure on hers. He already knew what was coming." I'm afraid that their car crash in France wasn't an accident. They were targeted and eliminated by the Shadow organisation. Afterwards, Antonio brought the minds of the Directors back under control and the Mèdici bank was his from then until he disappeared twelve years later."

Gina looked like rag doll with all the stuffing pulled out of it. She was silent for a while.

"Nothing is really as I know it, is it?" Gina said at last with resignation. She became aware that Callum was still squeezing her hand supportively.

"Not everything perhaps, but the world isn't all bad. What is good is worth fighting for Gina. It's what we do every day," she felt the warmth and sincerity of his smile.

Emanuel continued.

"One of two things happened to your late husband and none of us sat at this table believe in the suicide scenario," Emanuel raised a bushy white eyebrow at Gina, looking for her accord. He got it in the form of an almost imperceptible nod. "The Pindar will have long since considered the assets of your bank to be his in everything but name. Antonio was clearly skimming off monies, that is a documented fact. So, he either got greedy and found out by the Pindar and cut and ran, or he was eliminated by him. I suspect the second."

"I never considered that it might have been the Illuminati," Gina said, "but I have never doubted that he was dead. I *feel* people's presence, I always have. It must be part of those inborn skills that you talked of. I ceased feeling Antonio's presence during the first night that he was away. I remember waking up in a cold sweat and a feeling of deep dread. It must have happened then," Gina's face showed a trace of pity but no more than that.

"The Mèdici bank was certainly the cause of your husband's death but it might be your and your families' salvation. Well at least in the short term. Your insurance policy," Emanuel began. "We know that the Pindar has a three-year plan to evoke a Third World War and that key enabling acquisitions and funding are planned through Mèdici bank negotiations. We need to put in a 'safety net', such that if anything happens to you, then that automatically evokes some kind of contingency plan," Emanuel paused before adding the deadly caveat. "Of course, for it to work you would have to go public with the Pindar and declare your hand. You would be seen as his enemy but it would buy you an extra six months at best, before the Pindar has a fall-back plan in place," Gina looked ashen.

"And how long do I have without making myself his enemy? And how do you know about Mèdici acquisitions anyway?" Gina began to feel the safety of her castle walls tumbling down around her.

"Well that depends on how well advanced you are with the Pindar's acquisitions and finance agreements. To answer your question about 'how we know', well that's the business that we are in. We have offices all over the world like this and agents placed strategically in government, banking and commerce to name but a few. Even the Mèdici bank I am sorry to say, but now you see why."

Gina nodded in resignation. She realised that she had no options outside of the four walls of the Crystalita Room.

"I have completed the Pindar's acquisitions bar one, along with generous finance plans that are set to go through the roof in the short to near term. He now holds a minimum of 51% in each, but of course in the Mèdici name," Gina explained ashamedly. "When the interest rates become unsupportable, the Mèdici bank will withdraw funding and force their clients to sell the remaining shares to the bank."

"You said that all acquisitions bar one were in place. What then is the Pindar's final acquisition?" Emanuel asked spreading his big hands on the table as if to add weight to his question.

"The Mèdici bank," Gina said simply.

Emanuel and Callum exchanged looks. They both suspected as much.

"If you sign over 51% of the Mèdici bank to the Pindar, then you are also signing your own death warrant," Callum said with finality, "and they will have ways of making you sign."

Gina immediately thought of her children being taken and her blood ran cold.

"How can I resist? Either way the Pindar will have his way," Gina looked desperate.

"In truth, you cannot Gina. But you can buy time," Callum offered, "that insurance policy that we talked about. That is the Pindar's clear understanding that, if anything happens to you or your loved ones, you will trash the bank and all its assets. We can come up with the detail behind that plan for you," Gina looked unconvinced.

"So, I buy six months, max. What then?" Gina's raised her brow quizzically at Emanuel.

"In six months, we groom a girl to have half a chance of staying alive as opposed to none."

It was hard hitting and direct. Emanuel's stern expression showed Gina, that it was a fair appraisal of her hope for survival, just fifty-fifty. But it was an act. He and Callum both knew that, in reality, it was significantly less. Gina needed hope though, to keep striving. They could not afford to let her feel that it was impossible and give up without a fight. Humanity was depending on her.

"Great. I piss off the most bad-arsed man in history for hardly a hope in Hell's chance of surviving it. Thanks a bunch guys," Gina said with gallows humour, forcing a smile.

Callum interceded.

"As I've already told you, there's a woman that we want you to meet. She has endured against odds even worse than yours. Ava is your hope Gina and I would certainly trust her with my life," Callum said with absolute conviction.

Ironically, in another life that he was unaware of, he had trusted in her and lost his life to her.

As if on cue, there was a knocking at the door. An attractive, athletically slim woman entered with red hair and a captivating smile. She walked with the deportment and confidence of a dancer. Callum stood to greet her and they exchanged kisses. Their fondness for each other was profoundly evident to Gina.

"Let me introduce you to Ava Alexandrov-Kaplinski. She will be your mentor over the next few months," Callum said proudly.

Gina stood and held out her hand. It was the *Magician*; the one that Asmina had predicted would help her on her journey of discovery. She felt a superstitious shiver run down her back.

"We were just talking about you Ava," Gina said offering her hand. "I've been looking forward to meeting you ever since Leonardo spoke so highly of you."

They shook hands but Ava didn't let go. Instead she took the other and stood toe to toe with Gina and smiled at her captivatingly.

"Then we have both been blessed by meeting him Gina. I had my hour of need and his words of wisdom were the turning point for me. Unfortunately, it took me too long to see that, but I got there in the end and I came through. You will come through too Gina. You must always believe that."

Ava was clearly a sophisticated woman who spoke perfect English with an endearing Russian accent. Her eyes were the deepest blue with flecks of brown in them that seemed to dance in her expressions. There was empathy in them too, such that Gina felt completely at ease with this strikingly beautiful redhead. She quite naturally returned her smile.

"Are you prepared to share everything with me Gina, your life history, your thoughts and secrets? Can you trust me that much?" Ava was still holding Gina's hands and her gaze.

"I have to trust you Ava. Whatever it takes, I'm pretty low on options don't you know?" It was Gina's effort at making light of it.

"Did you join minds with Leonardo?" Ava asked, she was sure that Gina had.

"Only briefly, but it was the most amazing experience of my life; almost religious."

"Yes isn't it? That's because he is so pure of spirit. Probably the most perfect man that has ever existed," Gina could sense Ava's awe.

The two women stood in the middle of the room holding hands, were strangers to each other. Despite that, and being in the company of others, neither felt in slightest bit awkward.

"I am not perfect though Gina, far from it. My blood is mixed such that I have a dark side and I have done some terrible things. When we share minds, you will come to know all of my past and my innermost thoughts and secrets too. You will know more about me than anyone here in this room knows, even more than my husband, Yuri. Are you ready to do that?"

Gina was without any doubts or reservations and nodded her consent. Ava continued.

"You will see the potential in me that will give you an insight into your own possibilities. In turn, this will give you the confidence and strength you need to endure and I will be better able to understand you and your potential."

Ava turned to the men.

"Would you give us girls some time together to get to know each other? Take a coffee break perhaps?" Ava's statement was more than a request.

Emanuel and Callum left obediently, without protest.

"Will you sit with me Gina?" Ava asked, already leading her to the small two-seater leather sofa.

They sat knees touching and hands held. Gina felt a kindred spirit. Perhaps it was in their genes, but much more so. She sensed that this red headed beauty had suffered. Suffered and endured. She had the credentials of the Magician that she needed, that the Tarot cards and Asmina had predicted.

"Are you ready?" Ava asked with an encouraging smile. "My history will shock you Gina, more than any words of preparation could ready you for. I only ask that you don't judge me," Gina nodded and bowed respectfully.

Ava touched her forehead against Gina's.

"Relax and let your mind roam free Gina and then it will happen naturally," Ava whispered.

It happened more quickly than Gina could have possibly imagined. Their joining of minds was breath-taking. All at once, Gina was swept into the exhilaration of Ava's lived experiences. It was as if they were happening to her. Ava's thoughts and emotions, sensual and sexual, her pain and despair; were as if they were her own experiences. Even Ava's love of motherhood and devotion to her daughter, Mina and her love for her husband, Yuri, were being shared with her. It was like living a life in fast forward. Ava had exercised some control over the order of things though, so as not to shock Gina before she had become accustomed to the sharing of minds. But Ava had to let it all go for Gina to understand. She did.

Gina felt the terror and anguish when Ava's mother was brutally murdered by her absent father in front of her eyes, when she was just five years old. The years of hardship and guilt that followed at the Bolshoi. Her rape by her aunt's perverted boyfriend when she was still a child, and how she killed him in a fit of rage afterwards. Then Ava revealed her isolation and abuse in the Madrassas of Pakistan and how she killed one of her tormentors. There was the mental turmoil that she suffered as she was indoctrinated and radicalised to be a jihadist assassin. She lived first hand through Ava's suffering as her loved ones were eliminated. One of those murdered was her lover, Katarina. She was a petite ballerina who she adored. Their love was the most sensual of her life. Katarina was the one who helped her to try and overcome the demons inside her that wanted to possess her. Gina could see that Katarina was Ava's anchor, and how she was cast adrift when she lost her, then how those demons swiftly took over.

It was a rollercoaster of horror, unsupportable by any mere mortal but Ava's misery went on and on. Gina experienced how it was to take a man's life with your own bare hands in revenge when she executed Bortnik, the violator and murderer of her dearest friend and aunt. Her manipulation, rape and radicalisation by Demitri, who she was later to find out was her father, seemed to be where Ava's life story couldn't get any worse. But it did. She shared with Ava how she had executed the Hydra in another life and another dimension, then followed her father into the past and killed him. It was all surreal, a bad dream. Gina couldn't believe the enormity of the horror that Ava had endured and survived. All at once she understood why Ava had done this. To show her that you can survive the impossible, you just need to want to enough. Gina knew that she had two very good reasons to want to; Sasha and Isabella.

Gina felt that she had now shared all of Ava's darkest secrets but Ava had saved the worst until last. Gina saw Callum's smile at first. Then she experienced the love affair of a lifetime that Ava had shared with him. Then her pain and the guilt that followed as she poisoned him and how he died in her arms, manipulated to do this by her father. Her despair and suicide attempt as she needed to end the pain by seeking oblivion. Of all the scars that Ava had, this was the one that she still hadn't come to terms with and probably never would.

Gina became aware that Ava was looking into her eyes and that tears were streaming down her face. The sharing had been agonising for Ava and she looked destroyed.

"Oh Ava, I'm so sorry," Gina threw her arms around Ava and held her close. She could feel her body heaving with each heartfelt sob.

In those few minutes, it was as if Gina had personally experienced all the trials and tribulations of Ava's life; her fears, her grief, her passion and her love. Until the present, Ava's life had been a tragedy; a life of indescribable suffering. At last the storm within her abated and she was able to pull away from the comfort of Gina's shoulder.

"Thank you, Gina. I will be alright now. I've been dreading sharing my memories with you. I knew that it would open old wounds for me, I just didn't realise how much. You had to see it though, with your own eyes, or you would never have believed the possibilities that we share. If you didn't then I would never have been able to prepare you for your own struggle," Ava smiled through her smudged and streaked eyeliner. "Do I look a mess?" she asked innocently.

"Nothing that we can't fix together," Gina said supportively, taking Ava's hand and standing her.

They retired to the bathroom. Ava looked at her reflection in the mirror and gasped.

"Thank God I asked the boys to leave," she said as she filled the basin.

Since the joining of their minds, each felt perfectly at ease with the other as if they had been the closest of friends for years. Gina took a small bottle of Molton Brown face wash and poured it into the warm water, soaked a flannel and began to wipe away the black streaks from Ava's face. They talked about unimportant things, their children, men and disappointment. While they chatted, Gina helped Ava put on fresh makeup.

"Try this," Gina said rummaging through her own bag producing her mascara," it's so good, better than extensions. Trust me."

Gina thickened and curled Ava's lashes, then finished them with her pencil.

"There, you look amazing again," Gina said, and Ava smiled her approval through freshly glossed lips.

Their faces were only inches apart and had been so throughout the remake. Neither planned it, but they finished with a kiss. It was more lingering than they had anticipated and not clear to either who had initiated it. Perhaps it was both, but it felt like the natural thing to do. It was something less than sexual but more than friendly; somewhere between possibility and fantasy. It left Gina a little light headed and confused, unlike Ava who was liberated and without the encumbrance of heterosexuality. Ava released the tension of the moment.

"Come on Gina, we have much to talk about before the boy's return," Ava took Gina's hand quite naturally and led her out of the bathroom.

Moments later they were sat talking animatedly about each other's experiences. Although they had exchanged a plethora of information, some things needed context to fully understand. Women, being woman, were quick to focus on each other's love lives.

"I feel like I have wasted my womanhood compared to the tempestuous love life that you have experienced Ava. I'm no more than a blinkered runner in the course of life."

There was much regret in that statement. Gina had never been truly fulfilled. Ava picked up on it.

"Perhaps, Gina," she said placing her hand reassuringly on Gina's knee, "but you will have seen the unholy mess that men have made of my life. Perhaps somewhere between you and me lies the ideal. To be with a man who knows how to love a woman and not just how to take from her. Callum would be ideal for you," Ava added, almost as an aside.

"What?" Gina's jaw dropped in disbelief at what she had just heard.

That was all that Gina managed to say, before realising that Ava had accessed her innermost thoughts and desires in their union. There were concepts in that union that Gina didn't even begin to understand. Like how Ava had loved, then killed Callum in some 'previous life' but now he was here in another. It was unfathomable. Ava didn't need Gina to ask how it was possible, she could read minds and Gina's was an open book right now.

"You want to know more about me and Callum, don't you?" Ava's smile was conspiratorial.

"Well yes, but you already knew that from when we joined minds. I seem to be the only dummy here."

Gina sighed at the inevitability of it all. She was the pupil and Ava her teacher, just as Asmina had divined from the Tarot cards; the Magician.

"Much you already know Gina and what you don't will slowly filter into your consciousness. Our union has overloaded your mind but it will have stimulated your DNA such that your brain development will accelerate as will you physiologically. Soon your mind will be able to assimilate all the information that I have given you and manifest itself in your consciousness. Hopefully it will be the key to unlock those powers that have been dormant until now. Then we will find out what lies deep within that beautiful persona of yours. A veritable empowered tigress I suspect."

Ava smiled knowingly. Gina wasn't too dissimilar from herself she decided. Certainly, much more inexperienced and naive but equal in spirit. It made Ava recall how it wasn't so long ago that the Matriarch, Maelströminha, had taught her how to liberate her own powers, enabling her to choose her own destiny and not be the victim of somebody else's.

"But you are a woman," Ava continued, "and of course you cannot wait for enlightenment, not even for a minute. I will fill in the gaps about Callum so that you don't drive yourself mad with curiosity until then," Ava smiled knowingly, perhaps a little mockingly and began her tale.

She explained in more detail how she had been groomed by her sponsor Demitri, the man she later knew to be her absent father. How he manipulated her to become his lover, and how his end-game was for her to be his puppet, an assassin. Just a tool to use to destroy the Angel generals, and that one of those generals was Callum.

"I had been radicalised in the Madrassas of Pakistan. Demitri liberated me. He was my saviour, or so I thought. But he was my captor. I had lost perspective and was taught to believe that Callum was evil. Ironic isn't it to believe that your captor was your liberator? I was such a fool."

Gina saw that Ava's expression had become distant as she regressed into her horrific past. She could see that the telling of it was going to be painful. She noticed too, that the brown flecks in Ava's eyes had massed and grown in density, like storm clouds.

"You don't have to do this Ava, I will work it out for myself eventually," Gina offered.

"No I do. I need to say it and you need to hear it. All that I am about to say is in the past of another life so it never happened in this one. I haven't even told this to Callum. Nor Yuri," she added guiltily. "Neither knows that it ever happened and I have to live with that alone. No Gina, I *need* to share this with someone or I will eventually go mad."

She told of how she fell for him the moment she met him, and that he was simply the best lover ever; a man in a million. Gina felt that feeling again deep in the pit her belly at the mention of it. She flushed with anticipation but strangely not with embarrassment, despite knowing that Ava could read her every thought. They were as close as sisters now and there were no secrets between them.

Ava explained how her radicalised mind had separated her love for a mortal man from her duty to her God as a jihadist.

"I always thought that somehow God would grant him pardon, because I could see that he was a good man. Right up to the night that he died in my arms from the poison that I gave him, I thought that God would give me a sign to spare him of his wrath. He didn't, of course."

"Callum was the love of my life Gina and I sacrificed him to some undeserving God," Ava howled at the agony of it and tears of remorse flooded her eyes and ran in rivers down her face. "Even knowing what I had done, his last words to me were, 'I have always loved you Ava and I will always love you'."

Gina took Ava's shaking body in her arms and comforted her. Much later she continued.

"I live everyday carrying that sin. Every time I meet him I want to throw my arms around him and ask for his forgiveness and for him to take me back," Ava sighed. "But for him it never happened. *We* never happened. I came back to this alternative life with a child already born and a husband that I never married. Don't get me wrong," Ava added hastily, "I love Yuri. Honestly, I do. But I never *chose* him. You must think I'm mad," Ava said, suddenly feeling foolish.

"No Ava, I didn't choose my husband either. He chose me and I can't even blame alternative lives for it. I'm only just beginning to understand that life isn't as simple as just being here, now. Be patient with me please, I am a quick learner. But there is something that you want of me I can sense that. What is it?"

Gina felt it. Perhaps it was the start of her renaissance, her metamorphosis into the new being that she was supposed to be.

"You are very perceptive Gina. Yes, there is. I want you to right my wrongs. I want you to make Callum happy, he deserves that. Be all the things that I should have been for him. Love him with all your heart. That would ease my guilt and I would enjoy seeing him in love and being loved," it was the most generous request.

"What makes you think that he would want me," Gina asked incredulously, "and what makes you think that I would measure up to his libido? I doubt if I'm sexy enough, from what you say."

Ava could see the depths of Gina's self-doubt and her desperate need for reassurance. She countered Gina's doubts.

"The way he looks at you. How he reacts to each of the expressions that cross your face. How his heart raced when he brushed passed you as he left the room. And yes, before you ask, I can sense all these things. You might also soon. More than that, he will bring out your sexuality and you will find the woman within you. Have nothing to fear on that front," Gina held Ava's eyes. She could see that Ava hadn't said it all.

"There's more isn't there?"

"Yes," Ava confessed, "He's not happy and I don't think he ever really has been. There's a woman that he loves and never gets over, Kayla is her name. She's a black woman, strikingly beautiful and intelligent, but a nightmare dressed as a daydream. Callum has little resistance when it comes to beautiful persuasive women and certainly none at all when it comes to Kayla."

"I already know that," Gina said. "His Kryptonite, he called her. I checked her out on Google, I'm ashamed to say. She's quite some woman!"

"Indeed, but she is a woman for a season. Callum needs a woman for life and you would be perfect, trust me," Ava said assertively. "We will hatch a cunning plan."

"And we will go back to the bathroom and fix you up again," Gina countered, as much to change the subject as anything.

"You are just angling for another girlie kiss," Ava joked as they left the room.

The look in Gina's eye however, said that there was a just hint of truth in it.

Gina and Ava were already sat at the round table deep in conversation when the men returned. The subject was the development of Gina's genetic powers and her possibilities. What the triggers were that she should look out for and how to remain in control of them. Ava had never had the benefit of such an induction to enable her to cope with her powers. As a result, she had spent years in dread of their occurrence and lived in fear of their consequences. In her formative years, Ava was dangerous and out of control. She had killed a lecherous older man that had abused her trust and raped her, taking his life with just the power of her mind. It had taken a lifetime since then for Ava to reconcile that sin. She was determined that Gina would never experience that loss of control and the emotional burden that went with it.

"Can we join you?" Emanuel asked, not wanting to impose if it was too soon.

"Yes of course, we are about done anyway," Ava beckoned them in. "Besides Gina has no idea about how tired she is going to be over the next 48 hours, while her physiology undergoes the changes that I have initiated. Better that we get on and close as early as possible, then get Gina back to her hotel for some rest."

"But I'm fine," Gina protested. She felt like a child being sent to bed early because it was school the next day.

"You are alright now Gina, but it will hit you like a train when it starts. Trust me please," Ava's tone made it clear that she was no longer just giving advice. "The DNA in your body will undertake a relatively minor mutation but you will find the result life-changing. That chemical reaction will require an immense amount of energy so you will need to eat as much protein and carbohydrates as you can and sleep like the dead."

"OK Mum, I get it," Gina said surrendering graciously. "So much for going to the Bolshoi tonight then Callum," she quipped.

Callum smiled but looked a little self-conscious at the airing of his intentions.

"Quite," Emanuel began bringing the meeting back on track, "so, quickly then, before you leave us. Who currently makes up the Council of Thirteen? The secrecy of the Illuminati organisation at its highest level is even beyond our ability to infiltrate. We need to get a full profile on them to best help you Gina. So anything that you know, will help us," Emanuel's brow furrowed above his bushy white eyebrows as he listened intendedly to Gina's reply.

She went through the names of the councillors, one by one as they were sat at the Pindar's direction. She included as much detail as she could but it was scant. The Pindar had never encouraged the sharing of personal information. Each only knew what they needed to know to achieve his vision. Three names were of particular interest to Emanuel and Callum; the Mullah, Ismail Alansari, Illya Dracul and Hydie Papandreou.

"Tell us what you know of the Mullah Gina," Callum asked and reinforced the request with an encouraging smile.

114

Gina rubbed her brow before replying. A headache was coming on strongly. She was just about to ask if anyone had some aspirins when Ava pushed a packet across the table to her. She had read Gina's mind. With that act came a silent message that only Gina picked up, "Keep going Gina, you're doing just fine," simple words of encouragement but it helped lift Gina. It was yet more proof that these people had something that could not be explained. It felt so reassuring and it gave her hope.

"The Mullah," Gina began as she popped two aspirins, "well not so much really, he only joined the Council the night of the last summer solstice. He replaced number five, the man that they executed along with his innocent niece. It was a sacrifice meant to appease Satan," Gina said with disgust, "but I digress. He is a man of the desert, an international arms dealer with some influence over the warring Arab factions."

Gina was having trouble forcing the image of the human sacrifice out of her mind and her haunting thought that it was Isabella on the altar. Her voice was faltering and she had to dig deep to continue.

"When he walked into the meeting he did so without a nerve in his body. I have never seen a man in such powerful company look so calm, and dangerous," she added under her breath. "He wasn't even afraid of the Pindar, not even slightly."

"He is afraid of no one. They call him the 'un-killable man'," Emanuel interjected. "There is none better connected than him in the Middle East, nor any more ruthless. The Pindar has chosen well."

"And what then of Illya Dracul?" Callum asked. "He seems young to be in the company of the others at the Council."

"He has sat on only two Council meetings but has had meteoric rise. From number twelve to six in just one year. It's unheard of, apparently. He seems to have amazing skills in IT and media. The Pindar has aspirations that he will control the masses through the media. Quite how Mr Dracul is going to do this was not mentioned. Suffice to say that if he fails it will cost his life," Gina's matter of fact statement was without sympathy. "They will all reap what they sow; as in all probability, will I."

"No Gina! Don't even think that," Ava's tone was reprimanding. "They are there of their own volition. You are there through Illuminati manipulation. It is not the same Gina, get that thought out of your head right now."

That forceful statement showed that Ava was as adamant and forthright as she was beautiful. Gina counted this as a positive. Despite her public scalding, she needed Ava to be as hard and demanding on her as possible. No half-measures. Sasha and Isabella would never survive this if it was anything less.

"I'm sorry Ava, you are right of course," Gina said apologetically, "it won't happen again."

"What won't happen again?" Emanuel asked, looking confused.

"Ava having to tell me off for being such a wimp" Gina said. "I won't have those negative thoughts again, I promise," Gina meant it.

"But I didn't say anything Gina. Nothing at all, did I boys?" Ava looked at them for their support.

"No," they both replied in unison, still looking confused.

Gina felt on the spot as if there had been a conspiracy. She reacted defensively, feeling that she was being made out to be a fool.

"Yes, you did Ava! You said, *don't even think that*, when I was being negative about my culpability, and..."

Ava cut her off.

"No I didn't say that Gina, I only *thought* it."

"But you..." Gina stopped in mid-sentence. An expression of total disbelief came over her face and then a smile of enlightenment, "I read your mind then?" her mouth dropped and Gina covered it with her hand.

"Yes Gina, its beginning. Your metamorphosis!" they both burst out laughing simultaneously, it was their first sign of success.

"Wow! Oh, my God. This is insane," she looked at Callum and grinned impishly. "I wish I had discovered this before we dined last night. That would have kept you on your toes Romeo!"

The girls were in stitches and Callum and Emanuel, nonplussed.

"Going back to the point then," began Callum, "the other member of the Council that interests us particularly, is Hydie Papandreou. What of her?"

"Again, I don't think that I can be of much help. Hydie Papandreou is a strikingly beautiful woman and sophisticated too. She holds her own counsel and doesn't give much away. She is scarily self-contained and exudes power and confidence," Gina shivered. The woman's presence was that foreboding. "I know that the Pindar consults her in matters of finance, politics and the military but the detail of the meetings is always in the brown envelopes that we carry home. She sits at his right hand and they talk in whispers during the meetings. He clearly values her opinion, that is more than obvious. I'm sorry but that's not much to go on, is it?"

"More than you think Gina," Emanuel made that expansive gesture of spreading his big hands on the table again. "We now know definitively who the twelve members of the Pindar's Council are, something that we have only guessed at before. That enables us to focus our efforts, not just globally but particularly on those that you have named. As dangerous as the Mullah is, he will be of no consequence to you. His interests lie solely in the Middle East. I cannot imagine how Illya Dracul could pose you any problems, unless that is in cyber-warfare directed against the Mèdici bank, but that wouldn't make sense either. The Pindar will own your bank soon enough."

"That leaves Hydie Papandreou," Gina smiled. "I can count you know."

"Quite," Emanuel conceded. He had purposefully left her until last. "She is known as *the Hydra*. Few people know her personal name. She is the Supreme Senator of the Shadow organisation and the richest and most powerful woman on Earth, by a country mile. It will irk her beyond imagination that she is subordinate to the Pindar. The situation is untenable. Eventually one will kill the other and both know that," Emanuel shook his big shaggy head at the inevitability of it and continued. "Thankfully she may not be a danger to you Gina because she has bigger fish to fry. Was there nothing else about her that you have noticed?"

Gina considered that for a moment. The Hydra hadn't really paid her any attention at all over the two years that she had been a member of the Council, but there was something. Perhaps.

"Well," Gina began, "maybe it's only woman's intuition, but at the last meeting she was different."

"In what way?" Emanuel asked.

"She smiled at me. It wasn't a smirk for sure. I think it was an invitation for us to get closer."

"She needs an ally!" Callum said and clapped his hands together in triumph. "After 5,000 years on this Earth, the Shadows are looking to the Angels for support. It beggars belief."

Callum got up and paced around the room, deep in thought. He was trying to piece it together. He placed his fingers on his temples, closed his eyes and chuckled.

"That's it. The Hydra has conceded that she cannot take the Pindar on by herself. That means that her formidable powers are not a match on the Pindar's, which begs the question, 'what the hell are his'," Callum paused, "and *what* is he?"

"Not Angel or Shadow, that's for sure," Ava added with authority.

Ava had the accolade of killing the Hydra in her alternative life and knew just what they were up against. Hydie Papandreou had an intellect comparable with the highest born of the Angels, except for the Matriarch, Maelströminha and her sister Crystalita, that is. She was a formidable enemy who had endured as leader of the Shadow organisation since before the birth of Christ. For her to even consider an alliance with her arch enemies, the Angels, was like a monumental shift of the Earth's axis. All sat at the round table but Gina, understood the enormity of her simple statement, *I think it was an invitation for us to get closer*. They all realised instinctively that it was neither the time nor the place to discuss this openly in Gina's presence, so they let it go. Emanuel moved the subject on.

"While you girls were getting to know each other, we sat with our legal friends. They had an immediate answer to your dilemma Gina, and came up with a bullet proof way of you denying the Pindar's takeover if anything happened to you or your loved ones. But it would mean trashing the Mèdici bank by returning ownership of company shares to the bank's clients and the annulment of any financial obligations that they were under. It would lead to the collapse of the Mèdici bank and, unless you have already secured your position, you would be penniless," Emanuel's expression was grave. Gina's response was immediate.

"I have not *secured my position* as you say, but what is money if you have no family? Do it. I ask only one thing."

"Go ahead," Emanuel said.

"That you ask your legal friends to find a way to transfer the Mèdici estate to the local community under some kind of trust or equity sharing," Gina's expression was imploring. "Please, they are my family too and depend on me every bit as much as Sasha and Isabella do."

"We will find a way," assured Emanuel reinforcing the statement with his benign smile.

"Thank you, Emanuel."

Gina suddenly began to feel the effects of her transition and Ava was right. She felt it coming on like a speeding train.

"I think I need to go now and concede to Ava's good advice," Gina was shaking. "Can someone help me though, only I feel so strange?"

Emanuel pressed the intercom and called reception.

"Kristina, will you come here please?"

Moments later the pretty Russian receptionist entered the room with her air hostess smile.

"Would you please take Mrs Mèdici back to her hotel personally, and stay the night with her?" Emanuel asked politely.

It was an instruction politely disguised as a request that was dutifully received by the young woman.

"Of course, Mr Goldberg; Mrs Mèdici, are you ready?"

Gina got up, almost drunkenly. It was all happening so quickly. She desperately needed to get out of the room before she let herself down. Gina gathered her things hastily.

"Bye and thanks, it's been a pleasure," Gina blurted. She wasn't even facing the others as she finished her sentence; such was her desperation to leave the room.

"You must help me," Gina said to the Russian girl as soon as she was out of the room. "I'm not sure I can do this alone."

Suddenly Gina became aware of being swept down the corridor, as if she was on wheels. The slight receptionist had an unnatural strength about her as she got Gina efficiently out of the building and into a chauffeur driven car. The last words that Gina remembered saying as she gazed into the pretty girl's bright blue eyes were, "Are you an Angel?" the Russian's reply was unequivocal.

"Yes, Mrs Mèdici, and so are you."

"So," began Callum, "what do we make of the Hydra's unprecedented friendliness towards an Angel?"

He gave a wry smile that dimpled his face endearingly. Ava's heart fluttered at the memory of that smile being above her face as they had made love in another life. She bit her bottom lip at the thought of it.

"Desperate times call for desperate measures," he continued, "and these must be desperate times for the Hydra."

"Desperate for all of us Callum," Ava's clear blue eyes darkened to a soft brown. It was a classic harbinger of Ava showing her dark-side. "If the Hydra fears the Pindar, then he must be a formidable adversary and not from this Earth. So what in Hell is he."

"Well that might depend on how much credence you give to the 27th book of the New Testament of the Holy Bible," Emanuel replied. He was truly going to put the cat amongst the pigeons. "The Book of Revelation chapter 12:9 says:

"The great dragon was hurled down – that ancient serpent called the Devil, or Satan, who leads the whole world astray. He was hurled to the Earth and his angels with him".

It's common knowledge that the Pindar is referred to as Lucifer's representative on Earth. But what if he *is* Lucifer? It makes all kinds of sense, particularly given that the Hydra appears out of her depth for the first time in millennia," again, Emanuel spread those giant hands across the table.

Callum and Ava simply looked at each other. There was a mental exchange needing no words between them, they could handle this through their thoughts alone. At last they agreed that the Pindar could indeed be Lucifer or Satan. He turned to engage Emanuel.

"That is the scariest thought that we have ever considered," Callum admitted. "Worse, neither Ava nor I can fault it. If what you say is true, and we think it is, then this could lead to the fulfilment of then the End Time prophecy as described in the scriptures. Armageddon," Callum looked grey. Such was the magnitude of this possibility.

"It is simply fact," Ava said resignedly. "Now that you have opened my eyes to the possibility, I know it. You *feel* it too don't you Emanuel?" he nodded. "If you ask Kayla when you see her Callum, she will sense it too," this is bigger than us and bigger than the Shadows. *That* is why the Hydra needs us."

"I will need to consult with Maelströminha, as our leader on this," Emanuel conceded with a sigh. "I suspect that she has already seen this possibility in the mirrors of time though, but not yet shared it with us. She will be able to guide us towards the most favourable outcome, as she always does."

It reminded Ava of how it was the Matriarch Maelströminha, who had guided her to find her own salvation. She was a petite, dark haired woman with the face of a doll and the gentleness of a lamb. Despite those physical attributes, she was more powerful than anyone on Earth; powerful on a biblical scale. Suddenly Ava shuddered and the colour of her eyes turned dark brown as the premonition came upon her. She saw death and destruction all around her.

There was a menacing man in a dark habit. His head was cowled so that Ava couldn't see his face, just the glint of something metallic like a golden mask. The aura around him was the blackest that she had ever seen, and his intent was evil. She was stood in a circle facing him with three other women. They were also wearing cloaks with hoods so she couldn't tell who the other women were. Their attitude was one of attack, or defence. Ava wasn't sure. What was certain though, was that they were about to fight to the death. One of the women turned to her, dropping her hood as she did so. Ava recognised her immediately, it was Maelströminha. Somehow she was now holding a baby in one arm and the hand of an infant in the other. She spoke gravely to her in a voice that was lyrical and kind to the ear.

"Take my children Ava and look after them for me. Grow them up with love and talk to them often of me."

The vision faded and Ava's eyes turned back to blue but now they were filled with tears.

What's the matter?" Callum asked, alarmed by the sudden change in her. "You look like you've just seen a ghost."

"Perhaps I have," Ava's voice was unnaturally weak, just a whisper. "It doesn't end well Callum. It doesn't end well at all."

Chapter 14

Three days later.

Gina was walking through a field of poppies towards the two young people at the far end of the meadow. She called out to them and waved, "Sasha! Isabella!" She felt the joy of seeing them and quickened her pace. They were beckoning her on, encouraging her to hurry. Gina glanced down at the blanket of bright red flowers as her flowing skirts skimmed atop of them. She looked up again, but they were so much further away now.

"Stop, wait for me!" Gina shouted desperately, the rising panic sounding in her voice.

She was running now, but it was no longer through a field of poppies, it was through a cemetery. There were hundreds of identical white, polished marble crosses neatly laid out in rows. Gina was weaving her way through them at speed, but she never closed the gap between them. She was tiring. Her strides were shortening with each laboured effort. She was breathless and beaten. Gina gazed into the distance but they were gone. Now exhausted, she fell at the base of one of the crosses. Gina placed her hands on the arms of the cross to haul herself up and came face to face with the writing that was lovingly carved into it. Her expression turned to horror as she read it. The words hit her like a blow to the stomach, *"Isabella Mèdici."*

Kristina was in the bathroom when she heard Gina's frantic screams.

"No! Please God no! Forgive me Isabella, I wasn't there for you. I failed you, God help me," Gina howled at the physical pain of it

Kristina ran to Gina, who was sitting up in bed, not yet fully awake. Her hands were reaching out into nowhere and she was crying in helpless anguish.

"Gina, it's alright. Everything's alright, it's just a bad dream."

Gina's arms found Kristina's shoulders and she pulled her to her. In Gina's dream-crazed mind, the blonde Russian was her daughter.

"Don't you ever scare me like that again Issie, I thought I'd lost you," Gina was stroking Kristina's silky blonde hair.

"It's alright Mrs Mèdici, Isabella is safe. Everybody is safe," Kristina said soothingly.

She didn't try to pull away. Instead, she let Gina waken naturally from the horrors of her dream.

Gina slowly slipped free from the chains of her nightmare and realised that the woman in her arms wasn't her daughter. She still needed that comfort and reassurance though, and held the embrace a little longer. Eventually she released her.

"Thank you, Kristina, I'm glad you were here," they exchanged smiles without any awkwardness. "Have you been here all the time?" Gina asked drowsily.

"Yes," she replied taking Gina's hand. "You have been on quite some journey and your dreams have been troubled. You must be starving. Can I order you some breakfast?"

"God, yes please. I'm ravenous. Is it morning yet?"

"Yes, it's the morning of the third day Mrs Mèdici. You have woken and fed a few times but you were not really aware of it," the Russian smiled and loosed Gina's hand. "I'll fix breakfast for the both of us."

She stood and left Gina open-mouthed in disbelief.

"Three days? I've been asleep for three days?" Gina was shaking her head. Her mind began to clear and she suddenly looked concerned. "What about my kids?" she shouted after her. "They must be worried sick. I have never missed calling them before bedtime, never," Gina searched her bedside table for her phone.

"Ava has been talking to them and has made your excuses. They think that you are on an intensive training course, which is not too far from the truth, as it happens," Kristina grinned back reassuringly at her.

Gina relaxed, "I'll call them after breakfast then. At least that will give me time to think of a credible explanation."

Kristina was already on the phone to room service, ordering food enough for a small army. Gina was somewhere else entirely. She was backtracking through her dreams. The subjects of them bore no relationship to her own experiences; it was as if someone else had dreamt them, "Ava's dreams perhaps?" she wondered without any real reason.

One thing was clear to Gina though. She felt different. No longer the long-suffering Mrs Mèdici, a woman without options, living in a dangerous world of power-crazed tyrants. She felt empowered and resilient. A mother up for the fight!

"Let them dare touch a hair on their heads!" Gina challenged under her breath. "I swear to God, I will kill them all."

Gina waited impatiently in the plush and sumptuously furnished lounge of the Metropol hotel. Her bags were packed in readiness. Callum and Ava were collecting Gina to take her out to an old farmhouse in the country. She would be spending the next five months there alone with Ava, learning her skills. Kristina had left a couple of hours earlier, which had given Gina a chance to reflect alone on the changes that had already taken place in her.

The most apparent change was that her senses had become heightened, almost to the point of pain. Something that Gina was hoping she would become hardened to. Her first realisation of it, was when Kristina had been in the bathroom. Gina was wishing that the noise of the hairdryer would stop. It's one of those sounds that drive you mad at the best of times, but this morning it seemed unbearable to her.

"Close the door please," Gina had called out cupping her ears.

Kristina popped her head around the door and spoke through a mouthful of toothpaste.

"What was that Gina?" she said, then put the electric toothbrush back in her mouth.

"Nothing, it's not important. I'll tell you later," Kristina stepped back into the bathroom.

"Oh, my God," thought Gina, she was knocked over. It wasn't the hairdryer at all, just the gentle hum of Kristina's electric toothbrush. Her hearing had become that keen.

Then there were her eyes. For twenty years, Gina had been putting her contact lenses in every morning and taken them out at night. When Gina had woken up she could see clearly and cursed that she must have fallen asleep with her lenses in, knowing that her eyes would now be puffy and red. She raised a lid with one finger and tried to drag the offending lens to the corner of her eye.

"Ouch!" she cried out as her finger touched the sensitive tissue of her pupil, not the lens.

Gina tried the other eye with the same painful result, then went to the bathroom mirror to sort it out. She could clearly see her own reflection. It was crystal, so the lenses had to be in, but they weren't. Nor were her eyes puffy or red. In fact, the whites of Gina's eyes had never been whiter. Everything was perfectly clear; too clear to be normal. She looked around the bathroom to test her eyes. There were bottles of shampoo and conditioner stood on the shower tray at the far end of the bathroom. She read the labels easily. Working out which was which without her lenses in had always been a frustration to her.

"Why are the important words like 'shampoo' and 'conditioner' always so small that you can't read them and the irrelevant brand names so big that they scream at you?"

This was a question that Gina had asked herself a thousand times as she had squinted at the bottles through rivers of water running down her face. Now she could read the smallest print at a distance. It was beyond amazing.

Gina had another revelation. She was sat in the Metropol lounge, flicking through a copy of the *Vogue* magazine in English. It wasn't until she had gone through several pages that Gina realised that she was reading it at a page a glance in a foreign language. She dropped the magazine as if it had become red hot and put her hands to her face.

"No," she whispered to herself in disbelief.

Just then, she sensed that Callum was arriving and looked out of the window to see him pulling up in a white Bentley Continental. There were two others in the car. It was clearly Ava in the back, with her shock of auburn hair. The elegant woman sat beside Callum in the front was unfamiliar to her though. She was dark and slim with long, silky black hair. Her head was slanted towards Callum and Gina saw her hand briefly caress his cheek. A sign that she knew him intimately, Gina deduced. The girl was laughing enthusiastically at whatever he must have said. She tossed her hair back then drew it over her shoulder the furthest away from Callum, still looking at him and smiling. That simple feminine act exposed her long neck to him.

"That was no accident," Gina thought wryly.

Just at that moment, the dark-skinned beauty turned and faced Gina locking eyes on her. They were fifty metres apart and Gina was only one of many faces in the busy lounge but still the woman had picked her out. There was not a trace of that beautiful smile left on her face. Gina knew that it was a statement, "He's mine. Hands off!" she also knew that it had to be Kayla Lovell.

Gina was engineering her bags out of the hotel entrance when she smelt his fragrance. It was that same fragrance he had worn when they first dined at the hotel together, the same fragrance that had filled the lift when they had gone up to their separate rooms and that same sensuous smell of clean man. That was the other thing, her sense of smell. It had become so acute since her renaissance. She turned her head and looked up. Callum was still ten metres away but he filled her senses. She went weak at the knees. He did something to her that no other man had ever come close to. Gina was flustered.

"Let me," he said. His face had that usual easy smile.

Gina had to look away. It was all that she had waited for but the woman in the car had changed everything. His woman. Gina tried to be offhand but it was a thin disguise.

"It's OK. Really, I can manage," she flashed a smile and set off pulling her bags towards the Bentley.

Callum didn't argue, he just picked her bags up so that they wouldn't wheel.

"There are *pink* jobs and *blue* jobs Gina. This one happens to be a blue job."

Gina conceded and crossed to the car. To her surprise the dark-haired girl was standing next to the car with the back door open and a welcoming smile on her face.

"Gina! I have been looking forward to meeting you so much. My name's Kayla," her smile appeared to be genuine as she leant forward to exchange kisses. "Callum has told me all about you and I'm intrigued. I just can't wait to get to know you," again her smile seemed genuine.

"Pleased to meet you too Kayla. Callum has spoken highly of you and its nice now to meet the legend," Gina was engaging and her statement was honest, well apart from the underlying matter of rivalry.

Kayla was indeed a stunning beauty, Gina had to concede. She felt like a white whale stood next to a stick insect by comparison. She hoped that *voluptuous* did it for Callum. All the self confidence that had come from years of photo shoots and public acclaim, simply melted away like snow in springtime. Gina could tell that Kayla was pleased with her ampleness.

"Round one to you," Gina thought and sensed that Kayla concurred.

Ava greeted Gina like a long-lost friend, quickly distracting her from her concerns. They chatted animatedly as they headed out in a westerly direction from Moscow's city centre, crossing the second ring road then passing to the south side of Moscow's famous zoo. Ava suddenly became distant. The sight of it always gave her a frisson and a heavy heart. Her last fond memory of her childhood was at that zoo with her mother, on her fifth birthday; the same day that her mother was murdered in front of her eyes by her father.

They crossed the third ring road and then the Moskva river, leaving suburbia behind. The traffic thinned. Callum put his foot down as they joined the M-9 and the Bentley's powerful V-8 engine responded with an appealing roar. Moments later they were cruising effortlessly at 100 mph on the open road. Despite their speed, conversation was easy in the comfort and quiet of the Bentley's plush interior.

"Callum tells me that you have two grown up kids Gina, you must miss them so much," Kayla asked, leaning over the back of her seat.

"I do, very much," Gina confirmed," But as you pointed out, they are grown up now and this experience will probably do us all good. Of course, I call them every day and then there is Asmina, who is like a grandmother to them," Kayla nodded and smiled.

"Round two to you also," Gina thought without allowing any negativity to show on her face.

In that one sentence, Kayla had managed to underline a couple of facts. *Two kids* equals *baggage* and *grown up* equals *old Mum*. Gina already felt out of the competition and wondered whether she was being unfair on Kayla. Perhaps she was just making polite conversation; certainly her tone and body language seemed at ease. It all felt bizarre. She was sat in a car with Callum and his two lovers. Although his romance with Ava was in another life that he had remained oblivious to, it wasn't from Ava's point of view. She still harboured a deep love for him that was clear. Ava had already confessed it. She wondered what Ava might be thinking right then. However, there was no doubting the currency of Kayla's relationship with Callum as she turned to him, squeezed has muscular arm and planted a kiss possessively on his cheek.

The white Bentley struck out ever eastwards leaving the bustle of Moscow city far behind them. The grey concrete urban belt had long since given way to green countryside, where Russia's underlying poverty became increasingly apparent. Russia's status as a superpower had come at a price, one that the working class had paid.

They had been driving for nearly two hours. The conversation had been light and frivolous, mostly around the latest Moscow fashions and celebrity. Callum had contributed the least to the conversation, but then he was their driver and the only man amongst them. Even though he was of lesser blood and therefore the least empowered of them, it wasn't too difficult for Callum to sense the oestrogen in the car and the rivalry between the women. His mouth turned upwards at the corners into a wry smile and Kayla caught it immediately. It triggered a change in Kayla's cordiality.

"So Gina, you have been pretty much unaware of the powers of your birth right, which probably means that they are unlikely to be significant," it was Kayla's first open taunt.

"Round three to you Kayla," Gina thought, "a statement of your superiority."

Before Gina could offer her reply, Ava rounded squarely on Kayla in defence of her.

"I've joined minds with Gina and I know what a formidable woman lies beneath. She might just knock you off your perch one day Kayla, so watch out for who you mock."

Gina watched as the transformation came over Ava. It was clearly triggered by anger. She sensed a force being emitted by her that chilled her to the bone. Gina's jaw dropped. Somehow dark clouds were forming in the blueness of Ava's eyes until they were the darkest brown, almost black and smouldered like burning coals.

"Girls!" Callum's voice was commanding and they instantly calmed to it.

"No offence meant," Kayla demurred after several seconds.

"None taken," Gina replied.

The destructive energy in the car was almost palpable. Gina was just glad that it hadn't turned into the cat fight of the century, because it would have if Callum hadn't nipped it in the bud.

"As a matter of fact," Gina continued, glad to keep up the diversion, "those *powers* that you talked of seem to be manifesting themselves all the time now."

"Tell me," Ava urged, already over the issue.

Gina was amazed that Ava's eyes were once again a serene blue and couldn't fathom it.

"It probably seems nothing to you," Gina began, "but this morning Kristina was in the bathroom and the sound of her hairdryer was deafening me so I asked her to close the bathroom door. It turned out that she was only brushing her teeth with an electric toothbrush. My hearing has become so heightened. Then, I thought that I had fallen asleep with my contact lenses in, because when I woke, I could see so clearly. Incredibly clearly actually, but I hadn't. My eyes are just amazing now. The strangest thing though is that I sensed your arrival this morning and I get glimpses into your minds. It's all pretty garbled and I can't focus on anything yet but I definitely get something."

Ava looked triumphantly at Kayla with an *I told you so* look as she hugged Gina.

"That is all part of your renaissance and your changing DNA Gina and it will continue to change over the next few months. You are still an embryo Gina, none of us can predict where this will end, but I sense that you will be a force to contend with, if we can make you focus your emotions."

"Those words again. *An embryo*," Gina thought; Asmina's words.

Callum slowed the Bentley and pulled off the motorway, heading south towards Gorodishche. They drove through narrow lanes, that twisted like snakes down to a wind-chopped lake off to their right, and lush green meadows to their left. Trees hung to the grassy banks and leant out over the water, offering shade and protection to the multitude of water life that had congregated there. Two swans were startled by the burbling of the Bentley's 4-

litre engine and took clumsily to the air, inciting the other waterfowl to do the same. After fifteen minutes, they arrived at a quaint old farmhouse set amongst several small outbuildings and a huge barn. The place looked tired, like it had lacked the loving attention of a family for many years, but the structures were sound and weatherproof. All Angel safe houses were subject to regular maintenance and restocking.

The copious trunk of the Bentley was full. Other than day to day consumables, it had everything in it that Gina and Ava would need for the next five months. It took the four of them the best part of an hour to unload and settle them in.

Gina checked the fridge and cupboards. Someone had clearly been there earlier in the day, as there was fresh food and drinks enough to get them started and more besides. Amongst the groceries, was a fresh crusty loaf, butter, a selection of cheeses and a bottle of red wine. Gina augmented this with cherry tomatoes and pickles, setting them a small feast to refresh them before Callum and Kayla headed back for Moscow.

The minor standoff between Kayla and Ava had been forgotten. Conversation was now focussed around Ava's development and preparation. Preparation for what though, wasn't entirely clear to Gina. She kept that to herself. Anyway she wasn't too sure that she wanted to know right now.

Callum took them on a tour of the farm and it really was a *safe* house. It turned out that the quaint little farmhouse and agricultural outbuildings were nothing of the kind. The barn was a fully equipped gymnasium and assault course. The other nondescript outbuildings were research laboratories. These included experimental units for paranormal activities and a computerised operations room, or 'the Hub' as it was known as. It was equipped with a vast arsenal of every type of weapon that you could possibly think of. The farm could be turned into the Alamo in hours. Gina learned to her amazement that inside the Hub's agricultural facade, were one metre thick reinforced concrete walls and ceiling. The grounds around the farmhouse were covered by CCTV and riddled with electronic mines that could be detonated remotely from the operations room. Tunnels led away from the Hub and, short of an air strike, the Hub was virtually impregnable.

"Daunting. What the hell are they expecting?" Gina thought as they returned to the farmhouse, but it made her feel safe.

Despite their re-established cordiality, Kayla guarded Callum like a Doberman. She intercepted any personal advances with strategic diversions. Nothing that could be taken offensively, but both Gina and Ava felt her possessiveness. When lunch was over and Callum mentioned returning to Moscow, Kayla took up the opportunity to leave with both hands.

"If we go now we'll miss rush hour Callum," Kayla said enthusiastically, "then we'll still have time for you to take me to that little Bistro downtown. You know the one that you have been teasing me with for a romantic night together?" Kayla looked voracious and Callum, a little awkward.

"Round four," thought Gina. "You win again, he's yours."

Ava read Gina's mind and gave her a supportive smile for what it was worth, but the underlying secret message, sent mind to mind, was, "Fight the bitch!"

Gina had tired of Kayla's little games and was looking forward to seeing the back of her, even at the cost of losing Callum's company. She had even been offhand with Callum, not that it was really his fault, but he was guilty by association. Callum for his part, had regretted that he had brought Kayla along, but there is nobody more persuasive than Kayla Lovell when she wants something. Besides, a woman with Kayla's skill set seldom leaves anything to chance or freedom of choice.

"Let's get going and put your foot down Callum," Kayla said as she buckled her seat belt." We can just beat the traffic, if you thrill me. Don't keep a girl waiting when she's in the mood," she winked suggestively at Callum.

It was said for the benefit of her audience. Kayla closed the car door and rolled the window down.

"Have fun you two; we'll be thinking of you over a candlelit dinner," Kayla's smile was more of a smirk as Callum pulled away.

Gina felt a sudden static in the air. Her hair became alive with electricity and it floated bizarrely around her face. A frisson ran down her spine as she realised that something was wrong. Gina looked at Ava for reassurance and was both astonished and frightened at what she saw. Ava was stood motionless with her head stooped in the direction of the departing Bentley. Her arms were partly raised at her sides and her fists clenched so hard, that her knuckles had turned white. The bright afternoon sun was playing on Ava's long auburn hair that was stood up with the charge of static, such that it looked like her head was on fire. But it was the blackness of Ava's eyes that had frightened Gina. A look of hate. In fact, at that moment, there was nothing beautiful about Ava at all.

Gina was brought back to her senses by the explosion. Five hundred yards up the road, Callum's Bentley was yawing across the road with smoke coming from the back, kerbside tyre. A slim arm appeared out of the passenger window. Her hand was pointing up in the air, with all but the middle finger clenched. Gina looked back at Ava who was once again a blue eyed serene beauty.

"You?" Gina asked incredulously.

"Me," Ava confirmed. "Now let's see if the bitch can still get to that romantic dinner date in time."

They laughed conspiratorially, linked arms and trooped back to the farmhouse.

Chapter 15

Four months later. LuminaGames research and development facility. Berlin, Germany. November 7th 2017.

As Illya Dracul walked into the LuminaGames facility, he had every reason to look pleased with himself. It was official; the Dream App had gone viral. Illya had delivered the project six weeks early. Initial sales had outstripped that of any other game in history. It breezed by the sales of Grand Theft Auto IV, Halo 3 and even GTA V. The Dream App was the talk of all teenagers and hardened gamesters across the planet. With its costly upgrades and illicit sales of legal highs to enhance the dream experience, it was already a bigger money maker than Coca-Cola and as addictive as cocaine. The icing on the cake was that every dream had a subliminal, pro-Illuminati message in it. When it was time for the political movement to begin, the masses would follow.

"Has Doctor Schwartz arrived yet?" Illya asked the fastidiously dressed, plump receptionist.

"Yes Mr Dracul. He's waiting for you in your office. I'll bring coffee right away."

Illya Dracul nodded and walked on through into the atrium. He took the lift to the fifth floor, business sector. As the floor-counter ticked its way through naught to five, Illya looked at his reflection in the mirror. He was now one of the most successful IT project managers in Europe and possibly the world. He afforded himself a smile that showed his perfect white teeth. The image looking back at him was that of a confident young man with extraordinary looks. Dark eyes shone from his pale face, incongruous with his blonde cropped hair. He was a veritable Adonis but unfortunately, he knew it. He had a smugness about him that was almost tangible and a reputation for letting woman down, that made him infamous. The man was a scoundrel.

The lift stopped. Illya straightened his tie, grinned at himself in the mirror and strutted down the corridor to his office. The ancient Doctor Walter Schwartz was sat hunched in a chair to the side of Illya's desk. He was flicking through the pages of his note book until he found what he was looking for.

"Ah Dracul, nice of you to call in," it was a rebuke.

"I worked late yesterday," Dracul countered. Shadows were essentially nocturnal by nature and more active and productive at night.

"Have you seen the latest sales figures?" the doctor asked with pride. "It's already set to be the game of the century and it's still in its infancy."

"Yes Walter, I get updates by the hour. The Dream App has become self-publicising. Media interest is doing the marketing for us. It's the most talked about subject on Twitter, Facebook and chat-shows across the globe. Celebrities are falling over themselves to be interviewed on the subject because of its notoriety and the publicity rub off. Of course the use of legal highs does the rest, to assure it gets the headlines."

"Indeed," the doctor agreed. "Seemingly our only issue is the sudden intervention of the World Health Organisation, who classifies the game as 'Electronic Stalking & Mind Control', or ESMC as they say. They have called it the biggest risk to humanity, since the invention of the atomic bomb," he grinned showing all seven of his discoloured teeth.

"How perceptive of them," Illya smirked. "But it will all come to nothing. The FBI has been using ESMC for decades now and it suits their methods. There is no legislation to control it. Currently they are breaking no laws, so it's hard to imagine them putting any in their way," lllya was dismissive of the matter. "Anyway, everybody can be bought, or eliminated," he added, off-handedly.

"True," the old man conceded, "this is just noise in the grand scheme of things, not a barrier to success. That apart, I have some good news for you Illya. We are ready to move into the next phase of the programme, targeted personalised upgrades, and sales of hard narcotics to further enhance the addictiveness of the dream experience."

It was the news that Illya had been waiting for. They already had the registration details of tens of millions of clients. These developments meant that any individual on their client list could be targeted and receive a personalised upgrade and a conduit to buy hallucinatory drugs. That upgrade could include coded instructions to carry out a specific task, much like Bjorn had been programmed to carry out his assault on Heidi. It would soon be possible to place gamers next to high profile figures, such as the President of the United States, and then assassinate them. Even to incite a rebellion of the masses be a government coup.

"That's impressive progress Walter and highly commendable. The Pindar will be pleased beyond measure."

"Indeed, I hope so Illya. Because this option comes with a price tag," the doctor was pushing the boundaries of their agreement.

"The Pindar is not a man to try and take advantage of in business," Illya warned. "Three billion U.S. Dollars was the price you agreed and the contract that you signed."

"Call it inflation then. One billion U.S. Dollars is a small price to pay for this latest innovation," the doctor was not going to concede.

"Tell the Pindar that for this paltry sum, he gets total control of the gaming population within months. Tell him also that the first targeted upgrades can go out this week. After our targeted clients have played the game, they will have their individual missions implanted in their minds, along with an activation code. They could then lie dormant for months, even years. All you will need to do is call them and read out the code, or email it to them. From that moment onwards, they will be like guided missiles and all for just one billion U.S. Dollars."

"You are playing a dangerous game Walter and you place yourself at risk," Illya advised.

"Am I Mr Dracul? Am I really?" the old doctor looked quietly confident. "I don't think so, not at all. There is no one who can maintain this software or upgrade it other than me. I have designed in *insurance* to that end. The Pindar has the key to the young minds of the world and with that, immeasurable power. I am not a greedy man Illya, only asking for what my work is worth. He will concede to my request. As soon as the money is in my Swiss bank account, you will have the functionality to create targeted, personalised upgrades for your clients.

Illya Dracul pondered on it for a moment. There was no choice, he conceded, and four billion U.S. Dollars was a pittance for what Walter Schwartz had given them. Illya had the autonomy to make the financial arrangements on behalf of the Pindar, so that wasn't going to be an issue either. The Council of Thirteen were due to meet for the winter solstice in several weeks' time. Illya desperately wanted to present *his* success story at that meeting. One billion U.S. Dollars was consequential in the grand scheme of things.

"Very well Walter, I will make that transaction today with two conditions. The first is that the new functionality is in the Dream App software by the end of this week. Understood?" Walter Schwartz nodded. "The second condition is that this will be the last *inflationary* increase in the contract price on pain of death. Now is that understood?"

"Perfectly," the doctor agreed. "Anyway, four billion U.S. Dollars will be enough to see me through a long and expensive retirement," Walter Schwartz chuckled, stood and snapped his notebook shut.

"I will bid you good day then," he clicked his heels together in the old Nazi way, bowed his head briefly and was gone.

Illya considered the enormity of Doctor Schwartz's success. It was the last piece in the jigsaw and it entirely fulfilled the Pindar's requirements of enabling an army of automatons. In terms of cost the price tag was insignificant. The game alone would gross that, probably in its first year the way things were going. In terms of the power that it gave the Pindar, it was infinite. Illya started his computer, selected his finance software and transferred the money to Doctor Walter Schwartz's account.

The fastidiously dressed receptionist arrived with the coffee along with her apologies.

"I'm sorry Mr Dracul, only I didn't realise your meeting with Doctor Schwartz was going to be so brief," she set the tray down.

"Brief but fruitful," he gave her something close to a smile and she left.

Illya had only taken his first sip of coffee, when he heard the email alert come in. He went to his mailbox and opened it. The email was from the doctor. Clearly it had been prepared in advance of their meeting.

"Illya,

Thank you for expediting the payment, which concludes our financial arrangements.

I had already consulted with the technical team and uploaded the personalised dream software module in anticipation of the successful outcome of our business arrangements. I have just this minute activated it. All you need to do now, is follow the link at the end of this email to see an overview of its functionality. You will find that all the dream scenarios are there as we agreed, assassination, suicide, espionage, genocide and the like. After selecting your target, you need to contact our technical department with their personal details, email address etc. and an outline of their mission. Where assassinations are intended, supporting photographs of the victims would assist. Again, this is all detailed in the guidance. Our technicians will then research the project further and select the appropriate dream scenario, create the personal links and then voilà, you have your programmed automaton. He will be unaware and 'sleeping' until you activate him with the game code (Satan666).

I trust you will be doing field trials soon. Please be assured of my closest attention should you encounter any difficulties.

Regards,

Walter."

"Crafty old dog," Illya thought.

He realised that the personalised dream module was already good to go and probably had been for a while. The sharp old man was just waiting for the right time to press home his advantage and make another billion.

Illya allowed himself to indulge in imagining the Pindar's satisfaction at hearing of his project's undeniable success. The Dream App, along with the control of the press and video industry through Pindar acquisitions were the corner stones of delivering the second step in creating the New World Order, control of the people. It was just up to the Mullah now, to augment the success of the Dream App with his part by creating religious control in the Middle East, through radicalisation of the people. He had already heard of the Mullah's unprecedented successes. It was now almost inevitable. Together, he and the Mullah would have delivered the Pindar's plan to the letter.

Illya's mobile phone rang, taking him out of his reverie. Uncannily it was the Pindar himself.

"Dracul?"

"Yes Pindar. What can I do for you?" the sound of the Pindar's voice was instantly recognisable. It was somehow unearthly and always sent a shiver of foreboding down Illya's spine.

"After the Council's meeting of the winter solstice, the Mèdici woman will be of no further use to me. By then her strategic procurements will all be in place to enable the first step of our strategy, globalisation through conglomerates. I trust you will then find her of use in the further research and development of your project Dracul."

It was not a suggestion of redeployment; it was an instruction to execute Gina Mèdici.

"Of course, Pindar. Leave it with me."

The call went dead. Illya placed his phone on the desk and smiled. It was a heartless smile, devoid of any humanity. That brief conversation alone had just guaranteed him promotion from the sixth to the fifth seat on the Council of Thirteen, well once Gina Mèdici had been dealt with that was. He shook the mouse of his PC, still grinning with satisfaction. The screen sprang into life. He expertly navigated through the software until he found the sales records for the Dream App. First he sorted by country then by surname, then by first name.

"Yes!" he said triumphantly. *"Sasha Mèdici."*

Chapter 16

The morning lectures were over. Sasha was drinking coffee in the cafeteria with his longest standing girlfriend ever, Lucia. She was a tall slim, brunette. Pretty, with a bubbly nature and easy to talk to. The fact that Lucia was popular with Sasha's friends, made her odds on to last the distance. It was probably the first time that Sasha had met a girl who was popular on equal terms to him. She was a challenge and he adored her. They were deep in conversation when Sasha's friends, Giovanni and Carlo joined them.

"Hey Sasha, how's it going man?" Giovanni was a little lost in his rock image and came out with all the clichés. "You guys fancy joining us for a couples' dream night? It can be at mine if you like. I've got the latest movies for the Dream App. Got the house to myself and the keys to the old man's Bentley," he jangled the keys proudly in front of them. "It'll seat the six of us," he gave them his best winning smile.

"What do you think Lucia, are you up for it? It's Friday night, no studies tomorrow, "Sasha asked. He clearly was, but Lucia didn't look too keen. There was an issue.

"That depends. If it's drug-free, then I'll go along," she looked searchingly into Sasha's face. "Please Sasha," she implored.

Sasha held his hands up in the air, palms forward in capitulation.

"OK, I promise no drugs. They are only legal highs anyway Lucia, nothing heavy, just Pink Panthers and Magic Dragon."

"Just because you can get them on the internet doesn't make them legal Sasha. Ask your sister, she studies law," Lucia challenged. "But you won't, because I'm right and you know it. Isabella would freak out if she knew you were doing that stuff and your mother, would absolutely flip," Lucia was constantly fighting this battle and had been ever since Sasha got hooked on the Dream App.

"OK, I already said no drugs, didn't I?" Jesus Christ woman, give me a fucking break," Sasha snapped at Lucia.

It used to be uncharacteristic of Sasha to lose his temper, let alone swear. Recently, since becoming addicted to the Dream App, it had become the norm. She held her tongue, but only because they were in the company of his friends. Lucia had seen a big change in Sasha's character since his obsession. That was evident even before the recreational drugs had started, which had made it ten times worse. Also, he had lied about the *legal highs* bit. Lucia knew that he was taking cocaine too and that it was *the* major dream stimulant. Sasha had sudden mood swings now and signs of paranoia, both of which were entirely new found. She despaired of him.

He had been so charming, gentle and attentive before. Those traits were what had attracted her to him in the first place, but now they seldom showed. Lucia had noticed similar changes in Giovanni and Carlos, although not to such a degree. It seemed a bit of a *boy thing* too she had noted. Girls also enjoyed the game but they didn't generally get emotionally involved with it. Lucia was deeply in love with Sasha, but the Dream App was changing everything. This issue was something that they needed to sort in their relationship and soon.

"Cool. I'll swing by and pick you up at about seven then," Giovanni waved the keys to the Bentley again, as if they were a badge of honour. "Chow then."

As soon as his friends were out of range Sasha turned aggressively on Lucia.

"You really showed me up Lucia," he looked furious, "made me look a right dick in front of my mates. Don't you ever dare do that again. If you've got problems, then talk about it when we're alone. Got it?"

"If *I've* got problems?" Lucia was outraged. "Jesus Christ Sasha, I'm not the one with the drug habit, or hooked on a game that soaks up my brain and all my money. Look at yourself Sasha. Your studies are going down the pan and you don't have any interests anymore, other than that bloody game."

Lucia was beyond furious but Sasha simply ignored her tirade. She stood and pulled her coat open in frustration revealing her shapely figure and generous breasts.

"You don't even pay attention to this anymore Sasha, it's making you dickless for fuck's sake," Lucia pushed her chair away and stomped off in a rage.

Sasha watched her march out of the cafeteria without trying to win her back. Then, in guilt, he picked up his phone and searched for her number. Sasha was just about to call her but changed his mind at the last moment. Instead, he scrolled to the 'App Store', selected 'Dream App' then 'Upgrade'. He selected 'Buy' and authorised another €100 for the latest upgrade and associated movies.

Lucia cried all the way to her car. She was losing Sasha to the game and drugs. The pain of watching it happen, was just too much for her to bear. Their relationship, until the Dream App had come on the scene, had been perfect and as passionate as she could ever have imagined. Now it was anything but that and she felt helpless. Every time she had tried to help him, he just blocked her out. Lucia opened the door to her baby blue Fiat 500, got in and rolled the roof back. Her eyes were too full of tears to drive. Instead she just sat there and thumped the steering wheel in anger and frustration.

"You stupid bastard Sasha! Open your fucking eyes and see what's happening to you. For God's sake open your fucking eyes," she cried out in anguish.

Not only was she losing him, she was failing him too. He needed help. Lucia loved him more than life but she realised now that she couldn't do it alone. She needed help every bit as much as he did. Lucia rummaged in her bag for her phone and dialled the number.

"Isabella?"

"Speaking."

"Thank God you picked up. I need to talk to you Issie, it's about Sasha," Isabella sensed her distress.

"Oh, my God. Is he alright? You're scaring me."

"Sorry yes, he's safe. It's not that, but I'm so worried about him Issie. Can you meet me, only it's hard to do this over the phone? Don't call him though; it'll make him angry with me for talking to you behind his back."

"Where are you Lucia? I will come now."

"There's a bar, Luigi's. It's just down from the university at the traffic lights. You can park behind. I'll be there. Thanks, Issie," she cut the call.

Isabella walked from the heat and bustle of the city street into the cool serenity of Luigi's bar. It took several seconds for her eyes to adjust from the bright sunlight before she picked out Lucia, waving from a booth at the back of the bar. A waiter greeted her to take her to a table.

"It's alright; I'm with my friend over there. Would you bring me a Coca-Cola please?" Isabella said with an easy smile and continued to the booth.

Lucia greeted her a little too urgently, Isabella thought, as they hugged and exchanged kisses. It was a clear sign that she was deeply troubled and it sent a shiver of dread through her. They sat facing each other.

"Thank you for coming," Lucia said earnestly. "I don't know how to begin," she was desperately trying not to cry.

"By just relaxing would be a good start," Isabella said placing her hand supportively over Lucia's.

"Yes, sorry. I'm a mess. It's just I don't know what to do," despite having planned exactly how to tell Isabella, she had gone to pieces.

"Is there something wrong with Sasha, is he sick?" asked Isabella

"In a way. He's changed so much in these last week's Issie, since he got obsessed with the Dream App."

"Obsessed?" Isabella questioned. "You can hardly call Saturday nights obsessive."

"It's not just 'Saturday nights' Issie, it's been *every* night for at least the last six weeks."

"That's not possible; he's up in his room Mondays to Fridays studying for his exams. That only leaves Saturday and he turns in early on Sunday for a fresh start at university on the Monday," Isabella was adamant. "I should know Lucia, I live with him."

146

"Do you go to his room and check Issie?"

"No, I don't have to. He says so."

Isabella was starting to feel uneasy. It was true. She was only taking Sasha's word for it and it wasn't usual for him to tend to his studies to the exclusion of all else either.

"Issie, he hasn't produced any work at Uni for weeks, nor done a moment of studying. He's going to crash out this semester and he knows it, but he can't turn it around. When he goes to his room he goes straight on the App. Sasha is hooked on the adrenaline rush from the action movies and wakes in the morning with dream exhaustion and severe headaches. When he gets to Uni he's bad tempered, surly and sleeps through the lectures," Lucia wrung her hands in despair. "When I try to help him, he just shouts me down and when I say that I will tell you and your mother, he gets angry and violent."

Lucia untucked her blouse and rolled it up to her bra. Her ribs were covered in bruises. Isabella looked at the injuries in sickening disbelief and then back up to Lucia's face. Silent tears of shame were rolling down her face.

"Oh Lucia," Isabella said leaving her chair to come and sit beside her. She put her arms around her. "Thank you for telling me that must have taken a lot of courage" she kissed Lucia's cheek.

It was several minutes before Lucia could talk again. When she did, her words shocked Isabella like nothing in her life's experience ever had.

"Did you know that he's doing drugs Issie? Cocaine mostly but some LSD," Isabella went pale with shock.

The air seemed to rush out of the room. Isabella couldn't breathe and thought she was going to feint or be sick. Just at that moment the waiter arrived with her drink.

"Are you all right Signorina?" he asked with real concern.

"It's all right, she will be fine," Lucia smiled and dropped a note on his tray. "Keep the change," then dismissed him with a polite wave of her hand.

Isabella was distraught. In the last few minutes her world had been turned upside down. There was no man less likely to take drugs or hurt a woman than her brother, but somehow, he must have changed. Isabella was confused and lost in the magnitude of it. She wondered if she should tell their mother or just confront him and deal with it herself? She felt sick with despair. It was Lucia's turn to be positive for them both now.

"Between us we can do this Issie. We both love him so much and with that we can do anything, right? Anything Issie, do you understand that?" despite all Lucia's new-found strength, she was faltering. "Can't we?"

There was Angel blood in Isabella's veins and that didn't mean quit. She quickly found her natural grit.

"Yes, Lucia we can and we *will* do this. Together we'll bring him back from the brink. Love conquers all. I think I read that somewhere," Isabella admitted, "and I'm going to find out just who LuminaGames are and what their *real* game is!"

Isabella had that sixth sense just like her mother had. She knew that something was desperately wrong about the Dream App and LuminaGames. Just like she knew that Lucia was not telling her everything.

"What is it Lucia? What else is it that's breaking your heart?" Lucia looked desolated.

"We haven't made love for several weeks," she confessed with tears welling in her eyes again. "Dream sex is much better than me, apparently."

When Sasha got home, Isabella and Lucia were in the kitchen waiting for him. He sensed the atmosphere and was immediately on his guard. The look of guilt on Lucia's face told him all that he needed to know.

"You traitorous bitch," he said coldly. Lucia just looked at the floor and shook with fear.

"She's here because she loves you and because she cares Sasha. God only knows why she still does but she does. It's now for you to prove that you deserve that love, not to treat her like shit," Isabella's voice was strong and assertive. "Or beat her," she added accusingly.

"You sound like mother," Sasha mocked. "What lies has Lucia told you?"

"Everything Sasha. Every sickening thing. How could you be so weak? You had so much pride, so much promise. What happened to you?"

Sasha could see by the look on his sister's face that she had come in peace. There was no anger, only disappointment and sorrow. Sasha's reaction was precariously in the balance for several seconds. If it had fallen the other way, he would have gone into a black and violent rage. Thankfully it didn't. He saw the confrontation for what it was; an olive branch, a peaceful offer of their love, help and trust.

"What happened Sasha?" Isabella repeated firmly.

Sasha pulled up a chair and sat at the kitchen table. He felt humbled and put his head in his hands, too ashamed to look at her in the eyes. Lucia crossed the kitchen and stood behind him, wrapping him lovingly in her arms. Sasha took his hands from his face and covered hers with his, but he didn't look up. He couldn't look up.

"Thank you," he whispered and squeezed her hand. "I don't know how I got so hooked on it Issie. You know I like games and how much I was looking forward to this one. It's different though, it just consumes me to the exclusion of all else. It's better than life, much better. And my life was already good. You have no idea."

149

Sasha looked up at his sister for the first time. He needed her understanding.

"It's not just me Issie; all my friends are hooked too. Some more than others perhaps but all hooked. It's the biggest thing on the planet right now. The games are developing so fast and the dreams are out of this world, you just don't want to wake up."

"What about the drugs Sasha, how did that come about? You have always been so anti," that was Isabella's biggest concern and what puzzled her the most.

"Through the media. Everywhere you look there are reports on how certain drugs improve the experience, not just by a bit I don't mean, like massively. I was just curious I guess. It was supposed to be a one off but it was just too amazing. The rest is history I guess."

His confession was deeply cathartic and Sasha felt like the world had come off his shoulders, just through the telling of it.

"I know that it's changed me and I don't like who I've become. It's just that I can't stop it," Sasha looked desperate. Isabella sat next to him and leant her head against his.

"Oh Sasha, maybe you can't stop it but perhaps together *we* can. You have to want to though and you have to let us in. Will you?"

Sasha nodded his head. He was choked and couldn't trust himself to speak.

"Thank God Mum's been spending so much time away Sasha. There's no reason she should ever know about this if you can clean yourself up and get back on track. You must Sasha, even if it's only for her. She doesn't deserve this. Now Dad's gone, she needs you to be the man for all of us. Do you see that Sasha?" he nodded and smiled thinly back at her.

They were in a silent group hug for some minutes before Isabella spoke again. In that time, she wondered how many other families might have been broken by the Dream App. Millions possibly, she concluded.

"I want you to delete the Dream App tonight Sasha and clean yourself up. You can't be drug dependent this quickly, so if you stop now you shouldn't have a lasting problem in that respect," Sasha nodded but still didn't trust his voice to reply.

"I will come and stay with you every night until you are through this Sasha if that will help you. My parents will understand," Lucia said stroking his blond hair.

"I would like that Lucia, but not tonight. I think I need to be alone tonight if you don't mind. I don't deserve you right now," his voice was shaky and his smile showed just how fond he was of her. "I'm sorry for hurting you baby. It's like I lost my identity, like I was looking at life through a plate glass window. Nothing seemed real or important, other than the Dream App."

They talked about it for another hour, by which time all three felt positive about Sasha's salvation. When Sasha got back to the sanctuary of his room he felt like he had gone through the full twelve rounds of a heavyweight boxing match. He was just about to delete the Dream App when a message came in. It was from LuminaGames.

"Congratulations Sasha! You have been selected for a personalised dream experience. Just click on the link below for your own dream of a lifetime."

"Oh well," he thought, "one for the road. What harm can there be in that? Definitely no drugs though," he added with new-found resolve.

Sasha took the tobacco tin out from under the bed. It was his stash. Inside there was more than €400 of cocaine, in neatly folded tin foil packets. He took them to the bathroom and ran the

151

tap. Opened each and swilled the contents down the sink. He felt strangely liberated.

This was going to be his last dream experience, period. He was sure of it. Sasha pledged an oath there and then that he would not fail his family again and was thankful that his mother had not found out. He knew that Isabella and Lucia would keep his secret, well if he kept his promise, that is. Sasha clicked on the link, selected his own private experience and then lay back on his bed to watch his own personalised dream.

"Just this last time," he said to himself. "What harm can that do?"

Chapter 17

Gina and Ava had quickly settled into a routine at the farmhouse. They were up at five thirty every morning and straight into their running kit. Depending on the weather, they would run down to the lake and do a circuit. That would take an hour, and Ava set a hard pace. It was pure torture for Gina, being the heavier of the two girls by far and the least fit. Ava was like a gazelle to her by comparison and seemed to breeze along effortlessly. If the weather was bad, they would do the hour on the treadmill with a punishing gradient set on the machine. After that, it was a gruelling stomach regime followed by weights for the next hour, then shower and change for breakfast. After that ordeal, breakfasts had never tasted so good to Gina!

The saving grace for her was that occasionally Ava would break regime and fence with her. Despite Ava's highly tuned Angel skills, she was no match for Gina with the sword. Gina beat her comfortably on each and every occasion. Consequently, their sparring turned into coaching sessions instead, and Ava was coming on leaps and bounds. Fortunately, Gina's own developing Angel strength and skills, kept Ava at bay.

They would do the same punishing physical routine in the early evening before dinner, leaving the rest of the day free for lessons. Excess fat was just stripping off Gina but, bizarrely, her weight was increasing. This was something that she couldn't quite fathom until Ava had explained. Apparently, the restructuring of her DNA causes denser bones and muscles, stronger ligaments and a significant increase in physical strength. Gina would ultimately have the equivalent power of a male athlete. Thankfully though, her genes would always dictate that she would remain curvy. Gina was proud of that, and increasingly so as she developed. She loved to catch a glance at herself sideways in the mirror and see her flat tummy and how trim she had become. Gina had a six-pack for the first time ever, and often wondered if Callum would approve, or indeed if he would ever get the chance to. She imagined him running his fingers over the contours of her belly and it gave her a frisson every time.

After breakfast, Ava would set her challenging mental arithmetic that demanded a seemingly impossible degree of memory. It was to teach Gina to focus on detail whilst holding an overall picture of the problem in her head. The workings if you like. It was like having a mental notebook where you could record the various stages of the calculations, then see the whole picture. This led on to Gina developing a photographic memory. After the first week, Gina was able to memorise several pages of the telephone directory, and Ava would test her on it. All Gina had to do to answer the questions was to conjure up the picture of the relevant page and read from it as if it was there on the table in front of her. Ava made it all seem like fun though which helped ease the pain of it.

After the second week though, the novelty was wearing off and Gina was getting tired and testy. She needed a break and to see her children.

"I fail to see how any of this is going to help me to challenge the Pindar," Gina said in an uncharacteristic show of negativity and petulance, "unless of course I challenge him to a game of Trivial Pursuit or something equally as banal."

"You will when you are fully enlightened Gina, but for now it's all about fitness and focus. So just shut the fuck up and do what I tell you and we will get along just fine."

153

Ava's hackles were raised. Her eyes darkened by the second as the malevolence inside her took control. She was clearly tired too and losing it.

"I never had any control over my powers until I learned that," Ava said aggressively. "As a consequence, it cost the lives of my mother, my aunt and my best friend. Is that what you want for your children and loved ones?"

It was callous of her, but the memory of her own failure cut Ava like a knife. She spat out her final sentence.

"That'll do for today. You can go now. I don't actually give a fuck," she said with absolute finality.

Ava stormed out of the training room and marched back to the farmhouse. She was furious. It wasn't really so much with Gina but with herself. She had let her dark side come to the surface again over nothing. Perhaps she needed a break too, she wondered.

Ava went straight to the bathroom and stripped off, turned the shower on to cold and stepped in. She could see the reflection of her eyes in the polished stainless steel wall plate that housed the mixer tap. They were black as the night, just as she suspected they would be. She had let the beast out again.

"I'm a freak," she said simply, disappointed in herself, and began to cry.

When Ava stormed out of the training room Gina felt dreadful. What she had said was surly and ungrateful of her. She was tired and didn't mean it. She desperately wanted to run after Ava and apologise but somehow, a menacing aura seemed to have engulfed her and there was that same static in the air that had preceded Callum's exploding tyre. Gina was petrified and decided that now wasn't the moment to talk to her.

"I'll leave it ten minutes," she decided.

She followed Ava slowly back to the farmhouse to use up time. When she got there, she could hear the shower running in the bathroom. Gina decided to bite the bullet and get it over with. When she entered the bathroom, Ava was stood naked in the shower cubicle with her back to her. She had her hands over the mixer tap and her forehead leaning on them. Her shoulders were shaking as if she was sobbing and she seemed unaware of Gina's presence. Her auburn hair, that was normally a mass of unruly curls, was wet and scraped back. It stuck to her back in a sleek red swathe down to her trim waist.

Ava seemed so fragile and vulnerable stood there naked and crying. She looked like a lost little girl, all alone in the world and nothing like the powerful woman that had just raged out of the room minutes before, nor the one that had faced off Kayla. She was a paradox. Gina couldn't help but stare in admiration at Ava's lithe athletic body. She was perfect. Long strong legs, tight bottom and toned muscles with a waist to die for. No wonder Callum had fallen for her in that other life. Ava was such an attractive and sensual woman.

Then Gina did something that was so completely spontaneous and out of character, but somehow it just seemed so right. She took the hem of her white fitted tee shirt and pulled it off over her head. The action dragged her ample breasts upwards until they escaped the tightness of the cotton before falling back with a single bounce. Her plum coloured nipples were large and already hardened by the confusion of thoughts that were running through her head. Gina kicked off her sandals, loosened the belt of her jeans and wriggled out of them. She put her thumbs in the waistband of her black panties, drew them down in a single action and stepped out of them and into the shower.

Ava hadn't moved, but somehow Gina knew that she was expecting her. Gina reached around and placed her hands on top of Ava's, encompassing her in her arms. The coldness of the water took Gina's breath away but not as much as the act of Ava leaning her svelte body into hers. As Gina turned the mixer tap towards hot, she was conscious of her nipples touching Ava's back and the

155

almost imperceptible circling action of Ava's pert bottom as she worked it against Gina's mound. She hadn't expected that and gasped at the sensation. It was clear that Ava wanted her just as much as she wanted Ava. Her senses were on overload and her desire to be intimate with Ava, overpowering.

Gina swept Ava's wet hair over her shoulder and breathlessly began placing little butterfly kisses on her neck, nibbling off the water drops as she did so. She felt Ava shudder and groan almost inaudibly and the pressure of her gyrations increase. Gina cupped her small breasts and was both shocked and excited at the smoothness of them and the impossible hardness of her little nipples. It excited her like she couldn't believe. Gina had never touched another woman's breasts before, let alone fondled them. Now, at last she understood men's obsession with them. She reached for the soap dispenser and took a generous handful and began soaping Ava's breasts. The sensation of it sent a message straight to her groin and she gasped out loud at the magnitude of it. Sensing the moment, Ava again increased the pressure of her gyrations against Gina and a smile crept across her face as she heard Gina's breath catch as the pressure against her pelvis mounted.

Gina was quickly losing all inhibition. She ran her soapy hands down Ava's hard abdomen feeling the delicious ripple of her muscles. She stopped just above mound and worked them back up to her breasts again paying increasing amounts of attention to Ava's nipples each time that she repeated the caress.

The agony of Gina not quite touching her sex was driving Ava crazy. It wasn't that Gina didn't want to, far from it, but she couldn't muster enough courage to make that personal and tender invasion. Ava solved their dilemma. On the next soapy pass of Gina's hand, Ava took it firmly and guided it urgently over her mound and down to the cleft between her legs, spreading her thighs enough to allow the deeply personal act. By now, Ava's want was so intense that she cried out as Gina's fingers found their goal. She could have come at that very moment and had to fight off her desire for release. Those colourful lights in her head that were always the harbinger of Ava's orgasm were massing and growing in intensity. She knew that she only had moments but she needed Gina to come with her.

Ava reached behind and slipped her hand down between them and over Gina's pubis. She found the spot immediately and was thrilled by Gina's clear and apparent readiness for her touch. Her experienced fingers worked quickly and expertly bringing Gina to the brink. She was quickly lost in Ava's skilled touch. This was nothing like a man's uneducated fumbling, Gina thought randomly.

"Oh, my God, oh my God!" Gina cried out as her orgasm came crashing over her.

She was still trying to coordinate her own touch on Ava but the intensity of her climax denied all else. From somewhere on the other side of paradise, she heard Ava scream out and was faintly aware that she was convulsing in her arms and crying. The glorious feelings seemed to last forever coming in wave after wave.

They stayed like that with Gina pressed against Ava's back for some time. Neither spoke, it was too special a moment for words. Gina became aware that she was still cupping Ava's breasts and wondered at the glorious feel of it. Ava rotated in her arms, slippy with soap, until she was facing Gina. Their faces were only inches apart. Gina noticed that there was no longer even a trace of brown left in Ava's brilliant blue eyes.

"Hello lover," Ava whispered.

She cupped Gina's face in her hands. The look of love and devotion on Ava's face was clear and apparent. She was searching Gina's mind for her innermost thoughts and fears. At last she spoke again and her tone was solemn.

"When the time comes for you to fight Gina, I will be there at your side. I swear it. We will either be united in victory or we will walk into the next world together, hand in hand, if that is what the gods decide."

157

Gina knew that Ava meant it sincerely but, she had no way of knowing that she had already glimpsed the future in a premonition. Gina had no idea that her quest against the Pindar was to end so badly.

Ava kissed her full on the lips as if she would never see her again. That kiss lasted for several minutes as one's mouth and tongue explored the others. It was a tender and loving kiss, no longer tainted by the need for sexual gratification. They had already had that in abundance.

"I'm sleepy," Ava said at last breaking the kiss. "Will you lay with me a while?"

Gina nodded; it was what she wanted too. She was still lost in the aftermath of her experience and words weren't coming easily. It was outright the best and most meaningful sexual experience of her life but it confused her. She wondered if she had been gay all these years and not even known it.

They towelled each other off, which was another first experience for Gina, then Ava led her by the hand to her bedroom. They lay there with their faces almost touching and chatted openly about their lives, their hopes and their fears.

"How does it work with Yuri and Katarina? Do they know about each other?" Gina asked.

"Katarina knows of Yuri," she replied, "but then I'm married to him for God's sake. But he knows nothing of my affair with Katarina. Why should he?" Ava posed. "They are separate parts of my life and they don't affect him or my love for him. Why should I give him any issues and spoil his peace of mind?"

It was a valid point Gina conceded.

"Anyway, Katarina makes me complete and a better person and that is better for all of us."

Gina had another question but wasn't sure how to ask it, so she took the long route.

"Today was my best experience ever. Too good perhaps, but it has put so many questions in my head."

"Like what?" Ava asked, but of course she already knew.

"That perhaps I'm gay and have been for years, but never admitted it to myself," Gina blushed and Ava pecked her on the lips for the compliment.

"Don't worry Gina, you are not gay and what if you were? Would that matter? I think not," Ava looked knowingly at her. "I see the changes that happen to you the moment Callum walks into the room. I can tell that it squeezes your ovaries and that your thoughts are way past obscene," Ava had a devilish look in her eye.

"God, is it that obvious?" Gina's blush intensified threefold.

"Only to me Gina, but he's just a man who is as lost in you as you are in him. He's too blind to even notice. No Gina, you are not gay. You have just discovered other aspects of yourself that you were not apparent to you before. The difference is allowing yourself to accept possibility is all."

It was the reassurance that Gina needed to ask the most important part of her question.

"Will making love with Callum be anywhere near as wonderful as it was with you?" Gina felt embarrassed for asking the question and held her breath hoping for the right answer.

"Have no doubt on that score Ava. He comes with *benefits* don't forget and a stamina to go with it that you *won't* believe. Trust me on that."

Ava looked distant for a long moment while she reflected on her own love for Callum. She knew that she could trust her innermost feelings with Gina, without jealousy getting in the way.

"Callum made me love him by making love to me so perfectly. Since then, I can't get him out of my mind, my soul or my heart.

We made perfect love," she smiled at Gina fondly. "He will make perfect love to you too Gina, and then you will be as lost in him as I am."

Gina didn't know whether it was Ava's wicked smile or the talk of sex and Callum, but she felt flushed with excitement.

"Will you make love to me again Ava?" she asked timidly. The want in Gina's big blue eyes was clear and apparent.

"I thought you were never going to ask sweetheart," Ava said with a grin.

She kissed Gina passionately until she was left breathless. Ava smiled at her with that wicked look in her eyes, then slipped down under the covers.

"Oh God," Gina whispered, as she realised what was about to happen to her.

The weeks flew by after that. Gina had accepted that she needed the highest degree of concentration to fulfil her potential, and that nothing short of 100% effort was going to be good enough. She embraced the facts that focus and self-belief was everything. After that, her psychic powers grew by the day. They used the laboratories extensively, testing and measuring Gina's powers to the limits.

At the end of the second month Ava judged that Gina's mental development was advanced enough to introduce her to the concept of Noetic Science.

"It's time you understood the concepts behind the powers that the Angels have, the powers that exist in you," Ava began. "Have you read anything about Noetic Science, Gina? It's a relatively new science, causing a major upset amongst the professors."

"Well a little, but from what I've read, it's perceived as a bit of a myth and mostly given credence to by those with a spiritual or supernatural bent, who *want* it to be true," Gina had heard that it was as much based on human hope rather than anything tangible. Of course, Ava *read* her negativity.

"It's not quackery Gina; it's just that this world isn't quite ready to embrace the truth. That is, that the universe is a mental and spiritual creation. They are still holding onto the old Newtonian 'material universe theory', Ava began. "For some time now, physicists have been exploring the relationship between human consciousness and the structure of matter. Quantum physicists have discovered that matter, at its smallest observable level, is energy. Humans of high intellect can exert their influence on this subatomic matter through their consciousness and influence its behaviour, even re-structure it. Mind over matter if you like," Gina still looked dubious.

"It's what you have already achieved in the laboratories Gina, though to a modest degree. When we cooled a vessel of water to freezing point, I asked you to concentrate on the cooling and think peaceful and happy thoughts of your children. Remind me of what shape the ice crystals that formed were please," Ava asked.

"Well, they were small and regular, but you already know that," Gina replied puzzled at where this was going.

"And in the second experiment, when I asked you to think of the Pindar and the sacrificed girl, what shape were they then?" Ava's brow was cocked quizzically and there was a hint of a smile on her face.

"Again, you know Ava. Large irregular crystals with cracks and fissures, reflecting my mood," they had already noted the difference and the reason.

"Yes Gina, that was the reason but it wasn't the *cause*. The cause was that your consciousness affected the physical system at a subatomic level; psychokinesis. At its highest level, this subatomic restructuring can manifest itself as shapeshifting. I will be happy right now if you can just boil a kettle with your thoughts right now," it was a throwaway comment and Ava grinned.

"Don't you see Gina?" that is why so much of our work has been to increase your intellect and ability to focus." Ava searched Gina's face for understanding.

"When you were sat for five hours in front of the Random Number Generator, concentrating on numerical sequences, you brought an element of uniformity to the numbers generated. The chances of the RNG coming up with those occasional ordered results was less than one in fifty million," Ava's smile was no longer a hint, she was beaming. "Your consciousness had a profound effect on the physical system, again at subatomic level. As your DNA further evolves and your intellect increases, your ability to control the machine's outcome will increase exponentially. Eventually you will be able to make it generate any number sequences that you wish, mind over matter; noetics."

Ava explained away the results of all the other experiments that Gina had undertaken. Like how she could describe the contents of a locked room by imagining herself inside it.

"Astral projection Gina," Ava had explained. "You simply placed your consciousness there."

Another example was evidenced in Gina's remarkable ability to selfheal extraordinarily quickly. Ava had explained that the human body had most all it needed to regenerate. All that was required was to focus and have the belief that we can change our physiology; faith.

"Reality is only as the observer perceives it to be," Ava added finally. "It basically means that our limitations are only those imposed on us by our own intellect and imagination. The catalyst is faith Gina. You must believe in yourself, totally and without question. The day that you take that leap of faith is the day that you no longer need me," Ava had said that with an element of sadness and regret.

Gina immediately recognised Ava's vulnerability and embraced her.

"Ava, I will always need you and I need you now, desperately. Don't ever leave me," it was Gina now who was searching Ava's face for her understanding.

The long and urgent kiss that followed confirmed that they would always be friends and lovers, no matter how this all ended.

As the months passed Gina was tasked to focus more and achieve more. Her mental skills were fast approaching Ava's but her psychokinetic abilities were still weak by comparison and of great concern to them both. These would be essential if she was ever to take on the Pindar and have even the remotest chance of survival. Whatever Ava tried, Gina could not bring those powers inside her to the fore. Ava remembered, that in her early years, she could only summon those powers herself in rage. She decided to take a big chance, and prayed that it wouldn't backfire. She needed to tap into Gina's rage.

Ava had spent the morning challenging Gina's endurance to the limit. It started with their morning run. Ava had set an impossible pace. Gina had risen to the challenge and kept up as best she could, feeling proud of her efforts and expecting high praise from Ava at the end of it.

"That's pitiful Gina. Don't you have any pride in yourself at all?" Ava's disdain was palpable and Gina shocked.

"But," Gina began. Ava cut her off curtly.

"But nothing," Ava spat. "We'll do it again but for Christ sake try and keep up this time."

Ava set off at a pace and a bewildered Gina dug deep and matched her stride for stride, even though it was killing her. At the end of the second hour Gina was blown and cramps had set in. She was in crisis but the finish line was only minutes away. Everything inside Gina wanted to quit but she couldn't let herself. Gina's feet were blistered and her spirit broken, but she was almost there. She would not give up. To her horror, Ava sprinted past the finish line and called out over her shoulder as Gina stopped, gasping for breath.

"Come on Gina, give me one more circuit to prove that you even give a shit about saving your bloody kids," it broke Ava's heart to be so cruel but it did the trick.

"Fuck you!" she heard Gina scream out and then the sound of her heavy limbs hitting the ground as Gina forced herself on.

She ran for the next half hour, hardly seeing where she was going through her tears of anger and pain. Her feet were squelching in her trainers, as they filled with the blood and fluid from her blisters. She was only able to continue the impossible pace by focussing on her rage. Gina forced herself on, not wanting Ava to see her beaten. She had too much pride for that.

To her horror, Ava took the pace up a notch. Gina willed her legs to respond but it was too much for her. They gave under her and Gina sprawled headlong, face down in the gravel, coming to a crushing stop against the base of a tree. She lay there concussed and hurting.

"Why is Ava doing this? She was angry and confused.

As Gina recovered her senses the pain shot through her head like a lightning bolt, fuelling her anger. She opened her eyes to see Ava stood there, leering at her hatefully and defiantly.

"Get the fuck up bitch and run, you pathetic waste of space," Ava kicked Gina in the side again, knocking what little precious wind she had left, out of her. "Run for your bloody kids damn you," she yelled, hefting another kick into Gina's ribs.

Then it happened. Gina's eyes were murderous; it was like someone had flicked a switch inside Gina's mind. Her anger became all consuming. She sprang to her feet like a leopard and struck out at Ava in a black rage. Although her hands never actually touched her, the force field that left her body, did. Like a speeding truck.

Ava's slim body folded against the impact of some invisible entity and cartwheeled like a rag doll through the trees into the lake beyond. The wildlife seemed to sense the supernatural happening and scattered in frenzied panic. Gina stood there for a long moment stunned, looking at her hands in disbelief.

"Ava! Oh, my God Ava. What have I done?"

Gina clawed her way through the dense trees and plunged into the lake. Ava was unconscious, face down in the water. Her clothes and skin were shredded from the sharp branches and she wasn't breathing. Gina dragged her to the muddy bank and shook her, not knowing what to do.

"Breathe Ava, for God's sake breathe!"

There was a sudden groan as the air rushed into Ava's empty chest and her eyes opened, staring into space. The impact of the force field had driven the air out of her and caused her diaphragm to spasm leaving her winded. At last her eyes focussed and she smiled up at Gina, who was crying with relief.

"You did it Gina you did it," Ava said weakly.

"Yes but I'm sorry I'm truly sorry. How can you ever forgive me?" then added shyly. "Let alone love me."

"You are missing my point Gina. You have just proven that your powers are strong and there at your command," a shadow of pain flashed across Ava's face. "I taunted you to attack me. I wanted your rage and you gave it to me. You are not responsible for what happened Gina, and I am so proud of you."

"But I could have killed you. It was never worth that risk Ava. Never and don't ever do that again," a tear of regret ran down her face. "Can you stand?" Gina asked, pretty sure that she couldn't.

"Not without your help, I don't think," Ava said getting up on her haunches. "Just for the record, it was worth it to me."

Gina helped her up and Ava winced. Even the effort of standing was too much. She looked like a beautiful broken doll, Gina thought and swept her effortlessly up into her arms. The walk back was going to take the best part of an hour. Gina had to close her mind to the pain of her mutilated feet and trudge on. Ava hardly said a word on the way back. Her rib cage was severely bruised and complained at the effort of breathing let alone talking. Instead they communicated in their thoughts, each distracting the other from their own suffering.

Back at the farmhouse, they bathed each other and tended their wounds. It was a spiritual experience, to the point of being almost sensual and served to further cement the bond of love and friendship that had grown between them.

Ava felt horrified and disgusted with herself when she saw the state of Gina's feet. Even with her newly found Angel physiology, it would take a week for the skin on them to regenerate. Ava took hold of Gina's mind to distract her from the pain, while she rubbed in amniotic cream. It was a rare Angel medication that had been given to her by the Angel Matriarch herself. The cream was enriched with stem cells and would speed Gina's recovery.

Gina reciprocated in tending to Ava's wounds, starting with all the angry tears in her skin from the trees.

"No, don't use the amniotic cream," Ava said a little too hastily, "it's very precious and not of this Earth."

"But you used it on me. What makes you less precious?" nothing irked Gina more than dual standards.

"Because I am more mature in evolution and I can endure. My capacity for rejuvenation for this is measured in hours, not days or weeks like yours," Gina could tell that Ava wasn't just being brave. "That cream really does come from the stars and can't be replaced, is all."

Gina conceded and swapped the cream for an antiseptic one. When all of Ava's numerous cuts and grazes were tended to, she rolled up Ava's nightdress to cream the bruises on her stomach where the force field had struck her the most. Her jaw dropped. Now the bruising had come out, the magnitude of the impact was sickeningly apparent.

"Jesus Christ! What have I done to you?" Gina was horrified.

"All that I wanted you to Gina, but not near enough to make you safe. You must try harder baby," Ava mocked gently.

"I will never forgive myself," Gina muttered as she rubbed ointment into the black and yellow bruising to her belly.

Gina worked the cream gently into Ava's skin and stopped suddenly, as if she had become paralysed. But then she was. With shock!

"You're pregnant!" with her new heightened senses, Gina had felt the baby's heartbeat. A thousand panicked thoughts ran through her head. "What have I done? Oh Jesus. We need a doctor. Callum, call Callum, he'll know what to do..." Gina was falling into despair.

She felt the strong grip of Ava's hands around her wrists, the force of her mind and the calmness of her words.

"Baby's fine Gina. She's part Angel, just like us. He doesn't give in. We don't give in. Do you understand that?"

Gina nodded but she looked like she could just burst into tears. It was a twofold thing though; partly fear but a huge amount of joy besides.

"I will tell you all about it when you come to me tonight," Ava said, holding the suspense, "and you can share my joy."

Chapter 18

Thessaloniki, Greece. November 2017. One month before the winter solstice.

Hydie Papandreou had just arrived back to the sanctuary of her home in Thessaloniki after four months of relentless campaigning. She had used every bit of her political, economic and military influence to lay down the foundations for the Pindar's third step to secure world domination; the corruption of the politicians and leaders. The Hydra had met behind closed doors with the ruling elite of every significant country in the world. She had also met with their opposition, who were usually the most corruptible in their hunger for power and wealth. After securing the hearts and minds of those, sometimes with the use of a little blackmail and intimidation, the Hydra had held counsel with generals, terrorists, religious leaders and criminal organisations across the world. Indeed, anyone that held power and influence over the population.

She had been open and honest about the inevitability of the Third World War and explicit about how things would look post-war. You were either in with the Illuminati or you were out. She made it clear that *out* meant *removed*; a euphemism for dead. All those at the meetings, had either met the Hydra before, or knew of her legendary might. None were naive enough to think that she had come in peace or as a friend. They knew that they were being given hard advice. Not to take it, would be a risk to their lives and to those of their loved ones. The fact alone that someone as powerful and dangerous as the Hydra referred to the Illuminati with such respect, was reason for their deepest concern.

Hydie was on her balcony where she always relaxed in times of duress. She called her aide, Vassos. He was never more than a heartbeat away. He wouldn't have dared. Vassos came out of the shadows.

"Yes Kyrie," he bowed in supplication.

"Bring me a margarita and my notebook, would you," it wasn't a question despite the formation of the sentence.

Vassos left obediently and returned several minutes later with both.

"Will that be all Kyrie?" he asked dutifully.

"For now, but I'm thirsty tonight. Don't leave my glass empty. That's all," she dismissed him.

The Hydra sipped at her drink and relished the moment. Her palate exulting in the explosion of the contrasting tastes. The initial saltiness of the rim of the glass, then the sweetness of the Cointreau and the sourness of the lime juice, followed by the kick of the tequila. She always found the shock to her taste buds, helped to stimulate her thoughts. She sat on the cushioned wicker chair, flicking through her notebook, reading the conclusions that she had drawn from her numerous clandestine meetings. She found it ironic that the superpowers, who expounded peace and justice to their people, were the most fervent advocates for having 'a piece of the pie', post-World War Three.

Conversely, it was the lesser powers that were not initially up for selling their souls for the promise of power. That was up until their realisation that they really had no choice in the matter and would ultimately lose their countries and lives if they resisted.

It came as an absolute surprise to her though, that religious rulers entrusted their Gods alone to determine their future. But then all things are not always as they seem, she surmised. Anyway, this fell into the Mullah's territory. They would all be united in holy war and unwittingly become followers of Satan and the Pindar, under the Mahdi. Muhammad Akhbar.

In short, Hydie Papandreou could now put a dossier together for the Pindar, defining who his allies would be in case of war, what it would cost to buy their allegiance and who his enemies were likely to be.

This political rally had been simplicity itself for the Hydra and was not the issue that really concerned her. The issue was, that once the Pindar had the covert allegiance of the new United Nations, he would have no need for her. She considered the last meeting of the Council of Thirteen at length, the objectives and the attendees. She put herself in the Pindar's place.

"What would I do?" she posed the question. "Who would I keep and who would I kill?" there was no emotion, no fear, only objectivity.

Of the twelve councillors, eight were *grey*, functional heads only. None of them posed a threat or were of any real strategic importance.

"Drones in a beehive," Hydie concluded, "necessary to support the queen. No more, no less," these were safe and secure posts.

That left herself, the Mullah, Illya Dracul and Gina Mèdici. She considered each in turn.

The Mullah was pivotal to the Pindar's plans and would remain so even past the Third World War, as would be Muhammad Akhbar, the Mahdi. He would be the next to join the Council of Thirteen, she was sure of it.

"But replacing who?" Hydie wondered.

So, the Mullah was safe she concluded and moved on to Illya Dracul. She knew his deceased uncle Alexis well. He was the oldest and most astute Shadow in living memory, attaining some 8,000 years, before losing his life to a nothing young Angel in a duel to the death by sword. There had never been a swordsman in history that had even come close to Alexis' skills until then, yet he lost his life to a boy of only sixteen. Perhaps at last he was ageing, she surmised. The Hydra came back to the point. This young man was of his uncle's blood and therefore not to be underestimated. He also had a uniquely empirical understanding of the youth and their response to the media. This was a valuable skill for the Pindar, and an enduring one.

"No, I would not kill you Illya and neither would the Pindar," he was also safe she concluded.

Apart from herself, that left Gina Mèdici. Hydie could see that Gina was in as precarious a position as herself. Both were about to time expire. Once Gina had finalised the Pindar's procurements and created his conglomerate, she would be of no further value to him. He would simply take her bank and all that went with it. Worse still, the Hydra had sensed that she was the only person of Angel blood in the Council of Thirteen, and there under duress. That also presented a security risk. It didn't bode well for Gina Mèdici.

"She will be eliminated," she concluded, "as will I."

It was a conundrum. Damned if you do and damned if you don't. Both would be executed if they didn't fulfil the Pindar's requirements but then both will be after they had. The Hydra needed leverage, she needed an ally. Gina Mèdici. If they joined ranks, they were denying the Pindar two out of his three steps to creating the New World Order; financial control and control of the politicians and leaders. It would be transient though. He would find alternatives, but it would buy them some bargaining time; time to think, maybe six months, maybe less. It was a scant chance for both but a chance none the less.

Hydie cast her mind back to that last meeting of the solstice. She had watched Gina throughout, particularly through the rape and sacrifice of the young woman. It wasn't just *watch* though. The Hydra had the power to read minds and to control thoughts. She had read Gina's initial sense of panic, when she thought the girl on the altar was her daughter. Then her elation when she realised that she wasn't. The Hydra had even read her deep guilt for rejoicing in someone else's misery, and the words of every prayer that Gina had offered to her god in gratitude and penitence.

Those were simple observational skills for the Hydra. What she saw above all else, was that Gina was a woman of fortitude. Looking deep into her mind she could see a strength and intelligence that was hardly tapped into. It was her Angel ancestry that had become dormant in times of security and comfort.

"But inside you are a tigress Gina Mèdici. God help anyone who crosses you when you have found the powers of your birth right. God help them indeed."

Hydie Papandreou had the deepest respect for this woman, who in any other circumstances would have been her mortal enemy. Of course, they were poles apart in doctrine, but they shared one big attribute; courage. Right up to the moment that Gina had realised the girl on the altar wasn't her daughter, she would have fought to the death under impossible odds to save her. Hydie laughed out loud.

"I hope they find out who and what you really are one day Gina Mèdici, and I hope I'm there to see it!" she mused.

The thought of Gina fighting for her children's lives reminded Hydie of her own loss and it saddened her. Anaxis was his name, her only child. She had lost him over a thousand years ago, to the hands of Angels. It was still a bitter pill to swallow, and it tempered her pro-Angel thoughts of allegiance. But now there was a new and much greater threat. The Pindar!

Chapter 19

Milan, Italy. November 2017. One month before the winter solstice.

It had been over four months, since Gina had left for Moscow. Asmina had kept Castello di Mèdici running smoothly and ensured that Sasha's and Isabella's daily routines were as normal as possible. Only Asmina knew why Gina was away. Everybody else thought she was on an intensive IT course, in preparation for a whole new state of the art software system that was to replace the existing outdated one at the bank. Asmina looked forward to Gina's brief visits, as did they all, but they were too short and too infrequent.

"Ain't no sunshine when you gone, only shadows," Asmina would say each time. It was true. Gina was the spirit of the Castello.

In the late evenings, when they were alone, Gina would confide in Asmina keeping her enthralled with her progress. Sometimes, Gina would practice her newfound skills on her, like mind reading and moving small objects without touching them. Asmina would cross herself in delicious fear of it, sure that it was the Devil's own work. She couldn't come to terms with the concept that Gina's powers were scientifically based and not black magic. Each time Gina returned, her powers were more significant. Of course, Asmina took full credit for it, as it was she who had summoned up the Magician.

Asmina couldn't help but tease Gina over the Lovers card. She would demand a progress report on Gina's love life at each visit. She could tell that Gina had fallen in love, even though she wouldn't quite declare it so.

"He's already taken Asmina," Gina would say, time and again.

Asmina's response was always the same though.

"Cards don't tell no lies bibi. You gonna be in his bed one day, or he in yours," then Asmina would fall about laughing. It didn't help at all.

Gina remained perfectly unaware of Sasha's mini crisis. His secret had been buried. She was aware though, that he was vigorously fighting a cause along with Isabella, to have the much-awaited Dream App abolished. They were trying to get it criminalised, as it breached several laws and certainly a lot of ethics. Isabella had managed to get the World Health Organisation on board, and for them to try to classify the game as a breach of the law under the classification of 'Electronic Stalking & Mind Control'. Gina wondered how Sasha had become so anti the game when he was so in favour initially. Fortunately for Sasha, she didn't have the time to dig deeper.

Sasha had been true to his word, and had cleaned up his act. No dreams and no drugs. His last indulgence was watching his own personalised dream experience the night that he swore that he would quit. It was the most amazing experience of his life and he wouldn't have missed it for the world. He had literally ended on a high. What Sasha didn't know was that he was now a ticking bomb, only one activation code away from killing his mother and everyone else in the Mèdici family.

Isabella had spent weeks investigating LuminaGames. Each trail had come to a dead end, as if its history had been carefully wiped out. The only link she could find ended at the Mèdici bank. If her mother had been there, she would have asked her about it, but she wasn't. Isabella was a naturally intuitive girl, something she came by naturally. Something told her, that the answers would all be in the LuminaGames customer file at the Mèdici bank. She was free for the rest of the day, and decided to do a bit of undercover work.

Isabella walked in through the grand entrance of the Mèdici bank. The doors were original and dated back to 1397, when the bank was founded. Now they were framed by marble columns and a security portcullis that dropped at night. The interior of the bank declared wealth and success. An absolute pre-requisite for customer confidence in these troubled economic times.

As powerful as the Mèdici bank was, any loss of confidence that might lead to a run on the bank, could still topple it. No bank, holds enough fluid cash to support itself in such a crisis. Banking is all about customer confidence. As Isabella walked through to the offices at the back, the evidence of the bank's investment in image was apparent; marble floors and counters, with marble plinths and dwarf columns that supported expensive sculptures by Louise Bourgeois, Marc Quinn and Henry Moore, to name but a few. The walls were hung with art through the ages, including the Masters. All of which, could grace the finest gallery.

When Isabella reached the offices, she was immediately recognised and greeted by Phoebe, her mother's secretary.

"Issie! What a lovely surprise. How are you, how's Sasha?"

It took Isabella nearly twenty minutes to answer all of Phoebe's questions, including all she knew about her mother's progress in Moscow. Isabella didn't want to rush it as she needed a favour. Eventually she got her chance to ask it.

"I know it's not usual, but Mum wants me to tend to a few personal things that won't wait, apparently. She has told me her personal logon for her own files so I won't be in Mèdici bank affairs," Isabella assured and followed her request with a beaming smile.

"Well you shouldn't come in really. However under the circumstances, as its private information only, I will let you but just this once. If there is a next time Isabella, I will need it in writing from your mother. Is that clear?"

"Of course, Phoebe," it was as simple as that. She was in.

"Well done special agent Mèdici," she said to herself as Phoebe left her mother's office.

Isabella had watched her mother log on many times, and had quite naturally memorised the finger patterns. She entered the username and password.

"Access Denied," the error message read.

Isabella counted back the months since she had last seen her mother log on. It was probably six she determined, but she had been in Moscow for four of those. That meant the password would have had two updates since the one that she had just typed in. It currently ended with the number 96. She retyped the password now ending it in 98, crossed her fingers and pressed 'enter'.

"Bingo! Special agent Mèdici," she said out loud. The error message read, "Password Expired - Renew Password."

She typed in the new password ending in 99 and pressed 'enter'. The Mèdici bank homepage appeared, with her mother's folder structure.

"You are good, special agent Mèdici. You are real good," she smiled as her fingers clattered over the keyboard.

Isabella looked in the folder under 'Clients'. Her heart skipped a beat. There it was *LuminaGames*. They had been a client since 2013. She looked at who had opened the account with them. It was her father's name that appeared. She touched the screen and ran her finger lovingly over the words, *Antonio Mèdici*. She looked for the Directors' names and found them, Georgios Rossi and Sophia Williams. Isabella wrote them on her notepad. She was getting somewhere at last.

Next, she looked at their borrowings. In 2013, it was €0.8 million, in 2014, €5.2 million, in 2015, €14.2 million and in 2016, €40.6 million.

"Jesus Christ!" was all that Isabella could say, when she read the 2017 figures to date, €1.2 billion.

The figures were on an exponential curve.

"The launch of the Dream App was responsible for the change," she concluded, and it had only been on sale for a few months.

This was the most exciting discovery that Isabella had ever made. She had found a business on the up in a meteoric way, but flaunting the law to gain profits. It was a hell of a story if you were a journalist and an even greater achievement to be the lawyer that brought them down.

She searched the Internet to find out more about the despicable Directors of LuminaGames and wondered what kind of people could sink to the depths of depravity that they had, to prey on the young and vulnerable. Isabella would have them in prison, she was sure of it.

To Isabella's pleasure they were easy to find. It turned out that LuminaGames was the brain-child of two outstanding university graduates. They had fallen in love and created a business together, that used innovations un-thought of before, real cutting edge stuff. The industry was pursuing them to sell up. Apparently, they had their own vision of what *UniGames*, their original company's name, would be and had resisted any and all takeovers. It seemed that despite their poverty they had ambition and vision.

"Yeah but no fucking morals," Isabella said out loud disdainfully, reading on.

They had started with seed funding from an undisclosed source, and struggled for three years trading under the name UniGames, a play on words from their university days where it had all began. They had run up a debt that would have made Onassis edgy, but they remained undaunted. The Mèdici bank stepped in to fund their project in 2014 when their sales took off, reaching a turnover of nearly €90 million by the end of 2016. What Isabella read next, blew her away.

"Oh, my God!" Isabella stood and stepped away from the computer as if it was about to explode. "Dear God no."

The news clip read:

"On December 21st, 2016. Georgios Rossi and Sophia Williams were found dead in their €500,000 apartment in Milan. Reliable sources claimed that it appeared to be another ritual solstice killing with the Illuminati fingerprint."

Isabella read the clip over and over in disbelief before continuing her internet search. The next news clip, dated 19th January 2017, was about the sale of UniGames and again it rocked her world:

"LuminaGames, as a principal creditor, has taken ownership of UniGames. Thereby resolving their outstanding loan. Their spokesman said that it was a significant acquisition and good

news for their shareholders, although their thoughts and condolences are with the family and friends of the previous owners, Georgios Rossi and Sophia Williams.

The company is to be re-branded as part of 'LuminaGames' and sales projections for 2017 are expected to exceed €1 billion."

This meant that the murdered directors were innocent. Isabella felt pang of guilt for her hasty and unfounded conclusions. The Dream App wasn't marketed until after the takeover. Suddenly the text of the news clip took on a whole new context. She read it again to be sure, but there it was, plain to see. There was no doubt in Isabella's mind.

"Il-LUMINA-ti," she breathed the word out in disbelief.

That was it. LuminaGames belonged to the Illuminati, she deduced. Isabella wondered if Georgios and Sophia had unwittingly agreed initial seed funding from them, and couldn't get out. Isabella wondered too, if anybody else had seen this obvious connection with the Illuminati.

"Was it an in-house ritualistic killing by the Illuminati, just as the first newspaper clip implied?" she questioned. "And how is the Mèdici bank involved?"

Isabella searched the Internet, but came to another dead end. The trail had run cold. Nothing took the LuminaGames story any further. It was obvious though, that they had continued success after the founders' deaths, simply by their financial borrowing. According to Mèdici bank records, LuminaGames' borrowing was currently €1.2 billion, and sales of the Dream App were astronomical.

Isabella spent another hour searching the Internet for anything that she could find on the Illuminati. So much was 'conspiracy theory' though, so she had to be objective. When she searched for the top five families that were allegedly in the Illuminati, the list simply changed her world. It read:

"Rothschild, Rockefeller, Bruce, Kennedy, Mèdici..."

"Jesus, are we really an Illuminati family?" Isabella couldn't believe that it could be possible. "Perhaps it's another Mèdici family?" it was more blind hope than anything else. It was too much of a coincidence; it had to be her family.

Isabella was blown away and felt sick. The walls in the spacious office seemed to close in on her, until she couldn't breathe. She almost called Phoebe for help, but managed to bring her panic back under control. She sat there stoically at the computer and wondered what to do next. There were no more leads on the Internet. She had failed at the last hurdle. The name of the new owners of LuminaGames, who were probably the murderers of Georgios and Sophia, would remain anonymous.

Isabella began closing the files. She was about to exit the programme when she saw a file called 'Acquisitions'. Something inside her told her to open it. She scrolled down the list of acquisitions the bank had made over the last two years. It was immense, totalling over one hundred billion U.S. Dollars. Most were media acquisitions and arms manufacturers. Each one had at least 51% ownership by the Mèdici bank, and there amongst them, was LuminaGames. Isabella was way beyond furious. Every transaction had been done by one, 'Gina Mèdici'.

"Jesus Christ mother, who the fuck are you?"

Chapter 20

Moscow, Russia. Monday, December 18th 2017. Three days before the winter solstice.

It was the fifth month that Gina had spent in Russia at the old farmhouse. Most of it was exclusively with Ava, or the Magician, as the Tarot cards had divined her to be. In that short time, they had become the closest of friends and occasional lovers. It wasn't just through the mutual sharing of time and experiences though, it was because they often shared the same thoughts and emotions. They had become inseparable.

There were two things that had spoiled Gina's peace though. Not seeing her kids every day was the major one, and hardly seeing Callum at all, the other. Gina had managed to fly back to Milan every other weekend on what amounted to be little more than a 24-hour pass. It was enough though, to reassure her that her children were safe in Asmina's hands, but not enough for her to discover Sasha's addiction; fortunately for him. Although Gina now had the power to read their minds, she drew the line at prying into her children's personal lives.

The problem wasn't her children, they didn't seem in any immediate danger, or so she thought. It was finding time to spend with Callum. Every time Gina was free, Kayla seemed to sense it and was on the scene in no time. Sometimes, that had meant a flight halfway across the world for Kayla, but that never deterred her. Callum and Ava had warned Gina about Kayla's persistence and his inability to resist her. They did however manage to spend at least some innocent time together, but the sexual tension between them was mounting and becoming all consuming. Unfortunately for them, Kayla knew it. She *sensed* it. After all, she was half Angel and half Shadow with that same and rare genetic mix as Ava. With it came the same dangerous dark side. Not even Emanuel, who was of almost pure Angel blood, could protect his thoughts from her.

Now that Gina could read thoughts too, it went some way towards her being able to compete against Kayla on near equal terms. She could now use her own mind to pry into Kayla's affaires. Unsurprisingly, Gina didn't seem to have the same ethical problems about reading Callum's and Kayla's minds as she did those of her children.

"After all," Gina had justified, "a woman must employ all of her guile to secure her man. Kayla certainly had," she noted. In Gina's mind, that alone justified her innocent deceit.

It was clear that Kayla had come to regard Gina as a significant threat. Not just as a rival in love, but strategically as an empowered woman. Kayla had appraised that Gina had genetic potential inside her that might surpass her own. That simply wasn't something that she was going to come to terms with easily. To lose Callum in an affair of the heart was one thing, but to lose her position in the hierarchy of the Angel organisation was entirely another. Consequently, Kayla was jealous and constantly on the watch.

Ava had finally managed to engineer Gina's long overdue date with Callum. It was to see a performance of Tchaikovsky's ballet, *Swan Lake,* at Russia's famous Bolshoi. The prima ballerina playing the double-role of Odette-Odile was Ava's closest friend, and secret lover, Katarina Romanov. She had arranged VIP tickets for Gina and Callum. It was a strange thing. In another innocent life, before the madness of Angels and Shadows, Ava had been prima ballerina at the Bolshoi, playing that same part herself to packed audiences. Now Katarina and Ava's mother, Anastasia, were the only people on Earth that knew how splendidly Ava could dance. It was the price that Ava had to pay for saving her mother's life. Now she lived the thrill of the ballet through her dearest friend, Katarina.

It started perfectly. Gina had spent a decadent amount of time and money making herself beautiful and irresistible for Callum. Kayla was in North Africa, visiting family, and the night out had been planned at the 'eleventh hour'. The chances of Kayla turning up uninvited, was infinitesimally small, so Gina's anticipation and expectation of romance that night was way off the scale. Her fantasies of having him hold her, kiss her and touch her had become overwhelming. Those thoughts had kept her awake on many a lonely night. She felt like a giddy teenager again, and was more than a little afraid of throwing herself at Callum. That fear, was tempered by the fact that she had read his mind on a number of occasions, and knew that Callum felt the same.

"God it's going to be amazing," Gina had said to Ava, who quite unselfishly had enthused with her.

"Gina, my darling; you have absolutely no idea," Ava said conspiratorially. She knew from experience," just don't plan anything too strenuous afterwards, because you won't want to walk too far for a week!"

They had fallen about in fits of laughter, but all of this was simply adding to Gina's fantasies and fuelling the fire within her. She just could not wait! It had been more than fifteen years since a man had laid a hand on her and close to six months since she had even wanted one to. Callum!

Ava had accompanied Gina to the ballet. It was partly to settle Gina's nerves, but principally to see her lover, Katarina. Ava had rarely missed a performance of hers since their reunion.

They had agreed to meet Callum at the Bolshoi bar, a place of so many memories for Ava, both happy and sad. When they arrived, Callum was already there. He was quite coincidentally sat on the very same barstool where Ava had first seen and lusted after Demitri Papandreou in that other life; the man who later turned out to be a cad. That was before he had turned her into a murderess. Callum was even dressed similarly. Ava shuddered at the memory of it. Demitri had been many things to her and none of them good: absent father, murderer, lover, benefactor and manipulator. Ava had killed him for his sins and now cursed him again for sullying this precious moment. Gina had shared Ava's mind on many an occasion, and knew all these things and sensed the bad vibes. The bitter memory was now hers too and it haunted her every bit as much as it did Ava. The three exchanged kisses and pleasantries, then Ava unexpectedly made her excuses, leaving the expectant couple at the bar.

"Can we sit somewhere else please," Gina asked Callum urgently. She needed to leave that ugly memory behind her.

She took his hand and headed with him for the discreetness of the booths. Moments later their privacy was invaded and their expectations dashed.

"Surprise!" the glamorous dusky lady in red had chirped. She waved her ticket and planted the biggest kiss on Callum's lips. "I was so lucky! I managed to get a last-minute seat next to you Cal," she beamed at them.

Gina was livid and no longer naive. She knew that Kayla would have used her skills to divine the owner of that ticket and *suggest* that he, or she, gave it up. They would have had no freedom of choice in the matter; none.

"Bitch!" was Kayla's immediate thought and Gina had heard it loud and clear.

"Fuck you," was hers.

So, that was the end of that little covert tryst.

There had been other opportunities for Gina and Callum to meet romantically, but they had all got derailed one way or another by Kayla Lovell.

Boot camp at the farmhouse was finally over, and Gina back in the comfort of the Metropol. There was nothing more that Ava could teach her. The rest, and there was much more to come, could only manifest itself through maturity and experience. Gina's education was now all about understanding the Angel organisation, its resources and who their enemies were. On that subject, it had all become confused.

Historically, it had been straight forward. Their enemies were the Shadow organisation, various religious zealots and power crazed leaders. All of them forever wanted a bigger slice of the cake, no matter what the consequence. Now they had the Illuminati and the Pindar to contend with.

Gina was getting ready to go down to take a quick breakfast, before going to the Angel Associates offices in Moscow City. She was to meet with Emanuel, Callum and Ava to talk about the forthcoming winter solstice meeting of the Council of Thirteen. It was only a week away now. The options on the table were for Gina to simply not attend, take her kids and go into hiding at the fortified farmhouse, or to go and face the Pindar down and buy time. There were merits in both. The practicalities of going into hiding for an indeterminate time with teenagers and their wants and needs were, quite frankly, optimistic. It also went nowhere towards derailing the Pindar's plans for global control. On the other hand, to confront the Pindar with Gina's current level of readiness, was also a poor option.

"Damned if you do and damned if you don't," Gina mused.

The bedside telephone rang. Gina answered, hoping that it would be Callum. It was reception.

"I have a Hydie Papandreou here who would like to meet you. Can I send her up?"

"No!" Gina said sounding panicked.

It was the last thing in the world that she had expected. The image of the Hydra sat to the right of the Pindar smiling at her, came vividly to mind.

"She has come in peace," Gina thought, trying to reassure herself.

On reflection, she was sure of it. Callum had said that the Hydra needed an ally and here she was.

"Mrs Mèdici? Hello?" the receptionist prompted, thinking that he had lost the connection.

"Yes, I'm still here. Tell Mrs Papandreou that I will join her for coffee in the lounge in five minutes," suddenly the thought of breakfast was most unappealing to Gina.

The lift doors opened on the ground floor. Gina stepped out into the hotel lobby and crossed over to the lounge. There was no doubting which of the women there Hydie Papandreou was. A dark, strikingly beautiful woman in a navy business suit and expensive shoes was sat with her legs crossed reading the morning paper. She looked up the instant Gina entered the lounge, as if she had sensed her arrival. In actual fact, she had.

Gina's heart was in her mouth as she crossed to her. The woman exuded power and she felt inadequate by comparison. She walked toward the Hydra, holding her gaze. It was like Mowgli meeting Kaa, the snake in Jungle Book. Gina felt like a rabbit caught in the headlights as she held out her hand in greeting.

"Gina Mèdici," she said unnecessarily. It was stating the obvious, "but of course you already know that."

The Hydra shook her hand in friendly manner.

"Yes Gina, I do. But I would like to get to know the woman behind the name. I think we have common interests and concerns. Would you sit with me a while and share some thoughts?"

It was either the spider's web or a completely earnest meeting. Gina was inwardly preparing herself for this to go wrong and was desperately trying to remember Ava's teachings. She even glanced to see where the fire exits were. It took Gina moments only to realise that she was no match for the Hydra.

"The fire exits are the main entrance, two at the back and out through the stairwells," the Hydra confirmed, reading her mind.

"I'm sorry that was rude and foolish of me," Gina said, embarrassed and smiling thinly.

Hydie Papandreou raised an admonishing hand. Gina took the seat opposite her. She realised, all too late, that her knees were pressed too tightly together, her hands were clasped unnecessarily firmly and that she was grinning like a fool.

"Shit," she thought. "Good start."

The Hydra read Gina's body language and put her at her ease.

"Relax Gina and call me Hydie please," the Hydra said with an engaging smile. "I have come to help you. To help us, more's the truth and I will not forsake you, on my life."

It was a big up front statement but Gina intuitively knew that it was genuine and she immediately relaxed.

"Go on."

"I will not lie to you Gina. We are of different bloods and ethos. In any other situation, we would be enemies and show each other no mercy. Sometimes though, circumstances change everything and so we need to reappraise the world that we live in," the Hydra's eyes hardened. "That is where we find ourselves now Gina, in a death struggle against the Pindar."

"We?" Gina tested. "But you sit and advise at the Pindar's right hand. You have his ear and his confidence."

"And he would gladly kill me with his left hand Gina. Things are not always as they appear. I am safe, as you are, until he has no further need for us. That time is fast approaching and neither of us will make it much past this winter's solstice, unless we have collateral."

"Collateral?" Gina asked cocking an inquisitive brow at the magnificent woman in front of her.

"Yes, something that the Pindar needs from us, that he can't get elsewhere. Or at least can't get from elsewhere in the near term," the Hydra's expression was stern and business-like.

Indeed, Hydie Papandreou was akin to Kaa, the hypnotic snake. Gina was mesmerised by her looks. Stunning didn't even come close to describing her. The woman exuded power, confidence and sophistication. It shone from her face and sparkled like diamonds in her near black, lively eyes. There was cruelty and danger there too though, Gina noted. She imagined that few men would have the courage to make romantic advances toward her, and that it would be a formidable man with immense confidence who could. She wondered at what such a man might be like. An inquisitive look crossed the Hydra's face and a wry smile followed. Gina's dalliance had been picked up. The Hydra had *read* her again.

"Thank you for the unspoken compliment," the Hydra said and Gina looked mortified.

"I'm sorry, that was rude of me again," Gina said hastily.

"Not at all, we all have thoughts but not everybody can read them," the Hydra smiled as if in reverie. "There was a man once and he *was* formidable. Alas, since then, there have been none to compare. His name was Demitri and I lost him to the Angels, as I did my son, Anaxis. But that was many hundreds of years before."

"I'm sorry," Gina said lamely. She still found it hard to come to terms with the fact that these beings, both Angels and Shadows, had longevity that spanned millennia.

"Don't be. All's fair in love and war, as they say. And it was war. You can be sure of that."

The Hydra closed that line of conversation and swiftly moved on to matters more pressing.

"As individuals, we are no match for the Pindar," the Hydra began, "but together, and with the combined power of our organisations behind us, well perhaps we just may be."

Gina contemplated what the Hydra had said. It underlined what Callum had already deduced. Hydie Papandreou *needed* allies, which begged the question.

"How powerful is the Pindar then Hydie, and who is he?" Gina asked, not altogether sure if she really wanted to know the truth.

"Who indeed, or *what*," the Hydra began. "I assume your organisation has asked the same question and have no more idea than we have. He is not human or of our races, that is for sure. I cannot read him either, but I sense that he is immensely powerful; powerful beyond us, and ruthless too."

"Your assumption would appear to be correct Hydie. We can't come up with a photograph of him let alone a profile. It's as if he doesn't really exist," it was a sinister concept and it sent a supernatural chill down Gina's spine. "As ridiculous as it may seem, we have even considered the possibility that he actually *is* Lucifer."

Gina looked embarrassed at even mentioning what could only be nonsense in her mind. The Hydra picked up on that.

"Are you a religious woman Gina and do you believe in God?" Gina answered without hesitation.

"I have always been a staunch Catholic," she said with clear commitment, "and yes I do believe in God; absolutely."

"Then at the very least you must be open to the possibility that if God exists, then Satan or *Lucifer* might also."

It was a challenge that Gina hadn't exactly readied herself for. Her usual eloquence on the matter of belief and theology seemed to have deserted her. All she could muster was a nod.

"I don't have such beliefs," the Hydra said almost dismissively, "but I do believe in possibility. Nothing that I can come up with is any more credible than the Pindar being Satan. Even the chair that he sits on is carved with Lucifer's initial. Do you think that is a coincidence?" The Hydra questioned.

Gina had come to the same conclusion and the Hydra could see that. She genuflected yet again, feeling a need for God's protection. That simple, almost desperate act reinforced just how precarious Gina's life had become and how far out of her depth she was.

"Following that thought," continued the Hydra, "and if the scriptures have any truth in them at all. Satan was cast down from Heaven and his angels with him. There is no mention in the bible that Satan has mortality, only that he can be tortured and banished," the Hydra paused almost theatrically. So if that's true, we can't kill him, more's the pity," she said with spite. "It is written:

'And the devil that deceived them was cast into the lake of fire and brimstone, where the beast and the false prophet are, and shall be tormented day and night for ever and ever.'

Are you familiar with that Gina?"

"Yes. It comes from the Book of Revelation 20:10 and relates to God's three enemies being overthrown and driven from the Earth, which they had sought to destroy."

Gina's grounding in the bible had always been thorough. Now with her near total recall, she could quote it from memory.

"But that can't in anyway be taken literally though. It was written for the understanding of the relatively primitive people at the time," Gina justified. "Fire and brimstone, burning lakes of sulphur, Hell and damnation."

But then Gina had never believed in Angels & Shadows either, until months ago. Now she was feeling far from certain about anything that she had taken for granted. The Hydra thought for a while on how she could best and most credibly make her case.

"I am sure that your people have already told you that the reality we live in is only how we are intellectually able to perceive it and measure it at the time. Outside of our limits the possibilities are boundless. Anything is possible. A maker of the universe and a destroyer of it, both lie within the bounds of possibility."

189

Gina nodded in recognition of that simple fact. She had indeed discussed the principle of infinite possibility with Emanuel, Callum and Ava; even with Leonardo. It had all seemed pretty abstract then though. Now it was a stark reality that threatened her and her family's very existence. The Hydra continued.

"Everything that the Pindar is currently planning was written in the scriptures thousands of years ago," the Hydra began. "The incitement of the people through the False Prophet, and the coming of the Mahdi, would lead to the holy war exactly as prophesied. This holy war would quickly expand into the Pindar's Third World War, one so ghastly that the people would seek God in desperation. In those dire times, it would be easy to fool the people to accept Satan as Jesus Christ. Indeed, that is what the scriptures predict."

The Hydra levelled her gaze at Gina and drew her into her mind, allowing her to see first-hand what she herself had seen. Through the Hydra's eyes, Gina found herself gazing into the face a man in a dark habit only inches in front of her. His cowl shaded his features, but she could clearly see the golden mask that covered part of his face and one eye. The other eye was looking at her coldly, devoid of any feeling or compassion. He blinked and Gina gasped. It was a reptilian eye, the Beast as referred to in the bible. It was nothing like the eye of a mortal man. She was looking at the Pindar, up close, like she had never seen him before.

"Satan," Gina mouthed almost inaudibly. In that moment she knew it to be true. "The Pindar is Satan," she declared.

The Hydra's sleek limousine pulled up outside the Angelos Associates' office in Moscow's International Business Centre. The two women that stepped out and walked to the entrance were both elegant, although they could not have been more different. Hydie Papandreou was dressed in a navy suit with pencil skirt and white shirt. She was slim, athletically built and walked with a confident and authoritative stride. Her black hair was swirled into an up-do, carefully pinned and business like. Gina on the other hand, was voluptuous and femininely dressed. She had long since noted that Callum had an eye for a girl in a well-cut dress and had chosen to please him. The full length red and white floral one that she had chosen was young looking and sufficiently short of being conservative to quicken a man's pulse. Gina's hair was only similar to Hydie's in colour and length. She wore hers loose and flowing, asymmetrically swept over one shoulder. Her walk was more fluid and feminine, with the typical confident sway of a woman used to the catwalk.

They walked the steps up to the glass doors of the building briskly, and passed through into the foyer. As they crossed towards security, the alarms sounded. Uniformed, practiced guards, quickly took up their positions at the exits, lifts and stairs. Steel roller shutters crashed to the ground all around them. In less than ten seconds, they were locked down.

The difference in the women was again apparent. Gina was panicked by the occurrence and disorientated, whereas the Hydra went straight into survival mode. She had clearly been identified by photo recognition and knew it. She focussed her mind on the steel door that had dropped over the entrance. The higher born of the Shadow race had almost the same mental power as the Angels. They also could influence a physical system through thought. The steelwork began to frost and the temperature in the foyer dropped like a stone. The Hydra judged her moment then ran at the shuttered doorway. The super-cooled metal had lost its malleability and shattered like glass, as the Hydra hit it full on. Moments later, she was stood in the street on the opposite side of her limousine.

Gina had gathered her wits and came running out of the building after her.

"No Hydie, don't leave!" she yelled. "I will bring them out to you."

The Hydra got into her car and spoke quickly to the chauffeur, but they didn't leave. Gina disappeared inside again. Five minutes later she reappeared with Emanuel, Callum and Ava. Emanuel bade them to stay at the top of the steps, while he alone approached the Hydra. His shock of white hair caught the morning sunshine as he descended the stairs, making him literally look like an angel. He crossed to the black limousine and disappeared from view as he ducked to talk to the Hydra through the window.

It was a full minute before Emanuel stood tall and reappeared with Hydie Papandreou stood next to him. They walked together up to the steps, leading into the building. Emanuel looked his usual easy self, but in contrast, the Hydra was stiff and alert. Her eyes were darting around, taking in her environment and constantly assessing and reassessing her predicament.

Emanuel entered the building alone to instruct the guards to stand down. Shortly afterwards, the heavy steel shutters around and inside the building began to lift. Callum led them inside through the shattered remains of the steelwork. The Hydra remained cautious as if looking for some concealed trap. It was unheard of over the millennia of their histories, that one leader had trusted the other enough to meet face to face.

Emanuel was quickly at hand with a security pass for Hydie Papandreou. He handed it to her and summoned the lift.

"We are on the eleventh," Emanuel said, for no other reason than to engage with her.

Hydie Papandreou nodded in reciprocation of Emanuel's modest gesture and entered the lift, still assessing the situation. They exited on the eleventh. Emanuel led them directly to the Crystalita Room, much to the surprise of Kristina who was poised to greet them. He opened the meeting room door and ushered them in. All the while, Hydie Papandreou was learning her surroundings down to the smallest detail. She noted where the emergency stairs were and whether the doors opened, inwards or outwards. She even assessed the offices for anyone who looked capable in a crisis, making a mental note of each.

Emanuel invited them all to sit at the round table. Hydie Papandreou placed herself opposite Emanuel and next to Gina, immediately recognising him as the senior of the Angels present and Gina as her natural ally. Emanuel spoke first.

"Welcome to our offices Mrs Papandreou," his usual affable smile hid any signs of concern that he might have had. "I must say that this is a meeting that I could never have envisaged."

"Desperate times call for desperate measures Mr Goldberg," she replied evenly, "and you can be sure that these *are* desperate times; unsurpassed in fact."

"Why so?" Emanuel asked although he already knew.

"The Pindar," she said simply and Emanuel nodded.

"We see it that way too," Emanuel spread those big hands of his on the table, adding weight to the statement in his usual calm way. "You are closer to him and so perhaps you could enlighten us more?"

"Indeed, Mr Goldberg. I have already broached the subject with Gina and I think we have an accord," Gina confirmed the Hydra's statement with a nervous smile.

"You can drop the 'Mr'. Please call me Emanuel," he smiled and extended his hand. "I have a feeling that we might be working together for a while. I trust you know of Callum Knight?" he said unnecessarily.

"I know of all of you, as you will know of all of us. It is our business to know these things," the Hydra gave a wry smile and shook hands with both. "It's Hydie, well at least for now," she added in the certainty that they were never going to be best friends.

None there doubted that this was going to be anything more than a marriage of convenience, one that would evaporate when the time came. For now though, they had a shared interest.

There was a knock on the door. Ava and Kayla entered. They had already been briefed by Kristina that Emanuel, Callum and Gina were in conference with the head of the Shadow organisation. The Hydra recognised them immediately. Two of the most powerful of the Angels and her concern was immediately evident. She was now even more heavily outnumbered. Emanuel took the initiative to calm her.

"Ladies, let me introduce you to Hydie Papandreou. She has come in peace to discuss her concerns over the Pindar's intentions," he said with a disarming smile.

The girls introduced themselves cordially. Unsurprisingly, they both chose to sit each side of Callum. Kayla had never met the Hydra before. In one brief glance, as only a woman can, she took in every aspect of the Hydra's appearance. Kayla could have told you what dress size she was, the jewellery that she wore, even the brand of shoes she was wearing.

"The Hydra was elegant and sophisticated," Kayla concluded, "and far too attractive to trust!"

Ava however, had known the Hydra in a different life and knew what a formidable opponent she could be and was most wary of her.

"Beauty is only skin deep," Ava mused. "This woman was ruthless and cruel. Not one to cross if you valued your life."

Both women smiled openly at Hydie Papandreou and kept their counsel and guarded their thoughts from her. Their mental skills were at least on par with those of the Hydra.

"So, to bring you up to speed then," Emanuel began. "Both our organisations see the Pindar as singularly the biggest threat the world has ever faced. We have no idea who he is, nor where he comes from. We do know, however, that he is planning a Third World War. We also know from visions that our leader Maelströminha has seen, that not much survives it. Is that more or less how you and your people believe it to be Hydie?"

She simply nodded and let Emanuel continue.

"So what is this 'accord' or consensus that you and Gina have come to?" he cocked a white bushy brow inquisitively in the Hydra's direction.

"That the Pindar is not human nor of our kinds, not even of this world," she said authoritatively. "I have sat at his right side for some years now. Darkness is no obstacle to the Shadow race as you know, and no place to hide from us. Our eyes are almost as keen in the dark as in the light. I have seen his face as clearly as I now see yours Emanuel. Gina has shared my mind and seen that vision through me. Ask her what she saw," the Hydra now looked completely composed and at ease in the company of Angels.

"What did you see Gina," Emanuel asked.

It seemed a monumental task for Gina to respond and her eyes searched the Hydra's for support.

"Go on Gina," the Hydra prompted.

At last Gina did but she crossed herself again to ward off evil spirits before she spoke.

"I saw the Devil."

Gina was shaking so much that Callum put his hands on top of hers in an attempt to calm her. They felt like the fluttering of a trapped bird beneath his. Gina was the only one at the table who was a staunch believer in God. The possibility that the Pindar was the very Devil himself and active here on Earth was a shocking revelation for her and she appreciated Callum's support. Kayla was not amused by Callum's show of concern and tactlessly entered the fray.

"That's ridiculous. Perhaps we should focus on reasonable and rational explanations before we turn to God and the Devil," Kayla's tone was just a little short of mocking.

"Is it ridiculous, Kayla?" the Hydra countered. "If you were to tell humans that aliens like us exist on this planet and have done for thousands of years, would they not find that ridiculous?"

Callum knew Kayla well. He could see that this confrontation wasn't going to end well and so diverted the conversation.

"So, just assuming that the Pindar *is* Satan," he began, "what can we find to underpin that? For example, are there any credible historical accounts, ancient scriptures, religious interventions by the Church, Vatican records; anything that corroborates the possibility?"

The diversion worked and Kayla bit her tongue, something quite uncharacteristic of her. The Hydra was already prepared for their scepticism.

"This possibility is new to you but I have been considering and researching it for quite some time and am personally convinced. I have seen the Pindar's face and experienced his presence. I've seen the total blackness of the aura that surrounds him and experienced the feeling of deep menace that he exudes. Why might you be surprised that the Pindar is both Lucifer and Satan in both his guises? You already know that the very foundation of the Illuminati organisation is Satanism and that they worship Lucifer?"

It was a fair challenge. They already knew, that at the base of the Illuminati pyramid of power, was organised Satanism and the brotherhoods. Then there were the levels of novice and craft-practicing witches, and above them, the master witches that supposedly summoned demons and led the covens, and then the Freemasons. Above all of these at the top of the pyramid purportedly, was the Council of Thirteen ruled by Lucifer and worshipped as their God. This was all well documented and not at all secret. Even a quick search on Google confirmed the layers of power and even suggests the names of the families that form the Council. The Hydra continued.

"In our research, we have found nothing that proves the existence of Satan, but equally, nothing that categorically disproves it. The bible describes Satan as 'the father of all lies'. What better disguise could there be, than to create the belief that Satan is a myth? That way he could go about his business unchallenged."

The Hydra paused while they considered that possibility.

"The Pindar's business is to create a New World Order with a one-world government and a single monetary system. That New World Order can only come about through a catastrophic Third World War. After that the Pindar declares himself as God and takes global control."

The theological debate went on another three hours before it was the consensus of them all that it would be safer to assume that the Pindar *was* Satan rather than not. The Hydra's research had been in depth. She had trawled most of the ancient scriptures, Satanic rights, church exorcisms and the like for any signs of the Pindar's mortality but there was none. Her researches couldn't even find a change in the Illuminati leadership over the centuries, no deaths or succession. The Pindar seemed timeless. If this was true, then he was immortal and therefore could not be killed. They had one glimmer of hope though. Hydie Papandreou had come to the Angels for help which meant that the situation wasn't entirely hopeless. She had to have some kind of a strategy. They waited patiently for it to all unfold. Finally, the background was set and the Hydra ready to be objective.

"We would all agree that neither me nor Gina will survive much past the winter solstice next week," the brutality of the Hydra's simple and clinical observation fell like a blow to Gina and rocked her world.

"Go on," Emanuel prompted, nodding his head in agreement.

"By then, Gina will have fulfilled her part in achieving the Pindar's objectives. That is globalisation through the creation of a powerful conglomerate to operate in it," she turned to Gina. "All your procurements are in place, are they not?" Gina nodded.

"Yes, but with the exception of signing the Mèdici bank over to him," Gina shrugged at the inevitability of that happening at some stage soon.

"My part in the Pindar's plan is gaining absolute control of the politicians and leaders. Like Gina's assignment, my work is also

197

complete. I have gained the confidence and agreed terms and conditions with all of the major players in world politics. I have dossiers on them all and know just how to control them and how to hurt them. That includes the names and locations of their close family and loved ones. They will comply."

The implication of that last statement was said without emotion and it sent a cold chill down the spines of all there. Tactics like that were unthinkable to the others at the table. It underlined the difference between their two races and that a long lasting treaty would be untenable. The Hydra continued.

"Like Gina, I have not yet delivered the dossiers to the Pindar. So between us, we hold the keys to two out of the three steps that the Pindar needs to execute his plan. Well, at least temporarily," she added. "That just leaves the final step, control of the people through religion and the media. The Mullah Ismael Alansari and Mohammed Akhbar are to initiate a holy war in Syria. Regrettably, they are both Shadows but traitors and beyond our influence. They cannot be bought off and both know that I would have them killed but for the Pindar's protection."

The Hydra's disdain and hatred for these two traitorous Arabs was clearly written across her face. Her scowl took away her beauty, leaving nothing but hardness there.

"That leaves Illya Dracul, whose part was gaining control of the media and the minds of the youth. He is another traitorous Shadow, who has chosen to place his allegiance with the Pindar rather than to support me," again the Hydra's face was murderous.

"How is this Dracul going to control the media?" Callum asked.

"Partly through Gina's recent media acquisitions," the Hydra began. "The Pindar has bought into mass media through newspapers, television, radio, publishing, movies, and the Internet. Managed together, they will form a media conglomerate to rival and consume any that currently exists. After that, ruthless company takeover bids with the usual death-threat incentives to sell will ensure that the Pindar eventually gets the lion's share of the media industry."

"Ruthless indeed," Callum said, scratching his stubbly chin thoughtfully.

"That's only the half of it," the Hydra added. "Dracul is somewhat of computer geek. He has put a research team together and employed the infamous Doctor Walter Schwartz. Together they have created a computer game that targets the youth and is wholly addictive and manipulative."

"I know of him," Emanuel interjected. "Wasn't he a Nazi physician specialising in the field of human experimentation in the Second World War?"

"The very same; he has continued specialising in that field ever since and enjoying his work," the Hydra's voice was disparaging. As ruthless as she was, she could not abide violence and violation for self-gratification. "Between them, they have developed a game that has gone viral. In essence, it's a brainwashing tool that becomes totally consuming and addictive. After addiction, you can programme an individual, or even the masses, to do what you want. They call it the 'Dream App', designed and distributed by LuminaGames, another Pindar acquisition."

Gina went white with shock.

"But that's the game that my son's been playing," her mind was racing. "LuminaGames. Why didn't I notice that?" Gina was clearly shaken. "Yes, they are one of my bank's acquisitions for the Pindar. I didn't put two and two together when Sasha talked of how much he was looking forward to the game's release. Isabella said how dangerous it was and that it would never be allowed. Even then it didn't raise any immediate alarm in my mind."

"Then get him off it!" the Hydra ordered "before it's too late."

"He is, thankfully and now an activist with his sister. They're campaigning to get it banned."

199

"Then they are in mortal danger too Gina. The mass brainwashing of the people is paramount to the Pindar's plans. He will kill them," the sugar-coated version of a warning wasn't in the Hydra's repertoire.

Gina became panicked and stood to leave. She desperately wanted to get home to protect them. Ava read her mind.

"That is not the way Gina," Ava turned to Callum, her voice urgent and commanding. "Send Yuri to bring them to the Moscow safe house where we can protect them. The farmhouse is a fortress with an arsenal of weapons."

"My thoughts entirely Ava and they couldn't be in safer hands than Yuri's. It's his day job and there's no field agent better. I'll get on to it as soon as this meeting is over."

Callum looked confident and Gina smiled gratefully in response. She would never forgive herself if anything happened to them. Callum continued.

"December 21st is the winter solstice and the ritual meeting of the Council of Thirteen. It's a 'must attend' Gina, and less than a week away. If you fail to turn up and go into hiding, he would not know that you have secured your position. You need to be there to declare your hand, to tell him that you have left plans to trash the bank and his investments if anything happens to you, or your family."

"Callum is right Gina," the Hydra added. "You must go, _we_ must go and pull the rug from under the Pindar. Together we are twice as strong. Besides, we need to focus on the Pindar's weaknesses. How we take him down."

"How we take the Pindar down?" Kayla was impressed with the Hydra's positivity. "Now you have my full attention Hydie Papandreou!" Kayla was a girl who was always up for a fight.

The Hydra gave them a wry smile, "This might just be a bridge too far for Angels, because it's gloves off and going to get messy. Maybe you just won't have the stomach for it," she challenged.

"Wasn't it you who said that these are desperate times?" Emanuel said reassuringly. "Please continue."

She opened her Gucci handbag and produced a memory stick and handed it to Emanuel.

"On that stick, is a detailed breakdown of the Pindar's organisation, from businessmen and politicians to royal families and the Vatican. There are names and addresses, roles and responsibilities, weaknesses and strengths of all involved. It contains details of every critical asset and the numbers of most all the Illuminati's bank accounts. But that is for you to assimilate later," it was an impressive piece of espionage and Hydie Papandreou an impressive woman.

"You have clearly done your homework Hydie," Emanuel began, "so what is it that you want from us? You seem to have matters pretty much in hand."

"Resources," she replied in matter of fact manner. "To take the Pindar down is bigger than my organisation; bigger than ours combined, in all probability, but my plan has contingency built in."

"Go on, we are fascinated."

"Simplistically, we join together to dismantle his empire. Having been at the top of the Illuminati for several years, I know exactly how his business runs. I know who he depends on and who his enemies are. We recruit his enemies and incentivise them to assist in destabilising his pyramid of power. That is the *contingency* that I was talking about, just in case we get stretched too thin. All levels of the pyramid have to be hit simultaneously for the plan to work, including the emptying of his bank accounts through a cyber-attack."

The Hydra's voice was edging towards the fanatical. She was clearly becoming caught up in the moment, but her gaze was level and her mind clear. She continued.

"The cyber-attack is where your organisation comes into the plan. Your science and resources are significantly superior to ours and the emptying of the Pindar's banks is pivotal to the success of the coup. If it goes wrong and he can release money, then the Pindar will be able to buy himself out of trouble and we will suffer his wrath at our peril."

Hydie Papandreou paused to assess the response of her audience. It was positive, but then she hadn't got to the unpalatable part of the plan.

"Of course, there will bloodshed. Key players will need to be dealt with, but these aren't Sunday school teachers. They are despots in their own right."

"Desperate times indeed, "Emanuel looked at his colleagues and shook his big head at the inevitability of it. "Murder does not sit well with our kind Hydie, but neither does the destruction of mankind. We too fight for what we believe in, as you already know."

The Hydra already did. She had lost her husband, Demitri and her son, Anaxis to their beliefs; Demitri to Ava Kaplinski and Anaxis to the Matriarch, Maelströminha. Settling that score, was for another day. For now they were safe, but it would not always be that way.

"I know," she said simply, holding her own counsel about her own personal loss. "I only want you to target one person. Mohammed Akhbar."

"Akhbar' why so?"

"Because he is already being seen by the Arab factions as the Mahdi. The prophesied redeemer of Islam, who it is said will rule for five, seven, nine, or nineteen years before the Day of Judgment and rid the world of evil. With him alive, the movement towards a holy war will become unstoppable, even without the Pindar and his Illuminati. A holy war would provide a foothold for the Pindar's return, so that must not be allowed to happen," the Hydra said it as if was a command.

"I can put a small squad together for that Emanuel, and go in by stealth," Callum offered. "We have eyes in the air, satellites and reconnaissance aircraft. It won't be hard to track him down in the desert, then go in at night."

Callum's boyish smile was evidence that he thrived on skirmishes such as this. Desert warfare was his specialty and passion. Callum was a Major in the Parachute Regiment, before being selected as strategic and tactical advisor to the Prime Minister. He was consulted in all matters pertaining to terrorism and arms escalation, particularly in the Middle East.

"Who is available to go in with you," Emanuel asked, not surprised by Callum's enthusiasm.

"Whoever I want," he stated confidently. Nothing is more important than this. I would keep it small though. Just Ralph Robinson, Mike Jackson, Red Jake and his squad of four. These are all battle hardened veterans. I would pit them against a small army with surprise on our side."

"A bold statement Callum, particularly as the Mullah will be there with him. You would be wise not to underestimate him," the Hydra warned.

"The 'un-killable man'," Callum conceded. "We have come close to taking him on several occasions and each time he has simply melted into the desert. No Hydie, we don't underestimate him. But even a cat only has nine lives, and the Mullah will run out of luck soon."

"Well, Hydie, you have given us much to think on," Emanuel concluded. "Now we need to take a look at that memory stick and see the detail behind your plan, but I don't doubt that it holds together. Could we reconvene here tomorrow?"

"Certainly, I had anticipated that you would need some time alone to consult. At what time?"

"Ten o'clock would be ideal, if you could make that?" The Hydra nodded and Emanuel continued tentatively. "Excellent. Would it be alright with you, if that meeting was just between you, me and Maelströminha?"

Hydie Papandreou wasn't expecting that and was visibly disturbed. They had been arch enemies across millennia and both had lost loved ones to the other side. Hydie had always held Maelströminha personally accountable for her son's death. It wasn't that way though. Several hundred years ago, Anaxis was on nefarious activities associated with the tyrants of that time. These tyrants enjoyed the protection of the Shadow organisation in return for a percentage of their profits. Maelströminha had sent a squad in to neutralise those particularly associated with drugs and prostitution. Anaxis was unfortunately collateral damage in that campaign. Hydie Papandreou never knew that.

The Hydra, considered Emanuel's request. There would be more favourable times to address issues of the past, she decided.

"Of course," the Hydra said with a perfectly false smile, "I shall look forward to meeting her."

Chapter 21

It had been three weeks since Isabella's breakthrough. At first the World Health Organisation hadn't taken her seriously. "Another conspiracy theory," they had said, although they were still avidly pursuing getting the game banned on legal grounds. It wasn't until she stumbled across one of their lawyers who took a particular interest that her luck changed. Or so she thought. She had taken photographs of her mother's computer screen at the bank giving her full details of the Mèdici acquisitions portfolio, which included all details and movements on the LuminaGames account. That lawyer, Daniel Gray, saw enough in it to warrant coming to Milan with a man called Brad Harper, from the CIA. Isabella was under strict instructions not to mention it to her mother or brother, and was extremely excited about the whole thing, particularly so about her part in initiating the global banning of the insidious Dream App.

It was a last minute arrangement. Daniel Gray had called earlier that morning to say that he and Harper had arrived unexpectedly early, and could they meet around lunchtime that day. Isabella was in lessons at the time and had agreed midday at Luigi's bar, where she had met with Lucia at the beginning of their quest. It seemed appropriate. In her excitement Isabella had got there far too early, but she simply couldn't wait. The time was passing too slowly though and she was drowning in Coca-Cola.

She went to the bathroom and looked at herself in the mirror as she brushed her long, blonde hair. She felt inappropriately dressed for a business meeting, faded blue jeans, white vest and no bra. She looked too young to be taken seriously, she thought and put on lipstick and eye shadow to make her appear older.

"And now I look like a Lolita," she said to herself disdainfully, snapping her purse shut.

At last two men entered the dimly lit bar from the sunny street. They looked unseeingly into the gloom while there eyes slowly adjusted to the light. Isabella stood and called them over to her booth.

"Hello, I'm Isabella Mèdici," she said warmly, offering her hand.

"My pleasure Ma'am," the short one of the two replied as he shook it. "My name's Daniel Gray. We spoke on the phone, and this is Brad Harper."

Daniel Gray was a small, Middle-aged, fastidiously dressed American. He was anything but significant, a balding man with horn-rimmed glasses that seemed to magnify his eyes much more than whatever he was looking at. His smile was engaging though. The other American, Brad Harper, was entirely different. He was tall, in his early forties, strong looking and ruggedly handsome. His good teeth showed when he smiled but his eyes were cold.

"He's every inch a CIA man for sure," Isabella surmised as he shook her hand, but he held it just a little too long to be comfortable. Isabella was glad to withdraw it.

"Please sit," she offered and signalled the waiter.

"An Americana for me," Gray said.

"Make mine a large beer," Harper added without looking at the waiter.

"A drinker *and* rude," Isabella noted disapprovingly, "and it's still early."

She let it drop. They passed small talk about how hot it was, how congested, the lousy food in Italy and how nobody spoke English. He showed a typical foreigner's lack of appreciation. At last Gray came to the point.

"You've really put the cat amongst the pigeons Miss Mèdici. The CIA are reopening the Rossi and Williams case, in light of the question mark hanging over the Mèdici investments you've sent over. That's quite a goddam shopping list. It's what you might want if you were looking at starting a small war."

"Or a big one," Harper added. "If you rolled all that potential into one organisation, you could start World War Three."

"I thought we were here to talk about LuminaGames?" Isabella suddenly looked panicked. "You don't for one minute think that my mother is an arms dealer, do you?"

Daniel Gray was quick to reassure.

"No, not at all. She might be guilty of making some bad decisions is all, but we aren't looking at criminalising her," his eyes seemed to have grown to the size of saucers and Isabella was rapidly feeling out of her depth.

"Then why are you here then?" she asked, not too sure that she actually wanted to know the truth.

"To protect you," Harper said in matter of fact manner. "If these acquisitions are Illuminati owned, then they'll need to secure the situation before things get outta hand, you having gone public an' all. They'll need to silence you, that's for sure."

"Kill me, you mean?" Brad Harper didn't answer and that spoke volumes.

Isabella looked like a frightened rabbit.

"It's a whole heap worse," Harper added, his steely eyes drilling into Isabella's." You're heading up a movement to ban the Dream App. That's Illuminati owned too, so you're hitting their bank balance by over a billion Dollars a year. They ain't gonna have that young lady."

Isabella didn't like Harper's patronising manner, but let it go for now. It was something that she would nip in the bud later though, she decided.

"So what do we do? We can't just let them destroy the lives of all those young people without doing anything," Isabella implored.

"You ain't doing nothing young lady. You've gotta hole up somewhere safe and let us handle this. Your job will be to turn evidence against the Illuminati when it's all over an' make sure those killers hang."

"Hole up, I mean hide where? I'm not one for running away and I'll finish what I have started," Isabella's chin was jutted out in defiance.

It was getting off to a bad start, Daniel Gray could tell. He took over from Harper, giving him the full power of his bug-eyed, disapproving stare.

"My apologies Miss Mèdici, we're not being very eloquent here. Don't get us wrong, we need your input on this, big time. The work that you and your brother have done to raise the international profile of this despicable product, is commendable and we want you to continue," Isabella sat a little less stiffly in her chair at those encouraging words. "Thing is we already know someone's got a contract out on you and your brother. That's not saying it's the Illuminati, but Brad got a tip off. Might just be a Mob thing."

"The Mob is after me, the Mafia?" Isabella was horrified.

"This damn place is Italy ain't it? That's a Mafia country for sure," Harper added and got another disapproving stare from Gray that said 'shut up and leave this to me'.

"Someone is Miss Mèdici. We just gotta get you off the streets for a spell until we've got a handle on this," Gray's manner was reassuring. "Sometimes you just gotta lie low to make sure you can fight another day."

Isabella's mind was going at a hundred miles an hour. She couldn't just disappear, her mother would freak out. Then there was her mother's involvement in the acquisitions. She could end up in gaol and the Mèdici bank left in ruins. She was wishing now that she'd had it out with her mother in the beginning, but now it had gone too far for that.

"What about Sasha, he will be in danger too?" Isabella was far more concerned about him than herself. "You have to protect him."

"Don't worry; we've got that in hand. He's at your house right now and we've got a couple of guys watching over him there. We'll get you to a safe place first and then pick him up and whatever stuff you're gonna need for the next few weeks," Gray said it as if going with them was already agreed.

"I'll call Sasha and let him know what's happening," Isabella said, picking up her mobile.

"No! Don't do that," Harper said a little too hastily. "I mean your calls are probably being listened to. Don't use that mobile again. We'll pick one up at the supermarket with an unregistered SIM."

Isabella put her mobile down on the table quickly and pushed it away from her as if it was about to explode.

"Did anyone know you were coming here or anyone see you come in?" Harper asked, his eyes searching hers for the sign of any lies.

"No. I mean I don't think so. I didn't..."

Isabella was disorientated. It was all too much to take in and, unusually for her, she was feeling confused and dull witted.

"Is there a back way out?" Gray asked.

"You have to go out through the carpark," Isabella slurred, "its over there," she pointed.

Gray dropped a handful of notes on the table next to Isabella's mobile and purse. He stood, taking Isabella's arm while Harper took the other. They walked casually out through the bar into the carpark, supporting Isabella between them such that her feet barely touched the floor.

Chapter 22

Hydie Papandreou's limousine pulled up outside the Angelos Associates' entrance at precisely one minute before ten in the morning.

"Stay here," she said to the driver through the privacy hatch as she got out, "and be ready to leave at a moment's notice," caution being the better part of valour.

Hydie was dressed in exactly the same way as the day before, except that this time her business suit was charcoal grey. She took a breath and then walked briskly and confidently up the steps to where men were working on the installation of a new steel roller door. As she entered, she noted there were extra security guards in the lobby. Hydie wondered if they were there to keep her out, or to keep her in.

Emanuel was at the security desk making sure that there were no mistakes and that the guards were ready to let Hydie Papandreou in, without a recurrence of yesterday's lock-down. He sensed her arrival and greeted her with his usual affable smile.

"Ah, a woman who respects time," Emanuel said lightly offering his hand. It was meant as a compliment and taken that way. They shook hands. "How refreshing and, alas, not always the case in my experience. Shall we go straight up?" the question was rhetorical.

They took the lift to the eleventh in silence. Both had there own thoughts to consider. The Hydra's were mostly around survival. With the exception of the Pindar, Maelströminha was the only person on the planet that she was afraid of. Her given powers were biblical, but fortunately she was a pacifist by nature and only moved to violence by necessity. The Hydra was the opposite. She hoped that the difference might give her the upper hand, if the meeting went badly. The lift doors opened and they stepped out. Emanuel called over to Kristina.

"Would you bring coffee to the Crystalita room in ten minutes please?" Kristina smiled and nodded her acknowledgement.

When they entered the meeting room, a woman was already sat at the round table facing them. She stood in welcome. The Hydra was surprised at how petite she was. In her mind's eye, she had pictured Maelströminha as being Amazonian in stature. This woman was probably only five feet six inches tall with a slim, athletic build. Slightly boyish perhaps, but still looked every inch a woman. She had long black, lustrous hair, a baby face and astonishingly big, bright blue eyes. Striking looks the Hydra had to concede, and not a hint of animosity or danger about her manner. The woman was a pacifist by nature, she knew that but she wasn't fooled. Maelströminha had been known to decimate whole legions with her destructive powers in the past, when pushed to the limit.

"Hello, I'm May," she said with an air of unfeigned innocence, offering her hand and her smile.

Maelströminha seldom referred to herself by her diminutive name and this gesture was meant as an offer of friendship.

Despite herself, the Hydra reciprocated shaking May's hand.

"Hydie. It's a pleasure and long overdue perhaps," but there was no cordial smile.

"Please sit with me," May said taking her seat.

The other two were set so that they formed a sociable triangle, not two facing one. Emanuel took the role of chairman and set the scene.

"So Hydie, we spent several hours yesterday reviewing the data that you left with us. Quite frankly, we were astonished at the level of detail that you have managed to put together. We have no doubt that the Pindar's organisation could be neutralised, at least temporarily, using this strategy," Emanuel spread his big hands on the table in that stereotypical way of his. "There are two things that concern us though."

"Go on," the Hydra prompted. But she knew just what those concerns would be.

"Ethics and logistics," he said simply.

"You mean that you don't have the stomach for it," the Hydra accused, "but you would have us do it for you."

"It's not like that Hydie," May said. Her voice was soft and lyrical, which completely matched her appearance. "We have always done what is necessary, but have also stuck to our principles. Your plan is faultless but more ruthless than it needs to be. As it stands, too many innocent people will die as collateral damage and that is where we have difficulties. So we would like to agree a more *surgical* approach in some circumstances. Are you open to that?"

There was a sadness in May's eyes that reflected how uncomfortable she was with wholesale murder, no matter how good the cause. For her part, Hydie Papandreou was relieved that her adversary's misgivings were only to do with limiting the impact on the innocent, and not about the total elimination of the Illuminati brotherhood.

211

"I would concede to that, just so long that it doesn't compromise the efficient elimination of the specified targets. "

A fleeting smile escaped Hydie's mouth at this modest concession but she quickly reverted to her implacable self.

"I imagine you have drafted those alternative plans?" she countered.

"We do indeed and have them here to go through with you later," May said, pushing a copy of the memory stick across the table to her. "But that is just minor detail. Our biggest concern is logistical. For the mission to be a success, the level of coordination, collaboration and trust between us must be absolutely faultless. This could be a tall order for two conflicting organisations such as ours that have been at war for thousands of years; too tall an order perhaps. What are your thoughts on that Hydie?"

In the moments it took for Hydie Papandreou to compose her reply, May took the time to appraise her lifelong opponent. They had never met although May had seen her in the mirrors of time. Physically she was a fine specimen of a woman. May could see beyond the consummate business woman in her expensive suit and up-do. Dressed to please a man, she would be a rare beauty indeed. Slim, elegant, aloof and confident. But there was another side to her, typical of her species. There was no inner beauty. This was a hard and calculating woman, a risk taker. There was avarice about her. Hydie Papandreou was by nature and necessity, a dangerously powerful and deadly adversary.

"My thoughts?" she laughed, but there was no humour in it. "Give me an alternative and I will take it. But there is none and well we all know it. We have to make this work. It is in the interest of every Shadow, every Angel and all of mankind. If the Pindar succeeds in his plan then it is the end of us and the end of the world as we know it. Eventually it would lead to the end of all humanity."

May stood and walked over to the old ornate mirror that commanded the wall behind the sofa. She ran her fingers gently over the beautifully carved cherubs that adorned the gilt frame, as if it was a caress.

"I know that you are familiar with these Hydie, as your people have stolen or destroyed sixty of them. This is one of the precious forty remaining portals that we brought with us from Angelos, 5,000 years ago," it was a gentle rebuke. "What I don't know is how adept you are at using them?" May cocked a well-groomed brow by means of posing the question.

"They are somewhat beyond our science and capacity, but we have mastered simple movement through space," it was much as May had thought. The Shadows had not divined the mirrors full secrets.

"Just tele-transportation then?" May confirmed. "Then you haven't actually seen 'the end of the world as we know it'. Let me show you both what is likely to happen if we fail to unite as one against the Pindar and depose him. What you are going to see is only one of the possible futures. In fact we never know," she conceded, "but this is the one that occurs nine times out of ten when I consult the portal for a glimpse into the future.

May placed her hand on the mirror. They could hear a faint humming as the portal vibrated. The image of their own reflections, sat at the round table, receded and was replaced by something that resembled a forest fire at night. It was hard to say though, as there was dense smoke everywhere.

"This is Epping forest, just north of London, days after the nuclear holocaust." May said and swept her hands over the face of the mirror as if swiping to a new page on a tablet.

Again it was difficult to see through the smoke and blackness, but it looked like a scene after the blitz.

"This is London. Nothing survived here in fact nothing survived in Britain. After the warheads struck in London, Southampton, Cardiff, Dublin, Cambridge, Nottingham, Liverpool, Leeds,

Newcastle and Glasgow, the blasts and firestorms that followed consumed everything."

May swiped her small hands across the glassy surface of the portal once again. Now they were looking at the Earth as if from space. The whole of the northern hemisphere was swathed in a black shroud.

"This is three years later. It wasn't just Britain that suffered the holocaust. The Pindar set all the nations in the northern hemisphere with nuclear capability, against each other. Russia and America had a pact but they were hit by other powers, albeit to a lesser degree. Pakistan, India, Israel and Iran suffered the same fate as Britain. There is nothing left."

May's audience was too engrossed in what they were seeing to notice the tears of grief that were streaming down her face.

"300 nuclear warheads were detonated, sending 150 million tons of dense black, radioactive carbon smoke into the stratosphere, blocking out the sun. The northern hemisphere descended into eternal darkness and a nuclear winter followed with temperatures plummeting to lower than that of the ice age, 18,000 years ago."

May paused and looked at the effect that the images had on them. Emanuel had his elbows on the desk. His big hands were clenched into a ball with his chin resting on them. His face had gone as white as his hair. Even the Hydra looked moved, and compassion wasn't a strong emotion for the Shadows. May continued.

"Here, the Earth is cooling at an alarming rate, affecting evaporation. Global rainfall has almost halved and nightly killing frosts are preventing anything being grown north of the equator. Famine is killing many of those who survived the initial blasts and radiation poisoning, killing many more. The ozone layer has thinned by more than 50%, so those who have survived in the Southern Hemisphere, cannot go outside much in the day. Electromagnetic pulses from the nuclear explosions have wiped out much of modern technology, so industry has failed, along with infrastructure, agriculture and medicine. The Americans and Russians that survived the war, have populated South America and South Africa. They now administer their meagre control through the Pindar. It is truly Armageddon," May's voice was faltering and at last her audience could see how devastated May was. She had to dig deep to continue.

"Humanity has reverted to tribalism and turned to God for an answer, and the God that they have chosen is Satan. The Middle East was the initial battlefield and a dreadful land based war was staged there, Arab against America and her allies. This quickly escalated into the Third World War and the nuclear holocaust ensued."

The image of a destroyed world in the mirror receded until they were once again looking at a reflection of themselves.

"So you see Hydie, we cannot fail. We must unite and put our differences behind us. We cannot let this be. We cannot let humanity end this way."

Chapter 23

It was eleven o'clock in the morning when Yuri Alexandrov collected his hire car from the parking lot at the Milan-Malpensa Airport. Less than 24 hours after Callum's call. He had crossed America and then flown from New York to London on a British Airways flight, all in only seven hours. Then he had travelled onwards to Milan, on an Alitalia flight, in another four including transfers. Yuri had managed to grab a few hours of fitful sleep on the journey. So apart from a little travel stiffness, he wasn't feeling too bad. Anyway, there was no question of taking a break. He needed to find Gina's kids and get them on a plane to Russia at the soonest. Yuri was just praying that he wasn't already too late.

He had chosen a Range Rover Sport for its brute power and off-road capability. If they had to make a run for it, then there was no better 4x4 to do it in. Yuri was pleasantly surprised to see that the rear windows were all tinted black, obscuring vision in. This simple optional extra had proved a lifesaver in the past against snipers and unwanted observers.

Yuri was travelling light, carrying two leather holdalls only. The smaller, contained two changes of clothes and his washing kit. The second was considerably larger and contained a small arsenal of light weapons. Yuri enjoyed diplomatic status and the privileges that went with it. As long as his locked baggage was kept in the hold, he could travel freely.

Yuri opened the boot, tossed the bags in and took off his jacket. His powerful upper body filled his shirt, emphasising his muscular build. He had good arms and shoulders with a lean waist. Yuri was a man who worked out and worked out hard. He was a little less than six feet tall but looked shorter because of his stockiness. He had that typical Russian square face, rugged, but good looking with short-cropped blond hair and alert blue eyes.

He unlocked the padlock on the larger bag and unzipped it, took out the shoulder holster and strapped it on. His preference for a hand arm was a Walther P99, the Hi-Power version. Although it was a little heavier, it used the .40 calibre Smith & Wesson bullets with a capacity of twelve instead of the standard ten. Two extra bullets, in a shootout, could make all the difference and often had. Yuri took the gun and pointed it to the floor. He ejected the magazine, then pulled the slide back and went through the pistol safety check. It was standard practice for a trained man who trusted his life to 26 oz. of metal. He loaded three magazines with the Smith & Wesson bullets, inserted one in the gun and clipped the other two to his holster belt. Yuri was right handed. He rolled his trouser leg up to his knee on that side and took the hunting knife and sheath from the bag. He located the latex retaining band over the knife's pommel and strapped it to his calf, handle downwards, for quick and easy deployment. There were times when the sound of a gunshot was unacceptable and a silent dispatch necessary. Yuri settled the rolled up trouser leg, put on his jacket then zipped the bag shut. He was armed and ready.

"But ready for what?" he wondered.

His meticulous preparation was habitual and only varied according to information. For this mission however he had none, other than two names and address.

Yuri settled himself in the driver seat and started the big V-8 engine. It rumbled pleasingly as he set the Sat Nav to the address that he had for Castello di Mèdici. Next, he set the Bluetooth to his mobile and made a call. It was to Ava, his wife. The call connected almost immediately.

"Yuri?" the voice sounded anxious.

"Yes honey. I'm at Malpensa and leaving now," Yuri shifted into reverse and pulled out of the parking bay. "I want you to do something for me Ava."

"Thank God, I was getting worried about you. You didn't call," it was unlike Ava to be needy. She put it down to her *condition*. "Yes, what do you need?"

"Put a trace out on both the kid's mobiles and find out where they are. We don't know who's listening in, so don't call under any circumstances. I'm heading for the Castello as best guess, but might change that according to your search," then, as an afterthought. "Oh, and arrange a chartered jet on constant standby. I don't know what to expect yet, and we might need to get out of Italy fast."

"Will do Yuri," Ava said wistfully. "God I miss you; and baby misses you too," she added shyly. "It seems so long and you really turn me on when you talk masterfully like that," Ava was physically aching for him.

"Save it for when I get back honey," he said. But he knew Ava well enough to be sure that she would already be touching herself.

"You know I can't," she teased. Then, "Baby kicked today by the way. I think he's going to be a footballer."

"Oh, my God. Really? That's amazing! *She* might be playing for the girls' side then," he taunted.

"No Yuri, it will be a boy, just like May told me it would be," there was a tremor in Ava's voice.

"What's the matter darling?" Yuri was suddenly concerned.

"Nothing, it's just me being silly," she lied.

"What's the matter Ava?" Yuri said firmly.

"He's going to need a daddy. Make sure you come home safely to us," Yuri could hear her crying softly.

"Now stop this nonsense. I'll be home before you know it. Now get on with my shopping list," he knew that Ava was best kept busy, her pregnancy had changed everything.

"OK, will do. Love you Yuri,"

"Love you too darling. Bye," he cut the call.

Castello di Mèdici was just outside Lenta, in the Province of Vercelli. The Sat Nav estimated journey time was only 45 minutes. Even allowing for traffic, Yuri was sure that he would be there by midday.

He wasn't counting on Sasha or Isabella being there though, as it was Tuesday and term-time. It was a start though, until Ava had a fix on them through their mobile phones. As if preordained, his mobile rang. It was Ava.

"Yuri, it's me. I've got them," Ava said excitedly.

"Good girl! So where are they?"

"Sasha is at home at the Castello and Isabella's phone has been stationary for the last ten minutes, just a few hundred metres south of the University of Milan. There's a main crossroads there with bars and restaurants. It's one of those, we can't tell which though."

"OK, good work honey. Send me a picture of her so I can spot her in a crowd and keep tracking that phone, she might have moved on by the time I get there."

"Will do. Stay safe baby," Ava closed the call.

Forty minutes later, Yuri turned into the drive that wound its way up through the vineyards to the Castello. It took another five before he was walking up the stairs to the orange and red sculpted building that was Castello di Mèdici. The doors were solid oak and black with age, with no visible sign of a bell push or door knocker. Yuri guessed that they would be at least four inches thick and to rap on them with his knuckles would make about as much noise inside as beating a drum with a feather. Then he noticed an iron bar with a pull handle that ran up the door frame and disappeared into the soffit above. He gave it a tug and a bell chimed inside loud enough for him to hear.

"Must be some bell," he though idly.

Shortly afterwards, the huge door creaked open and Yuri found himself face to face with a short round, black woman with a beaming smile.

"I'm Yuri, you must be Asmina," Yuri said returning her smile. He had been briefed.

"No, that be the skinny white girl. Works in the kitchen," Asmina replied haughtily with her hands on her hips.

"I'm sorry but I thought..."

Asmina clapped her hands and howled with laughter at his predicament. Everything about her seemed to shake.

"You some kinda detective? 'Course I'm Asmina, ain't no other black woman workin' here," she said. "Anyhow I been expectin' you."

"Gina called then?" he was puzzled. She was not supposed to contact the house or mobiles in case it alerted their enemy.

"Nobody call. Sometimes a woman feel these things is all," Asmina said with authority and just a little smugness.

She led him to the anteroom and settled him there.

"Sasha's in his room. Sit yourself down an' I'll bring the boy," she left him with another beaming smile.

The room was quaint, set out in the old style with leather chairs and settees. There was even a chaise longue of the sort that a psychoanalyst might use. It clearly served as a formal waiting room for unexpected guests or dignitaries. The walls and shelves were crammed full of interesting artefacts to help the guests pass the time. These ranged from paintings and statues to family portraits and photographs, books and antiques. There was a corner cabinet full of trophies and pictures in frames that caught Yuri's attention. He crossed over to it.

"It appears that our Gina is a world renowned swords woman," he observed.

There were trophies and photographs dating back as far as 25 years, from her school days until recent years. They were winners' trophies and international ones at that. Not even one was a runner up. The last trophy was dated June 2015. Yuri wondered why she had quit when she was clearly still competing at the very top level of her sport. Yuri had read her file and couldn't help but conclude that it had something to do with her husband's death and the Illuminati. Asmina arrived with a handsome youth, breaking Yuri's reveries.

"You wanted to see me," he said with a concerned expression on his face. "Is this something to do with my mother?"

"Yes, in part. But she is alright so don't be alarmed. We need to talk about some serious matters," Yuri's tone was calm as he shook Sasha's hand. He didn't want to set hares running prematurely.

"I be leavin' you to it," Asmina said, dismissing herself.

"No, Asmina, please stay. Gina wanted you to hear it all too," he pointed to the lounge chairs for them to sit.

"We have a situation," he began directing the conversation at Sasha. "It would appear that your late father had dealings with a very dangerous and secret society. Those dealings involved procurements at the Mèdici bank, on their behalf. Since his unfortunate death, your mother has been held responsible for the completion of his contract."

"The Illuminati," Sasha said simply. "You are talking about the Illuminati aren't you?"

"Yes, but how do you know that?" Yuri wasn't expecting that.

"Issie was doing some, well how can I say, 'research' at the bank on Mum's computer. That's all," Sasha wasn't too sure about saying anything more.

"Listen Sasha, I'm not the police, nor here to judge you. My job is to get you and Isabella safely out of Italy." The colour drained out of Sasha's face. "Now, if you know anything, then you had better level with me. I don't want any surprises."

Now Yuri had Sasha's full attention.

"Have you heard of the Dream App?," he asked.

"I should think that everybody in the civilised world has. It's gone viral, hasn't it?"

"Yes, but its bad news. It changes you. I've been there and it takes over your whole life to the exclusion of everything. I got out, but only because Issie helped me. Most don't make it and it consumes them. Issie, I mean we, have been looking into getting it banned but the company, LuminaGames, has spun a web of secrecy around itself. The only lead we found ended at the Mèdici bank."

"So Isabella did a little espionage at the bank then? What did she find?" Yuri couldn't help but admire their commitment and good intentions.

"She found billions of Dollars of acquisitions relating to weapons and the media. One of the media acquisitions was LuminaGames. All of these transactions were done by our parents, mother mostly, and all are at least 51% owned by the Mèdici bank. Mother owns the bank," he reinforced. "She therefore owns LuminaGames, the company that we are campaigning to close."

"That's how I see it too, but I sense there is more," Yuri prompted.

"There is. Isabella searched through news clips around the time of the acquisition. Apparently LuminaGames, started life as UniGames and was fast becoming an industry leader, through some great innovations. Then, on 21st December 2016, the owners of UniGames were found murdered in their apartment. Rumours followed of it being an Illuminati sacrificial killing, celebrating the winter solstice," Sasha was clearly passionate about the episode, and continued with equal enthusiasm. "Then, LuminaGames stepped in as principal creditor. They took over, settling the outstanding debt and then rebranded the company as part of theirs. After that the Mèdici bank, a.k.a. Mother, acquired LuminaGames. So what does that make her?" Sasha challenged.

"A victim, just like you and your sister," Yuri's tone was disdainful.

Sasha was surprised, expecting some form of recognition for their covert findings, not his disapproval

"And you didn't think to ask your mother about it first?" Yuri continued.

"Well, no. It was quite clear from the accounts," Sasha defended.

"Clear enough for you both to play the parts of judge, jury and executioner?"

Sasha didn't answer that. He was wise enough to sense that there was more to this than both he and Isabella knew, and to just shut up and listen.

"Why are we all victims then?" he asked humbly.

"Your deduction that the Mèdici acquisitions are Illuminati inspired is correct Sasha. You are probably also right about the murders of the UniGames owners being Illuminati linked too. But that's where it ends. Your Mother had no choice but to make these acquisitions. If she had refused, they would have killed her along with you and your sister in all probability."

Sasha looked at Asmina for confirmation and she nodded. Her expression was grave.

"Bibi tell me this, an' I seen it in the cards too," Asmina said proudly.

"Is that why Mum's gone away? Is she in hiding?" Sasha asked Yuri, worried now and feeling guilty about their hasty assumptions.

"No Sasha, she's learning how to fight," then added, "for all of you."

Sasha reflected on that for a moment. His guilt over misjudging his mother and not consulting her was clear and apparent. He was close to tears.

"Why are Isabella and me in danger then, if this is Illuminati business?" Sasha asked. "We are not involved."

"Two reasons. Firstly for revenge and completeness," Yuri began. "The Illuminati doesn't tolerate disobedience, ever. Your family would be made an example of to the other Illuminati families. Fear rules. Secondly, you are involved. You were from the moment you decided to take a stance against the commercialisation of the Dream App. You have threatened their income to the tune of billions of Dollars by campaigning against it. That alone has already made you a target for elimination."

"Elimination?" Sasha had a sudden feeling of dread, "Where is Isabella? We have to call her, now."

Sasha fumbled in his pocket for his mobile. Yuri placed his hand firmly on Sasha's forearm.

"Easy Sasha, that's not the way. They probably have your phones bugged. If you call her and warn her, it might panic them into doing something prematurely. We have a trace on her phone. Right now she's in one of the bars, just south of the university."

"That'll be Luigi's, I know it. I can take you there," Sasha stood, ready to go.

"Right, Sasha. You've got five minutes to pack essentials for you and Isabella, no more. Now go!"

Yuri turned to Asmina to explain where he was going to take them and was shocked at what he saw. She seemed to be having some kind of a fit. Her eyes had rolled back, so that all he could see was the bulging whites of them. She was staring sightlessly into space. Deep guttural sounds were coming from her chest such that Yuri thought she was dying.

"Asmina! Asmina!" Yuri called out to her as he took her firmly by the shoulders, shaking her.

"Nana, what's the matter?" Sasha had come quickly to her side. "Nana!" he hadn't called her by that name since he was a child.

Suddenly Asmina's eyes flicked open and she was back from wherever she had been. Tears of relief began to flow down Sasha's face.

"Issie's not there no more in that bar. She gone. She someplace else. Someplace dark an' she scared," Asmina's face was twisted by the terror that she was feeling for Isabella. "You find her Mr Yuri, you find my baby now!"

"She sees things," Sasha explained lamely, "or thinks she does. Mum believes it though."

"Hush your mouth boy," Asmina was already fully recovered. "I see things. I don't *think* I sees, I sees. Look for water Mr Yuri, my baby gonna be close to water. She can hear it an' smell it. An' rats, there's rats everywhere. Bitin' rats an a big wheel that don't turn. Find her Mr Yuri, find my baby."

Chapter 24

Yuri set the Sat Nav despite Sasha professing to know the best way into Milan. It wasn't a case of lack of trust, navigation aids give you alternatives; Sometimes lifesaving alternatives. Yuri left the Mèdici drive with light wheel spin and raced through the vineyard down to the main road. Irate farmers shouted out and waved their arms disapprovingly at the apparent senselessness of it. From the elevated advantage of the hill, Yuri had a good view of the main road below. He could see that it was clear and slewed into it at a pace, tyres screaming disapprovingly. Sasha, let off a whoop at the madness of it as Yuri floored the accelerator on the straight. It was a ninety minute drive, with traffic, to the centre of Milan. Every minute saved, could make the difference between finding Isabella or not. Asmina's performance at the Castello had spooked him. He didn't really believe her, but for some strange reason he sensed that there was something wrong. Yuri called Ava for reassurance.

"Ava, its Yuri. What's the latest on Isabella's position?"

"She hasn't moved, she's still in one of those bars at the crossroads. She must be having a long lunch with friends."

"I hope so, I really do," his voice was tense and Ava picked up on it.

"What's the matter Yuri, what's happened?"

"Oh it's nothing. Asmina freaked me out, that's all. She had some kind of a premonition, but I thought she was having a heart attack. Sasha says she thinks she sees things. It's just Mumbo-jumbo, but it was scary to watch," it sounded even more ridiculous to Yuri after saying it out loud. He wasn't prepared for Ava's response.

"She does see things Yuri, what did she say?" There was urgency in Ava's voice.

"Not you too Ava, it's nonsense."

"It was Asmina who somehow managed to contact Leonardo through the spirits, and started this whole thing off. Don't just dismiss her Yuri," she knew that he was something of a sceptic when it came to the occult. "What did she say?"

"That Isabella has gone already, no longer at the bar. That she's in some kind of rat-infested place that's dark and she's scared. Oh, and she's near water and something about a wheel that doesn't turn," Yuri laughed, almost nervously. "Just like I said, nonsense, the woman is batshit crazy. Isabella is sat with friends in Luigi's bar, in Milan."

"I expect you are right Yuri. I'm going to have a think about what she said anyway and take a look at a map. Stay safe lover," Ava left the call feeling really uneasy.

Yuri was feeling more positive though. Isabella's mobile was still active at Luigi's and they were less than an hour away now. It was looking good. Something else was on his mind though. There was a black Audi behind them in the distance keeping pace with them. Sasha noticed that Yuri was paying noticeably more attention to his mirror.

"Are we being followed?" he asked, craning his neck to look behind.

"I don't know Sasha, but there's one way to find out."

Yuri adjusted the scale of the Sat Nav to get a better picture of the surrounding roads. He found what he was looking for.

"There's a right turn up ahead, do you know it?" Yuri asked.

"Yes but it doesn't go anywhere, it just brings you back onto this road a mile further up."

"That's what I thought," Yuri had a wry smile on his face. "So anybody that follows us in, and comes out on the other side, is up to no good. Right?"

"Right," Sasha confirmed, already excited about the possibility of a chase.

Yuri allowed the car behind them to catch up. He left it to the very last second, then braked hard and slewed right into the turning. When he glanced up at his rear view mirror, he saw the front of the Audi dip viciously. Tyres screamed as the driver tried to brake and take the sharp right-hander. He failed and overshot, then reversed. They gained some valuable distance while the Audi got back on track. Yuri floored the accelerator and gunned ahead, maximising the advantage. He took the next left, then left again following the narrow road down back down to the main road. Yuri glanced in the rear-view mirror. To his amazement, the Audi was right up behind them.

"Christ, what engine has he got in that?" Yuri cursed.

He was just about to turn right and re-enter the main road, when a sixteen wheel truck filled his view. Yuri slammed on the brakes and skidded to a halt. The tailgating Audi hadn't anticipated the sudden stop, and crashed into the back of them. It wasn't a major impact though. The crumpled Audi pulled back a few metres and two men got out. Yuri caught sight of them in the wing mirrors.

"Get down Sasha, they've got guns!"

Sasha did, and with haste. It had suddenly all become very real to him. Yuri slammed his foot hard down on the accelerator and the Range Rover lurched ahead into the oncoming traffic. Six gunshots cracked out and thumped into the bodywork. They went through into the sumptuous seats, soaking up the bullets' velocity. Somehow, they made it through the traffic and out onto the road towards Milan. A quick glance in his mirror confirmed that the Audi was back in pursuit. Yuri wasn't going to outrun them, he knew it, at least not on the highway.

"What do you know about the fields and tracks around here?" Yuri asked, and struck it lucky.

"I take my scrambler out here often. You can cut off left in a mile or so and go cross country, through the Parco Naturale. You'll have to find a way to cross the river Ticino though, to get to Milan. There are crossings. I can show you when we get there. Your biggest problem are the streams and ditches, they come at you out of nowhere. I just jump them. But in this, well I don't know."

"We'll get over them somehow. Off-road, I'd back this thoroughbred against the Audi any day," Yuri gave Sasha a cheeky sideways grin.

"It's left through that gate ahead," Sasha said, pointing to the almost hidden turning.

Instead of slowing down, Yuri accelerated hitting the ageing gate at over 50 mph. It shattered like matchwood, sending its remains cartwheeling into the field.

"What gate was that?" Yuri quipped, glancing sideways as they raced off through the field.

"Stay south of that tree line and head for that farmhouse," Sasha said pointing. "Just before you get there, make a hard right and follow the ditch until it runs out. The water goes underground there, for twenty metres or so, and then opens up to a ditch again. You can cross there and follow it down to the river on the north side," Sasha felt exhilarated by the speed and danger. "This is even better than the Dream App!" he shouted above the roar of the powerful V-8 engine and laughed recklessly.

Yuri smiled at the impetuousness of youth. He checked his mirror. They were outrunning the Audi, but not as fast as he had reckoned.

"It's a Quattro," he said resignedly. "Powerful *and* four-wheel drive. We need tougher terrain Sasha, something that bloody car can't do."

"Head north, up into the forest then. There are some challenging tracks up there; he'll bust a spring for sure."

Yuri swung hard to his left and sped towards the forest. Even the approach was more challenging and the Range Rover's suspension had to work hard to iron out the bumps. It was bread and butter for the four-wheel drive Rover though, and they continued to make headway on their pursuers. Yuri checked the rear view mirror again. He could see that the Audi had slowed and was now bouncing across the rough terrain.

"There's a stream ahead about five metres across. You can run the bank until you find a narrowing and a suitable bank to ramp up on and jump. If not, you'll have to head east and skirt the forest, then pick up the main road for a few miles," Yuri was impressed with Sasha's recall.

"Good work Sasha; we'll go for the jump and press our advantage. Skirting the forest and getting back on the highway only goes in their favour."

They met the stream head on, just as Sasha had said they would. Yuri slewed the Rover to the right, heading east, running the bank. They were both rapidly assessing the contours of the banks on both sides of the stream, looking for a suitable place to send two and a half tonnes of metal over it.

"There!" Sasha shouted. "That's the best you're going to get."

Yuri gave it a drive by to better assess exactly where he would take off from and land. It was worth the detour. There were boulders on the north bank that he wouldn't have seen if he had just gone for it. That would have broken an axle for sure. He judged that an angled approach would be better. It would mean an extra two metres in the air but he would be landing in soft mud. His forward momentum and four-wheel drive would do the rest. He hoped.

Yuri veered away from the stream and drove in a wide circle to come back on himself. They hit the bank at the exact spot they had identified.

"Here goes. Brace yourself for the landing Sasha," Yuri yelled just as they reached the apex.

It felt surreal. When the wheels left the ground, the engine revs peaked through lack of resistance. The bumping and bouncing ceased and time seemed to stand still. It felt totally serene in the air, up until the Rover came crashing down heavily on the other bank. Despite bracing themselves for impact, the air was driven out of them and they gasped. It was almost concussing. Yuri had the presence of mind to press his foot on the accelerator, keeping the wheels turning in the mud. The Range Rover laboriously began to find traction as it slowly snaked its way up the far bank.

The crack of two gunshots rang out, taking out the back window. Sasha turned to see the Audi stationary on the other bank. Two suited men were stood beside it with their guns levelled at them. This time he didn't need to be told to keep his head down. The heavy Rover finally broke free of the chains of the muddy bank and picked up speed. Two more futile gunshots rang out. They either missed the Rover completely, or thumped harmlessly into the seats through the missing back window.

Yuri headed directly for the safety of the forest where their pursuers couldn't hope to reach them. In his rear view mirror, he saw the Audi do the same big loop that they had done.

"They're going for it Sasha!" Callum couldn't believe it. "Crazy or what?"

They watched as the black Audi gunned hard at the south bank and took off. It disappeared from sight as it fell below their eye-line. Several seconds passed, then twenty. Then thirty...

"They didn't make it," Yuri said ruefully and swung the Rover round to head south again.

"What are you doing?" Sasha's alarm was evident. "They've got guns!" his voice was almost a scream.

"So have I," Yuri said between gritted teeth, "and some unfinished business."

He cut the engine 500 yards before the stream and coasted silently to the north bank, stopping just out of view.

"Stay here," he said commandingly and jumped out.

As he walked the final few yards, Yuri calmly drew the pistol from his shoulder holster. Sasha watched in awe. He saw Yuri extend his arm. He aimed the gun downwards into the cut of the stream. Ten shots rang out as he emptied the magazine into the Audi.

"Jesus Christ!" Sasha said out loud in disbelief.

He was horrified. It was so composed and so clinical, two lives taken in seconds, without emotion. He watched as Yuri turned around to walk back without giving the dead men a second glance. Yuri ejected the spent magazine and reloaded.

"Job done," he muttered as he replaced the gun in its holster.

"Right Sasha, now show me the quickest route to Luigi's," not a word was mentioned about the brutal killing.

It was two o'clock when they arrived at the parking lot at the back of Luigi's bar. Mercifully, the traffic in Milan had been reasonably light and they had made good time.

"That's Isabella's car!" Sasha shouted excitedly, pointing at a red Punto. "Thank God, she's still here."

"Told you so Ava," Yuri said to himself and smiled. He looked forward to teasing her about it later. "Women," he thought.

When they stepped from the hot sunshine into the cool gloominess of the bar, they had the usual customer difficulty in adapting to the change in light. The lunchtime rush was over and there were only several customers left. Isabella wasn't one of them.

"We must have just missed her," Sasha said and ran back out into the carpark, hoping to intercept her there.

"Do you speak English?" Yuri's asked the tall skinny waiter.

"Si signore. How can I help you?"

Yuri opened Ava's message on his mobile and showed the attentive waiter Isabella's photograph.

"Has this girl been in here today?"

The waiter recognised her immediately.

"Ah, si signore. You must have come for these," he reached behind the counter and produced a mobile phone and a purse. He looked pleased with himself for being able to assist. "I think the young lady was maybe a little drunk, her friends had to help her out."

"Her friends?" Yuri asked, opening the purse and emptying the contents on the bar. There were no clues, only her make-up, some money and her car keys. "What did they look like?" Yuri felt uneasiness in the pit of his stomach.

The skinny waiter stroked his goatee beard pensively.

"Two men, Americans. The smaller one was in a city suit, fat with glasses."

"And the other?" Yuri prompted.

"Bigger, stronger. He was loud and unfriendly. I'm sorry, that's all I remember. Was she your daughter?"

"No, not my daughter, his sister," Yuri said, pointing at Sasha as he entered the bar.

Yuri wondered at when it was that he had suddenly grown so old as to look like he had a sixteen year old daughter...

"Which way did they go out?" he asked.

"The same way you came in signore, from the carpark," the waiter was becoming a little concerned over the questioning and wondered where it was going.

"Have you got CCTV?" Yuri asked.

"Si, in the bar and the carpark signore," the young waiter was now deeply worried about what he was getting himself involved in.

Yuri took a €100 note from his wallet, "I want to see the video from when the men entered the bar until they left the carpark," he handed the note over, "and I want to see it now. The girl's life could depend on it."

Ten minutes later, they were sat in the back office. The waiter had shuffled the video to the point where the two Americans entered the bar. They watched as Isabella greeted them and the conversation at the table that followed. The CCTV camera couldn't have been in a better position and the picture quality was unusually good. So good, that Yuri made his own video-recording of it with his mobile. The big American looked a nasty pice of work, Yuri thought and his attitude toward the waiter spoke volumes about the man.

"I can't wait to get my hands on you," Yuri muttered under his breath, clenching his fists reflexively. Then he saw it. "Stop! Rewind a few frames.

The waiter shuffled the video backwards.

"There! Play it again. Watch the big guys hands."

The waiter pressed 'play'.

"Freeze!" Yuri ordered.

Captured in the frame, was the dapper American talking animatedly with Isabella to distract her. The other American's hand was over her glass, clearly dropping something in it.

"Rohypnol!" Yuri spat the word out in disgust. "She wasn't drunk at all."

Sasha turned to Yuri. He looked desolated and couldn't even form a sentence, his heart was bursting.

The dose must have been high, because its effect on Isabella was almost immediate. They watched in helpless rage as the men half carried Isabella out of the bar towards the carpark.

"Switch cameras. I want to see the rest," Yuri was hoping that he would get a lead from the next recording.

The waiter worked hastily and shuffled back to the moment that the three of them appeared outside. Isabella could no longer support her own head, let alone stand. It had lolled to one side and her arms were hanging loosely at her sides. The camera picked up an old couple getting into a car. There was a quick exchange of words between the two Americans, followed by a nod of agreement. The short one with glasses crossed to a white BMW and popped the boot while the other propped Isabella up against the wall. He pinned her there with the weight of his own body and draped her arms around his neck. He checked the couple leaving in the car and could see that they were looking at him curiously. The big man then held Isabella's head straight and started to kiss her passionately.

"The bastard! I'll fucking kill him," tears of rage were flowing down Sasha's face. Callum put his hand on his shoulder.

"Easy Sasha. Save your rage and stay focussed. We will find her and he will get what he deserves. One way or another, he's a dead man."

234

They continued watching the video. The couple in the car looked disapprovingly at Isabella as they drove past. The old man rolled the window down and called out something. Yuri could guess what it was. As soon as the car was out of view, the man by the BMW waved his friend over. The big American dragged Isabella to the back of the car and propped her there. They looked around quickly, then tipped her backwards until she fell into boot, swung her legs over and slammed it shut.

"No!" Sasha wailed helplessly in anguish.

Asmina's words seemed to ring out in Yuri's ears as if she was there beside him:

"Issie's not there no more in the bar, she gone. She someplace else. Someplace dark an' she scared."

The car boot was dark. Yuri felt a supernatural shiver run through him. The time that Asmina had said those words was exactly the same time as the digital clock now showed on the monitor. 12:15pm.

The Americans got in and drove out of the carpark, turned left and were gone. Yuri noted the number plate.

"Keep that recording for the police," Yuri said to the waiter, then made a call on his mobile. It only rang once.

"Ava, I want you to listen. Isabella has been taken. It's all on CCTV at Luigi's bar. I'm sending you the recording after this call. Two Americans, one looks CIA, check it out. The car's a white BMW, registration ZA 904 SZ. It's a Milan plate. Check all the hire car companies in Milan. They turned left out of Luigi's carpark, just after quarter past twelve. Get hold of the Italian authorities and run a check on the road traffic surveillance cameras," he paused before adding. "And check out any disused buildings close to water in a 100 mile radius and send me the short list. Then work on the next fifty," he cut the call.

"What do we do now?" Sasha asked in despair.

"Right now, we do the hardest thing possible," Yuri said. "We wait."

Chapter 25

Isabella slowly drifted back into consciousness. Her brain felt like a wet sponge. She was still suffering from the effects of the powerful narcotic, disorientated and cold. Wherever it was that they had taken her stank of rotting sacks and mildew. It was almost pitch black. The only illumination was from a narrow shard of light that cut through the darkness like a knife. Isabella guessed that it was the sunlight shining through a vertical crack in an outside wall, like it would through lapped boarding that had shrunk over time. Isabella had always had a fear of the dark and always slept with a nightlight at her bedside. She was suddenly filled with dread, knowing that when nightfall came, she would be in total darkness.

Isabella listened hard, trying to find something to orientate her. She could hear running water close by. She quickly ruled out the possibility of being in the hold of a boat, because there was no hint of movement, or the bumping of the hull on a quay. She listened harder. There was a scurrying. No, several scurrying's. Just at that moment she felt a sharp pain on her left ankle and screamed out in panic.

"Rats!"

Isabella shuffled backwards on her haunches until her back was against a wall. She took off a shoe and pulled her knees up to her chest, making herself as small as she could. She put her other foot on top of her unprotected one and held her shoe like a club. Something touched her toes. She lashed out at it with the shoe and heard a squeal. It worked, at least for the moment anyway.

The rats fled but they would be back, she knew that. Isabella was locked up with her two biggest phobias, darkness and rats.

She tried to piece it all together. The last thing she could remember was sitting in Luigi's bar with the two Americans from the World Health Organisation and wanting to call Sasha to warn him. She remembered that they had told her not to use her mobile. Now she knew why. Then she remembered that she had suddenly felt strange and being marched out of the bar. That's where it all got a bit hazy. She had some recollection of being shoved against a wall and a beery kiss. She wiped her mouth with the back of her hand as if to cleanse herself. Suddenly Isabella panicked and shoved her hand down her jeans and felt herself. She breathed a sigh of relief at the dryness of her panties.

"At least that hadn't happened," she thought. "I'd kill myself first."

The last thing she remembered was being shut in the boot of a car and not being able to move or even scream. It was like she was paralysed. She remembered too, how terrified she felt and thought that she was going to go mad. Things hadn't got a whole lot better, she thought as she fended off another rat attack in the dark.

Isabella had no idea what the time was or even if it was the same day. But it was daylight. She gauged how hungry she was and the answer was not very. That probably meant it was the same day. She had a watch on but it was just a dress watch, not digital or luminous. Her eyes were growing accustomed to the darkness such that she could make out shapes by various degrees of blackness. The thin shard of light made that possible. She put her shoe back on, stood and shuffled forward with her hands out in front of her toward the crack of light. When she got there, it was no more than a two millimetre gap in the vertical wooden planks that lapped together to form the outside wall. She was in some kind of barn, Isabella imagined. The air coming through the crack was fresh and smelled of the wilderness. She breathed it in and savoured the moment, wondering if she would ever be out, running free in the country again. The narrow stream of light was enough to illuminate the hands of her watch. It was half past three and she must have been taken from Luigi's a little after midday. That meant, that she could only be a maximum of three hours from the centre of Milan. It gave her comfort knowing that she wasn't hundreds of miles from home.

Isabella pondered the facts. Firstly, she was still alive. That meant that somebody wanted something from her, or she would be dead already.

"Probably a ransom," she concluded.

Her mother was one of the wealthiest women in the world. She hadn't been raped, so the motive wasn't sexual, or at least not on behalf of her captors. She worked out Madrid traffic conditions for the time she was abducted. It was lunchtime and Madrid was a traffic nightmare at that time. They could only have made fifteen miles in the first hour and no more than thirty in the second. In the third, they could have made another fifty. So, she was no more than ninety five miles from the city centre, she concluded.

But then Isabella had no idea how long she had been lying unconscious in the rat-infested and decaying outbuilding. It could have been hours, or only minutes, so she could still be somewhere in Milan. She thought on that and concluded that couldn't be. Real estate in the city is far too expensive to have old buildings doing nothing. No, it couldn't be in Milan, she was sure of it. They hadn't gagged her, which meant that nobody would hear her, even if she screamed all day. That was depressing, she thought. Isabella imagined the map of Milan and the surrounding area. To be that far out in the wilds and next to water, she would need to be at least fifty miles from Milan centre. That meant she had to be somewhere in an annulus between fifty miles and ninety five miles radius. If it was only ever for this reason, and this reason alone, Isabella was thankful for her near photographic memory. She could picture all the waterways and lakes on the map.

"I'm near water," she said to herself, "moving water, so where does that annulus cut water?"

There were just three possibilities. The lakes in the north, but she quickly ruled that out. They were static masses of water and silent.

"So it could only be the river Ticino, or the Po, to the west and south of Milan," she deduced. "But where?"

There was more than a hundred miles of waterway that fell in her circles of possibility. She wondered if it was an old riverside wharf or a disused mill, perhaps a granary? That would explain the rats and the smell of rotting sacks. So commercial premises, she decided, old and disused commercial premises of a bygone era, situated somewhere on the river Po or the Ticino.

So now she knew where she might be. It was a start. The next question was, why had they only driven for three hours when they were on the run? That didn't make sense. Or did it? She thought on that too. It could either mean that this already was her final destination and they were going to deal with her here, or it was the end of the first leg of her journey. Isabella didn't want to contemplate the thought that it was all to end here in this hell-hole, she couldn't bear it. She imagined her corpse lying on this cold floor being consumed by rats. Panic started to squirm like a snake in her stomach. Isabella was at the point of losing it.

"Focus you stupid bitch. Don't give in. You are a Mèdici for fuck sake!"

Isabella fought herself back from the brink. She focussed.

"So if this is the end of the first leg, then what does that mean?" she wondered, talking out loud to comfort herself.

It could only mean one thing, she decided. That was, that the second leg of her journey wasn't by car. She ruled out boat straight away, as they couldn't be by the coast and neither the Ticino, nor the Po, were navigable waterways. It couldn't be by train either; too public. So it had to be by air.

"Yes that's it, we are waiting for a plane!" she said as if someone was there to hear.

It would have to be a private one, she concluded and a private airfield. She pondered the map in her head again. There were two private airfields near to where she thought she was and both near the river Po. One was at a place called Casal Monferrato to the south west of Milan and the other was at Cremona, to the south east. She only knew of these because her father used to use them. There could be others though, she conceded. At least she could start to think about how she could escape or raise the alarm. They would need to take her there by car, she concluded, and that would present her with opportunities to escape. She had to have a plan ready; either to cry for help, or make a run for it. That would have to be when they transferred her from this place to the car, or on the journey. She wouldn't have much chance if they got her to the airfield, she decided, or if they drugged her again. That was likely too, she thought despairingly.

Now she needed to know more about her prison. Using the crack of light as a reference point, she started to feel her way around the walls in a clockwise direction. Glass crunched under her feet and her hands found a broken window above it. Long shards of glass were still located in the frame. She could smell fresh timber. The window had been boarded over from the outside. Isabella felt around the outside of the frame. There were the ends of twelve heavy nails protruding through the wood. Whoever had done the work hadn't bent the nails over on the inside.

"So maybe I could kick it out," she said into the darkness and made a mental note of where it was. Isabella moved on.

At the end of her search, she had found three similar windows and one door. The door was also new wood and featureless on the inside. No way out through there she concluded. Her search of the inside produced nothing but a light stick, useless as a weapon but it would serve to fend off the rats. She kept it. So Isabella now knew that the room was twenty paces long and fifteen wide and that she could run across it in the dark without fear of bumping into anything, for what that was worth. She was in an empty barn, made of timber, with a concrete floor, boarded up windows and a featureless door. Oh yes, rats and a stick too.

"Great," she said, as a feeling of dread and despair began to overcome her.

Isabella couldn't let herself succumb and capitulate, it was contrary to everything that she stood for. She had chosen a career to fight for the freedom and liberty of others. Now she had to use that same determination to fight for her own liberty. She found the corner furthest from the door, slumped into it and drew her knees up to her chest again. Isabella had never needed her mother so desperately. She was a child again, no longer the positive young woman. Tears of despair ran down her face as she sat there, in the dark, waiting for the rats to come.

"Find me Mum, please find me," she called out despairingly into the blackness of her prison.

Chapter 26

Ava had to break the news to Gina that Isabella had been taken. It was like an arrow through her heart. She was demented, and blamed herself for not being there. Nothing that Ava could say or do eased the pain, other than to get Gina involved in finding her. At first Gina had demanded to go to Milan. It took a mammoth effort on Ava's part to convince her otherwise and that her only real chance to save Isabella, was to attend the Council of Thirteen solstice meeting, in two days' time. At last, Ava was able to bring Gina into the investigation, where her local knowledge proved invaluable.

They had picked up the white BMW on a traffic management camera on the Piazza Velasca, heading south to the intersection with the Corso di Porta Romana, then again as it passed the University of Bocconi, still heading south. The trail came to a dead end where the Via Carlo Bazzi met the Via Lampedusa. There were four possible directions from there. Unfortunately, none of them had operational traffic management cameras. The

BMW had disappeared, but Gina got lucky. She was checking speed cameras in the area. A white BMW, registration number ZA 904 SZ, had triggered a camera on the A7 at Gropello Cairoli.

Gropello Cairoli was a small town, midway between the river Ticino to the north, and the river Po, to the south. There were no further records of the BMW being on the A7, so they assumed that the car had left the auto route there, and that the rest of the journey would be local. That gave them just fifty miles of waterway to analyse for riverside buildings, secluded enough to be of use to the kidnappers.

"What do you make of the kidnappers staying local?" Ava asked Gina, by way of starting a brainstorming session.

"It would be easier to pick up the ransom money perhaps?" Gina suggested.

"Yes if it was about money," Ava agreed, "but we don't think this is about money, do we?"

"No, it's about power; power over me. So why didn't they just get the hell out of there and put some serious distance between them and the scene of the kidnapping?"

"Maybe they are. They would know that they would eventually be tracked down by the car, so that was just to get them out of town. But out of town to where?" Ava posed, "They didn't choose the Malpensa airport, which would have been their easiest route."

"No Ava, they just didn't choose Malpensa," Gina was onto something. "There are several private airports around Milan that they could use," Gina unfolded a map and placed a well-manicured finger on it. "Here is where we think they left the main road at Gropello Cairoli."

"So where's the nearest private airfield to it?" Ava asked.

"Here," Gina pointed. "Casale Monferrato. It's maybe an hour or so to the west of Gropello Cairoli."

"So, if their intention is to fly out from there, then Isabella is hidden on the river Po somewhere between the two towns," Ava allowed herself an optimistic smile. "That eliminates the Ticino and gives us only thirty miles of river to search. Good detective work Gina."

"Call Yuri now Ava, and get him to the airfield. He can be driving while we try and work through satellite pictures and local real estate records. There can't be that many derelict riverside properties."

Ava called Yuri's mobile. He was sat at the bar with Sasha, drinking yet another coffee. He picked up immediately.

"Ava, what have you got for me?"

"Progress," she began. "They headed south out of Milan on the A7. We think they came off at Gropello Cairoli, heading west on the SP494. That road crosses the river Po. We think they have hidden her there in some old deserted waterside building between Gropello Cairoli and Casale Monferrato. And get this, there's an airfield at Casale Monferrato. It fits, doesn't it?"

"It fits," Yuri agreed. "So we are going with Asmina's premonition then?"

"What else do we have?" Ava countered.

"True. In which case what do you make of the 'big wheel that doesn't turn'? I've been thinking on that," Yuri admitted, evidence that he had at least not written off Asmina's words.

"And?" she asked.

"And, maybe she's in a disused watermill. One with a paddle wheel that's all ceased up."

"It was painfully obvious, now that Yuri had said it. Ava and Gina had been concentrating too much on where the car was to consider the bigger picture.

"We're on it Yuri. Get yourself to the airfield and work your way eastwards along the river from there. We'll get back to you as soon as we turn up anything."

Ava was just about to hang up when Gina stopped her.

"Let me speak to Sasha," her tone was urgent. Ava handed her the phone.

"Sasha, darling; stay close to Yuri, it's not safe. None of us are safe, but we will find Issie, I swear it to you," Gina felt like crying but wouldn't let herself, not in front of Sasha.

"What's going on Mum, why have they taken her?" Gina felt the agony in his voice. "Is it to control you?"

It was the cruel truth.

"Yes, Sasha, it's exactly that. She's suffering because of something that your father started that I have to finish. Issie is their insurance to make sure that I do."

"What are you going to do Mum?"

"Sasha, I don't know. I truly don't know, but we have some of the most powerful people in the world helping us. Have faith Sasha, and stay with Yuri and trust in him," the words felt inadequate. "I have to go darling. Yuri will bring you and Issie to Moscow with him and we will be together again. Stay with faith. Love you Sasha."

Gina put the phone down. All her strength and positivity deserted her and she fell to pieces in Ava's arms.

Callum had spent the last two hours running Yuri's videos through their photo recognition software. The Angel databases were linked to those at MI6, the FBI, KGB, Interpol and Mossad. At last two files began to download onto his workstation. He had a positive match for both kidnappers. It turned out that the big guy was Bradley Harper, a CIA man with nefarious links to

244

organised crime syndicates, one of them believed to be the illuminati.

"That figures," Callum muttered and read on.

Harper was implicated in numerous covert U.S. arms deals across Africa and the Arab factions, including the so called ISIS. Recent intelligence had placed him in Syria in the company of Mohammed Akhbar and the Mullah Ismael Alansari, seemingly with CIA endorsement.

The depths that governments would plumb to turn a buck sickened Callum. He sighed and opened the second file. Daniel Gray's.

Gray was a paper-pusher without ethics. He had spent his career seeking the next highest pay-cheque. He usually worked in law, but his forte was industrial espionage, selling secrets and insider dealing. He was a man of perfect timing, always knowing when to cut and run. They were an unlikely duo; chalk and cheese, in appearance and in nature. Harper was a killer and Gray was not. His victims only bled money.

Now that Callum knew who they were dealing with, their chances of finding Isabella had significantly increased. He immediately fed the names and photographs to the Polizia di Stato, in hope of sealing the borders. In truth though, Europe's open borders meant that they could just simply drive out of Italy. In parallel to the ID check, Callum was running a trace on the BMW's registration plate. He had tracked it down to the Hertz rental agent at the Malpensa airport. The names registered there against the car, were Samuel Brown and Peter Finch.

"Damn," Callum cursed, "they are on false passports."

He updated his communication to the border control police and then sent Ava, Gina and Yuri a full report. That was his part done, ll he could do now was wait and hope that Ava and Gina got a breakthrough soon. He couldn't even begin to wonder how terrified a sixteen year old girl would be in the hands of a man like Brad Harper.

Isabella estimated that it was about six in the evening. The sun had set at least an hour ago, taking away that comforting slither of light that was her reference point. It was now as black as ink in her prison and gloomier still in her heart. She was hungry and cold too, now that the sun's warming rays no longer heated up the outside of the building. She regretted her decision to only wear jeans and a vest this morning, and wondered how she would make it through the night. She stood stiffly and marched across the room, counting to twenty with her hands out in front of her. From the eighteenth, she slowed, touched the wall and marched back. Isabella repeated it a dozen times until her circulation was invigorated, then sat back down in the corner with her rat stick.

Another hour passed, she guessed and repeated her routine. It was totally silent now, not even the chirping of the birds or the cacophony of the crickets. Just silence. She must be some distance from a main road, she concluded, having not heard a car in all the hours that she had been there. Then, as if the thought had tempted fate, she could hear the sound of an approaching car in the distance. Her initial thoughts were of salvation, before reality set in. It would most likely be her captors.

"Who would come out here at night if they hadn't bothered in the day?" she wondered. "Only her captors, that was for sure."

She felt the fear rise within her, crushing her chest so that she could barely breathe.

The car was close now. Isabella could hear the rolling crunch of the tyres in shale or grit, and the rumble of the engine. It stopped outside. She heard the sound of doors opening and closing, followed by their footsteps in the loose stone. Isabella seemed to have forgotten how to breathe out. She just sat there holding her breath, making herself as small as possible in the corner of the room.

There was another sound too, like something being dragged.

"A coffin," she thought, irrationally.

Then there was an exchange between them, two American voices. It was Isabella's worst nightmare come true.

"Give me half an hour with her, then we'll get going," it was Harper's voice. Isabella was sure of it.

"Sure thing Brad, but don't bruise the merchandise," the other man laughed conspiratorially. It was Gray.

"Give him half an hour for what?" she asked herself, but it was rhetorical. She knew *exactly* what he meant and her fear leapt to a whole new level.

Moments later, Harper was right outside her door, still dragging something. She could see light coming in under it and the sound of a key in the lock. The door creaked open and light from his fluorescent lamp flooded in. The glare was painful to Isabella's eyes and it took several seconds before she could see. It was Harper leering at her. The object that he had been dragging was a double mattress. Her heart sank. The half hour was for that.

Harper dumped it in the middle of the room and set the lamp on the floor beside it. The upward illumination of his face, gave him a demonic look that made Isabella's blood run cold.

"We're gonna do each other a favour sweet-cheeks. You're gonna please me with that cute arse of yours, then I'm not gonna hurt you," it wasn't an idle threat. Harper was the kind of man who enjoyed beating up on women.

Isabella was petrified, but determined not to be a victim. She tried to be rational and reason with him.

"Daniel Gray, said not to 'bruise the merchandise' remember?" she kept her tone even so as not to anger him. "I must be worth more money to your employer, *intact*. Think of the willing girls you can buy with that extra cash."

"Who says I get off on *willing*?" he grinned. "Now, you gonna come over here willingly, or am I gonna drag you kicking 'n screaming?"

"No please, I'm still not much more than a child," she begged. "Don't you have children, a daughter maybe? You wouldn't want anybody to hurt her would you?" it was a desperate plea.

"I already know that you're sixteen an' old enough sweet-cheeks. Besides I don't have kids. Hate 'em to be honest. Now are you coming over here?"

Isabella shook her head and stared at the floor. She drew her knees up to her chest again, circling them with her arms and crushing them to her. She was rapidly going into shock and began to mutter the words of the Lord's Prayer.

Harper took a handful of blonde hair and dragged Isabella to the mattress, still praying. He dumped her rudely on it, then cuffed her across the side of her face with an open hand that almost burst her eardrum.

"Do as you're goddamn told, rich bitch!" the animal madness was upon Harper. He was about to take what he wanted.

The power of the blow concussed Isabella, such that she was unaware of him removing her shoes and pulling her jeans off. By the time her senses had returned, she was spread with Harper on top of her and her vest rolled up above her small breasts. She could feel his big hands taking rough pleasure from them and the gyration of his pelvis as he rubbed himself against her crotch.

"No don't," she begged again, trying to push him off her.

It was futile. He was a mountain of a man and her, just a slip of a girl. Instead of trying to push him away, Isabella grabbed the side of her panties defiantly, trying to hold them in place. Harper pinned her to the mattress with the bulk of his torso and reached down to free himself of his trousers. He was grunting and blind with desire. She felt his fingers force their way into her pants, grab the flimsy material, then ripped the gusset out of them in one savage wrench. He was probing at her labia with his hardness trying to enter her, nuzzling and licking her neck as he pressed against her hymen. Isabella felt sick as her tightness began to give to the pressure of his hard penis. Still she resisted, clenching herself until her pelvic muscles screamed.

This wasn't how she had imagined losing her virginity. It was supposed to be a romantic and sharing act of deep love, not this disgusting and brutal rape. She dug deep and made one last attempt to resist him.

Isabella found the softness of his ear with her mouth and encompassed it entirely, then bit with all her might, until her teeth cut through and ground into themselves. She shook her head viciously and Harper's ear severed in her mouth making her gag involuntarily. His scream was blood-curdling as he pulled away from her, clutching the bleeding mess that was once his ear. Isabella spat the remains out contemptuously in his face, and slithered out from under him. She kicked the lamp across the room shattering it, plunging the room into total darkness. Never before had Isabella ever considered darkness to be her friend, not up until that moment.

She backed away from the mattress towards the corner of the room furthest from the door.

"Think special agent Mèdici, what would they do in the movies?" she knew that she would be dead if he got his hands on her again. This would be her last chance and she had to get it right.

Harper was still disorientated and screaming with pain and anger. These were valuable moments and Isabella knew that she had to cash in on them. She had learnt the room absolutely and didn't need light to move freely. This was the only advantage that she had over him. She worked her way down the wall to the first of the boarded up windows and felt for the broken glass. Her fingers traced the cracks until she had identified a triangular shard of glass nine inches long and two inches wide at the base. It would make a perfect dagger. Isabella eased the shard from the frame and then quickly removed the remains of her torn panties.

Harper's screams had turned to curses now as he began to focus again. Isabella quickly wrapped the scant piece of material around the broad end of the shard so that she could grip it, then stood still and listened. He was breathing like a bull elephant, which helped her place him accurately in the room.

"One chance," she said to herself. "You've got just one chance to kill him. Get it right special agent Mèdici, I'm counting on you," it was ridiculous, but somehow, talking to herself like that helped bolden her and make her focus on what she had to do.

Isabella needed to get him close, very close, to be sure that she didn't only wound him. It had to be a fatal stabbing. He was moving now, coming her way. She guessed that he would head for the wall, so he could feel his way around. She side stepped and let him through. There was a light thump as he collided with the timber, then a shuffling as he made his way to his left along it.

Isabella continued to play it through in her mind. She needed to be sure that they met face to face so that her stabbing hand was effective. If he got her from behind, she would be helpless and it would be all over. She imagined what he would do first when they bumped into each other. A bear hug she decided, he would trap her in a bear hug. That meant that her knife hand would be pinned to her side and that she would be helpless.

"I'm coming for you sweet-cheeks an' I'm gonna find you," he began to laugh. "And when I find you, I'm gonna fuck you. Then I'm gonna bite your ears and nose off before I kill you an' make you ugly in death."

It took a monumental effort for Isabella to force herself into his path, but somehow she did. She stood motionless in the corner with both arms held high above her head. That way, when he grabbed her in that bear hug, she would still have both arms free. He was getting closer by the second until she could feel his beery breath on her face.

"Got you, you bitch!" he yelled in her ear as his arms closed around her.

Isabella thanked God that she'd had the presence of mind to think about raising her arms high, she would have been totally trapped otherwise. Now she knew exactly where his neck would be. Isabella brought the blade down with all the force that she had, driving it in right up to the hilt. Five inches of glass buried itself into the softness of his neck, before the handle snapped off in her hand. It severed his carotid artery and windpipe. She felt the wetness of his blood as it sprayed in pulses across her face and mouth. The metallic taste of it made her gag and she vomited over him.

He loosed her. Isabella staggered back several paces, clutching her hand. The shard had cut through the cotton of her panties and sliced into her palm. Harper never uttered another word. The improvised dagger had also gone through his larynx so that he couldn't even scream. Isabella heard him slump to the floor, then the sound of his head striking the concrete floor heavily. She could hear Harper's body go into spasm as his feet involuntarily kicked against the concrete, then silence as his life bled out of him.

Isabella stood there for several minutes, listening for signs of life. At last, she shuffled forward until she could prod him with her foot. She did and leapt backwards in case he grabbed her, like in the Hollywood movies. Isabella did it several more times, until she was as sure as she could be that he was dead. Reassured, Isabella got on her hands and knees and crawled over to him. She went through his pockets and found what she was looking for, his mobile phone. The comforting glow of the screen faintly illuminated the room, enabling her to find her clothes that were next to the dirty mattress. She dressed quickly and shuddered at the thought of what nearly happened to her there.

The phone was blocked with a PIN number, but it allowed emergency calls. Isabella dialled 112 and held her breath. The number connected.

"Police," a woman answered, "how may I help you?"

"I've been kidnapped," she blurted. "I haven't got long, he's coming back. You've got to help me."

"What is your name and where are you?" the police woman asked calmly, assessing if it was a hoax call.

"Isabella Mèdici. I don't know where I am but maybe south east of Milan in an old waterside building. There are two men. Well one man now, and he will be here soon and he's going to be mad with me. You have to come now. Please!"

While Isabella was talking, the policewoman was checking her records for people reported as missing. Isabella was on her list and she immediately took the call seriously.

"Why is he going to be mad with you?" She asked.

"Because I've just killed his friend, he was trying to rape me," Isabella burst into tears just at the mention of it.

"Listen Isabella, this is very important. If you hear the man coming, warn me and hide the phone but don't turn it off, it's our best chance of tracking you. It's better that you leave it on where you are, rather than be caught with it. Put it face down under something. Do you understand?"

"Yes," she said between sobs. "I think he's going to take me to a private airfield near here. It could be Casale Monferrato, but that's not much more than a guess."

"Do you know the men Isabella?"

"I don't know them really, but their names are Brad Harper and Daniel Gray, both Americans."

"We are tracing your call now Isabella, stay on the phone."

Isabella heard footsteps approaching.

"He's coming back, I have to go. Hurry, please hurry!" Isabella slipped the phone face down under the mattress and retreated to the wall on the door side of the room.

"Time's up lover boy, we got a plane to catch," Gray shouted and pushed the door open.

He was expecting the lamp to be on but was met by perfect darkness.

"Hey Harper, you gone all romantic on me, with lights off and cosy?" there was no reply. "Harper, stop fooling around, we gotta get going. Harper?"

Gray's mobile was already on torch mode, to help him through the old building. Its feeble light picked up the empty mattress in the middle of the room. He walked over to it, then on past to the back wall. He could just about make out a shape on the floor near the far corner.

"Harper?" he called out, as he approached. Then the full horror became apparent. "Jesus Christ!"

Harper was lying on his back, staring sightlessly at the ceiling. His left ear was missing and he looked like his throat had been cut. Daniel Gray had never seen so much blood. His face, neck and shirt were drenched in it. Gray wasn't a man of any metal. He immediately threw up copiously. He was however a survivor and realised that if the girl could do this, then he was in great danger too. Gray took the pistol from his pocket, a small Beretta. It was the kind that a woman would choose. He had never shot a gun before and it shook in his hands as if it had a mind of its own. He turned around and shouted out.

"Don't come near me, I've got a gun!" his panicked voice was shrill, like a woman's.

Gray quickly scanned the room. He was alone with a corpse, the girl had fled. He breathed a sigh of relief and then thought more on it. If he lost the girl, then he would soon be dead anyway. The men that he worked for didn't tolerate failure. Gray walked reluctantly to the door with his gun pushed out in front of him, still shaking. He had to find the girl.

It was about nine o'clock in the evening when Callum received the call from Policewoman, Victoria Marina. It was their first major breakthrough in the nine hours since Isabella's abduction. Typically, if victims weren't found with in twelve hours, then they stay missing. This call was a glimmer of hope. Callum immediately called Yuri to give him a head start, then Gina.

"Gina, its Callum. Listen. Isabella has somehow managed to get a call out to the police. They traced it to a small place on the river Po, called Valenza, about twenty five kilometres from the airstrip at Casale Monferrato. Yuri is on his way now and will be there in minutes."

"Is she alright, did she say anything else?" Gina was holding her breath in anticipation.

"As far as they know, she's alright. She confirmed the names, Harper and Gray, but get this; she's killed one of them!" Callum paused and then added. "She's a fighter Gina, just like you. She's not going to give up."

"Oh Callum, she's all alone out there and terrified," Gina's voice was shaky.

She couldn't trust herself to say anymore. The thought of her baby fighting for her life was just too painful.

"The police are sending squad cars to the airport and Valenza as we speak. Soon the place will be crawling with them and we have there Yuri too. I'll get back to you as soon as I can. Miss you," he said and put the phone down.

"Miss you?" he repeated to himself, and realised that he really did.

Valenza was literally Yuri's next port of call and only several minutes away. When Sasha first heard the news that his sister had managed to make contact, his relief was immense. Yuri had to temper that excitement.

"That call was made at least half an hour ago Sasha. This isn't over yet, she may not even be there now, but we are close."

"I know that. But it's still good news, isn't it Yuri? And they are one man down too," Sasha pointed out. There was now a healthy amount of doubt in Sasha's tone.

"It's still good news," Yuri confirmed, not wanting to take away Sasha's hope.

The police had issued coordinates for Harper's mobile phone, so navigating to the exact location was made easy. The old mill was completely hidden from the main road and only really discoverable from the river. It was a perfect choice; you would have to know it was there to find it. Five minutes later they came to a grass track, about a mile long, which wound its way down from the main road to the waterside. The crushed grass in the headlights showed that only several vehicles had used it recently, or one vehicle, several times. That was more likely, Yuri thought.

They approached a deserted, moonlit building. As they got closer, they could see that it was exactly as predicted by Asmina, an old watermill with a big, seized up paddle wheel set in a fast moving millrace.

"How the hell did Asmina work that out?" Yuri asked incredulously.

"She says that it's African tribal, something handed down through generations," Sasha replied, no longer sceptical. "Anyway, one thing is for sure, I'm not doubting her again."

"Me neither," confirmed Yuri, shaking off the superstitious shiver that had just run up his back.

Yuri cut the engine and coasted down the track with his lights off. He saw a turn-off and swerved the black Range Rover into it and into the bushes beyond. Satisfied that it would be hard to spot, he turned to Sasha.

"No heroics. Have you got that?" Sasha nodded.

Yuri took a torch from the glove box and stepped down silently onto the soft earth. Sasha followed his lead.

"Keep behind me and stay alert," Yuri said, taking his gun out of its shoulder holster.

They kept low and skirted round the tree line to the back of the building.

"Stay here while I check around the back, then we go in together."

Yuri stayed crouched and worked his way around the building, making use of any natural cover he could find. It took minutes only for him to establish that they were alone. He returned to where he had left Sasha.

"We're too late Sasha. They must've already left for the airfield," Yuri looked stricken and Sasha, more so. "We had better check the inside to be sure and then head for the airfield. The police should be arriving there soon too."

Their disappointment was immense. They could only have missed them by minutes. Yuri couldn't tell Sasha why they were still going in, but it was to make sure that Isabella wasn't already lying dead inside. Yuri led the way to the big double doors of the old mill at a pace. There wasn't any time for caution. He burst in gun first, sweeping it and his torch from side to side, looking out for the enemy. It was empty, just as he had expected. There was an old granary to the side, with a newly fitted door. It was open. Yuri signalled for Sasha to stay where he was, then crossed to it. He stopped with his back to the wall next to the door and turned his torch off. With his pistol in the high-ready position, Yuri dived in through the doorway, rolled and came to his feet near the centre of the room. His torch arm was extended to his side as he flicked it on, to draw any gunshots away from his body. He swept the room with it. The granary was empty, but for an old mattress and a body in the far corner.

"It's safe," Yuri called out.

Sasha entered cautiously and they crossed over to the body together.

"Jesus," Sasha's voice was an astonished whisper. "My little sister did this?"

"Good girl," Yuri said, with deep admiration. "I'm looking forward to meeting her."

There was one more thing that Yuri had to do before leaving. Find the man's mobile phone. It had to be hidden in the granary somewhere. Not many hiding places, he thought and lifted the mattress. There it was.

"This might lead us to the bad guys," Yuri said. "Now let's get going, we've got a plane to catch!"

Gray had his back to Isabella when he came across Harper's body and emptied his stomach onto the granary floor. Isabella used the distraction to slip out of the open door. She found herself in a corridor that went left and right. It was pitch black. Everywhere was pitch black. She recalled the sound of the mattress being dragged and was sure it came from her right and followed it that way. She faced the wall and pushed out with her left foot, sidestepping along it, feeling her way. After serval yards, Isabella's hands reached out into nothingness.

"A doorway, thank God," she thought and stepped forward.

There was nothing there and Isabella found herself overbalancing. She caught herself with her right hand on the opening and thankfully her foot touched ground. She was on the first step of a staircase. Isabella eased downwards. The ancient wooden stairs creaked and groaned with every step she took, as if calling out to her captor saying, "Here I am."

She reached the bottom and listened. There were footsteps above her, moving towards the stairs and a glimmer of light on the landing.

Isabella could feel the panic rising in her again. It was crushing her chest so that she couldn't breathe or think. She ran blindly into the darkness, straight into the upright shaft of the mill, striking her head on the crown wheel above. Isabella fell heavily and lay motionless on the floor. When she came to, she was lying face down with her hands cuffed behind her. The pain in her head was excruciating. Blood had run into her left eye and coagulated there. She felt a sudden sting in her bottom and screamed out. Gray had stuck her with a hypodermic, he wasn't taking any chances.

"Let me go, please let me go. I haven't done anything," she pleaded. "You could run before the police get here."

"The police ain't coming sister. Nobody knows you're here but me," Gray said sadistically.

"I called them on Harper's mobile, they're on their way. If you run now you'll make it," Isabella could feel the drug beginning to work and her own voice was starting to sound distant.

"You did what? Jesus Christ you stupid bitch!"

Gray dragged Isabella to her feet by the handcuffs, almost dislocating her shoulders. Gray couldn't run. He had to complete his mission on pain of death. Isabella was almost unconscious again and could only just support herself on her legs. Gray was thankful that he didn't have to carry her and steered her to the door, out into the moonlight. She was too stupefied to think of resisting and went where she was shoved. When they got to the white BMW, Gray popped the boot and pushed her in. Moments later, they were speeding up the grassy track to the main road. It was clear. Gray turned right and accelerated as fast as he could in the direction of the airstrip at Casale Monferrato. Moments later, a black Range Rover turned into the same grass track, heading for the old watermill. Yuri had missed them by less than ten seconds.

It was only twenty five kilometres from the old watermill at Valenza, to the airstrip at Casale Monferrato. Gray had a ten minute start but he wasn't even close to being the driver that Yuri was. He drove the Range Rover hard and to the limit. Again his choice of hire car was perfect for the country roads. He had no way of knowing that he had only just missed them at the mill and no idea at all that they were now only several minutes ahead of them. Sasha was shaking in the passenger seat. He had all that energy and anger of youth and no way of expending it. He felt useless.

"Listen, Sasha," Yuri began. "Don't beat yourself up and don't give up. They want her alive or they would have already killed her. This fight against the Illuminati has only just begun and you will have a part to play in it. Just stay positive and focussed."

Sasha nodded and visibly rallied himself.

"We got this all so wrong Yuri," he lamented. "Everything pointed to Mum being the owner of the Dream App and some high-ranking member of the Illuminati. I nearly got lost to the Dream App and it was only Issie that got me back. We couldn't share our thoughts with Mum, because we thought that she was the problem. But then we couldn't let the Dream App continue to destroy lives. We had to do something."

"Done with noble intent," Yuri agreed," but you pissed off some very powerful people. Now we've got to take them down. Isabella is just the start of it, but the storm is yet to come. Prepare yourself for the long haul Sasha, not just the day trip.

Yuri took the mobile phone from his pocket that he had found at the old mill house and handed it to Sasha.

"There's a bag of electrical stuff in the glove box, chargers and the like. In there is a SIM card reader. Put this one in and Bluetooth it to your mobile and then select 'upload'. Your mother and Ava will receive it in Moscow. They can start looking at who these guys have been talking to. That'll give us a second bite at the cherry if we miss Isabella at the airfield. "

It served two purposes. One was to keep Sasha occupied, and the other was to lower his expectations; at least for now. Yuri knew that the odds were stacked against them for rescuing Isabella. If the plane was ready to go, the transfer would be quick and she would already be gone. Two minutes late would be too late. Getting the SIM card to the girls quickly, would give them some lines of enquiry and hopefully a lead to where they were taking Isabella.

Sasha inserted the SIM into the card reader and pressed send just as Yuri swerved into the entrance to the airfield. At first, it appeared to be deserted; closed even. Then Yuri saw lights at the far end of the runway, about three quarters of a mile away. He floored the accelerator and drove down the middle of the runway directly at the light Cessna aircraft. As they got closer, Yuri could see a white BMW twenty or so yards to the side and a rotund man running towards it. The plane began to accelerate up the runway towards them on a collision course.

"They've already made the transfer Sasha; I'll try and force them to abort the take off. If I fail, try and read the registration number on the fuselage as we pass."

Yuri knew that he could only take this game of chicken so far, or he would kill them all. Light aircraft, on take-off, don't have much ability to change direction. It quickly became patently clear that the pilot wasn't up for aborting either. At the last second, Yuri wrenched the steering wheel to the right. The heavy Land Rover came up on two wheels, perilously close to rolling and then passed under the Cessna's port wing. For a split second, their headlights illuminated the side of the plane and Sasha read the registration number.

"OE-666!" Sasha shouted above the combined noise of the two revving engines.

The Range Rover came down heavily onto all four and Yuri headed directly for the white BMW.

Gray was way outside his comfort zone and sweating profusely. He was used to driving a desk, not a powerful car at high speed. That was Harper's job. The mutilated image of Harper on the granary floor, drenched in his own blood, was driving him insane. It could so easily have been him, he thought.

"He shouldn't have touched the girl," Gray cursed as he kerbed the BMW, taking a tight right-hander.

The airfield was up ahead. Gray checked in his rear-view mirror and was relieved to see that the road behind him was deserted. He bounced into the airfield, over the sleeping policeman, and his cargo thumped heavily in the car boot. The airport was dark and unattended. In the distance, Gray could see the red and green navigation lights of an aircraft, then a double flash of a headlight calling him on. He sped towards it, desperate to get rid of his baggage that was Isabella Mèdici. He screeched to a halt, yards from the idling Cessna. Gray spilt himself out of the door and waddled, rather than ran to the back of the car. He popped the boot. Isabella was unconscious. Even though she only weighed a little over eight stone, Gray couldn't lift her. He waved petulantly at the pilot for assistance. That assistance came by way of the pilot taking Isabella single-handedly in a fireman's lift over his shoulder. He discharged her into the passenger seat of the Cessna just as a black Range Rover slewed onto the airstrip.

"Go, go!" Gray screamed petulantly at the pilot as he settled his plumpness back in the driver's seat.

In his panic, Gray fumbled with the ignition, then stalled the engine. By the time he got the BMW started, the Cessna was already three hundred yards up the runway on a collision course with the speeding Range Rover. Gray watched in awe as neither plane nor car looked like they would give way to the other. Gray braced himself as if he was personally involved in the pending carnage. At the last second, the Range Rover veered to its right and headed straight towards him.

"Holy shit!" Gray mouthed, but the words hardly formed. Fear had struck him dumb.

Gray dropped the clutch and lurched up the road. His only way out of the airfield, necessitated him getting past the oncoming Land Rover. As the distance between them narrowed, Gray closed his eyes. He neither had the skill nor the courage to do anything else. The impact never came. Instead, the Range Rover swerved and came in a sweeping arc back to the side of his car. The quaking American looked into the emotionless face of his pursuer and saw death in his eyes. Panicked, Gray veered away from the exit route. He headed towards the administration buildings, as if he could hide and find solace there. To his horror, the Range Rover stayed stuck to his flank. They were locked eye to eye, doing seventy miles an hour. Gray was knocked sideways at the impact of the heavy four wheel drive Rover as it rammed into his front-left wing. It sent the BMW off at a tangent, towards the refuelling depot. He dragged his eyes away from the menacing face of the driver and looked ahead. Gray's eyes opened wide with shock, as he saw the fuel tanker only yards in front of him. There was no time to brake. The white BMW ploughed into it and was immediately consumed in a fire ball that billowed two hundred feet in the air.

Illya Dracul was spitting teeth.

"All they had to do was pick up two lousy kids," he was beside himself with anger.

Three of them were trained killers and all of them highly paid. The first that he had heard about the failed attempt at capturing Sasha Mèdici was breaking news on the BBC. Apparently, two armed men were found dead in their car in the Parco Naturale Vale del Ticino, near Milan. They had been shot several times. There were no witnesses and no apparent motive.

Dracul pondered it. These were trained men. Sasha would not have had a gun, so that meant he had a guardian.

"Guardian Angel," he said to himself.

He had wondered how long it would take before Gina Mèdici would have found that organisation.

"No matter," he mused. "He was just a luxury, a 'nice to have'."

He was placated by the fact that Sasha Mèdici had already been radicalised through the Dream App, so his fate was sealed. All that was needed to activate him and make him an assassin or commit suicide was the simple code, 'Satan666'. No, that wasn't a problem. But it would be an unnecessary embarrassment when he had to report to the Pindar. He needed some good news to compensate; he needed to know that Isabella Mèdici's abduction had gone to plan. Otherwise there would be no placating the Pindar. The last contact from Harper and Gray was mid-afternoon and that was nearly seven hours ago. It didn't bode well. At last his mobile rang and Illya Dracul swiped it off the desk.

"Yes?"

All he could hear at first was static and the loud roar of an engine.

"Can you hear me?" Dracul shouted.

"I hear you," was the reply. The voice was heavily Germanic.

"Have you got the merchandise?" Dracul sounded desperate and immediately hated himself for his show of weakness.

"I have the girl. She's drugged and handcuffed, looks a bit beaten up too," he added unnecessarily.

It was said in a matter of fact way, not at all as if he could give a damn.

"Are Harper and Gray with you?"

"Negative. Don't know about Harper, but Gray didn't make it. He fled and took out a fuel tanker. Two guys were in pursuit."

Whether Harper or Gray made it or not was of no concern to Dracul. The girl was *en route* for Ingolstadt and that was all that mattered.

"What's your ETA?" Dracul asked, in control of his voice once again.

"It's six hours with refuelling, so 0400 hours."

"I will meet you there personally," Dracul said and cut the call.

Chapter 27

Moscow, Russia. Wednesday, December 20th 2017. The day before the winter solstice.

Gina had collapsed when she heard the news that Yuri had missed Isabella at Casale Monferrato by only seconds. They had traced the Cessna to an owner in Austria but there were no recorded landings at any of the airports. The trail had gone cold.

"They've taken my baby away!" Gina had cried out in anguish.

It was way too much for her to handle. Gina had been living the last half day on a cliff edge. This latest shock took her over. She had needed sedation that night, in order to find solace in oblivion. Ava had stayed by her side comforting her through her frenzied dreams well into the afternoon of the following day. When she woke, Ava couldn't believe the change that had come over Gina. It was like she hadn't got a nerve in her body. Her first words underlined her newly found resolve.

"Get me to Ingolstadt now Ava. I can't wait here a second longer," Gina was determined. "I will go to tomorrow's solstice meeting and find out where they've taken Issie and bring her back, or die trying. I swear to God I'll kill everyone there, if they have harmed her," Gina had no doubt that it was the Pindar who had arranged Isabella's abduction.

Ava could sense that all the hard months of training had culminated in this moment. The focus that Ava had endeavoured to instil in Gina was now clear and apparent.

"She would be a force to reckon with now," Ava thought, "like a lioness protecting her cubs. Gina would be limitless in what she would attempt. Now, she clearly had the determination and motivation to possibly achieve it."

"Will you stay and receive Sasha for me?" Gina asked, squeezing Ava's hand imploringly. "I trust him in your care and I can't do what I have to do, without knowing that he's safe.

Gina paused, and then added.

"If I don't make it home, will you look after him for me?" a single tear escaped from Gina's eye. She knew that she almost certainly wouldn't be coming back.

Ava felt that too. She wiped the rogue tear away with the tip of her finger and kissed her.

"You know that I would, but you are coming back to us Gina. Always believe that. You must have faith. Just remember all that I've taught you and use your rage to fuel your ability. Once you commit, don't relent. There will be no place for compassion, just focus on your objective to the exclusion of all else.

Gina's smile was thin. She tried to look brave and hoped that she would find the warrior inside her that Ava seemed so sure of.

"Do you think that Callum would come with me? Not to the meeting of the Council, of course, but just to be there," Gina didn't want to be alone in the waiting period, lest she faltered.

"I don't think you could stop him," Ava replied with an honest smile.

Much to Kayla's displeasure, Callum collected Gina from Ava's apartment at a little after four o'clock that afternoon. The flight from Moscow to Munich was three hours. With transfers, they finally arrived at the Mandarin Oriental Hotel in the centre of Munich at eight o'clock. Gina had been distant throughout the journey, preoccupied with what lay ahead of her. By the time they had checked in, Gina had her head organised. She knew what she must do and had to trust a lot to fate. At last she was ready to be sociable.

"I don't suppose you would like to dine with me tonight?" Callum asked, as he called the lift, his lack of confidence showing.

"I would love to Callum," Gina stretched up and kissed him on the cheek. "And I'm sorry for being such lousy company."

They stepped into the lift car and Callum selected their floor.

"Not lousy, just distant and that's hardly surprising," Callum looked relieved at Gina's change of spirit.

"Today is for now Callum, for us. I want this to be a night to remember," Gina's eyes were soft.

She had become fatalistic and wanted to bank memories. Gina felt like this would be the only chance that they would ever have to be together. She didn't want to die, not knowing how it would be. Tonight she would push her dark thoughts away and live for the moment. Callum hadn't picked up the change in her. Perhaps it was him still feeling unsure after Gina's period of remoteness.

"Great!" he positively beamed at her as the lift doors opened on the third floor. "Shall we meet in the bar in forty five minutes?"

"Make it half an hour Callum, this girl's ravenous!" she smiled an enigmatic smile. He had no idea!

Gina was already sat at the bar when Callum walked into the hotel lounge. It was her turn to watch and admire Callum as he approached. He had that walk of earned confidence, not an arrogant strut or a swagger. He was dressed casually, but expensively. Open white Armani shirt and faded Versace jeans. In Gina's mind, nothing was more appealing than a man with that look. She felt that all too familiar warm feeling in the pit of her stomach. It was the feeling that often manifested itself when her mind dallied to thinking of him. She gasped involuntarily and took a sip of her gin and tonic to steady herself. His smile was engaging. She loved the way that he seemed to have a smile that was only for her, a smile that seemed to ignore everyone else in the room. It made her feel special. That smile parted his lips so that his even teeth showed momentarily. Gina so desperately wanted to kiss that mouth.

"You look lovely Gina," Callum said, leaning across to kiss her on the cheek.

Gina strategically turned her head at the last moment, so that his lips brushed hers. The look that she gave him made Callum perfectly aware that it had been no accident.

"To us," Gina said, handing Callum a large Bombay Sapphire and tonic.

Callum held Gina's gaze as they clashed glasses and drank thirstily.

"That hits the spot," Callum said with a sigh of satisfaction.

He sat on the barstool that Gina had strategically placed close to her. Their thighs touched innocently, just as she had intended. The conversation was easy and light, bearing no connection to the happenings of the last 24 hours. Gina wanted it so and Callum sensed it.

"Shall we dine?" he asked after their third drink.

"I think we better had. These gin and tonics are going to my head," Gina said, taking her lipstick and mirror from her clutch bag.

Gina applied the red lipstick, looking at herself in the miniature mirror as she did so. She did it slowly and a little theatrically, exaggerating her pout and pursing her lips to smooth the cream. She felt Callum's eyes on her. She had established on their first meeting, that he was a man that watched a woman's mouth. She was enjoying every second of him having his eyes on her and imagining what he was thinking.

As Gina tended to her makeup, Callum took in the moment. She appeared oblivious to his gaze, or so he thought.

"She's so kissable," he thought.

Gina was by far the most beautiful woman in the room, he concluded. She had that delicious mixture of sophistication and liberation; a woman who was confident in her ability, looks and sexuality. She certainly wasn't afraid to dress to please a man. The knee length black dress, cut to show her thighs when she sat and her generous cleavage, was testament to that. She wore her main of luscious black hair over one shoulder, a look that Callum had always found deeply feminine. Gina's intelligent blue eyes shone with vitality and were cleverly made up to accentuate their size and beauty. Callum was lost in her and his thoughts, such that he hadn't noticed that she had finished making up.

"Penny for your thoughts, lover?" Gina had caught him off guard.

Callum's thoughts had dallied to those of a carnal nature. It was of course exactly as she had intended. Callum had forgotten momentarily that Gina's development had included the ability to enter people's minds and Callum's guard was down.

"I'm sorry Gina, that was unforgivable of me," he began, but she cut him off.

"Only unforgivable if you don't carry those thoughts out," she trapped him again with her arched eyebrow and a mocking look.

Callum was still floundering when Gina came graciously to his rescue.

"But before you do all those delicious things to me, I think you should feed me. It seems that I might need all of my strength," a playful smile crossed her lips as they stood and walked arm in arm to the restaurant.

The atmosphere at dinner could only be described as electric. They had both yearned for each other over the long months. Waiting had enhanced their anticipation to impossible levels and both were distracted by that want. The lobster and premier cru Chablis was exquisite but both would be hard pressed to remember it by morning. Gina could only think of Ava's first-hand stories about what an attentive and accomplished lover Callum was. She was imagining his strong hands on her and the eternal kisses that she had talked of. Her body was aching for him and her brain, frazzled.

"Can we skip desert," Gina asked out of the blue and immediately blushed profusely.

"Of course," Callum replied, looking away to allow Gina a moment to recover her composure.

He called the waiter and ordered a bottle of Bollinger and two glasses to take up. Room service might have been a bit *clumsy*, he decided, given that they were both desperate for each other and would never have managed the wait.

The lift doors opened. They stepped into the empty car, so charged with excitement that they could both barely trust themselves to be discrete. Callum had the ice bucket containing the champagne in one hand and two empty glasses in the other. Gina selected the floor and totally lost control. She took advantage of his defencelessness the moment the doors closed. Gina put her hands behind his head and pulled his face to hers urgently, pressing her pelvis into his as she did so. The kiss was long and divine as their tongues entwined. She felt dizzy and confused by the messages it was sending to her groin. Gina was evidently conscious of the fact that Callum was experiencing the same symptoms of lust, and enjoyed the thrill of his excitement pressing against her.

They didn't notice the doors open. They were both were lost in the intensity of the moment.

"Ahem," an annoyed and unfamiliar voice said.

They broke their lovers' embrace and bundled guiltily out of the lift. The moment the lift doors closed and they were alone again in the corridor; they giggled like teenagers and shushed each other so as not to disturb the other guests. It took them a minute before they realised that they were on the wrong floor. They took the stairs.

"Your place or mine?" Callum asked with a boyish grin on his face.

"Oh, most definitely mine Callum. You can do the walk of shame in the morning, not me."

"There will be no shame. I shall wear your surrender like a badge of honour," he countered. "Besides, you might not be up to the walk."

"How presumptuous of you, and what a delicious thought," Gina said as she held the key card to her door.

The instant they were inside, Gina hungrily continued their interrupted kiss and began unbuttoning Callum's shirt. She had fanaticised so often about the simple act of unbuttoning his shirt and now it was happening. He was still holding the champagne and helpless to resist, not that he would have, or even could have. He leant his weight against her and walked her backwards towards the dressing table until she was backed up against it. Callum set the ice bucket and glasses down, then ran his hands down her back and over the roundness of her bottom, cupping them in his hands.

"Nice bum," he whispered into her mouth as he lifted her onto the table.

Gina instinctively knew what was going to happen to her and groaned at the eroticism of the thought. His shirt was free and she pulled it down from his shoulders, then reached down to his belt and unbuckled it. His chest was hard and muscular and he smelt clean and manly. Gina cursed when she found that the Versace jeans were buttoned and not zipped, and that his excitement had put an impossible strain on them.

"Help me Callum," she pleaded. "I need you."

While Callum was freeing himself of denim, Gina dropped the shoulder straps of her dress and released the clasp of her bra. Her heavy breasts broke free and Callum looked visibly stunned at the impressive display of her womanhood. Gina was about to remove her panties, when Callum stopped her abruptly.

"Don't you dare," he grinned at her. "I want that to be my pleasure.

He pressed his own briefs down and Callum's ample manhood sprung from them eagerly. Gina bit her lip in the glorious anticipation of having him inside her. He hooked his thumbs in the waistband of her panties at her hips and slowly drew them down. He didn't look down at her sex, as most men would. His eyes never left her face. Gina wasn't to know, but to see the look in a girl's eyes as she surrenders herself to her man and the inevitable was one of Callum's greatest pleasures. It was too special to miss and something to treasure for always.

Gina held his gaze, even though she was feeling so self-conscious and shy. Callum watched with delight as her expression changed from trepidation to modesty and then to want. When her ankles were at last free of the flimsy garment, Gina wrapped her long legs around Callum and dragged him into her. When their desires met, her softness gave in naturally to his hardness until she felt full of him in body and mind. Gina gasped at the delicious pain of the sweet invasion, the invasion that she had so desperately waited for. Even the very anticipation of it had hurried her mind and body forwards on her journey towards orgasm. When Callum's powerful rhythm began, it was already too much for her and Gina climaxed in the moment.

She clung to him crying out loud as her pleasure consumed her. Her arms and legs were spread around him, locking her pelvis into his with all her strength, lest he broke free of her. She found his face, his mouth, his tongue and devoured him as waves of ecstasy wracked her body. In those euphoric minutes, Gina was only aware of the colours in her mind, the sensations that were consuming her and Callum's powerful rhythm as he played her. Gina felt like she was floating weightlessly, unaware that Callum was carrying her to the bed. They were still coupled but now the rhythm was gentle and loving as she lay on her side with him planting butterfly kisses on her face and neck.

She opened her eyes and looked at Callum's face as if it was for the first time. It was *her* Callum now and it changed everything. No man had ever made her come before. It was something that she always did herself afterwards, using the erotic thoughts of the earlier encounter to guide her. But now she could feel herself climbing the hill yet again towards her next plateau, he was taking her back to paradise.

"Oh, Callum," she whispered breathlessly.

The world seemed to close in around Gina until there was only her, Callum and his endless rhythm.

Gina woke first. She checked the clock on the bedside table. It was already after eight and she was famished from the exertions of the night.

"I could eat a horse," she murmured in Callum's ear, but he was dead to the world. "Or maybe ride a stallion?" she suggested and giggled at the thought of it, but unfortunately he was lost in much needed sleep.

Callum was lying on his back with the covers down to his waist to cool. Gina pushed herself up and rested her chin on his chest, looking up at his face.

"You have a strong chin," she thought and ran her finger gently along the line of it.

The feel of the morning stubble on it sent little electric shocks to her brain. It was such a display of manliness. Gina thought about their night together but all she could put together was a series of random images in no particular order. He had *really* frazzled her brain. She realised that he had kept her at or over the point of orgasm all night. She had been in glorious confusion throughout. He had never, for a moment, let her come down from her cloud.

"No wonder Ava loved him so much," she thought. "And she hadn't exaggerated at all about his attentiveness. That was amazing."

She wanted to wake him, even if only to kiss him. Gina had prepared herself mentally that today would probably be the last day of her life. She was resigned to it and could face the prospect more easily now that she had experienced the loving of a real man. It would have been one of life's deep regrets if it hadn't happened. God knows, she had enough of those without that. Right now was for living though, and Gina was going to bank every moment of it.

She eased the bedclothes off Callum and straddled him, locating herself so that they touched intimately. She leaned forwards to kiss him and rocked her hips gently in a mutual massage. Callum emerged slowly from slumber to the taste of Gina's salty kisses and the sound of her breathlessness. At first he thought he was still dreaming. The moistness and pressure of her touch was rousing and he quickly responded to Gina's demands. The shy and retiring woman of yesterday had become the predator today. She had taken control. Their coupling was far from gentle as she drove herself down onto him, crying out as she did so. Gina swept her hair high up on her head with both hands, holding it there as she rocked her pelvis. It was a gift, so that Callum could watch her expressions and her breasts as they swayed to her gyrations. She already knew how Callum delighted in the visual display of her beauty. Having his eyes on her like that was so inspiring, that

Gina quickly found the thoughts that would take her to her destination.

At last she collapsed on his chest, drenched in perspiration and sated. It was another delicious memory to take with her to eternity.

They took a late and leisurely breakfast. Gina had called Luigi the night before to collect them in the Mercedes. It was only an hour's run from Munich to Ingolstadt, so she had told him six o'clock in the evening. That meant that she had the whole day to enjoy Callum's company.

"Heaven," she thought.

They did things that new lovers do, like sightseeing, although they only really had eyes for each other. They walked the Marienplatz, a large historical square at the centre of Munich. It was a mixture of old and new town, since the city was rebuilt after the blitz. They strolled arm in arm, through ancient and modern and took coffees and cakes when the fancy took them and dallied and chatted when it didn't. Gina seemed to like to feed Callum by hand when she could, placing tasty morsels in his mouth. It was part of missing her kids, Callum thought, and indulged in it for her. They window shopped and made a game of planning what would go nicely in their apartment. Gina knew that it was just fantasy though. There never would be 'our apartment' or 'us', but it was fun to imagine it so.

Gina had no appetite. It was a nervous reaction to the imminent meeting of the Council of Thirteen later that evening, she was sure of it. So instead of taking lunch, they grazed from the multitude of stalls. It gave Gina even more opportunities to feed Callum by hand and she delighted in it. Before they knew it, four o'clock had arrived and time to head back to the hotel. They had both avoided any talk of what might or might not happen at the solstice meeting, there would be time for that on the journey there. Besides, they had gone through it a dozen times before.

The only thing that had changed was the last minute kidnapping of Isabella. Even that was only educated conjecture that it was Illuminati inspired.

They passed a jewellers and it stopped them in their tracks. They stood outside the window gazing in. They were arm in arm, like a couple choosing an engagement ring to celebrate a long future together. The irony of it hit Gina hard and she couldn't help the tears that followed. There was no long and bright future on the horizon for her. Callum picked up on it.

"What star sign are you Gina?"

"Aries. Why do you ask?"

"March or April?" he asked wiping her tears away with his fingers.

"April, but nobody's fool," Gina was puzzled. "Why do you ask?"

"So that means your birthstones are diamonds and sapphires. Yes?"

"Yes," she replied, liking where this was going.

"Expensive girl to take on then," he quipped.

"Perhaps, but I'm worth it."

"Indeed you are. I have hands-on experience of that," he grinned roguishly and there was a hint of a blush from Gina. "It had to be Aries though, adventurous and ambitious but compassionate and loyal. A born leader apparently."

Gina was impressed.

"You are interested in astrology then, a believer?"

"No, not at all. Its poppycock, but a great way to chat up a girl," he teased.

"Well, Asmina believes in it. Under the circumstances, you would be hard pushed to discredit her," he got that raised and accusing eyebrow again.

"*Touché*," he conceded. "Let's go and choose you a keepsake."

She settled for the sapphire pendant and matching earrings to compliment her eyes.

"I shall treasure it for always," she said honestly, then thought to herself. "For however long that is."

It was just before six o'clock when Gina snapped the lock shut on her suitcase. She took one last look around the room, trying to remember every detail, particularly where and how they had made love.

"Pretty much everywhere," she decided and grinned, feeling that familiar rush.

She picked up her document valise, just as there was a knock at the door. It was Callum, right on time. He had offered to help with her case. Gina opened the door, cupped his face with her hand and gave him an affectionate peck on the lips.

"Thank you for a wonderful time Callum," she said as she ran her hand over his cleanly shaven chin.

It brought back memories of his morning shadow and the roughness of it on her breasts. She bit her lip at the thought but said nothing.

Luigi was immaculately dressed in black, waiting faithfully outside the entrance by the side of the car. He opened the back door as they approached.

"Buonasera, Donna Gina." he said, looking genuinely pleased to see her.

They exchanged niceties for a couple of minutes. Gina asked after his wife and children and in turn, Luigi expressed their deep shock and regret about Isabella's abduction. He asked if their was any news. Gina put a brave face in it.

"No Luigi, but we expect to have her back soon," she lied. There wasn't an ounce of fact to underpin that statement.

Gina quickly moved the conversation to business.

"We don't have to be at the castle until seven thirty. Plan to arrive just before then Luigi, rather than park and wait please," it would have been gruelling, killing time there, she thought.

When they got in, Gina closed the privacy hatch so that they could talk freely. It was time to come back to the real world. She opened her valise and pulled out a small sheath of papers.

"These are copies of all the acquisitions that the Mèdici bank has made in accordance with the Pindar's schedule. Each one is signed by me returning full ownership to the original shareholders without any financial encumbrance, should anything out of the ordinary happen to me, Sasha or Isabella. These signatures have been witnessed and the originals kept in the bank vault. Electronic copies are being held in six independent, secure databases. The Pindar would get nothing," Gina almost spat out the last sentence.

"Good work Gina. I would like to be a fly on the wall when he reads that," Callum mused.

"Then you would probably be watching me die," she said ruefully. "The risk is that he has me killed in a blind rage out of spite. Remember, if he is the Devil, then he has been on this Earth for 6,000 years. What is a wait of six months to a year to recuperate his losses?" she was right and Callum had no answer for it.

"My only chance is that Hydie is true to her word and pitches in with me," Gina continued. "Success to me is walking out of there alive, even if it's only for days or weeks. That, and finding out where Isabella is. In truth, if the Pindar offers me Isabella's life for the acquisitions, I will take it."

It wasn't what Callum wanted to hear, but he couldn't blame her. It was mother's instinct; something stronger than the ideal of peace on Earth.

"How will you handle the matter of Isabella's abduction?" Callum asked cautiously.

"I don't know. I truly don't know Callum," Gina looked in pain. "It sounds pathetic, but I'm hoping for some kind of divine intervention, or some inspiration in the moment."

"You will think of something Gina. Just you being there gives her possibility. Focus on that."

It was a pretty lame thing to say, but that was all he could. Callum desperately wished that it was him going in there, not her.

The conversation dried up and Callum just held her. She felt so small and vulnerable in his arms, not a lioness at all, just a scared little girl. It was like a journey to someone's funeral. He desperately prayed that it wasn't going to be hers.

At just before seven thirty, they took their place at number five in the cavalcade of thirteen black Mercedes parked outside the Gothic castle grounds at Ingolstadt. Gina put her coarse, dark habit on over her dark grey, pinstriped skirt and white blouse. The lead car set off at the precise time and they proceeded through the avenue of poplars towards the castle gates.

It was a moonless night with dark stormy clouds blocking out the heavens. No surreal light show, like there was on the evening of the summer solstice when the setting sun and then the rising moon lit the avenue. There was only blackness, cut by the harsh white headlights of the limousines that cast grotesque shadows that seemed to scurry into the fields beyond the trees as they passed. The gates opened automatically and the cavalcade continued on to the courtyard and castle entrance.

278

Gina had used the approach to focus her mind on the task ahead of her. She had revisited the mentoring that she had received from Ava.

"Your only limitations are those that you place on yourself Gina. You are limitless. You just have to want it enough," Ava's words rang in her ears.

"I want it," Gina muttered to herself. "I want Isabella back."

The rush of adrenaline that had made her feel weak initially, was now coursing through her veins. She felt focussed and energised. She turned to face Callum and kissed him forcefully on the lips.

"Just in case," she said, leaving him with a brave smile.

Callum called out after her.

"If you don't make it out of there, rest assured that no man will," he said, tapping the handgun secreted inside his jacket.

"The Pindar is not a man Callum," she lamented and joined the file of habited councillors.

The procession passed through the aged doorway into the castle, then down the arched hallway, with its avenue of suits of armour and tapestries, to the chambers beyond. The blackened oak door was already open. Gina shuddered as she saw the stone altar with the cartwheel of candles hoisted above it. Memories of what happened there were still haunting her at night. The annulus of thirteen chairs was set around it in the usual manner. The Pindar's ornate wooden thrown was set facing the doorway, with the bold letter 'L' engraved on it. There was no longer any doubt in Gina's mind that it belonged to Lucifer, the enemy of God and mankind.

The walls of the chamber were hung with huge, grotesque oil paintings that portrayed the nine circles of Hell as described in *Dante's Inferno*. There was pain and suffering all around her, but nothing to equal the misery in Gina's heart for the loss of Isabella. Interspaced with the paintings, were weapons of all kinds. The crossed sabres caught Gina's eye. She would so have loved to take one and then drive it through the Pindar's heart. It would have been futile though as she was pretty sure that he hadn't got one.

The councillors took their positions behind their seats, waiting for the Pindar's entrance. Gina used that time to appraise the other councillors. There was anxiousness about most of them. Each would have been given tasks to do and tonight they would be held to account by the Pindar. Only three councillors looked at ease, number twelve, the Mullah. Number six, Illya Dracul and Number one, Hydie Papandreou. Numbers twelve and six had been given pivotal roles in creating the New World Order.

"They must have delivered," Gina surmised, "which would explain their calm demeanour."

Gina looked at Hydie and caught her gaze. She had been watching Gina. There was an almost imperceptible exchange of nods of recognition between them and then the Hydra looked away. Gina wondered why she would be so calm, given that she too had been given a pivotal role and was about to betray the Pindar. But then she had an inner strength that would surpass all others barring the Pindar himself.

A shadow crossed the open doorway and the Pindar was in the room. It seemed to Gina that he had materialised, rather than entered.

"Perhaps it was just a trick of the light," she thought, as he moved silently to take up his throne.

That was the strangest thing too, Gina noticed. Even with her newly found and acute Angel senses, she hadn't heard the Pindar's footsteps. He was dressed as one of them, the only difference being the gold mask that he wore inside his cowl.

"Once again it is the sacred night of the solstice," the Pindar began in his deep Slavic tones. "Tonight you will all renew your vows of allegiance to Lucifer and offer him the gift of life in the customary way."

With the exception of the Mullah, Dracul and the Hydra, there was an air of uneasiness about the councillors, including Gina. Only these three didn't have family and were therefore immune to the pain of the Pindar's cruel sacrifices.

He sat and motioned for the Council to do the same.

"Tonight, we will delay the pleasure of the human sacrifice until after your progress updates. I believe that we have some significant achievements to share tonight that will make our celebration afterwards even sweeter," the Pindar's unearthly voice sent a cold superstitious shiver right through Gina's body, as if someone had stepped on her grave.

The Pindar broke protocol and invited the councillors to speak in reverse of their numerical order. He was clearly dealing with the scraps and saving the feast until the end. Gina, the Mullah, Dracul and the Hydra were the last four. Dracul was the first of them to be invited to speak. He stood and began confidently.

"Pindar, councillors. As you will remember, I was charged with the research, design, development and commercialisation of a mind controlling game. The Dream App," Dracul paused theatrically. "I can confirm that human trials were completed in July this year, demonstrating that subscribers can be conditioned to obey subliminal messages after just a single viewing of a formatted film through the Dream App. These trials successfully included targeted violence and suicide."

There was an approving murmur from many of the other councillors.

"Trials went on to prove that individuals could be targeted with their own bespoke dream experiences, with tailored subliminal messages that can be triggered at a later date. Effectively, we can create a nation of unknowing 'sleepers' that we can deploy with a simple activation code. These sleepers can be placed next to politicians, senior civil servants, even world leaders. It could be

281

father and son. On hearing or reading the activation code, 'Satan666', they become automatons and will carry out their programmed response to the letter."

"Bravo!" one of the councillors called out and was immediately endorsed by others.

Illya Dracul let the praise for his considerable achievements subside before continuing.

"The Dream App became available on the high street and internet at the end of August. Since then sales have gone viral, grossing over one billion Dollars in the first quarter. It is highly addictive, particularly amongst the male population and we are currently working on improving its appeal to women."

Illya Dracul could have waxed lyrical for another hour but he decided that less was more.

"You have delivered in spades number six," the Pindar said with genuine admiration. "You have already given us a small army of would be assassins and the beginnings of control over the electorate. I have been watching the growth factor and it is truly of epidemic proportions. In significantly less than one generation we will have governing control of all the counties that make up the developed world. Well done Dracul."

It was rare praise indeed from the Pindar and a tough act to follow. The Mullah was next. He looked unimpressed and unfazed. He did not stand and only addressed the Pindar.

"Pindar. You now have your Mahdi in the name of Muhammad Akhbar," he grinned wryly through clenched, gappy teeth. He is rising like the Star of David over the holy lands. Akhbar has the people's hearts and the militants' guns. They flock to him, already recognising him as the Messiah and he unites them all; Sunnis, Shiites and Kurds."

It was the first time that all those who formed the Council of Thirteen, could see tangible evidence that the corner stone of the End Time war was set; the precursor to the New World Order that they all strived for. The Mullah, now in guise of the False Prophet, continued. He had captivated his audience.

"Akhbar preaches of a war, promised in the Hadith, and delivered through the Mahdi. There is a fever raging in the Middle East now that can only be cured through the shedding of blood in a Holy War. The people are ready. The question is Pindar, are you?" it was a bold and undisguised challenge.

"Tonight we will find out number twelve," the Pindar countered. "We have two more councillors yet to speak and then we will know."

Challenge made, the Mullah leaned back in his chair. An enigmatic smile remained on his lips, or perhaps it was a smirk? The un-killable man had just guaranteed that he would now be even more so.

"Number one," the Pindar prompted.

The Hydra stood, though it pained her to do so. She had a much bigger fish to fry. It would have been foolish to start off on the wrong foot, she conceded.

"You challenged me with bringing the politicians, world leaders, criminal organisations and the like under control," she began. "You put no financial constraints on that, nor have I applied any. What you have from me is a full portfolio of contracted world leaders, politicians, militants, mobsters, religious leaders and zealots. Where the existing ruling elite have been reluctant, I have engaged their opposition. All these will annex themselves to your cause at an agreed price, whether that be financial, power sharing or both. There are no omissions and their contracts are all binding."

"Commendable," the Pindar said, nodding his head approvingly. "I note that you haven't put a price on that portfolio of contracted agreements," he scrutinised her through the single eye cutaway of his golden mask, the All-Seeing Eye of the *Novus Ordo Seclorum*.

283

"At this stage, it is sufficed to say that it surpasses the Gross National Product of the entire modern world. But I am expecting that you will see it as a one-off investment that you will recoup one hundred fold," the Hydra looked confident in her assumption.

The Pindar simply nodded. Hydie Papandreou looked into that single eye. It was as cold as the Siberian wind and devoid of any compassion. It was the look of death. She shuddered.

"That was the easy bit," she thought, "now for the tricky part."

"You might consider this presumptuous of me Pindar, but I include myself in that portfolio of power. Indeed, my organisation ranks as high as any of the superpowers as far as control is concerned. Our people have globally infiltrated every aspect of government, commerce and the military. For my part, I am not interested in wealth or power. I have those in abundance. My price is simply security."

That single eye flared with anger but the Hydra held its reptilian stare. There was no going back from where she had positioned herself. She continued.

"I have built into these contracts a number of binding clauses. Simplistically, that they are overseen and serviced by me and me alone. Of course, that needed a little incentivisation," the Hydra let that hang to prompt a response from the Pindar.

"Which is?" he was perfectly aware that he was being spoon-fed.

"That I have a dossier on each; the names and addresses of their family line, close friends and allies. Breach of contract would naturally incur punishment," the Hydra had a look on her face that made Gina's blood run cold. "I am talking about the entire elimination of their family line, should they default on the terms of their contracts; genocide."

None in the room doubted the Hydra's ability to carry out that threat.

The Pindar held his counsel and reflected on it. The woman had bought herself maybe two years that was all. It was moment in time only for a being that had walked this Earth over millennia. He would have his revenge. The Pindar decided to let it go and moved on to Gina without looking at the Hydra again.

"Clever girl," Gina thought, as the Pindar directed his attention towards her.

"Number five. What have you to offer?" the Pindar's Slavic voice still reflected his anger at Hydie Papandreou's trickery. It was not a great start, from Gina's point of view, certainly not the start that she might have hoped for.

"Pindar," she began, standing to face him. "Your acquisitions are complete with each transaction signed over."

Gina took the folder from her valise, opened it and leant it against her chest with the text turned to face the Pindar. She flicked slowly through the pages of the portfolio, showing only a glimpse of each acquisition with her flamboyant signature adjacent.

She was about to say that these were her signatures transferring ownership back to the original shareholders should anything untoward happen to her or her children. But at that moment she had a premonition, that divine intervention that she had prayed for. Gina quickly closed the file. Something told her that it was the wrong thing to do at that moment. The Pindar was left with the impression that those signatures were signing over Mèdici acquisition ownership of each to him.

"Excellent!" The Pindar's mood had changed. "Now we can truly enjoy tonight's ceremony," he declared and clapped his hands. "Let the sacrifice begin."

Isabella Mèdici was trying to piece it together. She had been drugged for days and had completely lost her bearings and sense of reality. The last thing she could remember with any certainty was that she had killed Harper. She would unfortunately take that vile memory to her grave. Then she vaguely remembered the mill and running away from Gray in a blind panic. She had run into something, she remembered that, then nothing at all of any clarity. She had flashbacks of being concussed on the floor. Gray was there, she recalled and then there was a feeling as if she had been stung in her bottom. That was it, then nothing again until she woke in a squalid room, handcuffed to an iron-framed bed.

There was a man who came to her, she recalled; a man with a mass of red hair. He would force her to drink water, then the bee sting again and then nothing. Isabella couldn't remember how many times that it had happened like that, but the last time was different. She recalled that the man had come to her and taken the cuffs off.

"Can I go now?" she had said, as he led her into another room.

The man hadn't replied. There was a bath full of rusty brown water, she remembered, and him undressing her. Her next memory was of him bathing her.

"Daddy?" she had said in her confusion. The last time a man had bathed her was her father, when she was six years old.

This wasn't her daddy though, she had soon realised to her horror. His probing rough hands were washing her breasts and between her legs for much too long. She remembered crying and saying something to him drunkenly.

"You will die for that, just like Harper," she had said, doubting that he ever heard it, let alone cared.

She remembered him drying her hair and brushing it, as she sat naked on a chair. Finally the red headed man had dressed her in a coarse white robe. The feeling of the rough, clean cotton on her skin and being covered from the man's lecherous eyes was the only pleasure that Isabella had experienced since this nightmare had begun. She remembered feeling alert enough to think of escaping, and then there was the bee sting again.

The next thing she remembered was being walked through huge oak doors into an old building made of stone.

"I'm in a church," Isabella thought as she walked unsteadily down a stone corridor.

A cowled man in a white robe was helping her. She looked up at him and strangely his face was silver. Either side of her, were rows of suits of armour and tapestries. There were old weapons on the walls, swords, spears, axes and the like.

"No, I'm in a castle," she decided.

They came to a big, black wooden door. It creaked open. Inside, there were people sat in a circle around some kind of stone table. A ring of fire was burning above it, but the light that it offered was too poor for Isabella to make any sense of what she saw. The man steadying her on her feet forced her forwards into the room towards the stone table. They all seemed to be looking at her expectantly. Isabella wondered in her confusion why she might be of such interest. The man attending her sat her on the cold stone and opened her robe.

"No," Isabella protested feebly.

Her words seemed to be muffled and lost, as if she was gagged. She raised her hand to her mouth and realised for the first time that she too was wearing a mask. Even in her stupor, Isabella began to realise what was going on and screamed a terrified silent scream. It was a satanic sacrifice, and she was to be the offering. Her limbs were too numb with narcotics to function. She looked into the faces of her audience for help. Even in the gloom and cowled, there was one that she recognised. Isabella held out her arms pitifully to her and uttered one word. It was simply, "Mummy."

The chamber doors creaked open and a man and woman entered. The Pindar beckoned them forward. They were dressed in white robes with cowls, just as at the last meeting of the Council of

Thirteen. In fact everything was the same. The woman even seemed to need the man's support, just as before. He steered her past the Pindar to the stone altar where he sat her and dropped her robe. The young, blonde and petite girl was naked but for the silver fitted mask that covered her face. The expression on the mask was the same ambiguous grin that Gina had seen on that dreadful night of summer solstice. It gave no clue whatsoever as to the girl's identity or her personal crisis. However Gina knew exactly who it was. In truth, she knew it in her heart even before the premonition. The girl seemed unaware of her nakedness and was confused and scared. She held Gina's eyes and extended her arms towards her as if in recognition. She said something. It would have been inaudible to most of the others there, but Gina's new highly developed senses picked it up load and clear, "Mummy."

The man dropped his robe. He was apishly muscular and extremely well endowed. His readiness for the act that he was about to perform was beyond doubt. The stud had unruly red hair that seemed to be on fire in the candlelight and his silver mask had the leer of a devil. He had his back to his audience as he began to arrange Isabella's limbs in preparedness for their copulation.

Gina stood. It was as if she was in a trance and all preordained. She walked calmly over to the wall and took down one of the sabres. The blade had not become dull, even over the centuries. It glinted in the meagre light of the chamber and looked alive in Gina's slim hand as she tested its weight with a series of cuts in the air. She relaxed and let the blade be still at her side, then walked almost robotically over to the altar.

The Pindar and the councillors looked at Gina stoically, fascinated at what she was about. The red headed devil was too occupied with his erection to notice Gina's return. The cold steel of Gina's blade only cut through the air twice. The first time, it severed his penis and the second, his throat. There was a sickening thud as his corpse slumped and his head struck the stone. His life blood gushed from his wounds, drenching the altar. Satan had his offering. Isabella seemed unfazed by the macabre killing; she simply continued to look trustingly into her mother's face.

Gina went over to her and pulled her robe up to cover her nudity.

"Mummy's here now darling," she whispered, then pointed the blade accusingly at the Pindar.

"You have what you want from me, now let us go," it was said as a demand, not a request.

The Pindar laughed a cruel laugh. I do not think so number five. You have disrespected me and deign to cheat Satan of his just reward," he raised his arm and six armed guards took their positions at the entrance to the chamber. Their guns were all levelled at Gina.

There was an air of consternation about the other councillors. This had never happened before. Nobody had ever dared defy or disrespect the Pindar. Gina simply looked back defiantly at the armed guards without a hint of fear. She bowed her head, raised her arms slightly and clenched her fists as she concentrated. It was exactly the same stance that Ava had taken when she exploded Callum's tyre, that day at the farmhouse. She focussed her mind on their guns and imagined them burning like coals.

The air in the room quickly became oppressive as the static electricity, generated from Gina's rage built. The weapons that adorned the chamber walls began to rattle and clatter against the stonework. Some shook themselves free and crashed to the floor where they continued to kick and dance. Moments later, the guards screamed out in unison. In the same way that Ava had excited the air molecules in Callum's tyre to rub together to create heat, Gina had done it to the atomic structure of the metal in the guards' guns. Within seconds, they were glowing red hot and blistering their hands. Smoke began to fill the chamber with a smell like roasting pork. The guards had to shake their gun hands violently to free the stuck weapons from their grips. Their screams were deafening and befitting of the paintings of purgatory and damnation that were hung around the chamber.

Gina turned to face the Pindar with a look of hatred that made the other councillors fear for their lives. She was about to take him on, one to one. Only the Mullah, Illya Dracul and the Hydra were immune to the malevolence of her stare. Illya Dracul saw his opportunity to impress the Pindar further.

"Pindar," he said as he stood. "There is perhaps a more sporting way to resolve this. That is if number five is prepared to fight fair with the sword and not use her considerable Angel powers."

Dracul stood and walked arrogantly to the wall. He took the second sabre from its hanger and wielded it with the flourish of the consummate swordsman.

"I propose a duel to the death Pindar. If number five lives, then they go free. If she dies, they both die and Satan will have had three lives tonight," Dracul's arrogance pleased the Pindar.

"And you can guarantee me that you will be victorious, number six?" the Pindar asked.

"My family has lived and died by the sword since our ancestor Vlad the Impaler. Duels have become a matter of honour and I am well practiced in them. You have my personal guarantee Pindar, on my life."

The Pindar waved his hand and dismissed the bleating rabble that minutes ago were his elite guards.

"So be it number six. On your life," he said.

Illya Dracul's prowess with the sword was legendary amongst Gina's sporting peers. She knew that her chances of besting him without using the power of her mind were slim at best. She prayed that the responsibility of saving Isabella would make the difference in the end.

"Do I have your word that you will free us if I win?" Gina challenged the Pindar.

"You have my word number five, just as long as the fight is fair."

Gina had no choice now but to park her Angel powers, fight fairly and trust in her God.

They took their positions on opposite sides of the altar. Dracul divested himself of his robe. Beneath he wore black trousers and a white, open shirt. He looked confident as he rolled his sleeves up to his elbows and smirked derisively at Gina. Dracul took up the classic fencer's stance. Knees flexed, sword arm extended and free arm curled above his head for balance. Gina's pencil skirt, cut to just above the knee, was not conducive to giving her the freedom of movement she needed. She reversed her sabre and thrust it through the pinstripe material just below her crotch, then ran the keen blade down and out through the hem. She kicked off her Gucci shoes and stood barefooted on the cold stone flags. Now free of any encumbrance, Gina took her position opposite him, adopting the same classic stance.

"*En guarde!*" she ordered defiantly.

They crossed swords with a loud crash, then broke free and circled the altar watching each other's every move. Illya Dracul looked menacing with his short-cropped blonde hair and black eyes that seemed to burn like coals in the dim candlelight. Isabella was sat motionless on the altar between them. The naked and mutilated corpse of her captor and would be rapist, was slumped beside her. His leering silver mask and shock of red hair made him look both grotesque and foolish in death. Isabella was still physically encumbered by the cocktail of drugs that the man had given her, but her mind was now sharpened by recent events. She watched Dracul with a look of pure hatred as he circled with the intent of killing her mother. She wanted to throw herself at him and claw his eyes out but her drug-ravaged body refused her commands.

"You are going to die Gina Mèdici and then your daughter, after we have raped her of course," Dracul goaded to enrage and distract her. "I know that you are a swordswoman but that's just girl on girl stuff. You have never raised a blade in anger," it was all said to put her off her game plan.

Gina ignored Dracul's jibe and focussed only on his sword and eyes. From experience, she knew that there is always an involuntary pupil contraction just before an attack. Spotting it, gives you a split second's warning which is often the difference between winning and losing a bout, or in this case, the difference between life and death.

Gina was the first to break the safety of having the altar between them. She stepped out to allow him to come between her and the blood-soaked slab. It was a tactical move on Gina's part and it worked. Dracul had disobeyed one of the golden rules of sword fighting. That was, to never get caught with your back to an obstacle. That he did was a sign of his complacency and how easy he thought the duel would be. He cursed his carelessness and cursed again when Gina advanced quickly, taking advantage of him not being able to retreat. His legs came to a stop against the altar and her blade caught him in the stomach. Dracul had been lucky. It was only a flesh wound, but it bled profusely, soaking the bottom of his shirt. It was enough to create a rage in him though. Gina had drawn first blood and made him look foolish in front of the Pindar and the Council of Thirteen.

Dracul counter attacked, coming in from high right but Gina parried his sabre with ease. The deflected blade caught number four full in the face. He screamed out in agony and pressed the sleeve of his habit into the wound to stem the blood flow. It was enough to send the rest of the councillors scurrying to the back of the chamber for safety. The empty chairs formed an island that they could move in and out of to try to gain advantage, one over the other.

Dracul advanced again, using those short, scuttling steps that fencers do. It gives them perfect balance and maximises leg, body and arm extension into the attack. Gina parried it again. Their blades ran up each other until they came face to face with the hilts of their sabres locked together. It was now a question of strength. Who could push who away and take advantage of the other's backward stumbling. Illya Dracul expected Gina's wrist to buckle against a man's pressure but she held firm and gave only a little ground. It was unnatural, a woman withstanding a man's weight and strength.

Gina saw a sudden look of concern in Dracul's eyes. He hadn't reckoned on her having the strength of a man. There was a hint of fear too. Gina could almost taste it.

"Angel versus Shadow," he grunted through gritted teeth as he strained against her, "and the Angel dies," he added with disdain.

His youthful arrogance was his Achilles heel though. He hadn't realised that Gina had given a little ground in the stand-off purposely to lull him into a false sense of security.

"Wrong Dracul," she said menacingly. "Not just Angel; Angel of Death!"

Gina called on all of her newly found strength and forced Dracul backwards. He stumbled before catching his balance and lost the advantage for a second time. She took the initiative and came at him with an advance-lunge that he only just avoided with a successful parry, and then replied with a counter-riposte. Their blades sang musically in the air, ringing steel on steel to the rhythm of the cuts and thrusts of the duel. The swordsmen had quickly got the measure of each other. It was attack and counter-attack, with the advantage ebbing and flowing from one to the other.

The fight was physically and mentally gruelling. Gina was thankful for the countless hours of relentless training that Ava had forced on her without mercy at the farmhouse. Now she could see why. She decided that she would kiss her for it, if she ever survived this fight. Her stamina was holding out well and a lot of that was also due to her motherly instinct to protect her daughter. That alone seemed to give her a limitless supply of energy to draw on. Dracul on the other was bleeding and starting to show signs of fatigue. Gina decided to keep him working hard and wait him out. He couldn't keep losing blood for long without going into an energy crisis. If she went in for the kill too soon, he might dig deep and find reserves sufficient to turn the duel to his favour.

"Be patient Gina," she said to herself, "and keep him working and bleeding."

The life of her daughter was ever present in Gina's mind, spurring her on. The clashing of their swords rose and fell in tempo as they traversed the arena, each testing the other. Gina worked Dracul back over to the island of chairs and kept him moving around it. She used a style of defence that encouraged him to attack her from high, keeping his arms above his head. This simple strategy significantly increased his cardio effort and loss of blood. He soon began to tire more rapidly. Gina suddenly reversed their rotation around the island and caught him flat footed. She brought her sabre down from high to Dracul's left, slashing down at his neck. He saw her intent at the last second and leant backwards. Instead of finding the soft flesh and carotid artery, she caught his free hand, severing two fingers.

Dracul yelped. The blood dripped like a tap onto his shoulder and down the front of his shirt. It was the turning point. Illya Dracul suddenly had a flashback to the only other time that he had duelled with an Angel. It was with Ben Robinson, who had run him through with his sabre. Dracul had fled for his life that day and narrowly escaped death. He knew now that his energy was nearly spent and rued his complacency at the beginning of the duel. That stomach wound, although not serious, had cost him too much blood and maybe the fight. History would repeat itself unless he took the initiative to end this now. He felt the panic begin to rise in him and coil like a snake in his stomach. It took all of his effort to crush the monster that was growing inside him, but he did. Fear had focussed him again and now he was looking for the kill.

Dracul realised all too well that he only had enough strength left for one last attack and that it could not fail. He went for the killer advance-lunge, driving hard off his back leg. He had expected to take Gina by surprise but she saw his eye reflex just in time and side stepped. She raised her sabre, bracing herself for his impact. The force of his own advance drove Gina's sabre through his chest and out through his back. For a moment, Illya Dracul stood there wide mouthed in disbelief.

"A woman?" he mouthed almost inaudibly. "A mere woman has done this to me?"

He buckled at his knees and looked back at the Pindar as if hoping for a miracle. The Pindar's stare was as cold as the grave. There would be no miracles, only his distain.

"That's for all the young lives you have blighted with your vile Dream App Dracul," Gina said with contempt as she put her foot on his shoulder and withdrew her sabre.

"And this is for Isabella," she said calmly as she reversed the blade and opened his throat down to his spine.

Dracul's black eyes flared momentarily, then stared sightlessly back at her as the final moments of his life ebbed away.

Gina turned to face the Pindar.

"You are next if you break your promise Pindar," Gina spat the words out defiantly at him. "You would be wise to fear the woman scorned!"

"Guards!" he called out in a black rage.

There were only two left. They entered the chamber reluctantly and raised their guns, barely able to point them for shaking. Gina immediately adopted that stance again and began to focus her kinetic powers. The air became oppressively charged with static as before. This time though, Gina's rage was so fierce that the weaponry on the walls didn't just vibrate, they flew off the wall and crashed around the chamber randomly. Gina whipped her arms around in circles creating a kinetic storm. The randomness of the crashing weapons became less apparent as Gina organised them into a vortex of deadly steel. This phenomenon was founded purely on Gina's undiluted rage and hatred. She was about to unleash that deadly storm of weapons on the Pindar when the Hydra interceded.

"Pindar!" Hydie Papandreou shouted urgently above the clamour of crashing steel. She placed her hand on his arm. "You gave your word. What will the councillors think if it has no value?"

The Pindar paused for a long moment while Gina's and Isabella's lives hung in the balance. Compared to the magnitude of his dark powers, Gina's little storm of 'cutlery' as he perceived it, was futile. The Hydra was right though; he conceded and dismissed Gina with a wave of his hand.

"Leave and take your sprog with you," he growled. "I have what I want, my acquisitions. You only live to die another day number five. Now go!"

The storm abated in an instant and the weaponry crashed to the floor, much to the relief of the terrified councillors.

Gina looked briefly at the Hydra to thank her, but she had averted her face for their joint safety. She did catch her thought though and that was simply, "Impressive Gina."

Gina slipped her arm under Isabella's and stood her up. Somehow Isabella had managed to find the use of her feet and Gina hurried her as best she could out of the chamber. As soon as they were outside the room, Gina swept Isabella up into her arms and flew down the arched hallway with her, down the avenue of suits of armour and tapestries and out through the main entrance. Seconds later, they were in the road, heading for the Mercedes. Gina ran for all she was worth, clinging to Isabella until she arrived breathless at the limousine.

Callum was already waiting for them in the street with his gun at the ready. He bundled them into the car and screamed at Luigi.

"Go, go, go!"

Luigi pulled away with burning tyres, even before the doors of the limousine were fully shut. As they sped past the castle entrance there was a bloodcurdling roar. It wasn't human, by any means. It was animal and it echoed around the castle battlements like thunder.

"I think the Pindar has just looked at my acquisition documents," Gina said simply with a wicked grin.

Chapter 28

The journey back to Munich airport was emotional. Isabella went into shock and slept all the way, curled up on the back seat with her head on Gina's lap. Meanwhile, Gina was trying to come to terms with her own sins. She was a staunch Catholic and had just brutally killed two men. It didn't sit well on her conscience. That was compounded by the fact that she had no remorse at the time of doing it, only the feeling of guilt after the event. It hadn't helped either that Callum said at the time, "Guilt. That's what Catholics do isn't it?"

He was trying to make light of it, but Gina wasn't in the right place for that, not right then.

Gina kept bursting into tears when she looked at Isabella's face. Her skin was white and almost transparent. There were dark circles around her eyes that looked like bruises and her lips were dry and cracked. It looked like she had a split lip too and a deep cut in her hairline above her forehead. Her arms were full of needle marks and she had a deep cut in the palm of her right hand. Isabella had been badly abused and God only knew to what extent. Gina didn't dare even think that she might have been raped too.

"I wasn't there for her," Gina howled on several occasions. "She must have been terrified," and the tears would start again.

Callum did all he could to comfort her but, right now what they both needed was sleep. First though, they needed to find a medic. He had called ahead and arranged for a private doctor to meet them at the infirmary at Munich airport. They had a private jet waiting there for them so, all being well; they would be in Moscow by morning.

Doctor Franz Müller met them at the infirmary. He was a small insignificant man in his fifties. He had an intelligent brow, thinning mousey hair and glasses. Isabella was on a wheeled stretcher with hospital blue blankets over her. She hadn't woken in the transfer and was so still that Gina kept checking her pulse to make sure that she was still alive.

Callum helped the doctor transfer Isabella to the bed. Doctor Müller gave her a quick examination to make sure that there was nothing immediately life threatening to deal with.

"She is dangerously dehydrated and low on body sugars. We need to give her an intravenous glucose infusion immediately before we examine her further," he said in the grave manner that doctors do. "They normally bounce back pretty quickly Mrs Mèdici, particularly at her age," he added reassuringly.

He prepared the drip and was about to insert the cannula in Isabella's arm.

"Goodness me," he sounded shocked. "Is she drug dependent?" he was looking at the angry bruises and needle wounds along the vein in her arm.

"No doctor," Gina said a little too defensively. "She was abducted and *they* did this to her."

The doctor nodded and tutted as he searched her other arm for a suitable place for the catheter. There was none, so he inserted it in her hand.

"Is there anything else that I should know?" he asked.

"Not that we can tell you," Callum said, "other than she has been captive for four days."

"I need to test her bloods to find out what they've been putting in her and then a full medical examination, as I have already said. I hope you were not intending to leave here tonight, that would be most inappropriate."

"Whatever it takes," Gina said. "Just bring her back to me."

"I'll go and stand the jet down and bring back some coffees. I think it's going to be a long night," Callum said and left. It was no place for him to be right now.

When Callum returned two hours later with the coffees, Gina looked a different woman.

"Issie's going to be fine Callum. She's responding to the drip and her medicine. She even woke for a few moments and smiled before she drifted off."

"Did she say anything?" he asked. Gina looked tearful.

"No, she was too weak. But I could tell that she felt safe with me there," Gina looked away from Callum. The emotion of that innocent trust was hard for her to contain.

"That's fantastic news Gina. Has the doctor said anything about when she might be fit to travel?"

"Subject to nothing serious coming back from her blood test, then tomorrow afternoon would be OK. More than anything now, she needs sleep and nourishment."

"And so do you Gina," Callum's good advice fell on deaf ears.

"I can't go Callum. I can't leave her. When she wakes, she's going to be frightened. I can doze here in the chair. You go and get some sleep."

"OK, you're right," Callum conceded. "I will go to the canteen and bring you something, then check into one of the airport hotels nearby. Call me when she wakes and I'll come back with some food for her and we can change over and you get some rest back at the hotel."

Gina agreed for the sake of not arguing. However she had no intention of leaving Isabella's side, not for a long time.

Gina had no idea how long she had been asleep, but her nightmares had been vivid. As ever with dreams, there was a relevance to current events but that was all. Isabella was in deadly peril several times over in her dreams. On each occasion Gina had fought for her but failed to save her. Throughout, there was an evil and malevolent presence; the Pindar. He had frustrated every attempt that Gina had made to rescue her. It was as if Isabella's fate was sealed. It seemed that one day he would get her, no matter what Gina did.

"Leave her alone!" Gina screamed out into the darkness.

"Mum, it's OK. It's just a dream," Isabella was knelt on the floor next to her mother's chair. "It's just a dream Mum. I'm here."

"Issie? Oh, thank God. I thought I had lost you again."

Gina wrapped her arms urgently around Isabella's neck and drew her protectively into her breast. They stayed like that in silence for some time, savouring the moment. Neither wanted to spoil it with words, nor could either trust themselves to do so without crying. At last it was Isabella who found the strength and broke the silence.

"I always knew that you would find me Mummy. I never gave up hope," Isabella pulled away from her mother so that she could see her face. "Thank you. You were awesome."

Isabella's emotions welled up inside her, choking her words. She had to pause a moment to gather herself.

"I thought that masked man was going to rape and kill me on the altar. I felt sick with fear and couldn't move a muscle to resist. Then I saw you and knew I would be safe. But then that young man challenged you to fight to the death to save my life. He was young and strong and so confident. I thought he was going to kill you Mum. I wanted to help you but I couldn't move."

"You were all the help that I needed Issie. You gave me strength and purpose to survive. Somehow we both helped each other."

"Did all that really happen Mum, or was some of it a dream? Like things flying around the room and those men with the guns," it seemed too fantastic for Isabella to believe.

"It all happened Issie. I know that it's beyond belief, but it all happened. I have learned so much in the months I've been away."

Gina ran her fingers thoughtfully through Isabella's hair and settled it behind her ear. That simple loving act spoke volumes about the bond between them. She was wondering how best to explain it all. There was so much; Angels and Demons, Shadows and the Illuminati. There was only one way, she decided.

"The world is nothing like the physical creation that we have both imagined darling. It's a mental and spiritual place where our minds can make things happen. You just have to dig deep and unlock the potential inside you," Gina paused and then added, "Just like you had to dig deep to survive your capture. I'm so proud of you that you did Issie. It would have destroyed me and Sasha if you hadn't. So many people would have given up and become victims. You had to fight for your life, we know that because we found the American. You were pretty awesome too Issie."

"But I was petrified Mum. I only did what I did to survive."

"I was petrified too Issie, petrified of losing you. The fear and the rage that went with it, was what made me able to find my potential," Gina took Isabella's hands. "I need to show you something that words can't explain. This is how I learned from

Ava, a new friend of mine. We join minds and share each other's thoughts and memories."

"But Mum, that's not possible. Is it?" Isabella was still sceptical. "And who is Ava?"

"You will meet her as soon as we get to Moscow," Gina assured.

"Moscow? We are going to Moscow?" Isabella asked incredulously. It just went from crazy to mad.

"All will become clear soon. Relax and let your thoughts run free Issie and don't be afraid."

Gina took over her daughter's mind slowly so as not to alarm her. She took her back to when her father first became involved with the Mèdici bank. Isabella needed to know all of it, particularly how the Illuminati were brought into their lives by her father. Gina could feel Isabella's disappointment and distain when she realised what he had done, and her guilt for thinking that it was her mother who had sided with the Illuminati. Then Gina felt her horror and rage when she learned that he had arranged the fatal car crash to eliminate her grandparents to take over the Mèdici bank. After that was the heartbreak and grief of her father's death by murder. Despite the terrible things he had done, he was still her father. Gina needed to comfort her through that devastating part of the story. All that had only taken seconds to impart. Gina watched the expressions on Isabella's face change as she told her tale, reflecting her anger and pain. She knew that those expressions would soon change to astonishment and disbelief when she introduced Isabella to the concept of Angels and Shadows and that they were themselves descended from the Angel race. Even that would seem credible compared to telling her that the head of the Illuminati, the Pindar, was probably Satan.

Ten minutes later, it was done. Isabella now knew the events of the last few years as if she had lived them herself. In the same way, Gina had lived the horrors of her daughter's abduction. They spent some time in silence just holding each other.

"What are we going to do Mum?" Isabella asked, feeling helpless.

"We join forces with the Angels and trust in them," Gina began. "When all this started, I swore to them that I would see this through. We are united in the war against the Pindar and his ambition to create his New World Order. Now that we've joined ranks with the Hydra and her Shadow organisation, we have a chance. We can't stand back and let mankind slip into a Third World War and Satanism. We just can't."

"You will have to show me how to fight and Sasha too," Isabella was already up for it. "We are in this together now Mum. Together."

After sharing Isabella's mind and witnessing first-hand what she had been through and how she had coped, Gina had no doubt at all that she meant it.

Callum was eventually woken at ten o'clock in the morning by Gina's call. Apparently Isabella had been awake for hours and they had already sent out for breakfast. Gina had let Callum sleep in. Anyway, there was nothing much that he could do, she had decided. When Callum arrived at the infirmary, Isabella was sat up in animated conversation with her mother. She looked up and saw Callum, then shot her mother an approving look.

"This is Callum," Gina said and blushed.

"Pleased to meet you," Isabella said, extending her hand to greet him. She winced momentarily as the cannula snagged. "Mum has told me a lot about you and we shared minds too," her smile was genuine and mischievous too, Callum noted. Just like her mother's.

"I hope your mother hasn't told you too much. She is prone to a little exaggeration you know?" he quipped.

"I can't wait to get to know you and Yuri," Isabella added as an afterthought. "And learn more about your secret organisation."

"Well, we had better not get your mum too involved in that secret organisation had we, given her track record of keeping secrets?" Callum cocked an accusing eye at Gina.

"It's family," Gina said in defence, feigning hurt.

"Are you up to the flight to Moscow then Issie?" he asked, changing the subject.

"Can't wait, and have I got a story to tell you on the way!"

Emanuel, Ava, Yuri and Sasha met them at Moscow airport. The reunion went way past emotional. Even Emanuel was moved to tears, which was something pretty much unheard of. He was a man practiced at keeping the British 'stiff upper lip', but the Mèdici reunion took him past his limits. Sasha and Isabella quickly separated off and exchanged stories. They were joined in the delicious danger of the conspiracy theory which was the Dream App and its connections to the Illuminati. Both had campaigned to have it banned and both had nearly lost their lives doing it. Instead of being put off, they were both reinvigorated to finish the job that they had started.

Ava had never truly expected Gina to survive the Solstice meeting and so the reunion for her was a precious gift. She swore that it would be the last time that she would ever let Gina face danger without being at her side. When Ava learned how Gina had fought against Illya Dracul, a fabled swordsman, and won without using her powers, she was both amazed and immensely proud of her. The fact that Gina was able to focus and call up her powers over nature as well, justified the months of tortuous training that Ava had put her through. Gina tricking the Pindar into believing that she had signed over the Mèdici portfolio of acquisitions and getting out of the castle alive with Isabella was masterful. Gina was now the complete package, Ava thought, "Beautiful, intelligent, empowered, ruthless and dangerous."

They all agreed though, that despite all of Gina's amazing deeds, she and Isabella were only still alive because of the Hydra's intervention. Now, after being made a fool of, the Pindar would hunt the Mèdici's down, irrespective of the consequence to his mission. It would be a matter of honour. In anticipation of the Pindar's reaction, Emanuel had mobilised a squad to further fortify the farmhouse where Gina, Sasha and Isabella would need to spend an indeterminate period of time. Ava, along with Yuri, had naturally volunteered to stay with them as bodyguards and arranged for her daughter, Mina, to stay with her mother, Anastasia, until it was all over. She was too young and the situation, too dangerous.

That was a massive personal sacrifice for Ava who was becoming increasingly maternal and needy in pregnancy. When she first saw Yuri at the airport, her heart somersaulted. It was in times of danger that she truly and deeply loved Yuri. He was her rock. It was in that 'other life' that Yuri had no idea of, that he had loved her and protected her. She owed everything to him, her life and her children. Ava threw herself into his open arms and kissed him as if there was no tomorrow. She whispered urgently in his ear, her voice husky.

"Get me home and quickly, I want you."

She glanced guiltily over at Callum. He was stood unnecessarily close to Gina and she was leaning into him closing the gap still further. Ava could intuitively tell that they had had sex and smirked knowingly. Just at that moment, Gina caught her eye. She looked away immediately and blushed.

"Callum's going to be all right now," Ava thought and smiled fondly.

She felt the burden of the guilt that she had carried from her alternative life, lift from her spirit releasing her at last. Callum's happiness was no longer her responsibility and she could now give herself to Yuri completely. She took his hand, pulling him away from the group.

"Let's go Yuri, they won't miss us now."

Ava's intimate smile promised Yuri the moon.

Gina was resigned to their incarceration and recognised the sense in it. She was however, deeply disappointed in being taken out of the fray and saddened that she would see little or nothing of Callum. That was made worse by the knowledge that Kayla was back in town and would be getting her claws back in him again. The silver lining to this dark cloud was that Callum would soon be leaving Moscow anyway. He had been tasked by Emanuel to go to Syria with a small squad of men. Their mission was to assassinate Mohammed Akhbar, now recognised by the majority of the Arab nation as the Mahdi. Gina had a feeling of great foreboding though. Something dreadful was going to happen, she knew it, but she couldn't divine what and to whom.

Chapter 29

Angelos Associates' offices in Moscow City. Friday, January 5th 2018. Two weeks later.

Callum Knight was sat informally on the desk at the front of the briefing room. He was considering his squad. All of them were experienced in desert warfare. They were the best of the best. Together, they formed an elite team of battle hardened veterans that he had commanded for over a decade and learned to respect. Callum could trust his life to each and every one in the room and indeed had, on many occasions. The atmosphere was relaxed but charged with expectation. The dangerous mission that Callum was about to ask them to undertake, was simply their day jobs. These men thrived on inherent danger and the opportunity to show off their professionalism. They were not encumbered by conscience or the morality of their actions. For them this was just another clinical mission of 'search and destroy'. The rest was for politicians to debate and agonise over.

Callum appraised his men as he always did before going to war. It was to make sure that he didn't lose sight of their humanity. They were men first and soldiers, second. Their safety and survival was always at the front of Callum's mind.

He had chosen Ralph Robinson as his second in command. Ralph was a Major in the SAS with his own command. In Angel hierarchy, they were on equal terms and Ralph could quite easily have led the squad himself. He was a strongly built man in his early forties, ruggedly handsome, with a broad smile, vivid blue eyes and fair hair that had started to grey at the temples. His dimpled smile had deepened into creases in recent years, testament to the strain that he continuously worked under. Callum knew that he could trust this man to get his boys home if anything happened to him. That was a key factor in his decision.

Then there was Staff Sergeant Mike Jackson, another from the SAS Regiment. He was in his late twenties, strikingly handsome with a quizzical look that made girl's hearts flutter. He had joined the army at the age of seventeen and had spent most of his ten years of service in the theatre of war. Mike had completed three tours in Afghanistan, working covertly in the villages. His swarthy looks and fluency in the language had helped him pass himself off as an Arab. Mike followed that working in and around Syria. He was tasked with gathering intelligence on the deployment of the ISIS and the elimination of their leaders. Although young by comparison with his peers, he was fearless, funny and just the man you would want next to you when things got tough. Mike would probably be the most important member of his team, Callum acknowledged. He had just returned from Syria so his up-to-date understanding of the ISIS deployment and their *modus operandi*, would be invaluable. More importantly, he could mix with the Arabs and pass as one of them. Callum turned his attention to Red Jake.

Jake was looking back at him with his usual scowl. He was a bull of a man, ginger, bawdy and in his fifties. He was a fighter, drinker, insomniac and a paradox. Although fearless and ruthless in battle, he could cry himself to sleep at night over some chick flick movie. This same man though, wouldn't think twice about cutting another's throat. Red Jake also held the prize for the most

307

'shot man' in the organisation and rated man-flu as a worse malaise. Jake would never send a man into danger if he could take that risk himself. Red Jake would never make old bones, Callum had to concede. One day, he wouldn't be coming home, but his men just might.

Chas and Joey caught Callum's attention next. They were engaged in animated conversation. Callum imagined that they were probably pre-guessing their mission. There was enough global publicity about the ascension of the Mahdi and the massing of the Arabs for them to do so. They were Paratroopers and devoted brothers who had joined less than a year apart. They had been inseparable throughout their service, each owing his life to the other on several occasions. It was their back-watching and total commitment, one for the other, that had been their salvation. Callum knew that if he was to lose one in the mission, then he would probably lose both. That would either be in support of his brother, or in blind revenge.

James, who was sat apart from the others, was an obvious choice for Callum. He was a forty year old RAF Weapons Technician whose skills with explosives were currently second to none. He had the accolade of being the most prolific surviving bomb disposal expert in the combined armed forces. James had commanded two Explosive Ordnance Disposal units in Iraq and another in Afghanistan. He and his team were tasked with the disabling of roadside IEDs, investigating the aftermath of roadside car bombings, and searching the villages door to door to uncover bomb-makers at their homes. James had probably spent more time in a bomb suit than any other living serviceman. This understated, solitary man was nerveless and Callum was grateful to have him in his squad. James had the technical skills to single-handedly take out more of the enemy with his pyrotechnics than the rest of his squad put together.

That left the Marines Zak and Rudy, both dangerous men on and off the battlefield. They were a wild pair in their early thirties and highly charged with testosterone. They were a nightmare off-duty though, getting into more trouble than was possible to imagine.

Callum knew that these men could turn a fight around when it really mattered, which made their social shenanigans just noise in the grand scheme of things.

Their medic, Craig Jamieson, was sat in front of him scribbling a report. He was in his middle forties too, handsome with a strong chin and bright blue eyes. He was the sort of man who exuded competence and confidence. His accolade was having administering morphine on the battlefield and taking bullets out of all of those currently in the room. Callum included. It was a sad indictment of the business they were in and not one to worry too much about your pension scheme.

Callum needed a helicopter pilot who was experienced in desert warfare. A man he could trust implicitly, not just to get them in but who would risk all to get them out. Sean O'Malley was his obvious choice. O'Malley, a middle-aged and rotund Irishman with a ruddy face and ginger hair, was sat patiently waiting for his instructions. He had the deepest respect for Callum and his men and considered himself their guardian angel. He had flown to their rescue on countless occasions and knew that this next mission would be no different. In warfare, everything was planned to the tightest of schedules, invariably too tight, which is when casualties happen. It was ironic that in alternative lives, O'Malley had been a traitor to the Angels. In those lives, he had a gambling addiction that the Shadow organisation had taken advantage of. In this version of life though, O'Malley had so far kept the gambling beast inside him at bay. He was focussed and loyal.

"Men," he said at last, "can I have your attention please."

The room fell quiet immediately. Their Officer Commanding had spoken and he had their full respect and attention. At that timely moment, Kayla Lovell breezed in. She was all smiles and confidence. The look on Callum's face was a picture.

"Kayla?"

"The one and only," she fixed him with an accusing look disguised as a smile. It spoke chapters. "You weren't thinking of taking on the entire Arab nation. Without me to protect your men, were you Callum?"

"It's not the *complete Arab nation* Kayla, it's just one man," he said lamely.

There was a lot of sense in taking Kayla along but a lot of complications too. Callum had purposely left her out for personal reasons. He could tell by the atmosphere in the room that his men were pleased to see her. Kayla brought with her a whole new dimension with her kinetic abilities and mind control, which had made a difference many times in the past. Callum had little choice but to concede. She would have somehow manipulated his thoughts that way anyway, he lamented. What Kayla wants, Kayla gets. He nodded and she sat a little too triumphantly.

"So," he began, "following the Arab Spring eight years ago, the political, social and economic unrest in the Middle East has escalated. Poverty and disillusionment have left the Arab nation ripe for rebellion and radicalisation. Worse still, manipulation," Callum added meaningfully. "You will all no doubt have heard of Mohammed Akhbar?"

There was a general rumbling of the affirmative from Callum's squad. Red Jake spoke for them all.

"We guessed that he'd be our target," Jake shook his big ruddy head. "That man seriously needs stopping Boss, before there ain't no stoppin' him. The man's got Allah on his side."

There was a superstitious murmuring amongst the squad. They had all heard the truths, half-truths and lies about Mohammed Akhbar. Callum needed to exorcise any thoughts that his men might be harbouring about *God* being involved in the meteoric rise to power of this man. The one perceived to be the prophesied redeemer of Islam, the Mahdi.

"Agreed Jake, the man does need stopping, but a *man* is exactly what he is and you have only half guessed the mission," now

Callum really had their attention. "Akhbar is an imposter and no more the Mahdi than I am. He is an ISIS, Illuminati puppet, put in place to cause unrest. Our greater goal is to take down the Illuminati and avert a Third World War. Eliminating Akhbar is only one of scores of operations, planned to take place simultaneously, to take down the Illuminati organisation."

The mention of a Third World War and wholesale Illuminati assassinations came as a complete shock to the squad and Callum's men uncharacteristically lost their discipline and began talking amongst themselves. Their individual intelligence sources had not indicated this as being a possibility.

"Men," Callum said evenly, bringing them quickly back on track. "It has never been a secret that the aim of the Illuminati is to create a New World Order, the *Novus Ordo Seclorum*, as they call it. To create that, they need a world war big enough to eclipse the last two; one that will bring the world to its knees. Mohammed Akhbar is their catalyst to make that happen. He is seen by the Arab people to be the Mahdi, the Twelfth Imam, who the scriptures say will lead them in holy war against the infidels and emerge victorious."

Sergeant Mike Jackson interceded. He had witnessed this recent Arab phenomenon. Only days ago he was in the crowds of pilgrims that had gathered at Aleppo in Syria to pledge their allegiance to the Mahdi. His swarthy looks and fluent Arabic had allowed him to walk freely amongst them, singling out ISIS activists for later elimination.

"I have heard Akhbar address the people," Mike cocked a brow in that quizzical way that he was famous for. "Imposter, or not, the man is charismatic and has the people's hearts and minds. His followers are leaving their homes in droves to unite with him. He talks of unity through war and retribution as laid out in the scriptures. One faith and one people, united in one goal. That goal is death to the oppressor, glory and martyrdom."

"Good background, Mike," Callum said. It was no more than he already knew but it had endorsed the reason why he had selected

Mike. "Can you add anything more? Who he's working with, for example," again Callum knew but there was merit in his men hearing from first-hand experience.

"Yes, there's more," Mike began with authority. "His orations are preceded by the arrival of the so called prophet, the Mullah Ismael Alansari. He whips up frenzy, preaching of the arrival of Mohammed Akhbar, the Mahdi and gives him his holy endorsement. When Akhbar arrives the next day, the crowds ululate and supplicate themselves to him, pledging themselves to his holy cause. They go from village to village, town to town and to every holy place like this, creating mass hysteria and it's growing with momentum every day."

"Are they armed?" Callum asked.

"For the most part no, or at least not yet, but that must be the next stage. That and weapons training," Mike added.

"I can add more to this," Kayla offered. Strategy and intelligence were her strengths. "We know that the Americans and Russians have been covertly supplying ISIS vast quantities of weapons since the beginning of the civil war in Aleppo, between the Presidents soldiers and the rebels. The Russians have been shipping on a regular basis from Novorossiysk on the Black Sea, through the Bosporus Strait into the Aegean. We know that the KGB has handshakes in place with the Turkish customs, so they can do this with impunity. The Americans are doing the same through their CIA, but flying them into Aleppo and Homs under the guise of *Agricultural Machinery*. All this disguised as international aid."

"So we can assume that Akhbar's army could be armed and trained in months then Kayla?" Callum asked.

"You can and they will be," it was a simple statement of fact on Kayla's part.

"OK, thanks Kayla."

She caught Callum's eye with a reprimanding look that said, "Don't try and squeeze me out of this."

Callum already knew that he could not. His mind briefly wondered to Gina and what she would think of Kayla going along. Kayla caught his thought and her eyes flared in anger but she bit her tongue, knowing that she had given him every right and reason to stray.

Kayla was a conundrum. Only Callum and Emanuel fully understood her. Perhaps that was why they forgave her and loved her for all her infidelities and tempers. She was a hybrid, a woman of mixed blood. Her mother was an Angel and her father a Shadow. With that heady mix of chromosomes, comes an impossibility of both temperament and ability; passion and wrath. She was desperately in love with Callum, above all else. In the good times, it went passed amazing for Kayla. When he tried to raise it to the next level and had even proposed, she panicked. Her dark side would immediately come into play, despite her efforts to fight the monster within her back.

Something would snap inside her and she would lose herself to other men, hating herself after each one. Kayla would be in pieces for months and sometimes, years. Eventually she would come back to Callum, normally when she sensed competition. For months she would be an Angel again, and then it would start over. The Shadow inside her would rise, and she would spoil everything. Sometimes she would consider suicide to make it stop, and then Callum would take her back and understand the conflicting powers that controlled her. Kayla loved Callum more than life itself, she just couldn't prove it.

Callum sensed Kayla's brewing rage and quickly moved on.

"So, that gives you a fair idea of what it's all about," he said, avoiding Kayla's eyes. "There are folders on the desks for each of you with all the detail. I want you to read these thoroughly and commit your parts in the mission to memory. Before I give you the overall brief, are there any questions?"

"Yes," it was Ralph Robinson. "I'm assuming that Akhbar's land based army must already be in the tens of thousands. Where are their supplies coming from? Just to feed them all would be hundreds of tons of freight."

"The United Nations mostly," Callum replied ironically. "The British Red Cross, Médecins Sans Frontières, Human Appeal. You name the charitable organisation and ISIS is diverting their essential supplies from the refugee camps in Aleppo to Akhbar's army. In short, the rest of the world is unwittingly funding and enabling the Illuminati's war effort."

"I guessed as much," Ralph lamented. "No more questions."

Callum looked around his audience for anymore. There were none.

"In two days' time at midnight, we will be leaving RAF Brize Norton in Oxfordshire, for the British Sovereign Base at Akrotiri, Cyprus. There we transfer to a Chinook with Syrian markings. It will already have been fully prepped and armed for our mission. O'Malley takes us from there to the Shayrat Air Base at Homs to refuel. That's a little over 200 miles. We have friends on the ground there. Mike, being fluent in Arabic, will be our liaison. The rest of us stay in the Chinook and keep our mouths shut. From there, it's on to Aleppo. We can't use the Menagh Military Airbase there, as it's heavily under ISIS control. We're currently looking at satellite images for a secure location nearby to base ourselves."

"I know a safe haven at Abu Jurayn," Mike volunteered. "It's about 25 miles to the southeast of Aleppo, by the Al Jaboul lake. There's an airfield there. The town has suffered badly at the hands of ISIS and are pro-British. Pro anybody that is in opposition to ISIS, actually."

"Thanks Mike, we will research that possibility," Callum nodded at Kayla who was best placed to make that assessment. "Kayla, will you field that please?" he asked.

Kayla was his natural choice, being vastly experienced in logistics and opportunity management. On that front, she didn't miss the opportunity of giving him a 'you couldn't do without me' look. Callum continued.

"At that point, we have 24 hours to locate and kill Akhbar. Any longer than that would be impossible to keep our presence secret, even if the natives are friendly. It only takes one. Besides that, we are committed to coordinate the attack with the others taking place around the globe, as I have said."

Callum could already see that his men were totally bought into the mission. They were hanging on his every word and you could have heard a pin drop. He continued.

"We know Akhbar is still in that region of Syria from satellite imaging received only hours ago. It's hard to hide the massing of several thousand people. Intelligence says that he is headed for Dabiq, a place of holy significance. Again, satellite imaging is already showing a massing of people there. Also, it's where the scriptures say that the holy war will take place."

Callum turned his direct attention to his Staff Sergeant, Mike Jackson.

"This is where you come into play Mike. I need you to take on pilgrim status and join them on the road from Aleppo to Dabiq. It's a thirty mile walk. I want you to mix with the pilgrims and learn what you can. Make friends, so that you can use them as cover and lose yourself in the crowd, at Dabiq, if necessary. We need to know where Akhbar is camped, the numbers and disposition of his guard and where they have cached their weaponry. Do you see any problems in that?" Callum asked.

"No, but I'm going to need to take out one of their guards during the night at the soonest. Dressed in his clothing, I'll be free to access all areas in darkness and give you the coordinates by GPS," he cocked that quizzical brow at Callum. "How long do you need to mobilise after I give you the information? Only after I kill the guard, I'll have four hours max before the body is discovered and all hell breaks loose."

"We'll be there in three Mike, to give you a factor of safety," Callum had quickly done the maths. "One hour tops to strategize and mobilise the attack. One more, to load any last minute supplies on the Chinook, scramble and fly to the drop-off point outside Dabiq. Then we need another hour to run in on foot. The closest we dare take the Chinook is three miles from their camp. Any closer, the rotors will alert the enemy. If we make better time, we'll push the drop-off back a mile. It will be well worth the pain for that extra element of surprise."

"OK," returned Mike. "I will look to take the guard out at about 2300 hours. That gives me an hour for reconnaissance and to get you those coordinates. That'll bring you into their camp at around 0300 hours, when the guards will be at their lowest ebb," Mike instinctively knew that would be in line with Callum's thinking.

"Good Mike. That is precisely the hour that we have coordinated the global attacks on the Illuminati to take place," Callum had heard exactly what he had expected to hear. "We have already strategized how we think this is going to go. The coordinates you give will be used for simultaneous cruise missile attacks on all targets. We already have coordinates for many other tactical points in the greater region and they will be included in the strike."

"OK," Mike had that quizzical look again, "so why are you guys coming in if it's all going to be done by air strike?"

"Ostensibly, it's to get you out Mike, but also to verify that Akhbar is dead. If he escapes the inferno of a cruise missile attack, then he truly will be hailed as the Mahdi and having God's protection. That is something that we cannot afford, something that the world cannot afford."

Callum spent the next three hours going over the known details of the mission, plus some "what if?" scenarios. At the close, each knew what his expectations were of them.

Callum was to lead 'A' squad with Red Jake, the two brothers, Chas and Joey and Kayla. Ralph would follow, leading 'B' squad, with James, Zack, Rudi and Mike joining them on retreat. In the confusion following the cruise missile attack, they would be verifying the kill. Mike would have already laid explosive devices, prepared by James, on the way in and out. This was to give them cover if things went wrong. O'Malley, the pilot and Craig, the medic, were to stay in the Chinook and come in closer for the pick up after the missile attack. Craig's task was to set up a combat field hospital in the Chinook and be ready to treat the wounded. They all knew, although none stated, that this mission was likely to have heavy casualties, at best.

Callum's men picked up their individual briefs and left with their usual swagger and bawdy humour, leaving Callum alone with Kayla. It was a situation that he feared more than the mission ahead. He could feel the storm inside Kayla brewing by the moment. And then it broke.

"So, when were you going to get round to telling me that you're fucking that Italian bitch?"

Kayla had those same eyes that Ava had, that could darken with rage. Right now, they were pitch black.

"It's not like that Kayla," Callum countered.

"Like you're not fucking her? Or like you are fucking her, but you're in love?"

Callum paused for just too long and Kayla read him.

"You are fucking kidding me Callum! You're in love with her?" Kayla looked shocked and even angrier, if that was possible. "I'll kill the whore when we get back from Syria, if I haven't already killed you first. Jesus!"

"Maybe if you hadn't left me a dozen times over the last ten years, you could have kept all of my heart, Kayla."

"Oh, so you're fucking her to teach me a lesson, are you Callum? Does she know that?"

Kayla was shaking with rage. Her hair began to dance around her head in curly black snakes, charged with the static of her fury. She looked like Medusa, the mythical Gorgon. Suddenly, all the glass in the room shattered. Papers flew around the room in a wild dance as if caught in a gale and tables and chairs tumbled.

"Fuck the both of you," she yelled at him petulantly and stormed out of the trashed room.

Gina had spent Christmas at the old farmhouse with Sasha and Isabella along with Ava and Yuri. She had got to realise what an amazing man he was and could easily see why Ava was so in love with him. Ava seemed more content too. It wasn't hard for Gina to see that it was partly because of Callum being happy at last and no longer her guilty secret. She could now devote herself to Yuri and her pregnancy and did with all of her heart.

Apart from the Christmas celebrations when Ava had little Mina stay with them, it had all been about preparing the house and grounds for a siege. That included weapons' training for all of them. After their recent near death experiences, Sasha and Isabella threw themselves into learning how to defend themselves wholeheartedly. They hardly noticed the constraints of their incarceration. For her part, Gina was struggling with Callum leaving for Syria in the morning. Although her premonition of great foreboding wasn't personified, she could feel that they wouldn't all be coming home. She had only just found Callum and couldn't bear the thought of losing him now. Gina tried to keep her concerns from the others, but Ava had sensed her anxiety. Worse still, Ava had a similar feeling of pending disaster. Gina was anxiously waiting for Callum's last call before heading for the

RAF base at Brize Norton, *en route* for Syria. It wasn't until ten o'clock that evening that she finally got the call.

"Gina?"

"Yes, it's me darling. I was starting to worry that you weren't going to call. I've missed you so much."

That sounded needier than she meant it to. She squeezed her knees together involuntarily and cringed.

"Sorry Gina. I've had my back to the wall. The logistics and timescale of this mission are really punishing. It's lucky that I've got Kayla here to help."

It was Callum's turn to cringe. He couldn't believe that he had been so obtuse as to have just come out with that. Gina was on him in a second.

"Kayla's there, with you?"

All the air seemed to have been sucked out of the room and Gina couldn't breathe for a moment.

"I thought you said that you hadn't included her, for obvious reasons," Gina sounded cross.

"I didn't. She just turned up as she always does," Callum assured her. "But then there is no sound reason not to include her. She's a lifesaver when things turn bad."

Callum couldn't have chosen better words if he had tried. Gina's greatest fear was that he might not make it home. If Kayla's presence could make the difference, then it was a price worth paying.

"Then you were right to include her Callum," she conceded, "just remember that I love you."

It was the first time that Gina had declared her love, other than when they were actually making love. It disorientated both of them and there was a pregnant silence for a while. Gina held her breathe through that long moment, worried about Callum's response.

"Kayla knows that I've fallen for you too," he admitted.

"You told her that?" Gina gasped.

"I didn't have to. She read me, trashed the room and left. Just try not to be around when she comes back," it was advice, not a joke.

"Aw, Callum, have you fallen for me?" her lips parted in the biggest smile. "You don't need to answer that," she added quickly. "And regarding avoiding Kayla, we are on equal terms now and you are worth the fight. Bring it on!"

Callum didn't doubt it, "Perhaps it's me who should stay out of the way," he thought.

"Look Gina, I have to go. They're waiting for me. I'll call you at about the same time tomorrow from Cyprus, before we take off for Syria. OK?"

"Stay safe Callum and stay close to Kayla. Love you."

"Love you too," he cut the call, wondering why Gina sounded so desperate for him to stay close to Kayla.

Gina stood there for several minutes. She was looking at her mobile phone as if it held all the answers. Out of the blue, she had told him to stay close to Kayla. Why? She would normally rather that they had continents between each other. A frisson ran the length of her back, leaving her cold and scared. Her premonition was taking shape. Callum had to stay close to Kayla at all cost, she knew that much now.

Chapter 30

Akrotiri, Cyprus. Sunday, January 7th 2018. Two days before the day of reckoning.

It was just before midnight when the dun coloured Chinook lumbered up into the cool night air, leaving the British Sovereign Base of Akrotiri behind. It headed due east out towards the Shayrat Air Base at Homs in Syria, some ninety minutes away. Taking on fuel there, would enable them to complete their mission at Aleppo and return to Cyprus without the need to refuel again. This would be of paramount importance if things didn't go to plan, particularly if they incurred casualties. Their major problem and potential mission impasse was attracting suspicion at an airfield that was infiltrated by ISIS soldiers and paid spies. The Chinook's Syrian markings, false documents and Mike Jackson's fluency in Arabic were all they had to pin their hopes on. Well, that and a briefcase with ten thousand U.S. Dollars in it.

The noise inside the twin-engine, tandem rotor Chinook rendered conversation to *essential* levels only. The squad were dressed in white, loose-fitting Bedouin robes. Only Chas, Joey, Zak, Rudy and Red Jake were engaged in any kind of banter. The others were pensive. By all passed standards, this was by far the most dangerous mission they had been on. They would be in the middle of several thousand Arabs whipped into frenzy by the imposter, Mohammed Akhbar. Getting in and killing the man they believed to be their messiah was going to be a challenge. To get out alive afterwards however, was entirely another matter. Callum looked at each of the other members of his squad and idly wondered what was going through their minds. He felt a great personal responsibility for their safety. Craig, the medic, looked deep in thought. He had been in this situation many times before and bore the responsibility of keeping the wounded alive. It was something that was becoming increasingly burdensome for him. Over the years, he had treated most all of those who worked in covert operations. Certainly all of those present in the Chinook. The problem was that these had become his friends, not just some hapless strangers. Craig was coming towards the end of his useful service career. The stress of such responsibility had taken its toll on him and he was starting to look haggard and grey before his time.

James, sat next to Craig, was the polar opposite. He didn't seem to have a nerve in his body and was already asleep. There are few people who can do bomb disposal long-term without eventually believing that their luck will run out one day. James had long since come to terms with the fact that it would, and so that didn't stress him. He had no family and few friends. Life was very much black and white to him and he was fatalistic about it. Besides, he was addicted to the adrenaline rush.

Then there was Ralph. He was looking anxious. Another man who had been on too many missions and it was telling on him too. He had recently become a grandfather to his son Ben's child and Elizabeth was expecting. Ralph's life was going through a change of phase and he desperately wanted to be around to share it with his family. Callum knew that one day; he would be in the same position and would want out too. It is the natural order of things. He could intuitively tell that Ralph was harbouring fears of his own mortality.

Callum looked across at Kayla, who was looking back at him contemptuously. She was still seething. He had no difficulty in guessing what was going through her mind. And so it was, until O'Malley's voice came booming through the tannoy.

"Fifteen minutes to landing," he said in his endearingly relaxed Irish brogue.

"OK guys, roll out your bedding. Get in and look sleepy with arms at the ready. O'Malley, dim the fuselage lights five minutes before landing," Callum was only repeating what they had already planned. "You are asleep unless kicked in the ribs. Got it?"

"Sir!" was the unanimous reply. Their transition from friends and colleagues to chain of command was immediate.

"Mike. Once O'Malley has killed the rotors, you get out alone and engage with the authorities. Hopefully, our man's there, but we can't count on that. Only you will be able to sense if it's a trap. You have to make a quick judgement on that and err to caution. If you are not comfortable or smell a rat, call out 'Mohammed' as if for some document assistance. We'll come out firing and keep firing at everything and anything until O'Malley spins up. Then we abort the mission and get the hell out of there. We can ditch the helicopter somewhere in the Lebanon before fuel runs out and make it to Beirut on foot. Clear?"

"Affirmative," was Mike's unequivocal answer.

O'Malley called out the 'five minutes to landing' warning. It heralded a silence while each prepared themselves mentally for the unknown as the minutes ticked down to touchdown.

The tailgate dropped. Mike Jackson stepped out into the stiff, cool night breeze blowing in from the desert. It was a little after one-thirty in the morning, which added to the reasonableness that those on board the Chinook would be asleep. His loose fitting clothes were caught in the night breeze and slapped uncomfortably against him. Moments later, the headlights of an approaching vehicle came into view. Pinpricks in the blackness at first, but they grew until he was floodlit and blinded by them. This was the moment of truth. He would soon find out if they were friend or foe. Mike knew that the lives of his friends and the success of their mission were precariously in the balance. Everything would depend on the decisions that he made in the next two minutes. By reflex, his hand increased its grip on the handle of the pistol secreted in his robes.

Mike turned his head away to avoid the direct glare of the headlights and protect his night vision. Two armed men stepped out of the tanker and approached.

"Ahlan wa sahlan, as salaam alaykum," was the greeting. Welcome, peace be with you.

The words were offered by the shorter of the two men. He was uniformed with an angular face and a friendly handshake. It was all that Mike could have hoped for.

"Salaam," Mike returned, touching his forehead and bowing deeply in the traditional Arab way.

"You are amongst friends," the official said in perfect English. "This is my brother-in-law, Salim and my name is Abu Bakr."

He quickly gave some instructions in Arabic to Salim, who bowed respectfully and retreated to the tanker. Moments later, he was rolling out his fuel line.

"We are most grateful for your help in the struggle against ISIS domination," Mike began, also in English. "You are doing your people a great service Abu Bakr."

"What we do is in God's name my friend and the money will bring relief to hundreds of refugees," Abu Bakr looked sad for his people as he extended his arm to take the briefcase. "This holy land has been war-torn for the best part of a decade. Until the ISIS have been driven out, there will be no peace."

The thirty minute wait for those inside the Chinook was intolerable. It was clear to them, from the sound of the refuelling, that Mike had met with their man. Their concerns were being descended upon by the airport police or ISIS soldiers with a helicopter full of fuel and explosives. They were sitting ducks in a bomb. When Mike finally appeared at the bottom of the ramp, with that quirky grin of his, the tension went out of the squad.

"Spin her up. The deal's done and we're ready to go."

Callum pressed the switch to raise the tailgate even while Mike was still walking up it. O'Malley started the engines. In less than a minute, the twin thumping rotors had lifted them from the hard standing, heading them north to the lake at Abu Jurayn. Their mood was significantly more upbeat now that the first obstacle was over, well apart from Kayla that is, who still had a face like thunder. Refuelling was the only part of the mission that was entirely beyond their control. It could have been a deadly show-stopper. Now that was over, they only had an hour's flight to their camp at Abu Jurayn and they were in high spirits.

Ali Bahar picked up the characteristic thump of the approaching Chinook when it was several miles away. He had chosen a landing site four miles from their village, out by the lake. There was a copse of trees there that was heavily foliaged, with a small tor of sandstone to the side. It offered perfect natural cover. Enhanced with camouflage nets, the Chinook would be almost impossible to see from the air. In readiness, they had set oil drums as beacons to guide the Chinook in. Ali Bahar ordered the drums to be lit at the last minute to minimise the chances of attracting unwanted attention.

"We have visual," O'Malley called out over the tannoy. "Sure, I'm going to sweep the area a few times before we go in, sure I am."

It was that lovely double affirmative that the Irish were famous for. O'Malley passed across the area three times, in that nose-down attitude, to maximise his view of the terrain. It was only six days after the full moon so they had the benefit of good natural light. Coupled with this, O'Malley had infrared night vision. Nothing he saw gave him any reason for concern.

"Seat belts for landing," he called out and made his approach.

"Arms at the ready," Calum added, "until we know that it's safe but keep them low. We don't want to scare our hosts."

O'Malley settled the Chinook in the centre of the beacons, which were extinguished the moment he did so. Callum lowered the tailgate and led his squad out with their Heckler & Koch submachine guns held pointing downwards in the alert weapons position. They formed a line in relaxed pose facing Ali Bahar and his eight men. They were dressed in loose-fitting robes, each sporting their preferred Russian AK-47 rifles. There was an exchange of questioning looks between them. Neither side was prepared to completely trust the other at this early stage of the encounter. Mike naturally walked forward to engage with Ali Bahar who greeted him in the Arab way. They exchanged the traditional pleasantries before talking of the business in hand. Both sides quickly came to a consensus of purpose, releasing the tension between them. Bahar seemed anxious to get the Chinook covered and leave and Callum detailed his men to assist in the task. Fifteen minutes later the job was done.

Bahar had brought the school bus for transfers. They all crammed in, Arab and westerner alike. Their close proximity further assisted in breaking down the barriers between them. In only minutes, they were exchanging cigarettes, chocolates and sharing photographs of loved ones.

Fifteen minutes later, the bus bumped into the grounds of a large but poor sandstone dwelling, with ramshackle outbuildings. It was just outside the town limits of Abu Jurayn and the featureless buildings seemed to melt into the monochromatic desert landscape.

"You are welcome to share my humble house for this night," Ali Bahar offered. There was a look of genuine regret on his face as he continued. "But just this one night and you must be gone after the sun sets tomorrow. Nothing remains secret in this country where man has forsaken his God and we have children here to consider."

Mike nodded and translated for the others, introducing Callum as their officer in command. Callum responded in his far from perfect Arabic.

"We will be gone as you ask and thank you for your kind hospitality. I ask just one more favour my friend," Bahar nodded his consent for Callum to ask that favour. "Will you take my sergeant into Aleppo tonight? I want him to journey to Dabiq tomorrow morning with those who seek to affiliate themselves with Mohammed Akhbar."

Ali Bahar bowed his head confirming his accord but his eyes were on fire.

"It will be done as you ask but I have one condition in return."

This time it was Callum's turn to bow his head in consent, "What is your condition old friend?"

"That you rid this holy land of the imposter Mohammed Akhbar and decimate his false disciples such that they are broken and impotent," Bahar's voice was disdainful and his look, murderous. "This unholy man is not of Islam. He brings with him only death and destruction."

"It is our intent to rain down the full fury of the Royal Air Force on his camp within the next 24 hours. For Akhbar, we will be the Angels of Death and he will reap what he has sowed," Callum met Bahar's expression with one equally as murderous. "I swear that we will rid Syria of this man and his Satanic followers, or we will die trying if that's what it takes."

Ali Bahar seemed humbled at their readiness to lay down their lives, if necessary, in a land that wasn't their own and for his people. He signalled to one of his men with a subtle move of his head.

"Have your man ready to leave in twenty minutes, Major Knight. I will take you and your men to your quarters where there is food and drink awaiting you," Bahar bowed his head respectfully and touched his forehead and chest in that Arab gesture. "This way please."

They were taken to one of the dilapidated outbuildings. It was made from bricks cast from the desert sand, with a rusted corrugated steel roof that seemed to have also taken on the colour of the desert. The windows were shuttered against the brisk desert winds that drove the sand in through every crack or opening. It was as if nature was trying to consume and bury man's efforts to abide there. Although weather beaten and dilapidated on the outside, the inside was tidy and well-scrubbed. Bedding had been laid out for them at one end and a refectory table with benches, at the other. The table was laden with humble fare. Bread and goats cheese was the main offerings, with pulled meat and fruit to accompany. The stoneware jugs were filled with cool water from the deep well, with white enamel mugs to drink from.

Mike Jackson already had his tapestry shoulder bag packed with the explosive devices and remote detonator that James had fastidiously prepared for him. There were twenty four in total. He took a napkin and wrapped some bread and cheese in it for his journey, poured some water and drank copiously. His bag also contained a Global Positioning System with satellite communication function, and a plastic bottle with two litres of precious water. He was going to need to refill that bottle several times on his long walk from Aleppo to Dabiq. Secreted on him, were his documents, money, a stiletto knife, pistol and ammunition.

Minutes later, they could hear the rumble of an engine and an overloud exhaust outside the entrance. It was followed by the unnecessary sound of a horn to announce its arrival. There was a hurried exchange of goodbyes. It was unnecessary to discuss Mike's mission, as that had been gone over a dozen times before. It was that awkward moment that brothers in arms have when one of them is going into battle without the others and none of them wanting to dwell on the danger of it.

"Leave some for us to kill!" Red Jake bellowed to the amusement of the others.

It was gallows humour, part of how soldiers cope in times of duress. Out of the blue, Kayla ran over to Mike and threw her arms around him as if it was for the last time. Somehow, she sensed that it was. The tears were rolling down her face when she whispered in his ear.

"Don't be a hero Mike. You have Elizabeth and little Edith waiting at home for you."

She kissed his cheek. Mike returned that cheeky quizzical look of his and cocked a brow at her.

"Nobody's going to take this bad boy down sister. I'll be on that helicopter getting the hell out of here. You can count on it."

With that and a cocky bow, Mike turned and was gone. Kayla knew then, without a shadow of doubt, that she would never see him again.

Chapter 31

Syria. Monday, January 8th 2018. The eve of destruction.

The road to Aleppo was broken and potholed. Somehow, the old eighties Toyota HiAce managed to stay in one piece as it rattled and banged its way along. Thirty years of sun, had blistered the white paintwork such that there was more rust than paint. It gave the old charabanc a natural camouflage to blend in with the desert. As they got closer to their destination, the evidence of the civil war was all around them. The driver had to swerve around bomb craters, abandoned and burned out vehicles and the multitude of pilgrims destined for Dabiq. Swerving around obstacles was clearly something that he was well practiced at and Mike, uncomfortable with. It would have helped if the driver was to have looked forwards from time to time, and not direct his conversation and attention directly at Mike. The only thing about the old Toyota, that seemed serviceable, was the horn. Mike imagined that if that broke, the Toyota would too.

As they approached the city, the horror of the so called ISIS occupation and civil war became apparent. Mike wondered at how anybody could have survived the blitz. Nothing looked like it could be habitable. Wild dogs roamed the streets and Mike dreaded to think what they were feeding on. Evidence of atrocities was all around them. There were crucifixion frames where the Islamic State soldiers had publicly tortured and killed those who opposed their rule, finally beheading them and leaving them as examples for others who might resist. There were multiple gallows in public places. Some still displayed the gruesome remains of their victims. Somehow, people still clung to life in this hell-hole, eking out an existence. The sight of this inhumanity, fully exonerated any doubts that Mike might have otherwise had about the carnage they were about to impose on this illegal and unelected regime.

It was a slow and painful journey through the streets of the city. Most roads were rendered impassable by the relentless bombing and those open, were jammed by the mass of pilgrims making their way to Dabiq. Finally, they reached the north side and Mike bade the driver farewell. Only after bestowing a multitude of blessings on him, did the driver turn and set off into the oncoming masses.

It was seven o'clock in the morning, when Mike began the thirty mile walk on the road to Dabiq. The sun was low in the sky offering no heat and there was a brisk, chilling breeze that cut to the bone. To make matters worse, his bag dug painfully into his shoulder under the weight of the explosives it secreted. It was going to be an endurance test. He walked for the first hour in silence, having to change shoulders several times to ease the pain of his burden. Finally he had to concede that he wouldn't make the distance continuing like that. He reluctantly stopped again and tore off the bottom ten inches of his robe to use as padding on his blistered shoulders. It exposed his military footwear, which was the last thing that he wanted to do, but he was without choice. If challenged, he decided he would say that they were trophies of war, "And why not?" he thought.

Feeling more sociable now, Mike began to talk amongst the others. He learned much about what he already knew. Like Dabiq, that was liberated by the Turkish Armed Forces and the Free Syrian Army in 2016, was once again under ISIS occupation. What was new and surprising, was that these men were not in the slightest bit militant. They were simply following their belief in the scriptures and the prophecies therein. To them, Mohammed Akhbar *was* the Messiah and they were simply doing their duty. Pawns caught up in lies and deceit, to be sacrificed for the Pindar's own gain. It made Mike review the nature of their planned assault. He was to be calling in a cruise missile attack, taking out most of the camp. Now, with this new knowledge, Mike couldn't live with that. These were innocent and honest believers in their faith, not terrorists like Akhbar, the Mullah and the so called Islamic State. He had to risk getting word out to Callum.

Mike left his group of newly found comrades on the pretence of a nature call. He used the cover of a sandstone scree, some twenty yards from the road. Relieved didn't describe how good it felt to shrug off the heavy shoulder bag. He sat near the top of the scree so that he could see if anyone approached, then took the sat phone from the bag and dialled the number that he had committed to memory.

"Callum," was the economical reply.

"We have a problem," Mike began. "I'm on the road, twenty miles from Dabiq and haven't seen any Islamic State presence yet. That's not to say there won't be at Dabiq, but there could be as many as tens of thousands of innocent believers there too. We can't go in with cruise missiles Callum, it's too indiscriminate. The death toll would be unacceptable and cause an international outcry. We need to scale down the air strike, use Apache attack helicopters and Hellfire missiles, perhaps?"

Callum considered that for a long moment before replying.

"I'll think on it Mike. Going in that way will significantly reduce our chances of getting out of their alive," Callum's first duty was to his men. "Not only that, but it threatens the effectiveness of the mission. Akhbar could escape and the world plunge into war."

It was a tough decision.

"I'll give you accurate coordinates of the targets, then it's your call Callum," Mike had done what he could for the pilgrims.

At that moment, three men left the road for the privacy of the sandstone scree.

"Gotta go. Not safe," Mike cut the call.

The short break was all that Mike needed to put a spring back in his step. Fifteen minutes later he had caught up with his group and three hours after that, he was on top of a hill, looking down over Mohammed Akhbar's encampment. He imagined that the hill would be the very place that Akhbar would hold his sermon the next day. It was also the place where O'Malley would pick them up from, at the end of their mission.

All around him was a sea of humanity. Mike noticed immediately that there was no randomness about the gathering at this holy place. Akhbar and his cohorts had set up what amounted to a village of tents with water bowsers and kitchens. There was a convoy of about forty supply trucks parked at the centre that circled another smaller group of tents. It was Akhbar's camp, Mike determined. At the outer perimeter of the encampment, were a dozen stockades. These would be his arsenal of weapons and ammunition, he assumed. It was going to be easier than Mike had first thought and he smiled a wry smile. He would be able to walk freely around the encampment, amongst the crowds. Recording the coordinates of the stockades would be just a matter of pressing the 'send' button on his global positioning device. That would just leave Akhbar's tent to record in the night and to verify that he was in it.

Mike left the solitude of the hill and joined that sea of humanity. He walked as if aimlessly but his route was carefully chosen to take him past each of the twelve stockades. As he passed, he pressed the button sending the coordinates of each to Callum for onward transmission to the RAF base at Akrotiri, Cyprus. Now, all he could do was to wait for nightfall to make a full reconnaissance of Akhbar's camp that formed the hub of the gathering.

Mike had spent the daylight hours walking around the encampment and surrounding area assessing Akhbar's military capability. It was pleasingly light. He had counted less than a hundred ISIS soldiers, two rocket launchers and four machine gun mounted trucks. Clearly Akhbar wasn't expecting an attack.

He had taken lunch at one of the kitchens on the inner perimeter, where he had a clear view of the ISIS camp at its centre. The tent at the epicentre was in a class of its own and so clearly Akhbar's. The ten surrounding it were for his guard. That was also clear, from the comings and goings of the men dressed in their traditional green camouflage Afghani robes, typical of their front line soldiers. Mike would need the coordinates of each of these tents, but that would be later. When the air strike came, only those on active guard duty would survive and they would likely be a dozen or so. The rest would be killed in their beds.

Mike was as prepared as he could be. All that he could do now was find a place in the shade and get as much sleep as possible between then and 2300 hours. He needed to be fresh for the fight; they were all depending on him.

It was ten minutes before three o'clock in the morning. Mohammed Akhbar and the Mullah were sat cross-legged on the carpeted tent floor. The old copper hookah was set between them and the air thick with the sweet smell of hashish. They had talked through the evening and half of the night. Such was their anticipation of the day ahead.

Akhbar drew deeply from the hose and held the breath for several seconds. As he passed it to the Mullah, he exhaled in a sigh of profound satisfaction.

"We are coming to the end of our journey old friend," Akhbar stated wearily. "Now we have arrived at Dabiq, the place of holy retribution, there is no stopping the inevitable."

It had indeed been an arduous journey. Their campaign of relentlessly choreographed and staged sermons was of biblical proportion, very much as intended. They had journeyed separately. The Mullah had set off one month ahead of Akhbar, whipping the towns into religious frenzy in advance of the coming of the Mahdi. His fanatical rhetoric and the increasing expectation over the fulfilment of the prophecy, was beyond infectious. Such was the anticipation of the people, that the moment the charismatic Mohammed Akhbar arrived, he was immediately proclaimed as the true Mahdi, the Twelfth Imam. This was testament to the power and persuasion of the Mullah's rhetoric. From there, and as they progressed through the Arab nation, it was self-perpetuating. Word spread from village to village, town to town and city to city. The religious fever was pandemic. The Mullah sucked at the hookah, nodding his head in accord.

"Tomorrow, in front of ten or twenty thousand worshippers and live television broadcast to the rest of the world, you will declare your divinity. No Muslim will dare to challenge your claim and your call for retribution will plunge this land into holy war," the Mullah smiled coldly through his gappy teeth, "and the Pindar will have his want. The platform set for World War Three."

"And our security and prosperity will be assured my friend," Akhbar had the same fanatical look in his eyes. "The Pindar will need his Mahdi and his false prophet indefinitely. Only great age will take us. Life will be good Mullah Ismael."

The Mullah was not a man to count his chickens. Complacency was not a word in his vocabulary.

"It is nearing three and the sun will rise in another three. I will bid you goodnight Mohammed, but not God's speed as we both know that there is not one. How gullible is mankind?" of this the Mullah was certain, but then he had no soul. "I will do my rounds before retiring, that we might sleep afterwards in peace. We cannot trust those lazy oafs to stay alert in the small hours."

The Mullah Ismael Alansari had not lived this long without having a healthy mistrust for the competence of his subordinates.

It was 0130 hours precisely, when O'Malley started the powerful engines of the Chinook. The flight would only take twenty minutes from lift-off to drop-off; just time enough for a final weapons check and to run through the basics. They were wearing their usual British Army desert battle fatigues, with flak jackets and helmets. Their faces were randomly striped with camouflage paint apart from Kayla's, where it had been meticulously applied to enhance her looks. There was no doubting that it was for Callum's benefit. She wanted him to know what he was missing and it worked. Callum had to admit to himself that Kayla was looking appealingly boyish.

Kayla was his nightmare, his Kryptonite. Until Gina came along and confused things, there was nobody else in the world for Callum. Even when Kayla wasn't there in person, she filled his mind and his senses. She was quite probably the third most powerful woman on the planet, but in his arms she was vulnerable and loving. He understood the storms that went on in her head that she had no control over; a conflict of temptress, devoted lover, needy child and bitch.

The problem was that Callum had endured more than a decade of Kayla's moods and affaires and he was used up. Understanding and accepting, was becoming harder. In front of everything though, he was deeply in love with her and always would be; as impossible and unsustainable as that was.

Callum had to quickly distract his mind to stay objective.

"Attention men," Callum began and Kayla's eyes flared.

He was immediately conscious of the disapproving look he had got from Kayla for using that form of address and it was clear that she was still seething over him and Gina.

"O'Malley drops us to the west of Turkmen Bareh at 0150 hours," he continued. "That gives us one hour to make the three and a half miles to the hill outside Dabiq, arriving there ten minutes before the air strike at 0300. From that elevated position, using night vision, we'll be able to assess the effectiveness of the strike. We anticipate that the civilians will flee in all directions in fear for their lives and superstitious dread. So we have to assume that those who choose to remain, are ISIS and we shoot to kill. Understood?"

There was a general rumble of the affirmative. Only Red Jake chose to be more explicit.

"I'm hoping a few of them butchers choose to stay an' fight. Then they can experience the Gospel according to Jake!"

His comment started some sabre rattling from the squad as Jake had intended. There was nothing like pre-combat banter to relieve tension.

"Careful what you wish for Jake," Callum countered. "Likely as not you'll get shot up again, as usual."

Jake just beamed back proudly. That would simply be another badge of honour to him.

"OK," Callum got them back on track. "As soon as the strike's over, Mike lays a line of explosives from the base of the hill below us, to the Akhbar's inner compound and then returns laying a second. Mike stays there to watch our backs. Remember that he'll be wearing ISIS uniform, so don't get trigger happy and shoot him by accident," Callum looked accusingly at Jake, who beamed innocently back at him.

"When we get the all clear from Mike, we go in two squads twenty seconds apart. 'A' squad on me is Red Jake, Chas, Joey and Kayla. Ralph heads up 'B' squad with James, Zack, Rudi and then Mike joins them as we retreat for the Chinook."

Callum had reluctantly put Kayla in his squad, although he would have preferred not to right now. It was simply because of promising Gina that he would, although he had not a clue why it was so important to her. To make matters worse, he could tell that Kayla knew that too. There was nothing that could be kept from Kayla. He put the matter out of his mind and continued.

"As we run past Mike, he detonates the explosives in front of us, giving us safe cover. As you already know, the planned cruise missiles have been substituted for Apache launched Hellfire missiles, which leaves a high likelihood of encountering un-killed ISIS and even Akhbar himself."

When Callum had told them about the proposed tactical substitution, he had put it to the vote. After all, he would be gambling with their lives, particularly as at that time they had no idea of the enemy's numbers or disposition. They had unanimously chosen to go with the option of reducing civilian casualties.

"We search the compound for Akhbar and we don't leave until we know he's dead. Clear!" again Callum got the affirmative. "Once confirmed, we call Mike and he detonates the explosives in advance of our return run, to clear our way and give us cover. Again we leave twenty seconds apart. Ralph and 'B' squad go first this time. Pick up point is on top of the hill where we started and O'Malley will be looking out for us. Questions?" he asked.

There were none and the pre-battle atmosphere, tense. Again Red Jake had his own way of relieving that tension. He turned to Kayla with a devilish look in his eye.

"Kayla, did you know that 70% of men *want* sex after going into battle and 95% of women *need* it?" he purposely smirked at her as he said it to get a reaction. He wasn't disappointed.

"I didn't think you could count to 95 Jake," she said sarcastically. "Anyway, where did you get those statistics from?" she asked.

"PIDOOMA," he said simply.

"PIDOOMA?" Kayla questioned.

"Yep. Plucked It Directly Out Of My Arse," Jake replied smugly, having set her up for ridicule.

He was beside himself with self-appreciation over his wit and would have fallen off the bench laughing, had he not been strapped in for the flight. The lads were in stitches too but Kayla was unmoved, in fact she looked deadly.

"And I can tell you something as an absolute fact Jake," Kayla countered. "If you were involved, 100% of those women would be left sitting in the wet-patch, hugely disappointed with a DIY job on their hands," Kayla's disdainful look cut him in half.

They were all in hysterics, well except for Red Jake. Kayla was the clear winner and Jake had to concede. He should have known by now, that he would never have the last word sparing with Kayla. There could have been no better way to go into battle though. Their spirits were high and their intent, deadly.

Mike Jackson had only slept fitfully until his alarm chimed at 2300 hours. After sunset, the temperature had dropped below freezing and there was no shelter for him anywhere. Every available tent was full and those left outside were huddled in groups to share their body warmth. Even wrapped in a sheet of polythene in the lee of the wind, Mike was chilled to the bone. He discarded the polythene and stood stiffly, shaking the cold from his limbs. He stomped and beat his arms around his body, encouraging the blood to flow to his extremities. Looking around him, he could see that he wasn't suffering the cold alone. Many others were running on the spot or pacing up and down. This was better than Mike could have hoped for. It meant that he would be able to walk around the encampment inconspicuously. He ambled in the throng of those trying to keep warm, as if without purpose, getting ever closer to Akhbar's inner compound. Once there, he walked the full perimeter. His keen eyes were picking out the guards, looking for any that were slothful. He counted twenty in all, two of which were either asleep or dozing. The unlucky one, about to die, would be the guard closest to Mike's dress size. It was a simple choice as the fortunate one was no bigger than a woman.

"One horse race," he muttered as he passed the guard for the second time and then slipped into the compound behind him.

The guard was sat on a plastic crate, set between two rusty oil drums with their tops cut off. His AK-47 assault rifle was propped against it. Mike crept up behind him; his footsteps fell silently in the soft sand. He could hear the rhythm of the guard's breathing that confirmed he was asleep. The killing of the guard needed to be silent and relatively bloodless so that he could use his uniform. Mike took the stiletto knife from his tapestry bag and opened it slowly so as not to allow the characteristic metallic click of the blade locking. To cut the man's throat would indeed be quick, but too messy. He would have bled like a pig, soaking the front of his uniform.

Mike went down on his hands and knees so that he was below the level of the drums and therefore invisible to the other guards. He crawled until he was directly behind the sleeping guard. He put one hand over the guard's mouth to gag him, and then drove the stiletto through his eye, deep into his brain with the other. The guard kicked once and was still, dispatched in only seconds. Working swiftly in the shelter of the drums, Mike stripped the corpse, pulled his own robe off over his head and put on the guard's uniform. He checked around quickly, then lifted the body and dumped it head first into one of the drums, covering it with his discarded robe. Mike then transferred the contents of his bag, apart from the explosives, into his webbing and pockets then hid the bag behind the drums. He picked up the rifle, ejected the magazine and checked it over. It was second nature to him to do so. Only a fool goes into battle with an unproven weapon. The rifle was sound and he had three full magazines. So far it simply couldn't have gone better. Mike allowed himself a crooked smile. All he needed now was to walk around Akhbar's compound and take the coordinates as he passed each tent. He checked his watch. It was a quarter to midnight, which meant he had fifteen minutes to complete.

"A walk in the park," he muttered to himself, setting off for the first tent.

It took an unpleasant ten minutes to get the coordinates of the guards' tents. As Mike passed each, the stench of humanity living in close proximity and poor hygiene hit him like a physical blow to the stomach, making him gag. Sleeping alone and rough in the cold, suddenly didn't seem so bad to him. He checked the perimeter guards to be sure that none were patrolling and then stepped through the guards' humble tents to that of Akhbar. It was a veritable palace by comparison, with gold lamé and velvet adorning it. As Mike got close, he could smell the sweet scent of hashish and the sound of two men talking conspiratorially. He needed to know definitively whether one of them was Akhbar and lay down as close to the voices as he could get. While he waited for a name to fall out of the conversation, he took the coordinates and pressed 'send' on his GPS. It was midnight precisely.

"Soldier's precision," he acknowledged with no small professional satisfaction.

As if as a reward, he heard one man address the other as 'Akhbar'. It was manna from heaven. Mike quickly keyed a message to Callum. It simply read, "Our friend is at home."

He scanned the area around him, then stood and made his way back to the drums and his hidden tapestry bag. He picked it up and walked calmly through the circle of trucks into the civilian camp, disappearing amongst the multitude there. Mike found the spot where he had slept and recovered the plastic sheeting, then wrapped it around himself. Apart from shielding him from the cold, it hid his ISIS uniform and AK-47 assault rifle. Ten minutes later he was in position at the foot of the hill where his squad would station themselves in a little over two hours' time. After the air strike, nearly all of the ISIS soldiers would be dead. All he would then have to do was the simple task of laying the covering explosives to and from Akhbar's tent and retreat for the safety of the Chinook.

"It's difficult to see how this could possibly go wrong," Mike thought as he laid back in wait for the attack.

The Chinook had barely touched the ground when Callum and his squad jumped from the tailgate. They quickly fell into that easy jog that trained and fit soldiers do, and can keep up for miles. Each was carrying thirty pounds of weapons and supplies, including Kayla. She had stamina enough to match any of the men and more. But then she had certain genetic advantages, typical of her birth right. If all went well, they wouldn't need that amount of ordnance and supplies. However, if things went wrong, it probably wouldn't be enough. In that case, O'Malley would be coming in as a gunship dropping supplies with Brett Jamieson on the side-mounted M134 Minigun.

They ran in squads with fifty yards between them, in case of ambush. Callum and Ralph naturally took the leads. The going was good underfoot and the terrain, mostly farmland and track. Their way was reasonably illuminated by the three quarter moon in the clear night sky. It was natural for them to run in single file and in each other's tracks. This was ingrained in their basic training, to reduce the risk of encountering land mines, although they had no reason to expect them. All the while, Callum was monitoring their progress against the clock. At the mid-way point, they had made good time, so Callum rested them. There was no point arriving early and 'blown'. When they reached the bottom of the hill, he stopped and signalled for them to come close.

"I don't like it," Callum whispered. "There's no cover between here and the top. If they've got a lookout up there, he couldn't fail to spot a squad of nine men. We would be out in the open and mowed down before we got half way to the top of the hill. Mission ended before it begins."

"We need a scout to go up alone Callum," Ralph offered. "I can take that."

Callum knew that he wouldn't be short of volunteers, but there was one whose qualifications trumped all others, Kayla. She had a sixth sense. She would know well before she got to the top if it was manned or not, even how many. She could somehow sense these things. Kayla was always one step ahead of the game. She would be able to have their minds under control without a shot being fired.

"Agreed about the scout Ralph, but it can't be you," Callum felt Ralph's bitter disappointment. "I need you to complete the mission and get the squad back if anything happens to me. Besides, there's one of us that can do this with their eyes shut."

Callum turned to Kayla, who already knew what was coming. "You," he said simply.

Kayla crawled across to Callum on elbows and knees, keeping her silhouette below the scrub line.

"I'll take a look, then go down the other side and circle back to here. Don't want to be surprised by any late arrivals," she smirked. "I know why you chose me."

"You do?" Callum asked.

"Yeah, so you and your boys can watch my cute ass wiggle as I go up that hill, on all fours. In your dreams boys!" she winked at him provocatively and set off.

As she made her way, Callum was certain that she was putting on a bit more of a show on the tail-wag than was really necessary. She had certainly captivated the men, who looked on appreciatively. Kayla had only really done it for Callum though, to make him think about what he was missing. It worked. She knew it and so did he.

As Kayla reached the upper section, her acute sense of smell picked up the aroma of Turkish cigarettes. She stopped and listened. There were the voices of two men in relaxed conversation. It was going to be too easy for her. Amongst Kayla's mental skills, was the ability to enter people's thoughts and manipulate them. It was something that she had used unfairly on Callum for a decade, "But that had kept him keen," she justified to herself. "Besides, he was rewarded for it with the best sex, ever!"

Kayla had a clear conscience on this. Her problem was that this new Italian bitch on the scene could do that too. Either that or that Callum was too infatuated with her. Now that she couldn't have Callum, she wanted him even more. She physically ached for him and it was clouding her judgement, even here on the hill and that was dangerous for them all. It was something that she swore she would sort out once and for all as soon as they returned from the mission.

Kayla focused her mind on their voices and slowly entered their thoughts. Without realising it, they became accustomed to her being there. They were still smiling at her as she cut their throats.

It was only eight minutes later, when Kayla reappeared after quickly circling the base of the hillock.

"All clear," she said in matter of fact fashion.

"Well done Kayla, I owe you one," he acknowledged with a smile.

"Much more than that Callum," she said raising a brow. There was no ambiguity in that look.

Callum and his men reached the top of the hill, three minutes before the planned air strike. Uncomfortably close to zero hour, but they were there.

None of them were prepared for what they saw. Two men, one lying across the other, both with their throats cut. They were open-eyed and drenched in their own blood. Everyone looked disbelievingly at Kayla.

"I wouldn't want to piss her off," Ralph whispered to Callum, shocked at what he saw.

"I think I already have," was Callum's fatalistic reply.

They had maintained radio silence up until then, to minimise the chances of being overheard. Now Callum needed to know if Mike was in position and still effective. There was always the chance that he had been taken out. In which case, they wouldn't get the cover of the explosives, in and out of Akhbar's camp, as planned. That was partly why James was with them, it gave him alternatives if things went wrong. Callum waited anxiously for the distant roar of the Apache attack helicopters. He would call Mike on the sat phone the moment that he heard them.

Mike already had the sat phone in his hand when the screen illuminated with Callum's name.

"I'm in position Callum," he confirmed, without wasting any words on protocols.

"Good work Mike. We've got audio confirmation of incoming Apaches."

"I hear them too. I'm good to go as soon as the strike's over. I'll cover you from the top of the hill afterwards, as planned. Good luck," Mike was just about to hang up and then added with his lop-sided grin. "Tell Red Jake not to shoot my arse off."

"Already have done, Mike. Out."

There were three Apache attack helicopters in all, coming in low from the south at nearly 200 knots. It was just distant thumping at first, as the rotors drummed the still desert air, increasing rapidly as the birds of death bore down on their prey. Once overhead, the noise was deafening, drowning out the rush of the deadly Hellfire missiles, as they were released inexorably seeking their targets. Below them, the darkness was torn by the firestorm. Akhmed's camp was an inferno. Nothing could have survived, Callum judged. The twelve weapon dumps on the perimeter also exploded in flame, enhanced by the ammunition they contained. As anticipated, people were running into the desert in all directions, desperate to escape this unholy retribution. The might of the targeted attack, had created a blast of wind that flattened the hundreds of tents in the civilian camp, adding to the confusion.

It was the moment that Mike had been waiting for. He grabbed his rifle and the tapestry bag, then ran towards the burning remains of Akhbar's camp, dropping explosives every thirty strides on the way. The shanty town of blown-down tents was already deserted, bar a few mothers shepherding their infants to safety. Mike was relieved that they would be long gone by the time he detonated the bombs. He briefly looked at Akhbar's inner

344

compound. It was decimated with no sign of any guards. Any lucky enough to have survived would probably have fled with the civilians, he assumed. The air strike had been pin-point accurate. Some of the supply trucks that formed the perimeter had been capsized in the blast. By pure fortune, their bulk had served to protect the civilians, probably saving hundreds of innocent lives.

It wasn't Mike's job to verify the dead in the camp, that job was for Callum and his men. Instead, he returned at a full run, again dropping a device at every thirtieth stride until he was back at the hill. He opened a new call on the sat phone.

"All yours Callum, I'll light them up in front of you as you run past me. Good luck, see you back at the Chinook."

Mike got the affirmative and cut the call. He took the detonator from his jacket pocket and sat there poised, finger on the button. Seconds later, Callum came into view with 'A' squad, running at full pelt towards Akhbar's burning compound. Mike immediately detonated the explosives. The path before the running men erupted in a simultaneous explosion, causing a dense dust cloud. It gave them cover as they ran over open ground and would likely have caused any enemy to run for safety too. Now all Mike had to do was to wait for Callum's call to detonate the second line of explosives in front of their return run. He felt helpless now. It was going to be an agonising wait.

The Mullah Ismael Alansari exchanged the warm hashish scented air of Akhbar's Bedouin tent for the icy desert wind. Although it was cold enough to cut to the bone, the Mullah found that it sharpened the mind. It took only minutes for the effects of the hours of smoking dope to be expunged from his body. He was once again that fearsome predator, the un-killable man.

The first thing that the sleeping guard knew of the Mullah's presence was the impact of his AK-47 rifle, as the butt of it took out his front teeth.

"Lazy dog," the Mullah spat in disgust. "Think on this next time you fail in your duty and know that it will be your last."

The guard's pained scream started a wave of signalling both ways around the perimeter, such that the Mullah had no need to repeat the lesson. As he walked around, his eyes were constantly searching for anything that was out of place or just wrong. He stopped and listened regularly. It even seemed like he smelt the night air, like a gazelle searching for the pungent smell of lion. A lifetime in the desert, and in one war or another, had honed his senses. He was the consummate survivor.

As he passed the two oil drums, the robe dumped in the top of one of them caught his eye. In times of war and poverty, clothing was precious and something to be reused or handed down. Not something to be discarded. It wasn't right. He lifted it with the barrel of his rifle, exposing a man's leg. A hundred thoughts went through the Mullah's mind in only milliseconds. In the forefront of all of them was his survival. It was then that he heard the distant sound of approaching jets, getting louder by the second. There might just be enough time to warn Akhbar, he judged. But then there might not. It was no contest. The Mullah disappeared quickly into the civilian compound, distancing himself from Akhbar's tent.

"Good luck my old friend," was his final sentiment as the Apaches thundered above, firing their Hellfire missiles.

Callum and 'A' squad ran into the dust cloud kicked up by the line of explosives, shortly followed by Ralph and 'B' squad. They were running in blind on a bearing, seeing next to nothing. It was the best way to make sure that they were invisible to the enemy, even if that was only for a minute. Callum almost ran into an overturned supply truck before he saw it. He managed to swerve at the last second, and lead his squad safely past into Akhbar's compound. The dust cloud slowly left them on the stiff desert breeze, revealing the carnage of the missile attack. Callum and his men quickly circled the perimeter. They worked clockwise, knowing that they would meet 'B' squad on the other side coming the other way. When they did, neither had encountered the enemy who were clearly either dead, or had fled along with the civilians. After a brief exchange, Callum's squad began searching for bodies in the centre of the strike with Ralph and his men taking the outer camp.

It was a gruesome sight and immediately apparent that it would be difficult to make a positive ID. Many of the corpses had been mutilated beyond recognition, or not even recognisable as corpses. They needed to be lucky, and they were.

"Callum," Kayla called out urgently. "I think I have him."

Callum came over to her through the chaos of the craters and debris of the attack. She was stood next to the upper torso and head of a man. His face had been spared the might of the blast and he was dressed in the tattered remains of fine robes. Around his neck were the star and crescent symbols of Islam, and a medallion with the word 'Allah' engraved in Arabic script upon it. There was enough of his face left to still be recognisable. Callum just nodded in confirmation and immediately opened a call on his sat phone.

"Mike. Kill confirmed. We're rounding up the men now. Detonate the return explosives in five minutes. Got that?"

"Understood, five minutes and counting," Mike confirmed and cut the call.

He smiled to himself as he thought about the outcome. They, a small band of brothers, had gone into the heart of ISIS territory and taken out their king pin, the one man who could unite the Arabs in a war that would bring about Armageddon.

"Just a walk in the park as I thought," Mike mused.

He was feeling good about the success of the mission. It had been like taking candy from a baby. Meanwhile, Callum opened another call, it was to Ralph.

"Mission accomplished Ralph. Regroup on me now; detonation imminent."

Ralph acknowledged and rallied his men, while Callum quickly took photographs of Akhbar, to allow for reliable facial recognition later. They had to be very certain of the kill. He looked up at Kayla, allowing himself a wry smile. In that moment, he noticed just how beautiful she looked in her military fatigues and war paint. He was just about to praise her efforts for all that she had done so far, but was stopped in his tracks by the sudden expression of terror on her face.

"No!" Kayla screamed, as she threw herself in front of Callum.

The air was suddenly split by the piercing crack-crack of an AK-47 rifle firing on automatic. Kayla's petite body danced like a puppet on strings in front of Callum's eyes as the bullets ripped into her. He looked on in horror at the man in Arab clothing, emptying his magazine into Kayla. The look in the man's eyes was maniacal as he grinned cruelly through gappy teeth. Callum instinctively swung his machine gun into position aiming at where the Mullah had stood but it was already too late, he was gone. The desert had once again consumed the un-killable man.

Red Jake, Chas and Joey immediately formed a defensive triangle around them against further attack, facing outwards as Callum tended to Kayla. The bullets had taken her in the upper leg, groin, shoulder and neck severing her femoral and carotid arteries. Kayla was going into shock fast.

"Stay with me Kayla!" Callum pleaded.

He jammed his fingers in her neck and groin, trying to stem the flow of blood but they both knew that it was hopeless.

"I'll get you to Jamie, he can save you," he said desperately.

"No Callum, I won't make it. Just hold me, I'm scared. I don't want to die," she sounded terrified and her voice was fading.

Callum abandoned his attempt to stop the bleeding and held her close to him, their faces almost touching.

"That's how much I love you Callum. More than my life," she coughed, spraying a mist of blood over his cheek. "There has only ever been you Callum; nobody else meant anything to me. Only you," her eyes searched his for forgiveness.

Tears of grief and rage were flowing down Callum's face as he listened to all that she had to say; personal things, shared memories, her regrets and her words of profound love for him.

"I won't rest until I find him and kill him Kayla, you have my word," Callum swore.

In that brief moment of the shooting, he had recognised her killer. It was the Mullah, a man worth dying for to avenge her.

"No Callum that would only be for you," her voice was fading. "Stay safe and live long for me. Make my death worthwhile. Please," Kayla's eyes were imploring. It was her last wish.

She started to ramble as her brain became starved of oxygen. Then she had a final moment of absolute clarity, as people do when they are about to pass.

"Don't leave me here in the desert Callum, I couldn't bear that."

"I swear you will be leaving on the Chinook with me Kayla and you will fly home in my arms. I swear it," Callum could barely speak through grief and despair.

"I would like that Callum," she said, offering him her last smile.

"I love you Kayla. You know that I always have," he said, no longer able to see her clearly through his tears.

"I know Callum and I will take that sweet memory with me."

Those were the last words that Kayla said that he was entirely sure of. In her final breath, he thought that she said, "Have a happy life with Gina, but I want you back when you die. You owe me that Callum."

Kayla's words faded as she died in his arms, leaving him unsure if he had heard them at all.

"No!" he screamed, looking up to the heavens, as if God could bring her back to him. He knew now why Gina had made him promise to stay close to Kayla. She had sensed something, something dreadful.

Callum felt a hand on his shoulder. It was Red Jake's. Even as big and as rough as he was, he was crying too.

"We have to go now sir. I'm sorry," his voice was broken with emotion.

Callum nodded. He had no words. They felt the ground shock first, and then the explosion pained their ears as Mike's corridor of retreat erupted from the earth. Ralph led them out at a slow trot, with Callum carrying Kayla like a sleeping child in his arms at the middle of the formation.

Kayla was right about one thing, that she would never see Mike Jackson again.

Chapter 32

Thessaloniki, Greece. Tuesday, January 9th 2018. The day of reckoning.

Hydie Papandreou scrolled down the list of high-ranking Illuminati officers on the screen in front of her. It was their top 100, spread globally. Each name on the list had been assigned an assassin from her organisation, along with a strategy for their elimination. The assassinations were scheduled to happen at 0200 hours Moscow time, coinciding with the attack in Syria at 0300 hours local time there. From London to Beijing, that would mean the simple strategy of killing them in their beds. For the rest of the world, depending on their time zones, it could mean killing them at their place of work, publicly in the streets or restaurants. Even in front of their families; wherever they were at 0200 hours, Moscow time. The assassins had been incentivised for their kills. In the fullness of time, they would be taking over the roles of the deceased in a new organisation. That organisation would be under Shadow rule, the rule of the Hydra. Well once the Pindar had been dealt with, she vowed.

Every level of the Illuminati organisation had been targeted. From the elimination of the remaining members of the Council of Thirteen, down to the political groups like the United Nations and the political elite of the Bilderbergers. Corrupt leaders of intelligence groups, including the CIA, FBI, KGB and organised crime were targeted. Educational organisations with their corrupt slants including UNESCO, the Commission on Global Governance and the media were on that death list. Religious groups, including the Vatican, the World Council of Churches and New Age cults were on it too. Everywhere that the Illuminati had infiltrated and corrupted, had been pedantically researched. The secret societies were particularly rife in their structure of power and corruption. The Hydra had targeted Senior Freemasons, the Order of Skull & Bones and the Orders of the Knights.

Hydie Papandreou checked her watch. Greece shared the same time zone as Moscow. It was 0145 hours. Just fifteen minutes before all hell was to be let loose in Dabiq, near Aleppo and across the civilised world.

One of those on the Hydra's list was Sylus Rosenbaum, The current incumbent of the chairmanship of the Bilderberg Group and one of the most corrupt men on the planet. He used the power and influence of that secret society for his own personal gain and that of the Illuminati.

Sylus Rosenbaum was sat in his quaint study at Redcliffe Mews in Chelsea, surrounded by a lifetime of memorabilia. He grew up in the suburbs of post First World War London where you had to be ruthless and tough to survive. It was dog eat dog then and Rosenbaum had kept that ethos ever since. Now, in his mid-eighties, he was as active as ever. Sylus Rosenbaum had spent a lifetime in politics, mixing with the ruling elite and forming alliances across the world, particularly between Europe and the USA. He was at the group's first conference in 1954 at the Hotel de Bilderberg in Oosterbeek, Netherlands. Several of them had met to discuss their concerns over growing anti-Americanism in Europe. Their honest aim was to promote Atlanticism, but this soon became a secret society with the conspiracy to promote free market Western capitalism and a one-world government. Not too different from the objectives of the Illuminati into which it morphed. Over the years, the good intent was diluted as power, greed and avarice took over. The political and economic decisions that they made were merciless, plunging other nations into war and famine.

Sylus looked at the old clock on the wall that hung amongst photographs of his estranged family. It was approaching eleven o'clock in the evening.

"Everything comes at a cost," he lamented as he looked over the faces of those that he loved once upon a time.

The thought was only fleeting, replaced by another of tomorrow's business deal that would net another five billion U.S. Dollars.

"Most gratifying," he murmured picking up the cup of hot chocolate.

He turned the lights off in the study and went up to bed. Fifteen minutes later he was asleep.

James Carter watched the Rosenbaum residence from the enclosed gardens of the privileged Chelsea mews. He was a balding man in his mid-thirties with a powerful build and retiring nature. He looked something of a gentle giant but he was a calculating killer. Carter had the strictest of instructions to eliminate his target at 2300 hours precisely, whatever the risk, on pain of death. He had no reason to doubt that failure would be dealt with in such draconian manner and none that he wouldn't be rewarded for his success. One way or another, his life would change tonight. Carter was an accomplished assassin and a believer in clinical dispatches. Professionalism mattered to him.

Carter had checked the house earlier in the day, gaining entry through a carelessly unlocked and un-alarmed window. Once establishing that his quarry lived alone, he immobilised the alarms and jammed the lock, then left to wait in the gardens. He had lain in wait for eight hours in the icy January night air waiting for the appointed time. At last the house fell into darkness. Carter checked his watch; it was a quarter to eleven.

"Perfect," he muttered under his breath as he shook the stiffness from his limbs.

Carter had no need to skulk in his approach to the house. It was a reasonable hour for people to be making their way home from the Hollywood Arms, located only a few hundred yards to the south of the mews. At seven minutes to the hour, Carter checked the road in both directions before opening the window and stepping quickly through into Rosenbaum's study. He moved lightly and purposely for such a stocky man. Carter had committed the layout of the townhouse to memory, including every obstacle or trip. At five minutes before eleven, he was stood outside his victim's bedroom. There was no sound from within. Carter meticulously counted the minutes down. Four minutes later, he took the Walther pistol from his shoulder holster. At five seconds before eleven o'clock, Carter opened the bedroom door and strode in, picking up a cushion from one of the chairs as he passed. He pressed it against Rosenbaum's face to silence the gun and fired two bullets through it. When he removed the cushion, there were two holes side by side through his forehead. At five seconds passed eleven, he pressed the button on his communicator confirming the kill.

Rosenbaum's death was the first to auto-confirm on the screen in front of the Hydra. Within twenty seconds, half were confirmed and after another minute, all but eight. Nothing aroused Hydie Papandreou more than the death of her enemy. When the last of the eight targets remaining confirmed positive kills, she was beside herself in rapture. The Hydra had cut the head off of the Illuminati organisation, ready to insert her own people. What Hydie desperately needed right then was a man. Not just any man, Demitri her late husband. It was at violent times like this that they had their best sex. Since his death at the hands of the Angels, there had been no man to compare. Right now she physically ached for him. She remembered how his touch felt, his manly scent and the urgency and power of his lovemaking. Hydie became lost in herself as she imagined him there with her.

"Demitri!" she called out to no one there, as she was consumed by her fulfilment.

In the aftermath, Hydie Papandreou swore that once the Pindar was dealt with, the tenuous peace between Angel and Shadow would end. Then there would be retribution for the lives of her beloved Demitri and son, Anaxis.

Chapter 33

Moscow, Russia. Tuesday, January 9th 2018. The day of reckoning.

Emanuel Goldberg was sat at his desk in the Angelos Associates' offices in Moscow City. He had the morning newspapers strewn in front of him. From The Times, to Der Spiegel and the Washington Post to China Daily, they all carried the same story's. Russia's Pravda was typical. It recounted:

"British strike helicopters were scrambled yesterday from the British Sovereign Base at Akrotiri, Cyprus for targeted airstrikes against the so called ISIS. Missile attacks were

focussed on Dabiq in Syria, where it is thought that the militant religious leader, Mohammed Akhbar, was preparing to amass an army and initiate a holy war against American and British forces. Unsubstantiated reports indicate that Akhbar was killed in the attack..."

And:

"News is coming in of a series of coordinated assassinations taking place around the world. These include high-ranking business men, officials, politicians and leaders of financial and religious organisations. They reach into governments, palaces and even the Vatican. All the killings took place at exactly the same time and nobody has yet claimed responsibility. A number of the dead have been linked to the Illuminati organisation. Our sources have confirmed that the police are considering the possibility of this being the result of a power struggle within the Illuminati..."

Emanuel sighed as he pushed the papers away. None of them had yet connected the two stories, but they soon would. He knew that, just as he knew that the police would never uncover the full story. It had all gone almost to perfection. But the word *almost* broke Emanuel's heart. He held his big shaggy head in his hands and his eyes filled.

"Oh Kayla," he lamented.

The news of her death had hit him hard. Emanuel was the father figure to them all and they were all precious to him, particularly Kayla. He had known her since adolescence, when she was sent to him by her despairing parents. It was when she was first experiencing the sheer magnitude of her psychic and telekinetic skills. It couldn't have happened at a worse time for Kayla. Her hormones were way out of control and she was full of rage. At that time her father was in the early stages of his illness and couldn't guide her. Emanuel had counselled her through it and dealt with the carnage that she caused during her teenage mood-swings. Since then, their closeness had endured the test of time and Kayla felt secure and comfortable in his presence. She trusted him and he considered her as a daughter. Now Emanuel felt that he had betrayed that trust and felt the unbearable weight of the guilt for having sent her to her death. Now he had the task of notifying her family and arranging her funeral. It would be with full military honours of course, with the last post sounding out loud and lamenting for the much decorated, Major General Kayla Lovell.

The Gothic castle near Ingolstadt shook under the sheer power of the Pindar's rage. In less than an hour, his plans for world domination were decimated and his organisation, decapitated. In all his six thousand years, he had never known such venomous anger. The world would suffer for this, but first Gina Mèdici would. This all started with her and she had made a fool of him. One phone call was all it took. He already knew where she was. Nobody could hide from a being like him. By tomorrow there would be no farmhouse at Gorodishche. No Gina Mèdici or her annoying children.

Gina and Ava were devastated by the news of Kayla's death. They were notified at six o'clock that morning, less than three hours after the sad event. Apparently, she had sacrificed her life to save Callum. Yuri was broken by the news too, but of course he had to be their rock and showed little of his grief. Gina was the worst hit, because she was carrying an element of guilt too.

"I sensed it," Gina confessed to Ava, "or at least I sensed something."

"Sensed what?" Ava cocked a shapely brow inquisitively.

"Danger, that Callum needed her protection. I told him to stay close to her. I didn't know why and I didn't warn him properly," then she added guiltily, "or her."

Ava took Gina by the shoulders and held her eyes.

"Gina, we don't know what we don't know. We get clues and feelings, but not often the facts. We are not all as gifted as Asmina, who sees the detail. Every women feels deep dread when her man goes to war and many could say, 'I knew it was going to happen' and mostly they are wrong."

Although it was the truth, it still didn't assuage Gina's guilt.

"It's more than that Ava. I never considered Kayla's safety, not for a moment. To be honest, I never liked her. But then I never knew her as a person, only as a threat to me having Callum. I thought she was using him," Gina burst into tears and gulped out the rest in sobs. "Then I find out that she loved him more than her own life. I'm such a bitch."

"No," Ava consoled, "just a woman in love. We have all been there."

"I don't know how I will ever live with my sin," Gina felt that she had irreparably damaged her spirit.

"It was no sin Gina. If Kayla loved Callum enough to die for him, then she valued his life more than hers. She would want him to be happy. Make him happy for her. Consider that as your penitence."

Ava's words struck a chord with Gina. She was a woman of deep faith, driven from her Catholic background. She silently pledged an oath to Kayla that she would be there for Callum, no matter what. Ava changed the subject to matters of the present.

"Callum returns from Cyprus tomorrow. Have you thought on that?"

"Yes, constantly," Gina admitted. "I don't know what to say, he will be broken. I know that he truly loved Kayla and that if she had been..." Gina struggled to find the appropriate words, "a little more faithful, then there would never have been me. All I know is that I want to hold him and let his grief come out. Then, we will see."

"We should be there to meet them tomorrow Gina, despite our confinement to this farmhouse. They will need us, all of them. Kayla was part of their family and they will all be grieving too," Ava said, although it was probably unnecessarily. "That gives us this afternoon to pack and get ready. Callum will need you more than you can imagine Gina," she said reassuringly.

"I know Ava and I want to be there for him. I'll go and see Sasha and Isabella now and get them started. They're bound to want something that's not washed and ironed. They usually do."

"I'll see if I can get Yuri to agree to us all staying at the Metropol tonight. Maybe it's not the safest thing to do, but it would make tomorrow so much easier and," Ava paused, uncertain of herself.

"And what?" Gina asked, knowing fine well what she was going to say.

"And maybe you could find some private time to be together with Callum. I mean to comfort him," she added hastily.

"Perhaps," Gina conceded, uncomfortably.

Chapter 34

Moscow, Russia. Tuesday, January 9th 2018. The day of reckoning.

It was midday when the Russian Chief Marshal of Aviation, Alexander Mikhailov, put the phone down and walked to his drinks cabinet. He poured himself a large Zyr vodka. When it came to vodka, Mikhailov was a snob and Zyr was the brand that currently pleased him. Normally he would smell its aroma, swill it in his mouth to savour it, and then enjoy the deep pleasing burn of imbibing it. Right now, he just needed to drink it. He poured the second and did the same.

Alexander Mikhailov was a portly man in his late forties. He was balding and heavily bearded with bushy eyebrows that he knitted imposingly in moments of displeasure. This was one of them. He had survived a number of presidencies, power struggles and attempted coupes. Alexander Mikhailov had always enjoyed the ear of the incumbent Presidents, but this was entirely a different situation. Presidents come and go, but the Illuminati is constant. To fail them would not only be a death sentence for him, but for his family too. The call that he had just received, was from the highest level within the Illuminati; the Pindar himself. His instructions were to arm MiG-35 jets and take out a civilian target at Gorodishche, near Moscow. He had been given the precise coordinates and the timescale that he had been given, was immediately.

Mikhailov had the authority to do this; there was no doubt about that. He could justify a sudden civilian attack, in the short term, as a matter of national security. How he would survive afterwards, though, was quite another matter. He would be acting without the President's authority. It was a career ending scenario and one that would result in his execution in the aftermath. The press would have a heyday and there would be a witch hunt. The Pindar had given him a death sentence. He poured another vodka and downed it.

This was the scenario that Mikhailov had always dreaded, Illuminati over country and conscience. Despite his rank and expectations of him, Mikhailov was essentially a pacifist. He believed in political solutions and the threat of war, rather than the initiation of it. To make matters worse, he had read the morning papers and was painfully aware of the mass elimination of high-ranking Illuminati members around the world. He couldn't help but conclude that this order was related in some way. Mikhailov picked up the telephone and dialled. It was a call that he had spent the last decade dreading. The pickup took much longer than he had hoped and time was of paramount importance. His family's future would depend on his decisions and their responses over the next few hours.

"Irena?" he confirmed.

"Yes Alex, how unexpected and lovely of you to call."

Irena was about to enthuse more when she had a sudden feeling of foreboding. Alexander never called her from the office, because of security restrictions.

"Is everything alright?"

Alexander Mikhailov didn't answer that question. He was going to defect and there was no time for niceties.

"Get the children home and pack what you really need, nothing more" he instructed. "Do it now. Book four tickets to America, Washington or New York will do. Get three tickets on the first flight you can get on and one for me that leaves Moscow after five o'clock this evening. Then don't use your credit card again, in fact destroy it. Do you understand Irena?"

"Yes, but you are scaring me Alex. What's happened?" She was beginning to cry.

"Just listen and trust me Irena. We don't have time."

Alexander Mikhailov was trying to keep his voice calm, sensing that Irena was close to panicking.

"I'll meet you in America and explain there. Next, I want you to destroy your mobile phone and Viktor's and Liliya's too. Take the SIMs out, put the mobiles down a road drain somewhere and flush the SIMs down the toilet. Have you got that?"

"Yes," she mumbled in shock.

"Good girl. Don't make any calls or tell anyone what you are doing, not even your mother Irena. Particularly *not* your mother!" he added with emphasis.

Alexander had problems with women keeping secrets.

"The same applies for Viktor and Liliya. All of our lives will depend on that. One mistake and we are all dead."

Irena was over the initial shock now and was into the mother bear protecting her cubs' mode. The change in her was palpable.

"What else must I do Alex? Tell me!"

"Go to the bank. See Grigorij and buy as many Dollars as you can. If they don't have them, then buy British Pounds. Ask them to transfer the rest to our Swiss account and then destroy your bank cards."

"Yes, I've got that. What then?" Irena was fully focussed.

"Buy two mobile phones, pay as you go, with cash. When you get to the airport, find the ladies toilets that are the closest to check-in. Write the number of one of them on the wall and hide the other somewhere in that block for me. I will find it. Don't call out and only accept a call if it's from me."

"Where will I go in Washington, or New York?" she asked, thinking it through.

"Anywhere you don't have to show them your passport. Play little girl lost or bribe them if necessary. You will find a way Irena, you always do."

He had always been proud of her resilience and resourcefulness.

"Be brave for me Irena. The children need you to be strong and I need you to be strong. I will call you as soon as I arrive in America and we will go to the embassy together. I love you."

Alexander had to cut the call. He could no longer trust his voice to stay strong and positive.

"I love you too," Irena whispered to an unhearing open tone.

She was a plain but pretty woman in her late thirties, ten years younger than her husband. She was blonde, as was the current Russian fashion, and petite. Irena's only concession to makeup was red lipstick and eyeliner, her skin still having a youthful flush about it.

By nature, she was pale, but the enormity of the situation had sent her white. Irena went weak at the knees with shock, needing to lean on the wall to steady herself. The floor flew away from her and she thought she was going to feint. Irena was about to succumb to unconsciousness when her eyes flew wide open.

"Viktor! Liliya!" she shouted as her brain cleared.

There was a scampering of feet coming down the stairs. The tone of her voice had frightened them.

"Mama, Mama!" Liliya screamed, half way down, as a nine year old might.

They ran into their mothers outstretched arms, panicked. Victor was two years older and already considered himself the man in the house when his father was not there. He immediately sensed that it was to do with him.

"Is Papa alright?" despite his bravado, Viktor's bottom lip was trembling.

"Papa will be fine. It's just that," Irena struggled to find the right words, "it's just that he's been sent to America and it will be for some time. So the surprise is that we are going too!" Irena gave them a big enthusiastic smile that seemed to work.

"When?" Victor asked suspiciously, running his hand up the stubble of his short crew cut.

"Now, you've got 15 minutes to pack a small bag each with your special things and then we are off to the airport. I will pack some clothes for us and we can buy new things there. Now go!"

They turned and ran upstairs. Victor paused at the kitchen door. He was not convinced and about to ask another question. Irena derailed it.

"Go!" Victor reluctantly obeyed. "And I need your mobiles now. I will buy you new ones in America," she added, following them up.

While the children were packing, Irena arranged the air tickets and taxi. She would stop by the bank on the way and hoped that Grigorij would be there to help her. It was too dangerous to call him in advance she decided and took the SIM cards from the mobiles. She wrapped them individually in toilet paper and flushed them down the toilet. That just left the mobiles themselves to get rid of, something she could do outside the bank.

Irena was a coper by nature, seldom fazed but this was taking her to her very limits. She shuddered suddenly, as if someone had walked over her grave. It left her with a feeling of great foreboding. Irena desperately wanted to be in the safety of the arms of her man again. The memory of him holding and kissing her goodbye that morning suddenly filled her head. For some reason that kiss had felt different, she recalled; more soulful. She wondered if that was a premonition of it being their last. She had to quickly put the thought out of her mind. She had to function.

The taxi arrived. Irena shepherded the children out of the house and closed the door. She briefly placed her hand lovingly on it. It wasn't just a house; it was their home with all their belongings in it. The house was their history, with photographs, jewellery, keepsakes and memories; even their fragrance. All they had of their past life now, were three pathetic bags. Irena couldn't help the tears as she said goodbye to it.

The taxi stopped outside the VTB Bank of Moscow. By chance, it had stopped over a drain cover. Irena paid the driver a retainer and discretely dropped the mobiles through the grating as she got out, leaving the children in the car and the meter running.

By chance, Grigorij was at his desk. He was a tall, gangly man with a personable face and cordial manner. He recognised Irena as soon as she entered and he called her over.

"Irena, what a pleasure it is to see you. Please, sit down," he said indicating the chair. "How are you and the children? It's been months."

"Oh, we're fine," she lied, "but we have a mini crisis and I need your help and discretion. And your haste," she added.

"Absolutely, Mrs Mikhailov; tell me what you need and it will be my pleasure to help you."

Grigorij had an innocent crush on Irena. He worked swiftly and accommodatingly for her. Thirty minutes later, Irena left the bank with a briefcase full of Dollars, their account transferred to Switzerland and a crest-fallen Grigorij. The short journey to Moldova Airport was thankfully traffic free. The cabbie played the radio loud, which provided good distraction for the children, particularly for Liliya who had an unusually keen memory for lyrics and sung tunefully. The broadcast was interrupted by breaking news. It was about an airstrike to the north west of Moscow, by Soviet jets. The rest of the news flash was purely speculative. Now everything made sense to Irena. Her husband was going to take the fall for this and she gasped out loud.

"Mama, what's the matter?" Liliya asked, fiddling with one of her neatly plaited pigtails.

"It's just bad news on the radio darling, nothing for us to worry about though. Look, we're here," she said, changing the subject.

They went straight to the flight desk and collected their tickets. Irena handed the stewardess a sealed envelope. It was a love letter that she had quickly penned in the taxi. If her beloved Alexander was going to die, she needed him to know just how much she loved him.

"Will you give this to my husband when he collects his ticket please? It's very important."

"Of course Mrs Mikhailov, I will pin it to his ticket," the pretty stewardess said with a stereotypical smile.

Irena had one more task to do. She purchased two *pay as you go* phones from one of the airport shops, and then returned to the check-in area where she quickly found the closest toilets.

"Come on, quickly. Go to the toilet now before we get on the plane."

Irena took Liliya in with her. To her horror, everything was flush-fitted. There was no place that she could hide the phone where it wouldn't be seen immediately. She went into one of the cubicles and shut the door. While Liliya was having a pee, she tried to lever off the top of the porcelain cistern. It was hopeless and they only had minutes before boarding. Irena could feel her panic rising.

"What are you doing Mummy?" Liliya asked, frowning.

"Just straightening the top, it looked crooked. Hurry up."

"There's no paper Mummy," she lamented.

"Eureka! Clever girl," Irena said to her very puzzled daughter.

She rummaged in her bag, found some tissues and handed them to her daughter. Then took one of the mobiles and stuffed it in the empty paper dispenser. The problem was going to be when the cleaners came to clean and refresh the toilets. They would find it for sure. Irena needed to put the cubical out of service. She lifted the toilet seat. Then, using all her body weight, wrenched it off its mountings.

"What are you doing?" Liliya asked in disbelief as her mother smashed the seat against the wall.

The noise of the toilet seat shattering and her mother's bizarre actions frightened Liliya. She began to cry.

365

"It's alright darling. Mama will explain later," Irena said with a cuddle and a reassuring smile.

"What's going on? Are you alright?" someone shouted from outside, trying the door.

"Yes, just a minute," Irena replied, rummaging in her bag for the marker pen.

Irena quickly wrote a telephone number on the inside of the door and a long arrow leading to the paper dispenser. Then she scrawled graffiti all over the cubicle, making sure that they would put it out of service. When she opened the door and walked out with Liliya, the cleaner was drop-jawed at what she saw.

"No toilet paper," Irena said, shrugging her shoulders. "Doesn't it make you mad?"

The woman was too astonished to reply. They left leaving her staring in disbelief at the trashed cubicle.

Alexander Mikhailov's next call was to the Ministry of Defence. He sold the unprecedented internal air strike on the grounds of averting an imminent nuclear incident; an incident that would be of immense international embarrassment. The Ministry had no reason to doubt such a high-ranking and trusted officer. One who was also a close friend of the President himself. Authorisation to load Krypton air-to-surface missiles onto two MiG jets was immediate. Two and a half hours later, at 1430 hours, the MiGs were airborne with their missiles programmed to the coordinates of the farmhouse and outbuildings at Gorodishche. Mikhailov's despicable job was done. The airstrike was scheduled to happen thirty minutes later at 1500 hours. It wasn't a military target. Mikhailov felt the heavy responsibility and guilt of initiating such an atrocity. He was sure that his soul would be damned forever, but he had no choice. His family were innocent too.

As soon as Alexander Mikhailov had confirmation that the jets were in the air, he went directly to the safe in his office. Thirty years of experience in the military had left him far from naive. He had prepared meticulously for this day. The day that he would be sacrificed like a pawn in a game of chess, just for someone's political gain. He had seen it dozens of times before and knew that one day his time would come too.

Mikhailov had diplomatic status and was therefore entitled to travel with his diplomatic bag. By international agreement, these bags were beyond scrutiny by the police and customs. He began to load it with the contents of the safe. It was basically his survival kit. As well as other essentials, there were fresh passports for each member of the family, along with birth certificates and other documents that underpinned their new names. There were cash and bank cards to access his Swiss account, a pistol with silencer, ammunition and a medical kit. The current eastern bloc fashion for dealing with dissidents and to discourage others, was to poison them. That was either with radioactive polonium, as was the case with Alexander Litvinenko in 2006, or VX nerve-agent used on Kim Jon-Un's brother-in-law in 2017. These recent deaths had influenced what Mikhailov had included in his medical kit. There were iodine tablets to block his thyroid gland, in case of radiation poisoning and atropine, along with pralidoxime, in case of a nerve-agent attack. He had included dressings for gun wounds too, but was fairly confident that a public shooting at the airport was unlikely. Importantly, Mikhailov had also loaded syringes with diazepam to prevent him going into shock if any of these scenarios happened. Injecting himself would be his first action; otherwise he might not be able to function to administer the others.

Diplomatic bag packed, Alexander Mikhailov left his office and took a taxi to the airport. He could only hope to not be missed for thirty minutes, maximum. After that they would be contacting him about the success, or otherwise of the air strike and for further instructions. He had diverted his calls to his mobile and could bluff for a while. That would take him to 1530 hours. After that, they would be looking for him. It wouldn't take them long to realise that it wasn't a sanctioned attack and that he had fled as a traitor. Malpensa Airport would be their first port of call to find him but it was his only chance.

It was only a short run to the airport. Time enough though, for him to reflect on the situation that had exploded on him without warning, and of his family. The explosion was the Illuminati. Ten years ago, they had a presence in Russia only. Now they had control. Even the President was compromised. Senior statesmen across the globe were becoming increasingly dependent on the far reaching Illuminati to gain, or stay in power. Their political decisions were no longer for the benefit of Russia, but for a more globalised agenda and economy; one that his beloved Russia would be subservient to. It was infinitely powerful and therefore infinitely corrupt and ruthless. Mikhailov's position had just become untenable. It would be made to seem that a 'rogue' senior officer, aka him, in Moscow's elite had acted alone. Or at least that would be how it would have been reported. In such a case a man would have no choice but to take his pistol and commit suicide; death before dishonour. But then he was a loving family man and loved by his family. He could not do that to them.

"But the President has to have immunity at whatever price," Mikhailov thought ruefully, "and that price is me, my wife and children. I will not pay in that collateral!" he vowed.

As the taxi turned into Malpensa Airport, there was a sound like distant thunder. Mikhailov checked his watch. It was 1500 hours precisely. He touched his forehead and then made the sign off the cross. Despite his choice of profession, he was a religious man.

"God forgive me," he said out loud in despair.

"I'm sorry sir, what was that?" the cabbie asked over his shoulder.

"Nothing, just drop me here," Mikhailov ordered, handing over more notes than he needed to.

He deliberately got out of the taxi 200 yards before the departures entrance. It was to allow himself time to take in his surroundings and accustom himself to the crowds. That would allow him to respond more quickly and positively to a situation, should his worse fears come to fruition.

Mikhailov walked towards the crowd, desperately trying to call on his field training. He hadn't always driven a desk. In the early days, he was in the field as one of the scores of secret agents that had been inserted into the west as spies in the Cold War. In those days, he survived by instinct. He only prayed that those instincts, once so perfectly honed, hadn't deserted him completely. As he joined the masses, he naturally avoided being drawn into the centre, where his enemy could come at him from all sides. He blended in from the outside, maintaining a safe-zone of 180 degrees by staying close to walls and obstructions on one side. That way, he didn't have to watch his back. He remembered to watch faces, not people. Intent always showed on a man's face moments before an assault. Even one second's notice could make the difference between life and death. Mikhailov wondered at how much pure fear could focus the mind.

He worked his way to the flight desk down walls, facing backwards on escalators, keeping safe family groups on one side and walking so briskly that he would recognise anyone running to keep up. At no stage was there even a hint of something suspicious. Mikhailov got to the desk, checked around him and collected his ticket from a stereotypically blonde and beautiful Russian hostess.

"Your wife left you this letter, Mr Mikhailov," she said accommodatingly.

He thanked her and left with alacrity. All he needed to do now was to pick up the mobile phone from the ladies toilet and check in. Once he was passed the security check-in, he would be safe.

It didn't take long to find the toilets closest to check-in. The problem was that there was a cue to use them. Mikhailov quickly decided that there was no discrete way of doing this, if he was ever to catch his plane. He bundled apologetically through the queue.

"Excuse me, excuse me; Airport security. Excuse me, airport security."

His authoritative manner parted the crowd like Moses parting the Red Sea. That was only half of the problem solved though. When he entered the toilets, all the cubicles were occupied and he had no time. There were six doors. He knocked loudly on the first.

"Security! Open this door now, we have a situation," Mikhailov yelled out, not giving the woman a choice.

"But I can't, I'm..."

"Open it!"

There was panicked shuffling. The door opened and the woman was sat down again even before he entered. Mikhailov looked behind the door and around the cubicle. There were no messages.

"Apologies Miss," he conceded and moved on to the next

He had the same result through the next four, although with significantly more venom.

The last cubical was locked with a sign on the door proclaiming that it was 'Out of Service'. He reached up; placing his hands on top of the door, then dragged himself up until he was head and shoulders above the door. He could immediately see the state it was in and the graffiti.

"Clever girl," he muttered as he dropped down the other side of the door.

Mikhailov followed the arrow to the paper dispenser and reached inside it. His smile said it all. He memorised the number. A photographic memory was just one of the many skills he had been forced to learn. Things like number plates, access codes and map coordinates were no problem for him to recall. He opened the cubicle door and walked out passed the queue of puzzled women.

"So far, so good," he thought.

His flight had already been called. Mikhailov made his way directly to security, his last obstacle. If they let him through there, then he was probably home and dry. He was still hoping that he had caused enough confusion at flight command, that they wouldn't have blocked him on the immigration computers, yet. Mikhailov maintained his vigilance, looking out for suspicious people whilst avoiding having anyone on both sides of him. Just before security, he stopped at a water vending machine and purchased a bottle. He took a swig as he carefully planned how he could best get through to security. Sadly, there was no way that he could get there without joining the crowd, which was the last thing that he wanted to do.

"Here goes everything," he said to himself, joining one of the queues.

Mikhailov looked at the people either side of him, quickly ruling out some of them so that he could pay more attention to the others. To his left was a group of white-haired men, loud and slightly inebriated.

"Golfers," he concluded. "No risk."

Then there was a family. The mother was in stress, dealing with a screaming baby while the father was diverting their little boy.

"No risk".

He eliminated other groups in the same way. It was the loners that he was worried about and began to pay them more attention, paying particular attention to their faces. One in particular looked awkward and wouldn't be drawn into eye contact. The queue to his left was moving the fastest and he had to re-appraise that one whilst still keeping an eye on the man acting suspiciously. Mikhailov noticed two girls next to him. Pretty and vital, hardly described them. One of them, the tall blonde girl, was making herself up and grooming her long hair in the slow moving queue. She was extrovert and affected. The girl was obviously in raptures about her journey, or perhaps slightly drunk. He took another swig from his water bottle.

Mikhailov was painfully aware that he had become distracted, watching the girls too much. He quickly swung his attention back to the suspicious man, but he was gone. Mikhailov couldn't believe his lack of professionalism and searched anxiously for the man, but he was nowhere to be seen. Mikhailov turned back to the girls. The blonde was holding a mirror looking at herself while she preened. She was tossing her hair to attract attention and about to spray it. The whole show was text book. Mikhailov should have seen it coming, but he didn't, until it was too late. The blonde's laughing eyes turned to steel as she turned suddenly and sprayed him directly in the face, then was gone.

At the last second, Mikhailov had managed to avert his eyes but his face and nostrils were covered in a mist of VX nerve-agent. His immediate feelings were a mixture of anger and stupidity; anger for having been so stupid. Stupid, because this was exactly how Kim Jon-Un's brother-in-law was killed, and precisely what he had planned to avoid. He was also angry, because he needed to stay alive to keep his family safe. Now he would fail them.

Valuable seconds were ticking by while he mourned his family, lifesaving seconds. Mikhailov's brain was suffering from inertia. Suddenly his survival instinct clicked in. He emptied the rest of his water bottle over his head, scrubbing his face aggressively with his hands. As the water flowed over his face, he sniffed and snorted to clear his nostrils from the deadly agent and blinked in case his eyes had been contaminated. The effect of the nerve-agent on him was immediate, despite having washed so much off. He was thankful that he had mostly protected his eyes. Death would have followed quickly if he hadn't.

Mikhailov knew that his life expectancy could be measured in minutes now if he didn't self-medicate. He barged backwards through the queue to the toilets. One man was about to enter one of the cubicles when he shoved him to the floor. He locked himself inside and sat down before he fell down. It took Mikhailov monumental effort to maintain his sensibility as his shaking fingers fumbled the combination lock on his briefcase for far too long. His body was starting to succumb to the initial stages of shock. Eventually it opened. Mikhailov found the syringe loaded with diazepam and quickly jammed it into his thigh. He searched for the phial of pralidoxime, the antidote for the nerve-agent, found it quickly and loaded it into the syringe. This needed to go directly into his bloodstream. He stripped off his shirt and tied the sleeve of it around his upper arm, like a tourniquet, to swell his veins. The one in the crook of his elbow plumped up nicely and he injected it in his final moment of consciousness.

Mikhailov slipped into oblivion as chemical warfare began to place in his body; the VX nerve-agent against the pralidoxime antidote. The battle would be fought in the next fifteen minutes and the outcome, final. His dreams had that clarity people get, near death. His particular dream was that his family had left him. No matter what he tried in the dream, they would not or could not come back. He was desperate, apologising for not being there, begging for their forgiveness and promising that he would never let them down again. Despite all his efforts, they scorned him and walked away into the darkness leaving him bereft.

The clouds began to lift from Mikhailov's mind. He slowly became aware of his surroundings and wondered for long seconds how he had been there. The memories of the attack came crashing in on him, bringing him back to the present. Mikhailov's first action was to check his watch. He had no idea if he had lost minutes, or hours. To his enormous relief, it was minutes only, but they were twenty precious ones. If his body could still function, he could still catch the flight. He stood gingerly, but had to sit again after only a few moments. Mikhailov dug deep and tried again.

"For the family," he said out loud, as he tried again."they won't make it without you."

It was just the catalyst he needed. Mikhailov got up on shaking legs, grabbed his briefcase and left the cubicle drunkenly. His need for medical attention was urgent but that would have to wait until he was out of Russia. To give himself up to the authorities would be suicide. They would make sure that he didn't recover from the nerve-agent, or at best, imprison him for life on charges of crimes against the State. He no longer had the powers of observation necessary to look out for his own safety, it was as much as he could do to just steer himself to security. Somehow he had to steel himself to not look drunk or ill; otherwise he would be refused boarding. More than that, he had to maintain the charade until the flight had left Russian airspace. In the event of him going into crisis, the jet would naturally be diverted to the nearest airport.

"Documents," the immigration officer asked impatiently.

Mikhailov's life and those of his family, now depended on how he handled himself in the next few minutes.

"Are you alright sir," he asked, concerned about the passengers pallor and shakes.

"I'm terrified of flying is all," Mikhailov lied.

"Just relax, it'll be fine," the officer said sympathetically handing his documents back. "You better hurry sir, the flight has been called."

Mikhailov braced himself, set his eyes on the departure gates and set off unsteadily.

"I'm going to make it," he said to himself, focussing on his family. "I'm going to make it."

Chapter 35

Milan, Italy. Tuesday, January 9th 2018. The day of reckoning.

It was a little over three weeks since Gina, Sasha and Isabella had gone into hiding and Asmina missed them immensely. The world seemed to have gone mad since then, she lamented. All day, the news had been about assassinations of powerful people all over the world, none of whom Asmina knew, but she pitied them and their loved ones none-the-less. There had been another airstrike in Syria too, and reports of a religious leader being killed. On the news they called him the 'Mahdi'.

"He ain't no Mahdi," Asmina tutted, "I knows these t'ings. If he the Mahdi, then I be Mother Theresa," she chuckled at the nonsense of it and her bulk wobbled like jelly on a plate.

She was busily going about her day, making sure that the house was perfect and ready for the return of her 'family'.

"Ain't no sunshine when they gone," she declared, this time in the plural. "An' that's a fact."

Asmina was plumping the cushions in the anteroom when she suddenly felt weak and about to faint. She lowered herself unsteadily onto the settee. She sat there with her head lolled to one side, eyes staring into nothingness, and then they rolled back until only the whites of them showed. Asmina's breath left her in a sudden loud rush, as she went into a trance and entered the spirit world.

Asmina found herself in the kitchen of a quaint rustic house. The table was set for five people. There was a loaf of bread and a wheel of cheese set in the middle, with a pitcher of water and a bottle of red wine. She could hear voices, young voices. They seemed excited about something.

"Sasha! Issie!" Asmina called out as they appeared in her vision.

Her voice was deep and guttural but it went unheard by them. Gina came into the room with another woman and a man that she didn't recognise. Again, she called out with a voice from the other side, the voice of the spirits, but no one heard her. They sat. Asmina could sense that there was sadness amongst them, like they had lost something precious. As Gina cut the bread, the old grandfather clock struck three. Suddenly, there was a deafening scream, like all the cats in Hell were about to fight. Asmina watched in horror as a fireball ripped through the room, stripping the flesh off all there, leaving only charred bone and black smoke. Asmina's eyes flew open.

"Gina!" she screamed in panic. "Gina!"

It was a premonition. She looked at her wrist watch. It was five minutes before one o'clock. Asmina knew that the time in Moscow was two hours later.

"Holy Mary, they got five minutes," Asmina uttered in horror.

She got up and hurried to her quarters, upsetting a table with a floral display on it as she went. The vase crashed to the floor and shattered, leaving a pool of water spreading on the polished oak flooring. Asmina found her bag and her mobile was thankfully there. Her hands were shaking so much that she could hardly open the display and find the speed dial. The call connected. The ringing tone went on and on until it went to answerphone.

"You have reached the number of Gina Mèdici. I'm sorry but I can't take your call right now. Please leave your name and number and I will get back to you."

Asmina looked disbelievingly at the display. It read, "12:57." She frantically dialled again. The phone began ringing.

"Pick up bibi, for God's sake pick up!" Asmina cried out in despair.

Their bags were packed and already in the Range Rover. Gina had prepared a late and simple lunch for them. Just bread and cheese with pickles and red wine. They would dine later at the Metropol in a more magnificent manner. The day had passed in sombre and surreal manner. None of them could really connect with the reality of Kayla having died. She was such a powerful and vital woman, with supernatural abilities that included glimpsing the immediate future. For her to have been killed, would have needed an uncharacteristic and unprecedented loss of perception, or concentration on her part. Gina's guilt was fuelled by the possibility that Kayla had become distracted by their love affair and wasn't on top of her game at the time of her death, thinking about her love for Callum beyond all else. It was worse than that.

Gina was *certain* that it was the case. She could relate to that, it would be just the same for her if the tables were turned.

It was just before three o'clock in the afternoon when Gina, Ava and Yuri walked into the kitchen. Sasha and Isabella were in animated conversation, looking forward to getting away from the farmhouse and the bright lights of the city. The sadness of Kayla's death was less potent to them as they had never met her. Just as Gina sat down, her mobile rang.

"It can wait," she said. "I'll call them back later."

The MiG jets came in side by side from the south east and flew over the farmhouse at Gorodishche. Their airspeed was just over 200 knots, flying low in reconnaissance. Smoke was coming from the farmhouse chimney and a Range Rover was parked in the yard, a short distance away.

"141 to flight control, come in flight control," the pilot called.

Gregorin was a man in his early twenties, on his first mission in active service. This wasn't how he had expected it to be though and was feeling uncomfortable. They were on time. It was just before 0300 hours.

"Flight control to 141; reading you loud and clear. Over."

"We have visual; it looks like the building is occupied. We have smoke and a car parked on the drive. Over," Gregorin confirmed.

There was a pause, as if flight control were getting confirmation. The pilots had taken off with armed missiles but no brief, other than to locate the farmhouse and stand by.

"141, you are instructed to destroy those buildings. Repeat, you are instructed to destroy those buildings. Confirm your understanding," it was an anonymous and emotionless voice.

"Message understood. Circling and climbing to 2,000 feet, then coming in from the North West for missile attack. 141 out."

Gregorin called his flight buddy in less formal terms.

"Did you copy that Ivan?" he asked.

"I copied. I'll fly on your wing tip and you take us in Gregorin. It doesn't feel right though, does it?"

"It doesn't. I guess we will read about it tomorrow. Hope its good news. Stay focussed Ivan. Out."

The jets climbed and circled, then came in at 400 knots from the North West with their Krypton missiles armed.

"Fire!" Gregorin ordered.

Both jets released their deadly cargo in unison. Seconds later the buildings disappeared in a sea of black smoke and fire. Gregorin made the sign of the cross.

"God rest your souls," he said as the jets climbed and headed back to base.

Gina had just begun to cut the bread when her mobile rang again.

"Persistent," Ava said. "Perhaps you better get it?"

Gina capitulated and left the room. The name on the display was Asmina's. She smiled fondly and opened the call.

"Asmina," she said lovingly.

"Get outta that house now bibi 'an run! Run for your life!"

"Asmina, you're scaring me," it was Asmina's tone as much as her words.

Get out bibi now. Run!" Asmina cut the call.

"That's the strangest thing," Gina said as she came back into the kitchen.

"What is?" Yuri asked with a quizzical look on his face.

"That was Asmina. She said to get out of the house and run. Now," Gina was staring at her mobile as if for an explanation.

It took Yuri only ten seconds to make his decision. He stood quickly and grabbed a machine gun from the worktop, his chair flying away behind him.

"If Asmina says get out and run, then it's good enough for me. Get out. Now and run, and keep running!"

The memory of Asmina's premonition about the waterwheel was still fresh in his mind. He had no reason to doubt her. Yuri bundled them out of the kitchen into the yard, just as the sound of the approaching jets filled the air.

"Run!" he yelled again.

Everyone did, too confused and alarmed to question or refuse. The air was suddenly filled with the rush of the Krypton missiles as they homed in on their targets. Gina clasped Isabella's hand and ran frantically away from the farmhouse.

"Sasha!" she screamed. "Where are you?" she was looking around frantically but couldn't see him.

First there was the ground shock, then the blast. It bowled them along in its wake, like tumbleweed. Then there was the intense heat that scorched their skin and their lungs, followed by oblivion.

Sasha was the first to rouse. He had no idea how long he had been unconscious. All he did know was that everything hurt. He stood painfully; it felt like he had been trampled by a horse. His ears were screaming from blast trauma and his sense of balance was seriously upset. Sasha staggered around, searching for the others in the backdrop of the burning farmhouse and outbuildings. He found his mother and Isabella first. They were closest to the farmhouse. Gina had covered Isabella with her body taking most of the blast. Her clothing was scorched on her back and legs and her hair was singed. He checked their breathing. They seemed OK and were both stirring. Next he found Ava and

Yuri lying together. He appeared to have protected her too. Both were unconscious but they appeared to be breathing steadily. He needed to get them to hospital. The Range Rover was still parked in the yard and looked like it had escaped the blast. Sasha hoped that the keys would be in it. Those hopes were suddenly dashed when he saw that the tyres had melted. At that moment, a black Mercedes estate car pulled into the drive. Sasha was relieved and began waving to them for help. To his horror, two men got out holding guns.

"Shit!" he exclaimed, falling flat on the floor.

Sasha lay still for several seconds and then raised his eyes above the long grass. He breathed out a sigh of relief. They hadn't seen him. He watched as they walked through the ruins of the farm.

"Checking for bodies," he spat. "I will give them two; theirs."

Sasha crawled back over to the unconscious Yuri and took his Heckler & Koch machine gun.

He was tired of being the target. Besides they had hurt his family and they would pay for that dearly. He crawled on elbows and knees, circling around to the back of their car. Whatever they were up to, they would eventually come back to their car. Of that there was no doubt

"And that's where I will wait and take you when you think its all clear," he vowed.

Sasha watched them as they poked through the debris with sticks. They were looking for some evidence of their kill. The physical shock of the explosion had passed. What Sasha felt now, was a burning rage and a desire to kill. The two men were clearly relaxed when they came back into view, feeling safe. Both had dropped their weapons to their sides and were talking almost casually. Sasha stepped out from the cover of the Mercedes and faced them. They were only ten yards apart.

"Boo," he said, with a smirk on his face.

The men's eyes flew open wide with astonishment. They had barely raised their guns to their hips, when Sasha emptied the magazine into them. They danced comically to the impact of the bullets and then fell in a heap.

"Don't fuck with the Mèdici's," he mocked, totally oblivious of the third man stood behind him with a gun held to his head.

The sound of machine gun fire cracked through the smoke-filled air, piercing Gina's mind, bringing her back to consciousness. She sensed it, before she saw it.

"Sasha!" she called out the warning, but the roar of the burning buildings drowned out her words.

Gina forced her burning eyes to focus. Three hundred yards away, Sasha was stood looking at the bodies of two men. He was oblivious to the third that was stood behind him with a pistol held inches from the back of his head.

"Drop the gun. Put your hands up and don't turn around," were the menacing words that made Sasha's stomach flip with fear. "Where are the others?"

Sasha flinched as he felt the cold steel of the gun barrel being pressed into the back of his skull.

"Where are the others? Don't make me ask you three times," the man spat out the words in contempt as he increased the pressure.

Sasha heard the metallic click of the gun echo through his skull as the man pulled back the breach, preparing to fire.

"Go fuck yourself!" he blurted with disdain.

Gina's mind was still befuddled from the blast. All she could think of was to run to Sasha. She broke into a sprint covering the ground like a lioness to protect her cub. Sasha saw her through the corner of his eye.

"No Mum, run!" Sasha screamed at her, but she came on like a charging bull.

"Your Mum, hey kid?" The man said cruelly, noticing that she was unarmed. "Wanna watch her die?"

He forced Sasha's head to the side to make him witness the event. The gunman waited until Gina was within certain killing range and then levelled the gun at her.

"Say goodbye to your Mummy, kid," he said kicking Sasha away, sending him spiralling to the floor.

Now that Sasha couldn't disrupt his aim, he increased the pressure on the trigger. Gina was only thirty yards away from saving her boy. She ran on trying to clear her mind and focus her rage, just as Ava had taught her. She remembered Ava's words.

"Anything is possible; you just have to want it enough."

She was close enough now to see the man's face. He was sneering at her, his eyes locked cruelly on hers. It was his undoing. Slowly the look on the man's face changed from sneer to bemusement as he struggled to pull the trigger. Ava had entered his mind. It was as if the trigger had become welded to the gun, impossible for him to pull. His finger refused to work. There was a look of sheer panic on his face as this woman bore down on him at impossible speed. He couldn't even find the sensibility to run. Gina hit him like full on at speed, sending him cartwheeling backwards in to the Mercedes. Even above the roar of the burning farm, the snap of his neck sounded like a gunshot. His last image in this world was the face of a mother scorned.

Spending the night at the Metropol was no longer a desire, it was a necessity. Fortunately, Yuri had loaded their bags into the Range Rover before the missile attack, so at least they had their clothes. The drive from the farmhouse had been intense. Yuri had suffered the worst from the blast, having wrapped himself around Ava as he forced her to the floor. His back, buttocks and legs were cut and bruised from the debris of the explosion. In truth, he should have gone to the hospital, rather than suffer the indignity of the girls digging out the debris from his buttocks with tweezers and drenching him in antiseptic from the car's medical box. Nobody else's injuries were significant though. They had been lucky. Yuri wanted Ava to go to the hospital to check their baby was OK but she was adamant that it was unnecessary.

"She's part Angel, for Christ's sake Yuri. Trust her!" on this, she was unmovable.

Yuri parked the Mercedes in a long term parking zone, near to the centre of Moscow and wiped it clean with baby wipes. Ava was well into her seventh month and had already prepared her baby bag. Now it went everywhere with her. She was a premature baby herself, but apparently that went with her mix of genes. By early evening, they were checked in at the Metropol. Sasha and Isabella has managed to get *leave passes* and planned a night out in Moscow's famous Soho Rooms. It was a famous and notorious night club, one that Ava had raved about. They had no idea just how wayward she was in those days. When Ava had said, "Don't do anything that I wouldn't do," she was pretty much giving them unlimited scope.

Yuri and Ava retired soon after dinner. The near death experience had made Ava even clingier and she wanted to be alone with Yuri. Gina put that down to imminent motherhood and forgave her for it. That left her alone with her sombre thoughts at the bar, drinking Dirty Martinis. They weren't helping in the slightest though. All she could think of was Callum and how much she missed him. More selfishly, she wondered whether he would ever get over Kayla's death.

"Can I join you?" the familiar voice asked.

Gina turned. Her eyes widened in delight.

"Callum!"

Gina was off her barstool and in his arms in seconds, oblivious to the onlookers who were amazed at her public show of emotion.

She held him for a long moment. Gina wanted to tell him how sorry she was for his loss but the words were lost in her chokes.

"Two more," Callum said to the waiter as he steered Gina to one of the booths.

"But you weren't supposed to arrive until tomorrow Callum. We are all so sad about it all and sad for you. You must be devastated," Gina had found her voice and cupped his hand with hers.

"Devastated and guilt ridden," he corrected. "I never knew that she loved me that much and can't believe that she would give..." Callum struggled to complete the sentence, "her life for me," he said, finally.

"I can believe it Callum," she squeezed his hand. "I could tell that she loved you that much. We all did Callum."

"She died in my arms Gina," he said in agony, "Then I carried her back to the Chinook and nursed her all the way back to Cyprus."

"She would have liked that Callum," Gina said.

"I know. I told her before she died that she would fly home in my arms and she said that she would like that," he recalled. "And there was something else in her dying breath, but I'm not sure. It was something profoundly generous, particularly for a jealous girl like Kayla."

"What was that?" Gina already knew. She could sense it.

"To have a happy life with you, I think," Callum said, looking into Gina's clear blue eyes. "But that she wanted me back when I die."

Gina reflected on that for a long moment then gave Callum her smile.

"I will settle for that Callum, it's more than I could ever have hoped for anyway," she said honestly, "and she has earned the rest of eternity."

Given that Gina was a deeply religious person that was not a throwaway statement.

"Gina," he said, looking sadly at her. "I can't even begin to think about us, not now and maybe not ever. I don't know. Perhaps after the funeral it will be different?"

Callum felt Gina's grip again as she steeled herself.

"There is no hurry Callum. Sometime on this side of eternity would be good though," her smile was thin and pained. Then she added. "Shall we get smashed?"

"I'll drink to that!" Callum said raising his glass, with just a hint of the boyish smile that Gina had grown to love.

"There is at least hope," Gina thought as they clashed glasses.

Chapter 36

Arlington National Cemetery, Washington, USA. Tuesday, January 30th 2018. Three weeks later.

The funeral procession passed through the iron gates into the Arlington National Cemetery. Ever since Union troops crossed the Potomac River and confiscated the land from the Confederate General Robert E. Lee in 1861, it had been used by the United States as a place to honour their fallen heroes. Today, America's fallen hero was Major General Kayla Lovell.

The hearse led the two black limousines past the mausoleum and on down through the cemetery towards where Kayla's memorial service awaited her. In the first of the limousines, were Kayla's parents and her close family. In the second, were Callum, Emanuel, Gina, Yuri, Ava and May. The rest of Kayla's mourners were already gathered at her grave. There had been a light dusting of snow during the night. It reflected the morning sun on the multitude of white marble crosses that were set out in perfect geometrical lines, standing like sentries guarding over their fallen heroes. The snow had also deadened all background sound, making the atmosphere seem even more surreal, like something out of a fantasy. It was hard to reconcile that this beautiful and serene setting was to be the final resting place of a charismatic and vibrant woman like Kayla Lovell.

The funeral cortège stopped to the side of a gun carriage, drawn by six white horses. Five were mounted by horse soldiers of The Old Guard in their dress uniform, and the sixth was rider-less, to signify the one fallen in duty. Kayla. In front, were the members of the military band and the flag bearer. There were another eight soldiers stood in columns either side of the gun carriage. They turned to order and marched to the back of the hearse. On command, they drew out the coffin that was draped in the American flag. Holding the coffin at hip level, they rotated in side steps until they faced the gun carriage, and then marched in short steps to the back of it. They loaded the coffin onto the gun carriage and took up their positions either side. Kayla's Mother and father stepped out of the limousine and took up their places several yards behind. Kayla was a child of a mixed marriage. Her mother was a black, jolly, buxom woman. She normally stood proud, but today she was stooped and broken. Her father was a tall, lean white man, able and confident. He was stood ramrod straight with his chin jutted out determinedly. It would not be apparent to another just how broken he was inside.

The funeral cortège drove on to where the ceremony was to take place, leaving Kayla and her parents to make the last few hundred solemn yards alone.

The band began to play, 'Praise to the Lord the Almighty the King of creation', and the procession moved off at a slow walk. Kayla's mother was crippled with grief and had to lean heavily on her husband for support. It only took the procession minutes to reach the grave, but it seemed an eternity to the Lovells.

Callum, Emanuel, Gina, Yuri, Ava and May joined the rest of the mourners at the graveside. Red Jake and the men were there, along with a small army of others. Kayla Lovell was leaving a multitude of close friends behind. You could have heard a pin drop as they watched the gun carriage approach. The blue and red Stars and Stripes stood out boldly in the whiteness of the snow, focussing everyone's attention on Kayla's last journey to her place of rest. Gina was stood next to Callum. She put her arm around him, sensing that he needed strength at that moment. He didn't look at her, but she felt the stiffness go out of his body at her touch. He was biting his lip; she noted and felt entirely useless. All she wanted to do was to hold him and tell him that it was alright to hurt, but this was not the time, nor the place. The carriage drew to a halt in front of them. Mr and Mrs Lovell continued onwards to the chairs that had been placed for them at Kayla's graveside.

The guards took their positions either side of the coffin and lifted Kayla, then marched her in short step to her grave and placed her above it. Mrs Lovell's bereavement was so acute that she couldn't bear to watch. Instead, she buried her head in her husband's shoulder and sobbed her heart out. The Chaplin spoke words to comfort the mourners, talking of Kayla's accolades both as a soldier and as a loving daughter and then offered prayers for her salvation. All the while, Callum and the others stood in shocked silence, each with their own thoughts of Kayla Lovell. When the Chaplin had finished, the pallbearers lifted the flag and folded it ceremonially into a triangle and handed it to Mrs Lovell. She took it and stared at it glumly. In her mind, it was no exchange for the life of her beautiful and vital daughter.

Seven riflemen loaded their rifles and fired three times into the air in unison. The shots rang out painfully in the cold winter air as each one, cruelly reminded Callum of those bullets that had taken Kayla's life out there in the Syrian Desert. It was a 21 gun salute for a fallen hero, for the woman he had failed to protect.

A lone bugler began to play the haunting tune of 'Taps', as was traditional. The lament sounded out loud and clear and deeply moving. Gina looked around her and could see that there was hardly a dry eye, she included. Red Jake was sobbing unashamedly. He loved and respected Kayla, as they all did in his squad. Gina had to look twice, not believing what she saw. At the back of the crowd of mourners, was Hydie Papandreou. She nodded in recognition and turned her attention back to the bugler just as he sounded that last long and emotive note. Callum grabbed Gina's hand for support and clung on to it in agony. His eyes were drilling into the coffin. That last long and lonesome note signalled the commitment of Major General Kayla Lovell to the earth.

"God forgive me Kayla, I'm so sorry," he whispered. "Wait for me darling; I will keep my promise to you. On this I swear."

All Gina could do, was simply be there for him.

The wake was being held at the Four Seasons Hotel, across the Potomac River in Washington D.C. The hotel had been block-booked. Other than the Senators and dignitaries, everyone there was either family, close friend or a military associate of Kayla. Hydie Papandreou was there too but she kept herself apart, waiting for another rare opportunity to talk with Maelströminha. The Hydra knew that she would not leave it too long before engaging with her.

In contrast with the solemnity of the funeral ceremony, the atmosphere in the reception hall was light and cordial. Jake and the boys were swapping war stories that included Kayla's many daring escapades.

"PIDOOMA!" Jake exclaimed over-loudly and roared with laughter. He was a little drunk. "She sure got the drop on me that girl. Done me up like a kipper, she did."

None could disagree.

All around, there were groups of people exchanging fond memories of Kayla. They ranged from family and friends, to politicians and generals and soldiers to suitors. Callum was just one of them and he was speaking directly from his heart to Gina.

"The thing that really hurt me was that each time she left for another, she took away her friendship and each time she never said good bye properly. You just cannot even begin to imagine how much that hurt me. You cannot. When you love someone as much as I loved her, and they cut you off without even saying goodbye, it goes past crippling," Gina could see that, even the memory of it, caused him almost physical pain.

"Some let me down gently words would have made all the difference. Even a simple Post-it note left lovingly on my computer screen," Callum continued, without self-consciousness. "All I felt was her disdain or even hatred when it happened. When she was with me, there was no doubting just how much she loved me, none at all. But when she left, it was always stone cold and without feeling. That is not something you get over. All I could ever do was wait and hope that she might gift me with a kind word from time to time. She never did."

"You must have loved her a lot, to keep forgiving her," Gina offered, feeling inadequate for him.

"I did. Don't get me wrong, when it was good it was amazing. That was what made it so bad when it wasn't," Callum lamented.

Callum became aware that he was bleating on.

"I'm sorry Gina, it's just..."

"I know," Gina said forgivingly. "You have to say these things and today is the right time and the right place."

Callum kissed her gently on the lips. It wasn't passionate, but it was a statement.

"Thank you for listening Gina. I know it was the last thing that you wanted to hear, but I needed to say it to move on. I can and I will, but I need time," the smile was back on his face.

"And I need a drink," Gina said proffering her glass and cocking a chastising brow for his negligence.

"Shall we get smashed again?" he asked with a cheeky grin.

"If that's all that's on the menu Callum, then you can count me in," the exact meaning of her offer fell on deaf ears.

Callum disappeared to refresh their glasses. While he was gone, Gina idly looked at the remembrance cards on the table. There were scores of them. One immediately caught her eye though. She instinctively knew that it was from Callum. The card was simply addressed, *"Ode to the love of my life,"* and signed off, *"Your eternal lover, Callum."*

It read:

"Hell hath no fury like a woman scorned,

Nor that of a self-righteous man who, in his own naivety,

Believes his innocence and that he has been wronged.

Yet here we are, torn and bleeding, sick with the impossibility of our love,

With no sustenance, one from the other,

'Cept shared memories, a glance and a fleeting smile lost on our lips.

No encounters or exchange of words that proclaim our love and desire,

Neither hold, nor caress to consummate and prove that love.

Meagre tools indeed to for us to ensure,

That such a perfect and reciprocated love endures.

And without sustenance even the most perfect flower,

Will wither and die, to become lost and irrelevant in the sands of time."

Gina was not to know, but Callum had written this at a time when he had been abandoned and cut off by Kayla. They were words driven out of her having broken his heart. They were words that became overtaken by events. Kayla had returned to him and so he had never sent them. Now, they were even more appropriate; his eulogy to her.

"Such words of love and devotion to his lost woman," Gina conceded.

She wondered how she could ever compete with Callum's love for Kayla. That thought laid as heavy as lead in her heart.

It was an hour through the reception when May finally caught Hydie Papandreou's eye. With an almost indiscernible tilt of her head, she indicated for the Hydra to follow her outside. May had changed from her formal black funeral suit to a long black dress. It was discretely cut but infinitely feminine, flattering her slim, athletic body. She wore her long, lush black hair up, which accentuated her long neck and fine features. Hydie had not been so vain. She was still suited and business like, although striking non-the-less. Her hair was also up, but in more of a practical manner. When they were outside and alone, it was Hydie who began the conversation.

"It is not over," she said simply. "A delay at best, but the Pindar will be back with a vengeance. What do the mirrors tell you?"

"No, indeed it is not over Hydie," May began. "It would appear that we have won twenty years, is all."

Twenty years was just a moment in time for beings such as Maelströminha and the Hydra.

"And then?" Hydie asked.

"And then Kayla Lovell died for nothing. It begins again."

391

"And we cannot let that be. I will not let that be," a voice from behind them said defiantly.

They turned. It was Gina, with Ava stood next to her. They had both arrived there in that moment but separately; both sensing that they should. Gina continued.

"I know the Pindar well enough. He will not rest now, until he has killed us all. And I am not waiting until I'm at another funeral, burying my children," Gina's expression was murderous. "I will go to Ingolstadt now and put a sword through his black heart."

"No," May said authoritatively. "We all go, or none of us go."

The Hydra read her. May had seen something else in the mirrors, she was sure of it.

"What have you seen?" the Hydra asked knowingly.

"In 95 out of 100 alternative outcomes, I see the Pindar's organisation growing in strength over the next twenty years. Then comes another Mahdi, another false prophet and Armageddon follows," May paused; in none of those 95 outcomes, do I see the four of us."

"What do you see in the other five?" the Hydra asked.

A long moment passed, while May considered how much she could tell them. She had seen it all, one hundred times over. Only five of them ended successfully, but with consequences. She decided to be vague.

"I see the four of us at the castle and the Pindar."

"Do you see the four of us leaving alive, in any of those outcomes?" Ava asked.

Deceit was one thing in May's eyes, but barefaced lying was another. It was with the greatest of difficulty that she kept the truth from them.

"It's not clear," she said simply.

Ava being the closest to May spotted the lie immediately and her blood ran cold. The premonition that she had of pending doom engulfed her, filling her mind. May's plea rang out loud in her ears:

"Take my children Ava and look after them for me. Grow them up with love and talk to them often of me."

"But May, I..." she began.

May glowered at her, forcing her to shut up. May had read her. The message to Ava was loud and clear. Ava's vision was to be their secret. The names of any of those who were not going to make it were *not* to be shared with the others.

It was late evening when Callum and Gina finally left the reception area. The others had gone some hours earlier. Callum had felt the need to be close to Kayla's memory and close to the bar. The journey in the lift up to their rooms was awkward; Gina, desperately wanting an invitation and Callum feeling too guilty to give one.

"Well goodnight then," Gina said, after a long and hopeful pause.

Everything inside Callum wanted to say, "Coffee at yours?" but that felt inappropriate and disloyal right now.

"Yes, goodnight," it was clumsy. "Look Gina, I'm boozed and a little disoriented. It will pass though, but just not tonight," his face showed his regret.

"That's alright Callum. Anyway I'm really not that easy," she said, unnecessarily.

She left him in the corridor and strutted, rather than walked to her room. Opened the door, entered and didn't look back. When she closed the door, she turned her back and leant against it.

"Jesus Gina. What the fuck was all that about? *I'm really not that easy.* You are such a dick," she wished that she could have wound back and replayed it. "The man's hurting for Christ's sake."

But then, so was Gina and she desperately wanted to be in his arms.

"That went well," Callum thought ironically.

He turned and walked to his room, amazed at how many bends there were in the straight corridor. He had drunk too much. Callum had minor problems with an uncooperative lock, before finally spilling into his room. He went straight to the drinks cabinet and poured himself a large Jack Daniel's. He toasted his reflection in the dressing table mirror and looked at himself critically.

"You are a mess Callum Knight," he observed, "a bloody mess."

He was, at a glance, still passable as a man in his prime. But on closer inspection, he was, greying. His features were blurring. The chin was not quite so chiselled, his dimples, more creased and his stomach, not quite so flat. He didn't like what he saw. Callum took his drink with him to the bathroom and poured it down the sink. He knew in that instant what he needed. He needed a woman to care for, who cared for him. He was no longer that enigmatic bachelor to be pursued by the paparazzi and feature in trivial magazines. But he was a man trapped; trapped by the heady memories of more than a decade of loving Kayla and the want to love again. To love Gina. He was in crisis and desperate to escape and he needed to sleep and turn his head off and find solace.

Sleep brought no solace though, only alcohol fuelled dreams, guilty ones, mostly. Kayla had died a dozen times in his arms during the night. Each time, he had sworn that he would save her. In his crazed mind, Callum had even clung to her, hoping that he could drag her back into his world. Each time he awoke, she was gone and his disappointment and guilt, immense. He couldn't break out of the repetitive cycle of despair, nor anchor himself to reality. It really was a nightmare.

Callum woke in the early hours, to the smell of Kayla's fragrance. It was *Shalimar*, by Jacques Guerlain, a perfume he had bought for Kayla on her thirtieth birthday. She had worn it ever since such that it had become part of her presence.

"Kayla?" Callum asked in sleepy confusion.

He felt the mattress compress next to him. Her perfume pervaded his brain, confusing him further.

"I'm here," she said, running her fingers through his hair.

It was strange. Her touch had no weight to it. It was like a summer breeze, blowing through a cornfield, invisibly moving every sheath. Just for a second, he believed he had brought Kayla back from his dream, but that could only be nonsense. It was just another dream, but it felt even more real this time; her smell, her voice, her presence. Callum certainly felt awake. He didn't want to open his eyes though for fear that she would evaporate if he did.

"Is that really you?" he asked clumsily. "I mean, *really* you."

"Touch me," she said.

Kayla took his hand and placed it softly on her breast.

"If you feel me, then I'm real."

"I feel you, but you can't be. We buried you yesterday so how can it be?" Callum doubted his sanity.

Kayla cupped his hand with hers, savouring his touch.

"*How* doesn't matter Callum, but *why* does. I can't leave you hurting and wasting your life like this Callum. You have to move on. Don't make the loss of my life worthless. It was my gift to you so that you can live yours to its full."

Callum still had his eyes squeezed shut; he didn't dare risk the moment.

"Can I touch your face?" he asked.

Kayla leant towards him and guided his hands to her face. He gently ran his fingers over her features, caressing each and every contour. As he traced the shape of her lips, he spoke.

"Can I kiss you?" he asked almost shyly.

"I was hoping that you would," she answered honestly.

He cupped her face in his hands and kissed her. Their kiss was long and earnest. Callum knew for sure now, that she was there. He could even taste her. Not necessarily real, but there. He ran his hands down to her neck, feeling the smoothness of it until Kayla pulled back, ending the kiss abruptly.

"No Callum, you can't touch me there, I'm not yet healed."

His hands had passed over the place where the Mullah's bullet had taken her life. The act had broken that special moment and Callum felt bereft for losing it.

"I cannot stay any longer Callum and I cannot return. I came to tell you to move on. I want you to enjoy Gina. She will love you and make your life complete. Swear it to me Callum. Swear it," she demanded.

"I swear it," Callum whispered obediently.

He covered her mouth with his for the last time. She faded with each passing second of their kiss until finally, there was only her voice.

"You signed your beautiful ode to me, *Eternally yours*, Callum. Don't ever forget that. I will be waiting for you."

With that, she was gone. All that remained was her scent that filled the room.

Callum opened his eyes and switched the bedside lamp on. He sat up and swung his legs over the side of the bed. He was trying to make sense of it. It all seemed so real, but it couldn't have been. How could she possibly have known of the ode that he had written to her on the card, after her death? A sudden thought struck him. He looked at where Kayla had been sat, or at least sat in his mind's eye. He stared in awe at the mattress as the memory foam slowly recovered its shape from the dent she had left there. Moments later, there was no evidence of her ever being there, other than the pervasive smell of her perfume that lingered on and the joy in his heart.

It had been a grim night for Gina too. She was in the same hotel at Callum, but might as well have been five thousand miles away in Moscow. She had fallen head over heels in love with him. That romantic time in the Mandarin Oriental Hotel in Munich, had cemented it for her. Despite the fear of death hanging over her, he had lifted her spirit and taken her to places that she had never been. Nobody had ever made such perfect love to her. Now that he was so completely in her head, all she had to do was think of him and her body would ache for his touch. To know that he was in a room just down the corridor and not interested, was agony. She had to leave the hotel. It was too much to bear.

It was only just after eight in the morning. Washington time was seven hours behind Moscow's and the flight, ten hours. That meant that if Gina was lucky with flights, she could be back in Moscow by one o'clock in the morning, their time. She could have a half decent night's sleep and still surprise Sasha and Isabella at breakfast.

"At least I'll get a cuddle there," she thought ironically.

Gina threw the duvet off and went quickly to the bathroom. She tried not to think of Callum while she showered, but failed. Even in her anger, she was turning on to her thoughts and had to force them out of her mind.

Gina was sat in her black underwear in front of the dressing room mirror, doing her makeup, when her mobile pinged. The message was from Callum. It simply said, "I NEED you Gina Mèdici."

Gina's legs could hardly support her as she walked in her dressing gown to Callum's room. She had gone completely weak at the knees and her heart was thumping with nervous anticipation. She tried the door, it was off the latch. When she entered, Callum was lying in bed. He was naked and muscular, with just a sheet on him and a crooked smile. The bed sheet had fallen to his hips, only just covering his manhood.

Callum grinned as he noticed Gina's eyes unintentionally drop to the bulge in the sheets. She bit her bottom lip as she imagined that bulge inside her. It literally squeezed her ovaries and she moaned involuntarily at the delicious thought of it.

"Last night," she said, "when I told you that *I really wasn't that easy*. Well I was clearly lying, wasn't I?"

"So it would seem," he agreed with a smirk, "but simply the sexiest and most gorgeous liar of all."

Callum could tell by Gina's body language and the look in her eyes, that she was already aroused. For Callum there was nothing more sexually attractive than a woman with intent. He eased himself onto his side to better feast his eyes on her.

Gina kept eye contact as she let her robe slip to the floor. She stood there trembling in her black underwear; all she was aware of, was the bulge in the sheets and the throbbing in her groin. Gina went towards him, unclipping her bra and letting her heavy breasts fall free. It was her time to smirk as she watched Callum's eyes raping her. The satin sheet could no longer contain the bulge of Callum's manhood. His attempt at modesty at last failed as his erection sprang free. The sight of his evident desire, made Gina feel light headed. All that she could think of was impaling herself on him and the thought of it drenched her.

Gina was acutely aware that her nipples were sticking out ridiculously and that Callum's eyes were fixed on them. He subconsciously licked his lips at the thought of taking them in his mouth. Gina read his intent and moved closer to him, offering her breasts to him. She unashamedly wanted his sex, needed his sex and demanded his sex. From the moment that Gina had noticed his generous manhood respond to her nakedness, below the tantalising cover of the sheet, she had imagined its hardness sliding into her. She imagined it filling the void inside her, both in body and in soul. Gina knew from past experience that his penetration would unleash the woman in her and that she would be lost in him.

Callum knew how to play her and that she loved the sweet agony of delay. Gina knew that she would have to wait for that glorious penetration and that she would be begging him to release her. He buried his face in her breasts, breathing in the scent of her. Gina's nipples were screaming for his touch. She was desperate and tried to manoeuvre his head to press her swollen nipple into his mouth. Callum merely circled it with his tongue and almost imperceptibly brushed his lips over it. That insignificant touch was like an electric shock running through her body. Gina gasped at the magnitude of it, sending delicious spasms down to the pit of her stomach.

It was too much. Gina forced the hardness of her nipple into the wetness of his mouth. Callum took the initiative. He skilfully teased her and then, sensing the moment, bit gently on her sending Gina into the frenzy of orgasm. Only Callum could put her there with such a simple touch. It was because he knew her thoughts even before she had thought them herself. He was in her head, in her heart and in her soul. Now Gina was desperate to have him inside her body too. She was his instrument and he knew just how to play her. There was a difference though.

Something had changed, something monumental. Gina could sense it. Callum had turned a page. He was her man now and the knowledge of it heightened her pleasure to an intensity that she had never experienced before.

Gina was still in the raptures of that orgasm, such that she hadn't noticed that she was now on her back with Callum above her. His penetration was long and slow. Afterwards, Gina was left in no doubt that she was a woman and what God had blessed her to do. Callum began his rhythm. Gina's journey to paradise had only just begun.

Chapter 37

Bavaria, Germany. February 6th 2018. One week after Kayla's funeral.

Callum had gone along as driver. There was nothing that his lesser Angel skill set could bring to the party. He would just be a liability, a distraction that could get the others killed. They had picked up Hydie Papandreou at the airport and Maelströminha, well she had just simply arrived. May had no need for transport as we know it. Riding with them, was the heavily pregnant Ava and Gina. Apart from the Hydra, they all had children to consider but there was no right time to do this. The Pindar was down and distracted. Probably with a black rage too, that could cloud his judgement. Anyway, the mirrors said that today offered them their best opportunity, statistically.

They had little by way of a plan and little chance of success, even if they did. Five percent apparently, which meant they would probably all die. Only Ava and May, knew that it was not possible for all of them to survive, whatever. They had each said goodbye to their loved ones, as if for the last time, in the knowledge that pitting themselves against the Devil was likely to be suicide.

Their only chance was their collective power. In the black limousine, were four of the most powerful, supernatural minds on the planet and they were armed with hope. None there came even close to having the mental skills of May, who was truly from the Stars, but she couldn't do it alone. They could have desperately done with the mental help of Kayla, but that wasn't to be. She would have had the next most powerful mind. Gina was as yet, uncharted territory and therefore a risk. There were two others that could have been brought to bear. That was May's sister, Crystalita and Elizabeth Robinson. However, the mirrors had told May that their success would not have depended on them. There were bigger astral forces at play. May wouldn't, or couldn't say what that was. They just had to trust her. They did; even the Hydra.

So, it was with an air of great sadness and immense hope that the limousine pulled into the avenue of trees that led up to the castle and the final showdown. They were reasonably confident of two things. The first was that the Pindar would be expecting them and infinitely confident of defeating them. The second was that there would be no armed guard to fight. The Pindar would not be feeling at risk. Besides, May alone could wipe out an army at will. No, this was all about the Pindar's vanity and his surety that he was invincible and he probably was. Besides, he could call on all the demons in Hell, if it amused him.

The four women in the limousine were dressed in simple black robes with cowls. It was probably an unnecessary precaution, but there was a possibility that they needed to be indistinguishable from others in the castle. Just before the car stopped outside the main door, May gave them one last briefing.

"Remember, leave your minds open to me and block out any attempt of the Pindar to infiltrate. Our minds will be as one. If he separates us, he wins."

May was painfully aware of how out of their depths the other women were. She had waited until now to brief them about what she had seen in the mirrors, to prepare them. If she had told them earlier, they would have had too much time to conjure up demons of their own.

"The Devil will cast many illusions to trick you. Trust your instinct, not your eyes. He will do this to confuse you and separate us. Remember that we are doing this for our loved ones. Keep that thought in your mind and it will embolden you."

It seemed strange to Gina, that this woman, the most diminutive and gentle of them all, was their leader and powerful on a biblical scale. All there had witnessed it, except her. May had power over Nature and over minds. She could summon thunderbolts from the skies, make the Earth tremor, create firestorms and take over the minds of a multitude. But these were only party tricks for a being like the Pindar. All in the limousine knew it.

"There had to be something else," Gina thought. "Something that May was counting on; otherwise it just didn't make sense."

All that May was asking of them right then was for their trust and to have faith. May led them out of the limousine, holding a large silver cross. She pulled her cowl over her head and the others followed suit, each holding their own silver crosses. Gina was the last to leave the limousine. She turned desperately to Callum.

"If I don't make this," Gina began.

"Then I will watch over your children," Callum completed her sentence. "But you are leaving here with me, just as you did last time. Go and make me and your children proud."

Gina pressed her lips desperately against Callum's.

"I love you Callum, but I wanted you for longer. Our time together has not been enough."

With that, she was gone; certain that she would never see him or her children again.

The big oak door leading into the castle was unlocked and ajar, as if inviting them in. They followed May down the corridor that led to the chambers with its avenue of suits of armour and tapestries.

The master chamber, with its sacrificial altar and thirteen chairs was empty but even the sight of it sent a shudder down Gina's spine. The memories of the sacrificial girl and Isabella on that same altar were still vivid and sickening to Gina. She was glad to get past it and out into the open courtyard, with its cool night air.

In front of them, was something resembling a small Greek amphitheatre, surrounded by battlements. Stone seats, set in a circle, stepped down to a raised stone platform at the bottom with and altar at its centre. Stood in the centre of the platform, was a man wearing a cloak and cowl. As he looked up at them, the moonlight glinted on his golden mask. It was the Pindar.

May led the others to the top circle of seats. As they walked around, she bade each to stop in turn at each of the four quarter points of the compass. May, herself had her back to the North Star, as if by way of ritual. It was exactly as she had seen it in the mirrors.

They looked down at the Pindar on centre stage. Only May wasn't afraid, she had spent months studying the mirrors and knew absolutely how it would end and the path that she needed to follow to make it so. Kayla's death was to be the salvation of the world, if May could just get it right. She addressed the Pindar in Enochian, the language of satanic ritual. It was a language older even than Sanskrit and sounded like a mixture of Arabic, Latin and Hebrew. The others understood May's words, only through her thoughts.

"Your time on Earth is spent Lucifer, for you and your demons. There is no place for you now," they were brave words from a mortal to an immortal.

The Pindar's laugh was loud and soulless. It shook the very battlements of the castle and placed fear in the hearts of all there, barring May. The Pindar sensed it and wondered why she might be so brave, or so foolish?

"Do you have any idea how futile your resistance and your pitiful silver crosses are?" the Pindar thundered.

Suddenly the crosses in their hands became too hot to hold. All dropped them, except for May. She stood their defiantly, with smoke billowing from her hands; implacable. Just for a moment, the Pindar seemed concerned, or was it amused, May wondered?

"You will leave this world and be banished to Gehenna where the lakes of burning sulphur will be your torture for eternity, just as prophesied in the *Book of Revelation*," May's voice echoed in the night courageously.

May's hands were now aflame. She unflinchingly held out the glowing red silver cross in defiance, locking her gaze on the Pindar's single eye, trying to enter his mind. He glared back at her hatefully through the gold mask. Their minds were locked in a duel. May was willing him to banish himself while he concentrated on soaking up her life force, her essence; her spirit. May knew that her intellect would never be enough. She called in the minds of Gina, Ava and the Hydra, immediately feeling the power of her mind surge to an entirely different level. The Pindar felt it too and increased his effort easily, soaking up all that she could give, like a sponge does to water.

The Pindar dropped his cowl and dragged the golden mask from his face. Satan stood before them in all his malevolence, and it was a terrifying sight. Ava immediately buckled under the combined weight of baby and terror. The Hydra lifted her to her feet.

"Focus Ava, do it for your baby!"

Ava struggled to her feet and looked aghast at the Pindar. Now he had a trident in his hand and a baby impaled on it, screaming in agony. She looked down at her stomach and it was flat. Ava placed her hands on her stomach to prove it and screamed out pitifully.

"No!"

The word went on seemingly forever, until the Hydra slapped her mercilessly across the face.

"Focus bitch!"

In an instant, there was no trident or impaled baby. Ava once again felt the weight of her pregnancy, thanked God, and brought her mind back into the contest. It was one of the Devil's illusions that May had warned them of.

The minutes ticked by. In the darkness, the intense mental energy from the three women to May and from her to the Pindar shone like powerful torch beams between them. It was like they were all wired together. The Pindar was playing with them though, like a cat does with a mouse before he kills it. There were many more games to play to torment and distract and the Pindar was enjoying every second of the one-sided contest.

Somehow, the Pindar was no longer alone on the stone stage. Two people in white robes, with blonde hair and silver masks, had joined him; a man and a young woman. The man dropped the girl's robe, revealing her nudity. She looked directly at Gina and pulled her mask off. She smirked and then threw her head back laughing raucously.

"Come on Sasha, show Mum what a close family we are!" Isabella shouted gleefully, opening her legs encouragingly as she did so.

Gina screamed and surged forwards, only to be restrained by Ava.

"It's not your daughter Gina! It's not your daughter!"

Ava had to break free from their union of minds to bring Gina under control. The loss of both Gina and Ava to the Devil's deception caused May to scream out in agony, as she was forced to take up the slack. In an instant, she looked decades older after that momentary loss of mental support.

With their four minds once again united, the young couple at the altar no longer looked human and took on their true forms as demons, winged and dragon like, breathing fire. They swooped menacingly around the four brave women. May allowed a small part of her immense intellect to set one demon upon the other.

They immediately began to tear each other to bits, howling and screaming in a gruesome sideshow to the main event.

In fury, the Pindar raised the duel to impossible heights. May met him, but at a cost. She began to age visibly in front of their eyes, using up her life force in futile effort to resist the Pindar. The other three tried to raise their games too, but they couldn't give any more. It was now all on May to endure. Still the minutes passed and May held the cross out with the same defiance. Now though, it was only the charred bones of her hands that were locked around it.

Again, the Pindar raised his game and May matched him. Now though, she was ageing at a rate that she couldn't sustain for much longer. Death would come very soon and there was nothing she could do about it.

The Hydra was the first to falter. As a Shadow, she was a lesser being than those with Angel blood. It was killing her. May sensed it and severed the mental connection between them. The act saved the Hydra's life and she collapsed, exhausted. May took her load, but to her further detriment.

The Pindar was smirking at them, enjoying watching their suffering. He raised his mental level one final time. Ava screamed out as her waters broke. The immense mental and physical stress that she was under had sent her into labour. Never-the-less, she kept her mental link with May and the light shone brightly between them. Still the minutes ticked by until May sensed that Ava's baby was in deep distress. She shut her down too, dowsing the light between them. It was now just her and Gina, who fought on doggedly.

Out of the corner of her eye, May saw that the Hydra had crawled over to Ava to help her. It was something that no Shadow had ever done for an Angel in 5,000 years. It touched May's soul, that in this time of adversity, two warring civilisations had united as one. It was now up to her and Gina to hold on long enough for it to happen. And then it did.

A shaft of light fell from the heavens, illuminating May. Tears of relief rolled down her wrinkled face. She looked like a frail old lady caught on stage by one of the floodlights.

"Kayla?" she whispered.

There was no reply, only a sensation that it was her and the pervading smell of her perfume. Then the miracle happened; Kayla had opened the gateway. One by one, the steps of the amphitheatre filled with ethereal beings. There were 298 of them in all, and each was known by name to May. She had lived with them, decades, centuries and some even millennia ago. They were from the original colonisation of 300; fellow Angels of pure blood. All of them had the same intellect and power over Nature. They were facing May with their minds open to her, increasing her cerebral capacity. It was much the same as adding additional memory to a computer to enhance its performance. The power of their thoughts illuminated the castle, as shafts of light left their minds and entered May's. The power of their combined minds, focussed through May, hit the Pindar like a laser beam. He physically rocked on his feet and put his hands to his ears as if his brain was about to explode.

The amphitheatre was suddenly filled by myriad of screaming demons, swarming to protect their master.

"Be damned Pindar!" May cried out, in a voice that belied the frail old lady that she had become.

There was a sound like all the souls in purgatory had screamed out in unison and the Pindar and his demons were gone. Gina ran to May and caught her before she hit the ground, holding her closely. She wrested the flaming cross from the charred bones of May's hands, oblivious to her own pain.

"Kayla brought them," May said to Gina, pointing to the ethereal crowd that was still smiling benignly back at her as they slowly faded from sight. "Just as the mirrors said she would. He is gone Gina, but not forever. His followers will bring him back one day, but probably not for over a thousand years, if we are vigilant."

Hydie Papandreou helped Ava over to May's side, who smiled feebly back at them. She looked like a ninety year old woman in a cancer ward. Her face was old and wrinkled and her body withered and emaciated. She was little more than skin and bone now. May's eyes were still bright blue and clear though, and they shone with love. Her mind was still keen, despite her great age and frailty. At last she turned to Ava, who was already in full labour.

"This is that second baby that I promised you in that other life Ava, when we met in your other past. I want you to name him *Ben* for me. It means son of the right hand. You are my right hand now Ava."

Ava nodded but couldn't reply. She was in the act of birthing Ben and screamed at the agony of it.

"Take my children Ava and look after them for me. Crystalita will take my place and times will be hard for her, such that she will not have the time. Grow them up with love and talk to them often of me. They will be much the same age as yours and will grow to love each other."

Tears of regret flowed from May's bright eyes, knowing that she would never see them again, nor her beloved husband. It was just as Ava's premonition had predicted. Ava dug deep to find the words to say between her cries of agony.

"I will be honoured to have them for you."

The sentence ended with one final scream as baby Ben was born on the cold flag stones of the Gothic castle at Ingolstadt. It was the very same moment that Maelströminha's spirit left her body to return to the stars and her friends, that had waited so long for her.

Chapter 38

LuminaGames development facility. Berlin, Germany. February 13th 2018. One week later.

Since the unfortunate accident that had befallen Illya Dracul, Doctor Walter Schwartz had taken to working at the LuminaGames facility. The Pindar had requested that, since the collapse of the Illuminati organisation, he mothball the project until things had recovered. Ten years, he was told. Not long in Shadow terms. Schwartz fully expected to be there to reap the rewards.

He had not attended the office for some time and was sifting through the mail. One letter caught his eye immediately. It was in the unmistakeable hand of the Pindar; bold and striking, with angular slashes. He opened it, with intrigue. Letters from the Pindar were rare and usually involved death, one way or another, and money. He opened the letter with great optimism and wasn't disappointed. It simply read:

"Sasha Mèdici. Activate.

Pindar."

Doctor Schwartz smiled broadly. His thin lips were like that of a snake and his blood, just as cold. He turned to the computer and selected 'Accounts' and entered the name. Under 'Customer Details' was Sasha's email address. He sent a short message. It simply said:

"Satan666"

The old doctor already knew what scenario had been written for Sasha Mèdici in his own free personalised dream experience. After all, he had designed it and records showed that Sasha had watched it. In fact records showed that it was his last login on the Dream App. The doctor knew, with the deepest satisfaction, that the moment Sasha opened his message the whole Mèdici family line would be doomed, including Sasha himself.

Doctor Walter Schwartz was still smiling to himself as he opened the door of his Mercedes. It was parked in the street at the back of the facility, where he always left it. He got in, still sadistically imagining how the Mèdici saga might play out. Son in the kitchen, he gets the message. Mother and sister are in animated conversation over something inanely trivial. Son takes the kitchen knife and dispatches them both mercilessly, then cuts his own throat.

"Yes, that would do it perfectly," he thought as he adjusted the driver's rear view mirror.

The aged doctor's eyes widened in horror at what he saw, it was a young blonde woman who looked vaguely familiar. The look in her eyes, spelled death. Heidi was sat on the back seat leaning over him. Her left hand grabbed him by the chin, bending his old, stiff neck impossibly over the back of his chair until his throat was as taught as a drum. He found himself looking up into her ice-blue eyes.

"Do you remember me doctor, the pregnant girl?"

She held the cutthroat razor in front of his eyes so that he could feast them on it.

"Do you remember Bjorn? The young man who brought us here, looking for protection," Heidi's words were spoken with pure hatred.

Doctor Walter Schwartz couldn't reply, his neck was under too much tension but his eyes spoke volumes. He was petrified beyond imagination.

"Do you?" she demanded.

She pressed the razor into his neck, just below his ear and first blood flowed freely from the wound. Not being able to talk, the doctor blinked his acknowledgement.

"Well this is for him," she said, drawing the blade firmly across his throat, cutting him to the bone.

The doctor's eyes bulged at the shock and pain of it. He could feel the wetness of his blood, gushing down his chest and shoulders.

"And this is for our baby," Heidi said evenly, as she reversed the blade and drew it back the other way.

The doctor's life ended there and then with one final violent exhalation that splattered the windscreen with blood. Heidi got out of the car carrying a petrol can. She unscrewed the lid and doused the interior liberally with petrol, then dropped the half empty can inside. She reached into her pocket for the Zip lighter, lit it and tossed it through the open door. The explosion almost bowled Heidi over but it was done. Bjorn and their unborn baby were avenged. Now she could return to Sweden and begin again.

Chapter 39

It had been the most extraordinary and challenging week of Gina's life. She had gone through every emotion imaginable. Fear and hate, from the duel to the death with the Pindar, to the joy of the birth of baby Ben; and from the grief of May's death to the relief of securing the safety and security of her children and mankind. Kayla, through May, had given them deliverance and given her the joy of having Callum. It was a time to rejoice and a time to grieve. Gina now knew that May had known all along that she would have to die to save humanity. Even in the knowledge of that, she went to her death unflinchingly, giving them the most precious gift of all. Hope.

May was to be laid to rest in Greece, where she had lived with her husband and two children. There was to be no equivalent of military honours, no fuss; just a simple service with her close family and friends attending. Those friends were to be limited to Ava and Gina only for May's children's sake. May didn't want them to grow up in exile, like she had. Her sister, Crystalita, would now take on the daunting role of Matriarch and Ben, her husband, would be her full time emissary. That was why May wanted Ava to help raise her children. She wanted them to have a normal life and not become damaged like her.

The journey back to the Castello in Italy was a time for Gina, Sasha and Isabella to reflect. Life would never be the same for them, now that Gina had found her powers and the responsibility that went with it. Then there was the pending marriage. Callum had proposed to Gina directly after her dual to the death with the Pindar. It had made him realise how fragile and tenuous happiness was and how much he loved her. He had lost Kayla and had been given a second chance to be happy. He had taken it with both arms, literally.

So, Gina's joy was immense on the journey home, however touched with the sadness of the price that May had paid for their happiness.

When they arrived at Castello di Mèdici, Asmina was waiting on the steps for them. Gina hadn't called her, she simply knew as she always did. Like Asmina's premonition of where Isabella was being held captive and the airstrike at the farm. Gina owed her so much, everything in fact.

As soon as Luigi stopped the car at the steps to the main entrance, Sasha was off at a pace. He ran up the steps to Asmina, lifted her up despite her bulk and planted a dozen kisses on the top of her head, then spun her around.

"Put me down boy, put me down!" she demanded, loving every second of it. "You not too big for a good whooping boy."

Sasha kissed her several times more and put her down. Asmina stood there, hands on hips scalding him.

"Don't you never do that to me again. I'm tellin' you Sasha. I'm tellin' you!"

Sasha just grinned back and winked cheekily. Isabella was next. She threw her arms around Asmina, nearly squeezing the life out of her. It was the first time they had met since her kidnapping.

"Thank you for helping them find me Asmina, Yuri told me all about it," Isabella whispered, then kissed her cheek.

"Don't know what you talkin' about Miss Isabella. You was a big brave girl fightin' that man. An' Donna Gina, brave too."

Asmina had respectfully used Isabella's and Gina's formal addresses. She was so immensely proud of her adopted family.

Gina waited patiently for her turn while Isabella embraced Asmina and Luigi unloaded their bags. At last Isabella left Asmina with yet another kiss and tripped lightly up the steps, disappearing indoors. It took all Gina's willpower not to run up the steps and throw herself at Asmina like a little girl. Instead she walked up slowly to her holding her loving gaze. Asmina's bountiful smile spread across her big face as she approached and it touched Gina's heart. She had missed the comfort and safety that Asmina smile brought. She was Gina's constant and Gina adored her.

"I've missed you Asmina, more than words can say," Gina gulped in the saying of it.

Their embrace was long and meaningful.

"I felt your presence every step of the way Asmina. It was like you were protecting me and my children. Somehow you led us to Isabella when she was taken and needed you. Then, at the farmhouse, somehow you knew something terrible was going to happen. How, I don't know, but you saved us all that day."

Gina was past emotional and losing it. Asmina, her rock, stepped in and made light of it.

"I'm a black witch is all bibi, an' I knows things," she laughed that belly laugh that shook her bulk." Like I knows you found the man that the Lovers Tarot card said you would."

"How could you possibly know that?" Gina was astonished.

"Goddammit girl. I don't need to be no witch to see that iceberg on your finger!" Asmina howled with laughter at her own wit. "You been bumping bones wi' the man?"

"Shh Asmina, remember the children are around. Of course I haven't. Don't be so silly, I hardly know him," Gina lied.

Asmina put her hand on Gina's belly.

"Then you tell me how you got pregnant."

Asmina folded her arms and gave Gina a knowing look. Gina just looked shocked.

"That's just rubbish Asmina, you can't know something like that," Gina subconsciously placed her hands maternally on her tummy.

"An' I didn't know 'bout the High Priestess, the Magician, the Fool, the Lover, the Devil an' Death?" Asmina pointed out haughtily.

She had her hands on her hips and head to the side. Asmina was enjoying the moment, watching Gina squirm.

"An' I didn't know 'bout the mill an' the farm? Come bibi. I'll make tea an' you can tell me all 'bout the man. An' I means *all* bibi. Don't you hold out on me, you hear? You owes me girl. I sent the boy to you in the cards. Don't you never forget that."

Gina followed Asmina up the steps obediently, still holding her tummy in shock. She had to concede that Asmina was never wrong about these things.

"Is it a boy or a girl?" Gina blurted, and then flushed with embarrassment.

"They brother an' sister," Asmina said in matter of fact fashion.

"Christ. You mean twins?" was all that Gina could manage to say in unbridled shock.

For Sasha and Isabella, it was just nice to be home with all its comforts. In exile, they had not been allowed to use their phones, the internet and social media. They were both bursting to get back in touch with the outside world, now that they were safe and the family happy again. Sasha and Gina had been through so much, but they had endured. The Mèdici's had always endured. Their family line had survived every threat over the centuries; it was if God had charmed their very existence. The Mèdici's were invincible.

Sasha and Isabella were sat in the kitchen on their iPads while their mother and Asmina talked incessantly. Clearly there had been some special news that they were both excited about, but they weren't sharing it right now. That didn't matter to Sasha and Isabella though; they were both too involved catching up with friends to worry too much about it.

Sasha announced his return on Facebook and then went to check his emails. There were hundreds of them, so he just skimmed over the most recent. One caught his eye immediately. It was from LuminaGames.

"Just wait 'till I tell Callum," he heard his mother say. "Do you think he will be pleased?"

She looked so happy, he noticed; happier than he had ever seen her before. He smiled and looked at Issie. Her face was flushed with excitement too. She seemed to have picked up on the good news too, whatever that was.

Sasha opened the email. It simply said, *"Satan666."*

Chapter 40

Bavaria, Germany. June 21st 2018. The evening of the summer solstice, four months later.

The cavalcade of thirteen black Mercedes limousines passed down the avenue of poplars leading to the castle gate. The magnificent trees flickered in the mysterious orange light of the sunset as they passed. The gate opened without command as usual, and the cars drove on to the courtyard. A single person dressed in the cowl and black habit of a monk exited each of the cars. They walked in silence to the grand oak doorway of the castle and the thirteen filed through. They passed down the avenue of suits of armour and tapestries, into the candlelit chambers facing them. Thirteen chairs surrounded a stone altar. Twelve were of simple hewn oak, numbered one through twelve. The thirteenth was an ornately carved throne with serpents and dragons entwined on it. At the top of the backrest was a carved shield with the letter 'H' prominently declaring its owners name. The Hydra!

The End

AUTHOR's NOTE

I hope that you enjoyed 'Scorned' as much as I did writing it for you. If you did, then I would be forever grateful if you could leave a review on Amazon. This is essential to help me up the 'search engine' and be noticed as a writer. Without that 'Scorned' is almost invisible. If you could also recommend a friend, then that would be immense.

The first two books in the series, 'Angels & Shadows' and 'Forsaken', are available on Amazon and the fourth, 'The Assassin', is in the writing. I hope you read them to understand and enjoy the whole journey.

Thank you.

Chris Savage